Alexander Charles Ewald, George Farquhar

Dramatic Works of George Farquhar

Edited, with Life and Notes by Alex. Charles Ewald: Volume the Second

Alexander Charles Ewald, George Farquhar

Dramatic Works of George Farquhar
Edited, with Life and Notes by Alex. Charles Ewald: Volume the Second

ISBN/EAN: 9783337055370

Printed in Europe, USA, Canada, Australia, Japan

Cover: Foto ©Andreas Hilbeck / pixelio.de

More available books at **www.hansebooks.com**

Publisher's Note.

Five hundred and twenty copies of this book printed for England and America, and each numbered. Type distributed.

No. 262

THE

DRAMATIC WORKS

OF

GEORGE FARQUHAR

EDITED, WITH LIFE AND NOTES

BY

ALEX. CHARLES EWALD, F.S.A.

AUTHOR OF "STORIES FROM THE STATE PAPERS," ETC.

IN TWO VOLUMES

VOLUME THE SECOND

LONDON

JOHN C. NIMMO

14, KING WILLIAM STREET, STRAND

MDCCCXCII

CONTENTS OF VOL. II.

	PAGE
THE TWIN-RIVALS	1
THE RECRUITING OFFICER	115
THE BEAUX-STRATAGEM	237

THE TWIN-RIVALS.

A Comedy.

———

Sic vos non vobis.—VIRGIL

This comedy was produced at Drury Lane on December 14, 1702. *It is the most accurate of all Farquhar's productions. The plot, though improbable, is well constructed and sustained, the dialogue lively and entertaining, whilst the characters of the Younger Wouldbe, Mrs. Mandrake, and Teague are so naturally drawn as to appear real personages, dependent little upon the art of the actor or the imagination of the author for their creation. We have also here less of that "pert low dialogue" of which Pope complained. The play was, however, not a success, and was soon withdrawn.*

The original cast was:—*Elder Wouldbe*, WILKS; *Younger Wouldbe*, CIBBER; *Richmore*, HUSBAND; *Trueman*, MILLS; *Subtleman*, PINKETHMAN; *Balderdash* and *Alderman*, JOHNSON; *Clearaccount*, FAIRBANK; *Teague*, BOWEN; *Constance*, Mrs. ROGERS; *Aurelia*, Mrs. HOOK; *Mrs. Clearaccount*, Mrs. MOOR; *Mrs. Mandrake*, Mr. BULLOCK.

TO HENRY BRETT, ESQ.*

THE Commons of England have a right of petitioning ; and since by your place in the senate you are obliged to hear and redress the subject, I presume upon the privilege of the people to give you the following trouble.

As prologues introduce plays on the stage, so dedications usher them into the great theatre of the world ; and as we choose some stanch actor to address the audience, so we pitch upon some gentleman of undisputed ingenuity to recommend us to the reader. Books, like metals, require to be stamped with some valuable effigies before they become popular and current.

To escape the critics, I resolved to take sanctuary with one of the best ; one who differs from the fraternity in this, that his good-nature is ever predominant, can discover an author's smallest fault, and pardon the greatest.

Your generous approbation, Sir, has done this play service, but has injured the author ; for it has made him insufferably vain, and he thinks himself authorised to stand up for the merit of his performance, when so great a master of wit has declared in its favour.

The muses are the most coquettish of their sex, fond of being admired, and always putting on their best airs to the finest gentleman : but alas, Sir ! their addresses are stale, and their fine things but repetition ; for there is nothing new in wit, but what is found in your own conversation.

Could I write by the help of study, as you talk without it, I would venture to say something in the usual strain of dedication ; but as you have too much wit to suffer it, and I too little to undertake it, I hope the world will excuse my deficiency, and you will pardon the presumption of, Sir, your most obliged, and most humble servant,

G. FARQUHAR.

December 23, 1702.

---

* Colonel Brett, who married the divorced Countess of Macclesfield. He was a great theatre-lover, and was for some time a sharer in the Drury Lane Patent. See Cibber's *Apology*, chap. xi.

THE PREFACE.

THE success and countenance that debauchery has met with in plays, was the most severe and reasonable charge against their authors in Mr. Collier's " Short View ; "* and indeed this gentleman had done the drama considerable service, had he arraigned the stage only to punish its misdemeanours, and not to take away its life ; but there is an advantage to be made sometimes of the advice of an enemy, and the only way to disappoint his designs, is to improve upon his invective, and to make the stage flourish, by virtue of that satire by which he thought to suppress it.

I have therefore in this piece endeavoured to show, that an English comedy may answer the strictness of poetical justice ; but indeed the greater share of the English audience, I mean that part which is no farther read than in plays of their own language, have imbibed other principles, and stand up as vigorously for the old poetic licence, as they do for the liberty of the subject. They take all innovations for grievances ; and, let a project be never so well laid for their advantage, yet the undertaker is very likely to suffer by't. A play without a beau, cully, cuckold, or coquette, is as poor an entertainment to some palates, as their Sunday's dinner would be without beef and pudding. And this I take to be one reason that the galleries were so thin during the run of this play. I thought indeed to have soothed the splenetic zeal of the city, by making a gentleman a knave, and punishing their great grievance—a whoremaster ; but a certain virtuoso of that fraternity has told me since, that the citizens were never more disappointed in any entertainment : " For," said he, " however pious we may appear to be at home, yet we never go to that end of the town but with an intention to be lewd."

There was an odium cast upon this play, before it appeared, by some persons who thought it their interest to have it suppressed. The ladies were frighted from seeing it by formidable stories of a midwife, and were told, no doubt, that they must expect no less than a labour upon the stage ; but I hope the examining into that aspersion will be enough to wipe it off, since the character of the midwife is only so far touched as is necessary for carrying on the plot, she being principally deciphered in her procuring capacity ;

* Jeremy Collier's "Short view of the Immorality and profaneness of the English Stage," published in 1698.

and I dare not affront the ladies so far as to imagine they could be offended at the exposing of a bawd.

Some critics complain, that the design is defective for want of Clelia's appearance in the scene ; but I had rather they should find this fault, than I forfeit my regard to the fair, by showing a lady of figure under a misfortune ; for which reason I made her only nominal, and chose to expose the person that injured her ; and if the ladies don't agree that I have done her justice in the end, I'm very sorry for't.

Some people are apt to say, that the character of Richmore points at a particular person ; though I must confess I see nothing but what is very general in his character, except his marrying his own mistress ; which, by the way, he never did, for he was no sooner off the stage but he changed his mind, and the poor lady is still *in statu quo.* But upon the whole matter, 'tis application only makes the ass ; and characters in plays are like Long Lane clothes,* not hung out for the use of any particular people, but to be bought by only those they happen to fit.

The most material objection against this play is the importance of the subject, which necessarily leads into sentiments too grave for diversion, and supposes vices too great for comedy to punish. 'Tis said, I must own, that the business of comedy is chiefly to ridicule folly ; and that the punishment of vice falls rather into the province of tragedy ; but if there be a middle sort of wickedness, too high for the sock, and too low for the buskin, is there any reason that it should go unpunished? What are more obnoxious to human society, than the villanies exposed in this play, the frauds, plots, and contrivances upon the fortunes of men, and the virtue of women? But the persons are too mean for the heroic ; then what must we do with them? Why, they must of necessity drop into comedy ; for it is unreasonable to imagine that the lawgivers in poetry would tie themselves up from executing that justice which is the foundation of their constitution ; or to say, that exposing vice is the business of the drama, and yet make rules to screen it from persecution.

Some have asked the question, why the Elder Wouldbe, in the fourth act, should counterfeit madness in his confinement? Don't mistake, there was no such thing in his head ; and the judicious could easily perceive, that it was only a start of humour put on to divert his melancholy ; and when gaiety is strained to cover misfortune, it may very naturally be overdone, and rise to a semblance of madness, sufficient to impose on the constable, and perhaps on some of the audience ; who, taking everything at sight, impute that as a fault, which I am bold to stand up for, as one of the most masterly strokes of the whole piece.

* Long Lane, which reaches from Smithfield to Aldersgate Street, was in Farquhar's time a famous place for second-hand clothes dealers.

This I think sufficient to obviate what objections I have heard made ; but there was no great occasion for making this defence, having had the opinion of some of the greatest persons in England, both for quality and parts, that the play has merit enough to hide more faults than have been found ; and I think their approbation sufficient to excuse some pride that may be incident to the author upon this performance.

I must own myself obliged to Mr. Longueville for some lines in the part of Teague, and something of the lawyer ; but above all, for his hint of the twins, upon which I formed my plot. But having paid him all due satisfaction and acknowledgment, I must do myself the justice to believe, that few of our modern writers have been less beholden to foreign assistance in their plays, than I have been in the following scenes.

<h2 style="text-align:center">DRAMATIS PERSONÆ.</h2>

HERMES WOULDBE, *elder Son and heir to* LORD WOULDBE.
BENJAMIN WOULDBE, *his Brother.*
RICHMORE, *a gay dissipated Rake.*
CAPTAIN TRUEMAN, *his Nephew, and friend to* HERMES WOULDBE.
SUBTLEMAN, *an Attorney.*
FAIRBANK, *a Goldsmith.*
BALDERDASH, *a Vintner.*
CLEARACCOUNT, *Steward to* LORD WOULDBE.
COMIC, *a Poet.*
JACK,
FRISURE, } *Valets to* BENJAMIN WOULDBE.
TEAGUE, *Valet to* HERMES WOULDBE.

CONSTANCE, *betrothed to* HERMES WOULDBE.
AURELIA, *her Cousin, beloved by* CAPTAIN TRUEMAN.
MRS. CLEARACCOUNT, *Wife to* CLEARACCOUNT.
MRS. MANDRAKE, *a Midwife and Procuress.*

Alderman, Constables, Gentlemen, Mob, Maid, *and* Footmen.

SCENE.—LONDON.

PROLOGUE,

BY MR. MOTTEUX.   SPOKEN BY MR. WILKS.

An Alarm sounded.

WITH drums and trumpets in this warring age,
A martial prologue should alarm the stage.
New plays, ere acted, a full audience near,
Seem towns invested, when a siege they fear.
Prologues are like a forlorn hope, sent out
Before the play, to skirmish and to scout:
Our dreadful foes, the critics, when they spy,
They cock, they charge, they fire, then—back they fly.
The siege is laid,—there gallant chiefs abound,
Here foes intrench'd, there glittering troops around,
And the loud batteries roar—from yonder rising
    ground.
In the first act brisk sallies (miss or hit),
With volleys of small shot, or snip-snap wit,
Attack, and gall the trenches of the pit.
The next the fire continues, but at length
Grows less, and slackens like a bridegroom's strength.
The third, feints, mines, and countermines abound,
Your critic engineers safe underground,
Blow up our works, and all our art confound.
The fourth brings on most action, and 'tis sharp,
Fresh foes crowd on, at your remissness carp,
And desperate, though unskill'd, insult our counter
    scarp.

Then comes the last ; the general storm is near,
The poet-governor now quakes for fear ;
Runs wildly up and down, forgets to huff,
And would give all he has plunder'd—to get off.
So, Don and Monsieur, bluff before the siege,
Were quickly tamed—at Venloo, and at Liege :*
'Twas *Viva Spagnia! Vive France!* before ;
Now, *Quartier! Monsieur! Quartier! Ah, Señor!*
But what your resolution can withstand?
You master all, and awe the sea and land.
In war your valour makes the strong submit ;
Your judgment humbles all attempts in wit.
What play, what fort, what beauty can endure,
All fierce assaults, and always be secure!
Then grant 'em generous terms who dare to write,
Since now that seems as desperate as to fight :
If we must yield, yet ere the day be fixt,
Let us hold out the third, and, if we may, the sixth.†

* Taken by the English under the Duke of Marlborough in 1702.
† The author's nights.

THE TWIN-RIVALS.

ACT I.

SCENE I.

Benjamin Wouldbe's *Lodgings.*

Benjamin Wouldbe *discovered dressing,* Jack *buckling his shoes.*

Ben. Would. Here is such a plague every morning, with buckling shoes, gartering, combing and powdering!—Psha! cease thy impertinence, I'll dress no more to-day.—[*Exit* Jack.] Were I an honest brute, that rises from his litter, shakes himself, and so is dressed, I could bear it.

Enter Richmore.

Rich. No farther yet, Wouldbe! 'tis almost one.

Ben. Would. Then blame the clockmakers, they made it so; the sun has neither fore nor afternoon. Prithee, what have we to do with time? Can't we let it alone as nature made it? Can't a man eat when he's hungry, go to bed when he's sleepy, rise when he wakes, dress when he pleases, without the confinement of hours to enslave him?

Rich. Pardon me, sir, I understand your stoicism—
you have lost your money last night.

Ben. Would. No, no, Fortune took care of me
there—I had none to lose.

Rich. 'Tis that gives you the spleen.

Ben. Would. Yes, I have got the spleen; and
something else.—Hark'ee—   [*Whispers.*

Rich. How!

Ben. Would. Positively.   The lady's kind reception
was the most severe usage I ever met with.   Shan't I
break her windows, Richmore?

Rich. A mighty revenge truly!   Let me tell you,
friend, that breaking the windows of such houses are
no more than writing over a vintner's door as they do
in Holland, *Vin te koop.*   'Tis no more than a bush
to a tavern, a decoy to trade, and to draw in customers;
but upon the whole matter, I think, a gentleman should
put up an affront got in such little company; for the
pleasure, the pain, and the resentment, are all alike
scandalous.

Ben. Would. Have you forgot, Richmore, how I
found you one morning with the Flying-Post * in your
hand, hunting for physical advertisements?

Rich. That was in the days of dad, my friend, in
the days of dirty linen, pit-masks, hedge-taverns, and
beefsteaks; but now I fly at nobler game; the Ring,
the Court, Pawlet's, and the Park: I despise all
women that I apprehend any danger from, less than
the having my throat cut: and should scruple to
converse even with a lady of fortune, unless her virtue
were loud enough to give me pride in exposing it.—

* A leading newspaper in the reign of Queen Anne, issued three
times a week.

Here's a letter I received this morning; you may read it. [*Gives a letter.*

Ben. Would. [Reads.] *If there be solemnity in protestation, justice in heaven, or fidelity on earth, I may still depend on the faith of my Richmore. Though I may conceal my love, I no longer can hide the effects on't from the world. Be careful of my honour, remember your vows, and fly to the relief of the disconsolate* CLELIA.
The fair, the courted, blooming Clelia !

Rich. The credulous, troublesome, foolish Clelia. Did you ever read such a fulsome harangue? *Lard, sir, I am near my time, and want your assistance!* Does the silly creature imagine that any man would come near her in those circumstances, unless it were doctor Chamberlain ?* You may keep the letter.

Ben. Would. But why would you trust it with me ? you know I can't keep a secret that has any scandal in't.

Rich. For that reason I communicate: I know thou art a perfect gazette, and will spread the news all over the town: for you must understand that I am now besieging another; and I would have the fame of my conquest upon the wing, that the town may surrender the sooner.

Ben. Would. But if the report of your cruelty goes along with that of your valour, you'll find no garrison of any strength will open their gates to you.

Rich. No, no, women are cowards, and terror prevails upon them more than clemency: my best pretence to my success with the fair is my using 'em

* Hugh Chamberlain (or Chamberlen) was a noted *accoucheur.*

ill. 'Tis turning their own guns upon 'em, and I have always found it the most successful battery to assail one reputation by sacrificing another.

Ben. Would. I could love thee for thy mischief, did I not envy thee for thy success in't.

Rich. You never attempt a woman of figure.

Ben. Would. How can I? this confounded hump of mine is such a burden at my back, that it presses me down here in the dirt and diseases of Coventgarden, the low suburbs of pleasure. Curst fortune! I am a younger brother, and yet cruelly deprived of my birthright of a handsome person; seven thousand a year in a direct line, would have straightened my back to some purpose. But I look, in my present circumstances, like a branch of another kind, grafted only upon the stock which makes me grow so crooked.

Rich. Come, come, 'tis no misfortune, your father is so as well as you.

Ben. Would. Then why should not I be a lord as well as he? Had I the same title to the deformity I could bear it.

Rich. But how does my lord bear the absence of your twin-brother?

Ben. Would. My twin-brother! Ay, 'twas his crowding me that spoiled my shape, and his coming half an hour before me that ruined my fortune. My father expelled me his house some two years ago, because I would have persuaded him that my twin-brother was a bastard. He gave me my portion, which was about fifteen hundred pound, and I have spent two thousand of it already. As for my brother, he don't care a farthing for me.

Rich. Why so, pray?

Ben. Would. A very odd reason—because I hate him.

Rich. How should he know that?

Ben. Would. Because he thinks it reasonable it should be so.

Rich. But did your actions ever express any malice to him?

Ben. Would. Yes: I would fain have kept him company; but being aware of my kindness, he went abroad. He has travelled these five years, and, I am told, is a grave sober fellow, and in danger of living a great while; all my hope is, that when he gets into his honour and estate, the nobility will soon kill him by drinking him up to his dignity. But come, Frank, I have but two eyesores in the world, a brother before me and a hump behind me, and thou art still laying 'em in my way: let us assume an argument of less severity. Canst thou lend me a brace of hundred pounds?

Rich. What would you do with 'em?

Ben. Would. Do with 'em! there's a question indeed! Do you think I would eat 'em?

Rich. Yes, o' my troth, would you, and drink 'em together. Look'ee, Mr. Wouldbe, whilst you kept well with your father, I could have ventured to have lent you five guineas: but as the case stands, I can assure you, I have lately paid off my sister's fortune, and—

Ben. Would. Sir, this put-off looks like an affront, when you know I don't use to take such things.

Rich. Sir, your demand is rather an affront, when you know I don't use to give such things.

Ben. Would. Sir, I'll pawn my honour.

Rich. That's mortgaged already for more than it is worth; you had better pawn your sword there, 'twill bring you forty shillings.

Ben. Would. 'Sdeath, sir.—

[*Takes his sword off the table.*

Rich. Hold, Mr. Wouldbe! suppose I put an end to your misfortunes all at once?

Ben. Would. How, sir?

Rich. Why, go to a magistrate, and swear you would have robbed me of two hundred pounds. Look'ee, sir, you have been often told, that your extravagance would some time or other be the ruin of you; and it will go a great way in your indictment, to have turned the pad upon your friend.

Ben. Would. This usage is the height of ingratitude from you, in whose company I have spent my fortune.

Rich. I'm therefore a witness, that it was very ill spent. Why would you keep company, be at equal expenses with me, that have fifty times your estate? What was gallantry in me, was prodigality in you; mine was my health, because I could pay for't; yours a disease, because you could not.

Ben. Would. And is this all I must expect from our friendship?

Rich. Friendship! sir, there can be no such thing without an equality.

Ben. Would. That is, there can be no such thing when there is occasion for't.

Rich. Right, sir; our friendship was over a bottle only; and whilst you can pay your club of friendship, I'm that way your humble servant; but when once

you come borrowing, I'm this way — your humble
servant. [*Exit.*

Ben. Would. Rich, big, proud, arrogant villain ! I
have been twice his second, thrice sick of the same
love, and thrice cured by the same physic, and now
he drops me for a trifle. That an honest fellow in
his cups should be such a rogue when he's sober !
The narrow-hearted rascal has been drinking coffee
this morning. Well, thou dear, solitary half-crown,
adieu !—Here, Jack !

Re-enter JACK.

Take this ; pay for a bottle of wine, and bid Balderdash bring it himself.—[*Exit* JACK.] How melancholy are my poor breeches ; not one chink !—Thou
art a villanous hand, for thou hast picked my pocket.
—This vintner now has all the marks of an honest
fellow, a broad face, a copious look, a strutting belly,
and a jolly mien. I have brought him above three
pound a night for these two years successively. The
rogue has money, I'm sure, if he will but lend it.

Enter BALDERDASH *with a bottle and glass,*
JACK *attending.*

Oh, Mr. Balderdash, good morrow.

Bald. Noble Mr. Wouldbe, I'm your most humble
servant. I have brought you a whetting-glass, the
best old hock in Europe ; I know 'tis your drink in a
morning.

Ben. Would. I'll pledge you, Mr. Balderdash.

Bald. Your health, sir. [*Drinks.*

Ben. Would. Pray, Mr. Balderdash, tell me one
thing—but first sit down : now tell me plainly what
you think of me ?

Bald. Think of you, sir! I think that you are the honestest, noblest gentleman, that ever drank a glass of wine; and the best customer that ever came into my house.

Ben. Would. And you really think as you speak?

Bald. May this wine be my poison, sir, if I don't speak from the bottom of my heart!

Ben. Would. And how much money do you think I have spent in your house?

Bald. Why truly, sir, by a moderate computation, I do believe that I have handled of your money the best part of five hundred pounds within these two years.

Ben. Would. Very well! And do you think that you lie under any obligation for the trade I have promoted to your advantage?

Bald. Yes, sir; and if I can serve you in any respect, pray command me to the utmost of my ability.

Ben. Would. Well, thanks to my stars, there is still some honesty in wine!—Mr. Balderdash, I embrace you and your kindness: I am at present a little low in cash, and must beg you to lend me a hundred pieces.

Bald. Why, truly, Mr. Wouldbe, I was afraid it would come to this. I have had it in my head several times to caution you upon your expenses: but you were so very genteel in my house, and your liberality became you so very well, that I was unwilling to say anything that might check your disposition; but truly, sir, I can forbear no longer to tell you, that you have been a little too extravagant.

Ben. Would. But since you reaped the benefit of

my extravagance, you will, I hope, consider my necessity.

Bald. Consider your necessity! I do with all my heart, and must tell you, moreover, that I will be no longer accessory to it: I desire you, sir, to frequent my house no more.

Ben. Would. How, sir!

Bald. I say, sir, that I have an honour for my good lord your father, and will not suffer his son to run into any inconvenience. Sir, I shall order my drawers not to serve you with a drop of wine. Would you have me connive at a gentleman's destruction?

Ben. Would. But methinks, sir, that a person of your nice conscience should have cautioned me before.

Bald. Alas! sir, it was none of my business. Would you have me be saucy to a gentleman that was my best customer? Lackaday, sir, had you money to hold it out still, I had been hanged rather than be rude to you. But truly, sir, when a man is ruined, 'tis but the duty of a Christian to tell him of it.

Ben. Would. Will you lend me the money, sir?

Bald. Will you pay me this bill, sir?

Ben. Would. Lend me the hundred pound, and I will pay the bill.

Bald. Pay me the bill, and I will not lend the hundred pound, sir. But pray consider with yourself now, sir, would not you think me an arrant coxcomb, to trust a person with money that has always been so extravagant under my eye? whose profuseness I have seen, I have felt, I have handled? Have not I known you, sir, throw away ten pound of a night upon a covey of pit-partridges, and a setting-dog? Sir, you have made my house an ill house : my very chairs will bear you no longer. In short, sir, I desire you to frequent the Crown no more, sir.

Ben. Would. Thou sophisticated tun of iniquity, have I fattened your carcass, and swelled your bags with my vital blood? Have I made you my companion to be thus saucy to me? But now I will keep you at your due distance.   [*Kicks him.*

Jack. Welcome, sir!

Ben. Would. Well said, Jack.   [*Kicks him again.*

Jack. Very welcome, sir! I hope we shall have your company another time. Welcome, sir!

[BALDERDASH *is kicked off.*

Ben. Would. Pray wait on him downstairs, and give him a welcome at the door too.—[*Exit* JACK.] This is the punishment of hell; the very devil that tempted me to the sin, now upbraids me with the crime—I have villanously murdered my fortune ; and now its ghost, in the lank shape of poverty, haunts me : is there no charm to conjure down the fiend?

Re-enter JACK.

Jack. O sir, here's sad news!

Ben. Would. Then keep it to thyself, I have enough of that already.

Jack. Sir, you will hear it too soon.

Ben. Would. What! is Broad below?

Jack. No, no, sir ; better twenty such as he were hanged. Sir, your father's dead.

Ben. Would. My father!—Good night, my lord!— Has he left me anything?

Jack. I heard nothing of that, sir.

Ben. Would. Then I believe you heard all there was of it.—Let me see.—My father dead! and my elder brother abroad!—If necessity be the mother of invention, she was never more pregnant than with me.—[*Pauses.*] Here, sirrah, run to Mrs. Mandrake, and bid her come hither presently.—[*Exit* JACK.] That woman was 'my mother's midwife when I was born, and has been my bawd these ten years. I have had her endeavours to corrupt my brother's mistress; and now her assistance will be necessary to cheat him of his estate; for she's famous for understanding the right side of a woman, and the wrong side of the law.

[*Exit.*

SCENE II.

A Room in Mrs. MANDRAKE'S *House.*

Mrs. MANDRAKE *discovered.*

Mrs. Man. Who is there?　　　　　　　[*Calls.*

Enter Maid.

Maid. Madam!

Mrs. Man. Has any message been left for me to-day?

Maid. Yes, madam: here has been one from my lady Stillborn, that desired you not to be out of the way, for she expected to cry out every minute.

Mrs. Man. How! every minute!—Let me see.— [*Takes out a pocket-book.*] Stillborn—ay—she reckons with her husband from the first of April; and with Sir James, from the first of March.—Ay, she's always

a month before her time.—[*Knocking at the door.*]
Go see who's at the door.

Maid. Yes, madam.   [*Exit.*

Mrs. Man. Well, certainly there is not a woman
in the world so willing to oblige mankind as myself! and really I have been so ever since the age of
twelve, as I can remember. I have delivered as
many women of great bellies, and helped as many to
'em, as any person in England; but my watching and
cares have broken me quite, I am not the same
woman I was forty years ago.

Enter RICHMORE.

Oh, Mr. Richmore! you're a sad man, a barbarous
man, so you are! What will become of poor Clelia,
Mr. Richmore? The poor creature is so big with
her misfortunes, that they are not to be borne.

[*Weeps.*

Rich. You, Mrs. Mandrake, are the fittest person
in the world to ease her of 'em.

Mrs. Man. And won't you marry her, Mr. Richmore?

Rich. My conscience won't allow it; for I have
sworn since to marry another.

Mrs. Man. And will you break your vows to
Clelia?

Rich. Why not, when she has broke hers to me?

Mrs. Man. How's that, sir?

Rich. Why, she swore a hundred times never to
grant me the favour, and yet, you know she broke her
word.

Mrs. Man. But she loved, Mr. Richmore, and
that was the reason she forgot her oath.

Rich. And I love Mr. Richmore, and that is the reason I forgot mine. Why should she be angry that I follow her own example, by doing the very same thing from the very same motive?

Mrs. Man. Well, well, take my word, you'll never thrive. I wonder how you can have the face to come near me, that am the witness of your horrid oaths and imprecations! Are not you afraid that the guilty chamber above-stairs should fall down upon your head? Yes, yes, I was accessory, I was so; but if ever you involve my honour in such a villany the second time—Ah, poor Clelia! I loved her as I did my own daughter—you seducing man!

[*Weeps.*

Rich. Heigh-ho, my Aurelia!

Mrs. Man. Heigh-ho, she's very pretty!

Rich. Dost thou know her, my dear Mandrake?

Mrs. Man. Heigh-ho, she's very pretty! Ah, you're a sad man! Poor Clelia was handsome, but indeed, breeding, puking, and longing, has broken her much. 'Tis a hard case, Mr. Richmore, for a young lady to see a thousand things, and long for a thousand things, and yet not dare to own that she longs for one. She had liked to have miscarried t'other day for the pith of a loin of veal.—Ah, you barbarous man!—

Rich. But, my Aurelia! confirm me that you know her, and I'll adore thee.

Mrs. Man. You would fling five hundred guineas at my head, that you knew as much of her as I do: why, sir, I brought her into the world; I have had her sprawling in my lap. Ah! she was as plump as a puffin, sir.

Rich. I think she has no great portion to value herself upon; her reputation only will keep up the market. We must first make that cheap, by crying it down, and then she'll part with it at an easy rate.

Mrs. Man. But won't you provide for poor Clelia?

Rich. Provide! why, ha'n't I taught her a trade? Let her set up when she will, I'll engage her customers enough, because I can answer for the goodness of the ware.

Mrs. Man. Nay, but you ought to set her up with credit, and take a shop; that is, get her a husband. Have you no pretty gentleman your relation now, that wants a young virtuous lady with a handsome fortune? No young Templar that has spent his estate in the study of the law, and starves by the practice? No spruce officer that wants a handsome wife to make court for him among the major-generals? Have you none of these, sir?

Rich. Pho, pho, madam! you have tired me upon that subject. Do you think a lady that gave me so much trouble before possession shall ever give me any after it? No, no; had she been more obliging to me when I was in her power, I should be more civil to her now she's in mine: my assiduity before-hand was an overprice; had she made a merit of the matter, she should have yielded sooner.

Mrs. Man. Nay, nay, sir; though you have no regard to her honour, yet you shall protect mine. How d'ye think I have secured my reputation so long among the people of best figure, but by keeping all mouths stopped? Sir, I'll have no clamours at me. Heavens help me, I have clamours enough at my door early and late in my t'other capacity! In short, sir, a husband for Clelia, or I banish you my presence for ever.

Rich. Thou art a necessary devil, and I can't want thee. [*Aside.*

Mrs. Man. Look'ee, sir, 'tis your own advantage; 'tis only making over your estate into the hands of a trustee; and though you don't absolutely command the premises, yet you may exact enough out of 'em for necessaries, when you will.

Rich. Patience a little, madam! I have a young nephew that is a captain of horse: he mortgaged the last morsel of his estate to me, to make up his equipage for the last campaign. Perhaps you know him; he's a brisk fellow, much about court, Captain Trueman.

Mrs. Man. Trueman! ads my life, he's one of my babies! I can tell you the very minute he was born —precisely at three o'clock next St. George's day Trueman will be two-and-twenty; a stripling, the prettiest, good-natured child, and your nephew! he must be the man; and shall be the man; I have a kindness for him.

Rich. But we must have a care; the fellow wants neither sense nor courage.

Mrs. Man. Phu, phu! never fear her part, she shan't want instructions; and then for her lying-in a little abruptly, 'tis my business to reconcile matters there, a fright or a fall excuses that. Lard, sir! I do these things every day.

Rich. 'Tis pity then to put you out of your road; and Clelia shall have a husband.

Mrs. Man. Spoke like a man of honour! and now I'll serve you again. This Aurelia, you say—

Rich. Oh, she distracts me! Her beauty, family, and virtue, make her a noble pleasure.

Mrs. Man. And you have a mind for that reason to get her a husband?

Rich. Yes, faith; I have another young relation at Cambridge is just going into orders; and I think such a fine woman, with fifteen hundred pound, is a better presentation than any living in my gift; and why should he like the cure the worse that an incumbent was there before?

Mrs. Man. Thou art a pretty fellow! At the same moment you would persuade me that you love a woman to madness, are you contriving how to part with her.

Rich. If I loved her not to madness I should not run into these contradictions. Here, my dear mother, Aurelia's the word. [*Offers her money.*

Mrs. Man. Pardon me, sir!—[*Refusing the money.*] Did you ever know me mercenary? No, no, sir; virtue is its own reward.

Rich. Nay, but, madam, I owe you for the teeth-powder you sent me.

Mrs. Man. Oh, that's another matter, sir!—[*Takes the money.*] I hope you like it, sir?

Rich. Extremely, madam.—[*Aside.*] But it was somewhat dear of twenty guineas.

Enter Footman.

Foot. Madam, here is Mr. Wouldbe's footman below with a message from his master.

Mrs. Man. I come to him presently.—[*Exit* Footman.] Do you know that Wouldbe loves Aurelia's cousin and companion, Mrs. Constance, with the great fortune, and that I solicit for him?

Rich. Why, she's engaged to his elder brother! besides, young Wouldbe has no money to prosecute an affair of such consequence. You can have no hopes of success there, I'm sure.

Mrs. Man. Truly, I have no great hopes; but an industrious body, you know, would do anything rather than be idle: the aunt is very near her time, and I have access to the family when I please.

Rich. Now I think on't; prithee, get the letter from Wouldbe that I gave him just now. It would be proper to our designs upon Trueman that it should not be exposed.

Mrs. Man. And you showed Clelia's letter to Wouldbe?

Rich. Yes.

Mrs. Man. Eh, you barbarous man! Who the devil would oblige you? What pleasure can you take in exposing the poor creature? Dear little child, 'tis pity, indeed it is!

Rich. Madam, the messenger waits below: so I'll take my leave. [*Exit.*

Mrs. Man. Ah, you're a sad man! [*Exit.*

ACT II.

SCENE I.

The Park.

Constance *and* Aurelia *discovered.*

Aur. Prithee, cousin Constance, be cheerful; let the dead lord sleep in peace, and look up to the living; take pen, ink, and paper, and write immediately to your lover, that he is now a baron of England, and that you long to be a baroness.

Con. Nay, Aurelia, there is some regard due to the memory of the father for the respect I bear the son; besides, I don't know how, I could wish my young lord were at home in this juncture. This brother of his—some mischief will happen—I had a very ugly dream last night. In short, I am eaten up with the spleen, my dear.

Aur. Come, come, walk about and divert it; the air will do you good; think of other people's affairs a little. When did you see Clelia?

Con. I'm glad you mentioned her; don't you observe her gaiety to be much more forced than formerly? her humour don't sit so easy upon her.

Aur. No, nor her stays neither, I can assure you.

Con. Did you observe how she devoured the pomegranates yesterday?

Aur. She talks of visiting a relation in Leicester-shire.

Con. She fainted away in the country dance t'other night.

Aur. Richmore shunned her in the Walk last week.

Con. And his footman laughed.

Aur. She takes laudanum to make her sleep at nights.

Con. Ah, poor Clelia! What will she do, cousin?

Aur. Do! why nothing till the nine months be up.

Con. That's cruel, Aurelia, how can you make merry with her misfortunes? I am positive she was no easy conquest; some singular villany has been practised upon her.

Aur. Yes, yes, the fellow would be practising upon me too, I thank him.

Con. Have a care, cousin, he has a promising person.

Aur. Nay, for that matter, his promising person may as soon be broke as his promising vows. Nature indeed has made him a giant, and he wars with heaven like the giants of old.

Con. Then why will you admit his visits?

Aur. I never did : but all the servants are more his than our own. He has a golden key to every door in the house; besides, he makes my uncle believe that his intentions are honourable; and, in-deed, he has said nothing yet to disprove it. But, cousin, do you see who comes yonder, sliding along the Mall?

Con. Captain Trueman, I protest! the campaign has improved him, he makes a very clean, well-fur-nished figure.

Aur. Youthful, easy, and good-natured. I could wish he would know us.

Con. Are you sure he's well-bred?

Aur. I tell you he's good-natured, and I take good manners to be nothing but a natural desire to be easy and agreeable to whatever conversation we fall into; and a porter with this is mannerly in his way, and a duke without it has but the breeding of a dancing-master.

Con. I like him for his affection to my young lord.

Aur. And I like him for his affection to my young person.

Con. How, how, cousin, you never told me that.

Aur. How should I? He never told it me, but I have discovered it by a great many signs and tokens, that are better security for his heart than ten thousand vows and promises.

Con. He's Richmore's nephew.

Aur. Ah, would he were his heir too! He's a pretty fellow. But, then, he's a soldier; and must share his time with his mistress, honour, in Flanders. No, no, I'm resolved against a man that disappears all the summer like a woodcock.

Enter Captain TRUEMAN *behind them, as passing over the stage.*

True. That's for me who ever spoke it.—[*The* Ladies *turn about.*] Aurelia!

Con. What, captain, you're afraid of everything but the enemy!

True. I have reason, ladies, to be most apprehensive where there is most danger. The enemy is satisfied with a leg or an arm, but here I'm in hazard of losing my heart.

Aur. None in the world, sir, nobody here designs to attack it.

True. But suppose it be assaulted, and taken already, madam?

Aur. Then we'll return it without ransom.

True. But suppose, madam, the prisoner choose to stay where it is?

Aur. That were to turn deserter, and you know, captain, what such deserve.

True. The punishment it undergoes this moment —shot to death.

Con. Nay, then, 'tis time for me to put in.— Pray, sir, have you heard the news of my lord Wouldbe's death?

True. [*To* CONSTANCE.] People mind not the death of others, madam, that are expiring themselves.—[*To* AURELIA.] Do you consider, madam, the penalty of wounding a man in the Park?

Aur. Heyday! Why, captain, d'ye intend to make a Vigo* business of it, and break the boom at once? Sir, if you only rally, pray let my cousin have her share; or, if you would be particular, pray be more respectful; not so much upon the declaration, I beseech you, sir.

True. I have been, fair creature, a perfect coward in my passion; I have had hard strugglings with my fear before I durst engage, and now perhaps behave but too desperately.

---

* In Vigo Bay, on 23rd October 1702, the Spanish " Plate Fleet " was destroyed by the English and Dutch, who broke the boom that defended the harbour.

Aur. Sir, I am very sorry you have said so much; for I must punish you for't, though it be contrary to my inclination.—Come, cousin, will you walk?

Con. Servant, sir!   [*Exit with* AURELIA.

True. Charming creature!—*I must punish you for't though it be contrary to my inclination.*—Hope and despair in a breath. But I'll think the best.   [*Exit.*

SCENE II.

BENJAMIN WOULDBE'S *Lodgings.*

Enter BENJAMIN WOULDBE *and* Mrs. MANDRAKE, *meeting.*

Ben. Would. Thou life and soul of secret dealings, welcome!

Mrs. Man. My dear child, bless thee!—Who would have imagined that I brought this great rogue into the world? He makes me an old woman, I protest.—But, adso, my child, I forgot; I'm sorry for the loss of your father, sorry at my heart, poor man!—[*Weeps.*] Mr. Wouldbe, have you got a drop of brandy in your closet? I an't very well to-day.

Ben. Would. That you shan't want; but be pleased to sit, my dear mother.—Here, Jack, the brandy bottle.—[*Calls to* Servant.] Now, madam, I have occasion to use you in dressing up a handsome cheat for me.

Mrs. Man. I defy any chambermaid in England

to do it better. I have dressed up a hundred and fifty cheats in my time.

Enter JACK *with the brandy bottle.*

Here, boy, this glass is too big; carry it away, I'll take a sup out of the bottle.   [*Exit* JACK.

Ben. Would. Right, madam. And my business being very urgent—in three words, 'tis this—

Mrs. Man. Hold, sir, till I take advice of my counsel,—[*Drinks.*] There is nothing more comfortable to a poor creature, and fitter to revive wasting spirits, than a little plain brandy. I an't for your hot spirits, your rosa solis, your ratafias, your orange-waters, and the like: a moderate glass of cool Nantes is the thing.

Ben. Would. But to our business, madam.—My father is dead, and I have a mind to inherit his estate.

Mrs. Man. You put the case very well.

Ben. Would. One of two things I must choose —either to be a lord or a beggar.

Mrs. Man. Be a lord to choose :—though I have known some that have chosen both.

Ben. Would. I have a brother that I love very well; but, since one of us must want, I had rather he should starve than I.

Mrs. Man. Upon my conscience, dear heart, you're in the right on't.

Ben. Would. Now your advice upon these heads.

Mrs. Man. They be matters of weight, and I must consider.—[*Drinks.*] Is there a will in the case ?

Ben. Would. There is; which excludes me from every foot of the estate.

Mrs. Man. That's bad.—Where's your brother?

Ben. Would. He's now in Germany, in his way to England, and is expected very soon.

Mrs. Man. How soon?

Ben. Would. In a month or less.

Mrs. Man. O ho! a month is a great while! our business must be done in an hour or two. We must—[*Drinks*] suppose your brother to be dead; nay, he shall be actually dead—and, my lord, my humble service t'ye!

Ben. Would. O madam, I'm your ladyship's most devoted! Make your words good, and I'll—

Mrs. Man. Say no more, sir; you shall have it, you shall have it.

Ben. Would. Ay, but how, dear Mrs. Mandrake?

Mrs. Man. Mrs. Mandrake! is that all? Why not mother, aunt, grandmother? Sir, I have done more for you this moment than all the relations you have in the world.

Ben. Would. Let me hear it.

Mrs. Man. By the strength of this potent inspiration, I have made you a peer of England, with seven thousand pound a year.—My lord, I wish you joy.

[Drinks.

Ben. Would. The woman's mad, I believe!

Mrs. Man. Quick, quick, my lord! Counterfeit a letter presently from Germany, that your brother is killed in a duel; let it be directed to your father, and fall into the hands of the steward when you are by.—What sort of fellow is the steward?

Ben. Would. Why, a timorous, half-honest man,

that a little persuasion will make a whole knave. He wants courage to be thoroughly just or entirely a villain; but good backing will make him either.

Mrs. Man. And he shan't want that! I tell you the letter must come into his hands when you are by; upon this you take immediate possession, and so you have the best part of the law on your side.

Ben. Would. But suppose my brother comes in the meantime?

Mrs. Man. This must be done this very moment. Let him come when you're in possession, I'll warrant we'll find a way to keep him out.

Ben. Would. But, how, my dear contriver?

Mrs. Man. By your father's will, man, your father's will:—that is, one that your father might have made, and which we will make for him. I'll send you a nephew of my own, a lawyer, that shall do the business. Go, get into possession, possession, I say; let us have but the estate to back the suit, and you'll find the law too strong for justice, I warrant you.

Ben. Would. My oracle! How shall we revel in delight when this great prediction is accomplished! —But one thing yet remains, my brother's mistress, the charming Constance—let her be mine.

Mrs. Man. Pho! pho! she's yours o' course; she's contracted to you; for she's engaged to marry no man but my lord Wouldbe's son and heir; now, you being the person, she's recoverable by law.

Ben. Would. Marry her! no, no, she's contracted to him; 'twere injustice to rob a brother of his wife, an easier favour will satisfy me.

Mrs. Man. Why, truly, as you say, that favour is so easy that I wonder they make such a bustle about it. But get you gone and mind your affairs, I must about mine.—Oh—I had forgot—where's that foolish letter you had this morning from Richmore?

Ben. Would. I have posted it up in the chocolate-house.

Mrs. Man. Yaw!—[*Shrieks.*] I shall fall into fits; hold me—

Ben. Would. No, no, I did but jest; here it is. But be assured, madam, I wanted only time to have exposed it.

Mrs. Man. Ah, you barbarous man! why so?

Ben. Would. Because, when knaves of our sex, and fools of yours meet, they make the best jest in the world.

Mrs. Man. Sir, the world has a better share in the jest when we are the knaves and you the fools. But look'ee, sir, if ever you open your mouth about this trick, I'll discover all your tricks; therefore, silence and safety on both sides.

Ben. Would. Madam, you need not doubt my silence at present; because my own affairs will employ me sufficiently; so there's your letter.— [*Gives the letter.*] And now to write my own.

Mrs. Man. Adieu, my lord!—[*Exit* WOULDBE.] Let me see.—[*Opens the letter and reads.*] *If there be solemnity in protestations* — that's foolish, very foolish! Why should she expect solemnity in protestations?—Um, um, um.—*I may still depend upon the faith of my Richmore.*—Ah, poor Clelia!—Um, um, um.—*I can no longer hide the effects on't from the world.*—The effects on't! How modestly is that expressed! Well, 'tis a pretty letter, and I'll keep it.

[Exit.

SCENE III.

A Room in Lord WOULDBE'S *House.*

Mr. *and* Mrs. CLEARACCOUNT *discovered.*

Mrs. Clear. You are to blame, you are much to blame, husband, in being so scrupulous.

Clear. 'Tis true; this foolish conscience of mine has been the greatest bar to my fortune.

Mrs. Clear. And will ever be so. Tell me but one that thrives, and I'll show you a hundred that starve by it. Do you think 'tis fourscore pound a year makes my lord Gouty's steward's wife live at the rate of four hundred? Upon my word, my dear, I'm as good a gentlewoman as she, and I expect to be maintained accordingly. 'Tis conscience I warrant that buys her the point-heads and diamond necklace? Was it conscience that bought her the fine house in Jermyn Street? Is it conscience that enables the steward to buy when the lord is forced to sell?

Clear. But what would you have me do?

Mrs. Clear. Do! now's your time; that small morsel of an estate your lord bought lately, a thing not worth mentioning; take it towards your daughter Molly's portion. What's two hundred a year? 'twill never be missed.

Clear. 'Tis but a small matter, I must confess; and as a reward for my past faithful service, I think it but reasonable I should cheat a little now.

Mrs. Clear. Reasonable! all the reason that can be; if the ungrateful world won't reward an honest man, why let an honest man reward himself. There's five hundred pounds you received but two days ago, lay them aside. You may easily sink it in the charge of the funeral. Do my dear now, kiss me, and do it.

Clear. Well, you have such a winning way with you! But, my dear, I'm so much afraid of my young lord's coming home; he's a cunning close man, they say, and will examine my accounts very narrowly.

Mrs. Clear. Ay, my dear, would you had the younger brother to deal with! you might manage him as you pleased. I see him coming. Let us weep, let us weep. [*They pull out their handkerchiefs, and seem to mourn.*

Enter BENJAMIN WOULDBE.

Clear. Ah, sir! we have all lost a father, a friend, and a supporter.

Ben. Would. Ay, Mr. Steward, we must submit to fate, as he has done. And it is no small addition to my grief, honest Mr. Clearaccount, that it is not in my power to supply my father's place to you and yours. Your sincerity and justice to the dead merits the greatest regard from those that survive him. Had I but my brother's ability, or he my inclinations, I'll assure you, Mrs. Clearaccount, you should not have such cause to mourn.

Mrs. Clear. Ah, good noble sir!

Clear. Your brother, sir, I hear, is a very severe man.

Ben. Would. He is what the world calls a prudent man, Mr. Steward. I have often heard him very severe upon men of your business; and has declared, that for form's sake indeed he would keep a steward, but that he would inspect into all his accounts himself.

Mrs. Clear. Ay, Mr. Wouldbe, you have more sense than to do these things; you have more honour than to trouble your head with your own affairs. Would to Heavens we were to serve you!

Ben. Would. Would I could serve you, madam, without injustice to my brother.

Enter Footman.

Foot. A letter for my lord Wouldbe.

Clear. It comes too late, alas! for his perusal. Let me see it. [*Opens and reads.*

Frankfort, Octob. 10, *new style.*

Frankfort! where's Frankfort, sir?

Ben. Would. In Germany. This letter must be from my brother; I suppose he's a-coming home.

Clear. 'Tis none of his hand. Let me see.

[*Reads.*

My Lord,

I am troubled at this unhappy occasion of sending to your lordship; your brave son, and my dear friend, was yesterday unfortunately killed in a duel by a German count—

I shall love a German count as long as I live.—My lord, my lord, now I may call you so, since your elder brother's—dead.

Ben. Would., Mrs. Clear. How?

Clear. Read there.

[*Gives the letter,* WOULDBE *peruses it.*

Ben. Would. Oh, my fate! a father and a brother in one day! Heavens! 'tis too much.—Where is the fatal messenger?

Foot. A gentleman, sir, who said he came post on purpose. He was afraid the contents of the letter would unqualify my lord for company; so he would take another time to wait on him.   [*Exit.*

Ben. Would. Nay, then, 'tis true; and there is truth in dreams.   Last night I dreamed—

Mrs. Clear. Nay, my lord, I dreamed too; I dreamed I saw your brother dressed in a long minister's gown (Lord bless us!), with a book in his hand, walking before a dead body to the grave.

Ben. Would. Well, Mr. Clearaccount, get mourning ready.

Clear. Will your lordship have the old coach covered, or a new one made?

Ben. Would. A new one.   The old coach, with the grey horses, I give to Mrs. Clearaccount here; 'tis not fit she should walk the streets.

Mrs. Clear. [*Aside.*] Heavens bless the German count, I say!—[*Aloud.*] But, my lord—

Ben. Would. No reply, madam, you shall have it: and receive it but as the earnest of my favours.— Mr. Clearaccount, I double your salary, and all the servants' wages, to moderate their grief for our great losses.   Pray, sir, take order about these affairs.

Clear. I shall, my lord.

[*Exit with* Mrs. CLEARACCOUNT.

Ben. Would. So! I have got possession of the castle, and if I had but a little law to fortify me now, I believe we might hold it out a great while.   Oh! here comes my attorney.

Enter SUBTLEMAN.

Mr. Subtleman, your servant.

Sub. My lord, I wish you joy; my aunt Mandrake has sent me to receive your commands.

Ben. Would. Has she told you anything of the affair?

Sub. Not a word, my lord.

Ben. Would. Why then—come nearer.—Can you make a man right heir to an estate during the life of an elder brother?

Sub. I thought you had been the eldest.

Ben. Would. That we are not yet agreed upon ; for you must know, there is an impertinent fellow that takes a fancy to dispute the seniority with me ; for, look'ee, sir, my mother has unluckily sowed discord in the family, by bringing forth twins. My brother, 'tis true, was first-born ; but, I believe from the bottom of my heart, I was the first-begotten.

Sub. I understand—you are come to an estate and dignity, that by justice indeed is your own, but by law it falls to your brother.

Ben. Would. I had rather, Mr. Subtleman, it were his by justice and mine by law ; for I would have the strongest title, if possible.

Sub. I am very sorry there should happen any breach between brethren : so I think it would be but a Christian and charitable act to take away all farther disputes, by making you true heir to the estate by the last will of your father. Look'ee, I'll divide stakes ; you shall yield the eldership and honour to him, and he shall quit his estate to you.

Ben. Would. Why, as you say, I don't much care if I do grant him the eldest, half an hour is but a trifle. But how shall we do about this will? who shall we get to prove it?

Sub. Never trouble yourself for that, I expect a cargo of witnesses and usquebaugh by the first fair wind.

Ben. Would. But we can't stay for them ; it must be done immediately.

Sub. Well, well ; we'll find somebody, I warrant you, to make oath of his last words.

Ben. Would. That's impossible ; for my father died of an apoplexy, and did not speak at all.

Sub. That's nothing, sir : he's not the first dead man that I have made to speak.

Ben. Would. You're a great master of speech, I don't question, sir ; and I can assure you there will be ten guineas for every word you extort from him in my favour.

Sub. O sir, that's enough to make your great-grandfather speak.

Ben. Would. Come then, I'll carry you to my steward ; he shall give you the names of the manors, and the true titles and denominations of the estate, and then you shall go to work.   [*Exeunt.*

SCENE IV.

The Park.

Enter RICHMORE *and* Captain TRUEMAN, *meeting.*

Rich. O brave cuz! you're very happy with the fair, I find.   Pray which of those two ladies you encountered just now has your adoration ?

True. She that commands by forbidding it : and since I had courage to declare to herself, I dare now own it to the world : Aurelia, sir, is my angel.

Rich. Ha !—[*A long pause.*]   Sir, I find you're of

everybody's religion; but methinks you make a bold flight at first. Do you think your captain's pay will stake against so high a gamester?

True. What do you mean?

Rich. Mean! bless me, sir, mean!—You're a man of mighty honour, we all know.—But I'll tell you a secret—the thing is public already.

True. I should be proud that all mankind were acquainted with it; I should despise the passion that could make me either ashamed or afraid to own it.

Rich. Ha! ha! ha! prithee, dear captain, no more of these rhodomontados; you may as soon put a standing-army upon us. I'll tell you another secret— five hundred pound is the least penny.

True. Nay, to my knowledge, she has fifteen hundred.

Rich. Nay, to my knowledge, she took five.

True. Took five! how? where?

Rich. In her lap, in her lap, captain, where should it be?

True. I'm amazed!

Rich. So am I; that she could be so unreasonable. —Fifteen hundred pound! 'sdeath! had she that price from you?

True. 'Sdeath! I meant her portion.

Rich. Why, what have you to do with her portion?

True. I loved her up to marriage, by this light.

Rich. Marriage! ha! ha! ha! I love the gipsy for her cunning. A young, easy, amorous, credulous fellow of two-and-twenty, was just the game she wanted; I find she presently singled you out from the herd.

True. You distract me!

Rich. A soldier too, that must follow the wars abroad, and leave her to engagements at home.

True. Death and furies! I'll be revenged!

Rich. Why, what can you do? You'll challenge her, will you?

True. Her reputation was spotless when I went over.

Rich. So was the reputation of Mareschal Boufflers; but d'ye think, that while you were beating the French abroad, that we were idle at home? No, no, we have had our sieges, our capitulations, and surrendries, and all that. We have cut ourselves out good winter-quarters as well as you.

True. And are you billeted there?

Rich. Look'ee, Trueman, you ought to be very trusty to a secret, that has saved you from destruction. In plain terms, I have buried five hundred pounds in that little spot, and I should think it very hard if you took it over my head.

True. Not by a lease for life, I can assure you, but I shall—

Rich. What! you han't five hundred pounds to give? Look'ee, since you can make no sport, spoil none. In a year or two, she dwindles to a perfect basset-bank; everybody may play at it that pleases, and then you may put in for a piece or two.

True. Dear sir, I could worship you for this.

Rich. Not for this, nephew; for I did not intend it, but I came to seek you upon another affair. Were not you in the presence last night?

True. I was.

Rich. Did not you talk to Clelia, my lady Taper's niece?

True. A fine woman.

Rich. Well, I met her upon the stairs, and handing her to her coach, she asked me if you were not my nephew; and said two or three warm things, that persuade me she likes you. Her relations have interest at court, and she has money in her pocket.

True. But—this devil Aurelia still sticks with me.

Rich. What then! the way to love in one place with success, is to marry in another with convenience. Clelia has four thousand pound; this applied to your reigning ambition, whether love or advancement, will go a great way: and for her virtue and conduct, be assured, that nobody can give a better account of it than myself.

True. I am willing to believe from this late accident, that you consult my honour and interest in what you propose, and therefore I am satisfied to be governed.

Rich. I see the very lady in the walk. We'll about it.

True. I wait on you.   [*Exeunt.*

SCENE V.

A Room in Lord WOULDBE'S *House.*

BENJAMIN WOULDBE, SUBTLEMAN, *and* CLEAR-ACCOUNT, *discovered.*

Ben. Would. Well, Mr. Subtleman, you are sure the will is firm and good in law?

Sub. I warrant you, my lord: and for the last words to prove it, here they are—look'ee, Mr.

Clearaccount—*Yes*—that is an answer to the question that was put to him (you know) by those about him when he was a-dying—yes, or no, he must have said; so we have chosen yes—*Yes, I have made my will, as it may be found in the custody of Mr. Clearaccount my steward; and I desire it may stand as my last will and testament.* —Did you ever hear a dying man's words more to the purpose? An apoplexy! I tell you, my lord had intervals to the last.

Clear. Ay, but how shall these words be proved?

Sub. My lord shall speak 'em now.

Ben. Would. Shall he, faith?

Sub. Ay, now—if the corpse ben't buried. Look'ee, sir, these words must be put into his mouth, and drawn out again before us all; and if they won't be his last words then—I'll be perjured.

Ben. Would. What! violate the dead! it must not be, Mr. Subtleman.

Sub. With all my heart, sir! But I think you had better violate the dead of a tooth or so, than violate the living of seven thousand pound a year.

Ben. Would. But is there no other way?

Sub. No, sir. Why, d'ye think Mr. Clearaccount here will hazard soul and body to swear they are his last words, unless they be made his last words? For my part, sir, I'll swear to nothing but what I see with my eyes come out of a man's mouth.

Ben. Would. But it looks so unnatural.

Sub. What, to open a man's mouth, and put in a bit of paper!—this is all.

Ben. Would. But the body is cold, and his teeth can't be got asunder.

Sub. But what occasion has your father for teeth now? I tell you what, I knew a gentleman, three days buried, taken out of his grave, and his dead hand set to his last will, (unless somebody made him sign another afterwards,) and I know the estate to be held by that tenure to this day; and a firm tenure it is; for a dead hand holds fastest; and let me tell you, dead teeth will fasten as hard.

Ben. Would. Well, well, use your pleasure, you understand the law best.—[*Exeunt* SUBTLEMAN *and* CLEARACCOUNT.] What a mighty confusion is brought into families by sudden death! Men should do well to settle their affairs in time. Had my father done this before he was taken ill, what a trouble had he saved us! But he was taken suddenly, poor man!

Re-enter SUBTLEMAN.

Sub. Your father still bears you the old grudge, I find. It was with much struggling he consented; I never knew a man so loath to speak in my life.

Ben. Would. He was always a man of few words.

Sub. Now I may safely bear witness myself, as the scrivener there present: I love to do things with a clear conscience. [*Subscribes.*

Ben. Would. But the law requires three witnesses.

Sub. Oh! I shall pick up a couple more, that perhaps may take my word for't. But is not Mr. Clearaccount in your interest?

Ben. Would. I hope so.

Sub. Then he shall be one; a witness in the family goes a great way; besides, these foreign evidences are risen confoundedly since the wars. I hope, if mine escape the privateers, to make a hundred pound an car of every head of 'em. But the steward is an honest man, and shall save you the charges.   [*Exit.*

Ben. Would. The pride of birth, the heats of appetite, and fears of want, are strong temptations to injustice.—But why injustice?—The world has broke all civilities with me, and left me in the eldest state of nature, wild, where force, or cunning first created right. I cannot say I ever knew a father; 'tis true, I was begotten in his lifetime, but I was posthumous born, and lived not till he died. My hours indeed I numbered, but ne'er enjoyed 'em till this moment.—My brother! what is brother? we are all so; and the first two were enemies. He stands before me in the road of life to rob me of my pleasures. My senses, formed by nature for delight, are all alarmed. My sight, my hearing, taste and touch, call loudly on me for their objects, and they shall be satisfied.   [*Exit.*

ACT III.

SCENE I.

A Room in Lord WOULDBE'S *House.*

BENJAMIN WOULDBE *is discovered dressing.* FRISURE *attending.* CLEARACCOUNT, COMIC, *and a levee of* Gentlemen, *in waiting.*

Ben. Would. [*Aside.*] Surely, the greatest ornament of quality is a clean and a numerous levee ! Such a crowd of attendance for the cheap reward of words and promises, distinguishes the nobility from those that pay wages to their servants.—[First Gentleman *whispers.*] Sir, I shall speak to the commissioners, and use all my interest, I can assure you, sir.—[Second Gentleman *whispers.*] Sir, I shall meet some of your board this evening : let me see you to-morrow.— [Third Gentleman *whispers.*] Sir, I'll consider of it. —[*Aside.*] That fellow's breath stinks of tobacco.— O Mr. Comic, your servant !

Com. My lord, I wish you joy ; I have something to show your lordship.

Ben. Would. What is it, pray, sir ?

Com. I have an elegy upon the dead lord, and a panegyric upon the living one.—*In utrumque paratus,* my lord.

Ben. Would. Ha ! ha ! very pretty, Mr. Comic.

But pray, Mr. Comic, why don't you write plays? it would give one an opportunity of serving you.

Com. My lord, I have writ one.

Ben. Would. Was it ever acted?

Com. No, my lord; but it has been a-rehearsing these three years and a half.

Ben. Would. A long time.   There must be a great deal of business in it surely.

Com. No, my lord, none at all.   I have another play just finished, but that I want a plot for't.

Ben. Would. A plot! you should read the Italian and Spanish plays, Mr. Comic.   I like your verses here mightily.—Here, Mr. Clearaccount!

Com. Now for five guineas at least.   [*Aside.*

Ben. Would. Here, give Mr. Comic, give him— give him the Spanish play that lies in the closet window.—[*To a* Gentleman.]   Captain, can I do you any service?

Fourth Gent. Pray, my lord, use your interest with the general for that vacant commission: I hope, my lord, the blood I have already lost may entitle me to spill the remainder in my country's cause.

Ben. Would. All the reason in the world.— Captain, you may depend upon me for all the service I can.

Fifth Gent. I hope your lordship won't forget to speak to the general about that vacant commission. Although I have never made a campaign, yet, my lord, my interest in the country can raise me men, which, I think, should prefer me to that gentleman, whose bloody disposition frightens the poor people from listing.

Ben. Would. All the reason in the world, sir; you

may depend upon me for all the service in my power.
—Captain, I'll do your business for you.—Sir, I'll
speak to the general ; I shall see him at the house.

Enter Alderman.

Oh, Mr. Alderman, your servant !—Gentlemen all, I
beg your pardon !—[*Exeunt* Levee.] Mr. Alderman,
have you any service to command me ?

Ald. Your lordship's humble servant !—I have a
favour to beg. You must know, I have a graceless
son, a fellow that drinks and swears eternally, keeps
a whore in every corner of the town : in short, he's
fit for no kind of thing but a soldier. I am so tired
of him that I intend to throw him into the army, let
the fellow be ruined, if he will.

Ben. Would. I commend your paternal care, sir !
Can I do you any service in this affair ?

Ald. Yes, my lord : there is a vacant company in
Colonel Whatd'yecalum's regiment, and if your lordship would but speak to the general—

Ben. Would. Has your son ever served ?

Ald. Served ! yes, my lord, he's an ensign in the
trainbands.

Ben. Would. Has he ever signalised his courage ?

Ald. Often, often, my lord ; but one day particularly, you must know, his captain was so busy shipping
off a cargo of cheeses, that he left my son to command in his place—would you believe it, my lord? he
charged up Cheapside, in the front of the buff-coats
with such bravery and courage, that I could not
forbear wishing, in the loyalty of my heart, for ten
thousand such officers upon the Rhine. Ah! my

lord, we must employ such fellows as him, or we shall never humble the French king.—Now, my lord, if you could find a convenient time to hint these things to the general——

Ben. Would. All the reason in the world, Mr. Alderman—I'll do you all the service I can.

Ald. You may tell him; he's a man of courage, fit for the service; and then he loves hardship—he sleeps every other night in the round-house.

Ben. Would. I'll do you all the service I can.

Ald. Then, my lord, he salutes with his pike so very handsomely, it went to his mistress's heart, t'other day.—Then he beats a drum like an angel.

Ben. Would. Sir, I'll do you all the service I can—
     [*Not taking the least notice of the* Alderman *all
          this while, but dressing himself in the glass.*

Ald. But, my lord, the hurry of your lordship's affairs may put my business out of your head; therefore, my lord, I'll presume to leave you some memorandum.

Ben. Would. I'll do you all the service I can.
                              [*Not minding him.*

Ald. Pray, my lord,—[*Pulling him by the sleeve*] give me leave for a memorandum; my glove, I suppose, will do. Here, my lord, pray remember me—   [*Lays his glove upon the table, and exit.*

Ben. Would. I'll do you all the service I can.— What, is he gone? 'Tis the most rude familiar fellow!—Faugh, what a greasy gauntlet is here!— [*A purse drops out of the glove.*] Oh! no, no; the glove is a clean well-made glove, and the owner of it—the most respectful person I have seen this morning; he knows what distance—[*Chinking the purse*] is due to a man of quality.—But what must I do for this?—Frisure, do you remember what the alderman said to me?

Fris. No, my lord, I thought your lordship had.

Ben. Would. This blockhead thinks a man of quality can mind what people say—when they do something, 'tis another case.—Here, call him back. —[*Exit* FRISURE.] He talked something of the general, and his son, and trainbands, I know not what stuff.

Re-enter FRISURE *with* Alderman.

Oh, Mr. Alderman, I have put your memorandum in my pocket.

Ald. Oh, my lord, you do me too much honour!

Ben. Would. But, Mr. Alderman, the business you were talking of; it shall be done, but if you gave a short note of it to my secretary, it would not be amiss.—But, Mr. Alderman, han't you the fellow to this glove, it fits me mighty well—[*Putting on the glove.*] It looks so like a challenge to give a man an odd glove—and I would have nothing that looks like enmity between you and I, Mr. Alderman.

Ald. Truly, my lord, I intended the other glove for a memorandum to the colonel, but since your lordship has a mind to't— [*Gives the glove.*]

Ben. Would. Here, Frisure, lead this gentleman to my secretary, and bid him take a note of his business.

Ald. But, my lord, don't do me all the service you can now.

Ben. Would. Well, I won't do you all the service I can.—[*Exeunt* FRISURE *and* Alderman.] These

citizens have a strange capacity of soliciting sometimes.

Re-enter CLEARACCOUNT.

Clear. My lord, here are your tailor, your vintner,
your bookseller, and half-a-dozen more with their bills
at the door, and they desire their money.

Ben. Would. Tell 'em, Mr. Clearaccount, that
when I was a private gentleman, I had nothing else
to do but to run in debt, and now that I have got
into a higher rank, I'm so very busy I can't pay it.
As for that clamorous rogue of a tailor, speak him fair
till he has made up my liveries: then about a year
and a half hence, be at leisure to put him off; for a
year and a half longer.

Clear. My lord, there's a gentleman below calls
himself Mr. Basset, he says your lordship owes him
fifty guineas that he won of you at cards.

Ben. Would. Look'ee, sir, the gentleman's money
is a debt of honour, and must be paid immediately.

Clear. Your father thought otherwise, my lord.
He always took care to have the poor tradesmen
satisfied, whose only subsistence lay in the use of
their money, and was used to say, that nothing was
honourable but what was honest.

Ben. Would. My father might say what he pleased,
he was a nobleman of very singular humours : but
in my notion there are not two things in nature
more different than honour and honesty. Now your
honesty is a little mechanic quality, well enough
among citizens, people that do nothing but pitiful
mean actions according to law ; but your honour flies
a much higher pitch, and will do anything that's free

and spontaneous, but scorns to level itself to what is only just.

Clear. But I think it a little hard to have these poor people starve for want of their money, and yet pay this sharping rascal fifty guineas.

Ben. Would. Sharping rascal! what a barbarism that is! Why, he wears as good wigs, as fine linen, and keeps as good company, as any at White's; and between you and I, sir, this sharping rascal, as you are pleased to call him, shall make more interest among the nobility with his cards and counters, than a soldier shall with his sword and pistol. Pray let him have fifty guineas immediately. [*Exeunt.*

SCENE II.

The Street before Lord WOULDBE'S *House.*

Enter HERMES WOULDBE, *writing in a pocket-book.*

Herm. Would. *Monday the* 14*th of December,* 1702, *I arrived safe in London, and so concluding my travels—* [*Puts up the book.*

Now welcome country, father, friends,
My brother too, (if brothers can be friends :)
But above all, my charming fair, my Constance.
Through all the mazes of my wandering steps,
Through all the various climes that I have run,
Her love has been the loadstone of my course,
Her eyes the stars that pointed me the way.
Had not her charms my heart entire possessed,
Who knows what Circe's artful voice and look
Might have ensnared my travelling youth,

And fixed me to enchantment ?
Here comes my fellow-traveller.

Enter TEAGUE, *with a portmantle, which he throws
down and sits on.*

What makes you sit upon the portmantle, Teague?
You'll rumple the things.

Teague. Be me shoul, maishter, I did carry the
portmantle till it tired me; and now the portmantle
shall carry me till I tire him.

Herm. Would. And how d'ye like London, Teague,
after our travels ?

Teague. Fet, dear joy, 'tis the bravest plaase I have
sheen in my peregrinations, exshepting my nown brave
shitty of Carick-Vergus.—Uf, uf, dere ish a very
fragrant shmell hereabouts.—Maishter, shall I run to
that paishtry-cook's for shix pennyworths of boiled
beef?

Herm. Would. Though this fellow travelled the
world over he would never lose his brogue nor his
stomach.—Why, you cormorant, so hungry and so
early !

Teague. Early ! Deel tauke me, maishter, 'tish a
great deal more than almost twelve a-clock.

Herm. Would. Thou art never happy unless thy
guts be stuffed up to thy eyes.

Teague. O maishter, dere ish a dam way of distance,
and the deel a bit between.

Enter BENJAMIN WOULDBE *in a chair, passing over
the stage, with four or five* Footmen *before him.*

Herm. Would. Heyday, who comes here ? with
one, two, three, four, five footmen ! Some young

fellow just tasting the sweet vanity of fortune.—Run, Teague, inquire who that is.

Teague. Yes, maishter.—[*Runs to one of the* Footmen.] Sir, will you give my humble shervish to your maishter, and tell him to send me word fat naam ish upon him.

Foot. You would know fat naam ish upon him?

Teague. Yesh, fet would I.

Foot. Why, what are you, sir?

Teague. Be me shoule, I am a shentleman bred and born, and dere ish my maishter.

Foot. Then your master would know it?

Teague. Arrah, you fool, ish it not the saam ting?

Foot. Then tell your master 'tis the young lord Wouldbe, just come to his estate by the death of his father and elder brother.   [*Exit.*

Herm. Would. What do I hear?

Teague. You hear that you are dead, maishter; fere vil you please to be buried?

Herm. Would. But art thou sure it was my brother?

Teague. Be me shoule, it was him nown self; I know'd him fery well, after his man told me.

Herm. Would. The business requires that I be convinced with my own eyes; I'll follow him, and know the bottom on't. Stay here till I return.

Teague. Dear maishter, have a care upon yourshelf: now they know you are dead, by my shoule, they may kill you.

Herm. Would. Don't fear; none of his servants know me, and I'll take care to keep my face from his sight. It concerns me to conceal myself, till I know the engines of this contrivance.—Be sure you stay till I come to you; and let nobody know whom you belong to.				[*Exit.*

Teague. Oh, ho, hon, poor Teague is left all alone!
				[*Sits on the portmantle.*

Enter SUBTLEMAN *and* CLEARACCOUNT.

Sub. And you won't swear to the will?

Clear. My conscience tells me I dare not do't with safety.

Sub. But if we make it lawful, what should you fear? We now think nothing against conscience, till the cause be thrown out of court.

Clear. In you, sir, 'tis no sin; because 'tis the principle of your profession: but in me, sir, 'tis downright perjury indeed. You can't want witnesses enough, since money won't be wanting, and you must lose no time; for I heard just now that the true lord Wouldbe was seen in town, or his ghost.

Sub. It was his ghost, to be sure; for a nobleman without an estate is but the shadow of a lord. Well, take no care; leave me to myself; I'm near the Friars, and ten to one shall pick up an evidence.

Clear. Speed you well, sir!				[*Exit.*

Sub. There's a fellow that has hunger and the gallows pictured in his face, and looks like my countryman.——How now, honest friend, what have you got under you there?

Teague. Noting, dear joy.

Sub. Nothing? is it not a portmantle?

Teague. That is noting to you.

Sub. The fellow's a wit.

Teague. Fet am I; my grandfader was an Irish

poet. He did write a great book of verses concerning the vars between St. Patrick and the wolf-dogs.

Sub. Then thou art poor, I'm afraid?

Teague. Be me shoule, my sole generation ish so. I have noting but thish poor portmantle, and dat itshelf ish not my own.

Sub. Why, who does it belong to?

Teague. To my maishter, dear joy.

Sub. Then you have a master?

Teague. Fet I have, but he's dead.

Sub. Right! and how do you intend to live?

Teague. By eating, dear joy, fen I can get it, and by sleeping fen I can get none: 'tish the fashion of Ireland.

Sub. What was your master's name, pray?

Teague. [*Aside.*] I will tell a lee now; but it shall be a true one.—[*Aloud.*] Macfadin, dear joy, was his naam. He vent over vith King Jamish into France. —[*Aside.*] He was my master once. Deere ish de true lee noo.

Sub. What employment had he?

Teague. Je ne sai pas.

Sub. What, can you speak French?

Teague. Oui, monsieur, I did travel France, and Spain, and Italy. Dear joy, I did kish the pope's toe, and dat will excuse me all the sins of my life; and fen I am dead, St. Patrick will excuse the rest.

Sub. [*Aside.*] A rare fellow for my purpose!— [*Aloud.*] Thou lookest like an honest fellow; and if you'll go with me to the next tavern, I'll give thee a dinner, and a glass of wine.

Teague. Be me shoul, 'tis dat I wanted, dear joy ; come along, I will follow you.

[*Runs out with the portmantle on his back,*
SUBTLEMAN *following.*

Re-enter HERMES WOULDBE.

Herm. Would. My father dead! my birthright lost! How have my drowsy stars slept o'er my fortune?—Ha! [*Looking about*] my servant gone! The simple, poor, ungrateful wretch has left me. I took him up from poverty and want; and now he leaves me just as I found him. My clothes and money too!—But why should I repine? Let man but view the dangers he has passed, and few will fear what hazards are to come. That Providence that has secured my life from robbers, shipwreck, and from sickness, is still the same; still kind whilst I am just. My death, I find, is firmly believed; but how it gained so universal credit I fain would learn.—Who comes here?—honest Mr. Fairbank! my father's goldsmith, a man of substance and integrity. The alteration of five years' absence, with the report of my death, may shade me from his knowledge, till I inquire some news.

Enter FAIRBANK.

Sir, your humble servant!

Fair. Sir, I don't know you.   [*Shunning him.*

Herm. Would. I intend you no harm, sir ; but seeing you come from my lord Wouldbe's house, I would ask you a question or two.—Pray what distemper did my lord die of?

Fair. I am told it was an apoplexy.

Herm. Would. And pray, sir, what does the world say? is his death lamented?

Fair. Lamented! my eyes that question should resolve; friend, thou knewest him not: else thy own heart had answered thee.

Herm. Would. [*Aside.*] His grief, methinks, chides my defect of filial duty.—[*Aloud.*] But, I hope, sir, his loss is partly recompensed in the merits of his successor.

Fair. It might have been; but his eldest son, heir to his virtue and his honour, was lately and unfortunately killed in Germany.

Herm. Would. How unfortunately, sir?

Fair. Unfortunately for him and us. I do remember him. He was the mildest, humblest, sweetest youth—

Herm. Would. [*Aside.*] Happy indeed had been my part in life if I had left this human stage whilst this so spotless and so fair applause had crowned my going off.—[*Aloud.*] Well, sir.

Fair. But those that saw him in his travels, told such wonders of his improvement, that the report recalled his father's years; and with the joy to hear his Hermes praised, he oft would break the chains of gout and age; and leaping up with strength of greenest youth, cry, *My Hermes is myself. Methinks I live my sprightly days again and I am young in him.*

Herm. Would. Spite of all modesty, a man must own a pleasure in the hearing of his praise.   [*Aside.*

Fair. You're thoughtful, sir—had you any relation to the family we talk of?

Herm. Would. None, sir, beyond my private concern in the public loss. But pray, sir, what character does the present lord bear?

Fair. Your pardon, sir. As for the dead, their memories are left unguarded, and tongues may touch them freely : but for the living, they have provided for the safety of their names by a strong inclosure of the law. There is a thing called *scandalum magnatum*, sir.

Herm. Would. I commend your caution, sir ; but be assured I intend not to entrap you. I am a poor gentleman ; and having heard much of the charity of the old lord Wouldbe, I had a mind to apply to his son : and therefore inquired his character.

Fair. Alas ! sir, things are changed. That house was once what poverty might go a pilgrimage to seek, and have its pains rewarded. The noble lord, the truly noble lord, held his estate, his honour, and his house, as if they were only lent upon the interest of doing good to others. He kept a porter, not to exclude, but serve the poor. No creditor was seen to guard his going out, or watch his coming in : no craving eyes, but looks of smiling gratitude. But now, that family, which like a garden fairly kept invited every stranger to its fruit and shade, is now run o'er with weeds. Nothing but wine and revelling within, a crowd of noisy creditors without, a train of servants insolently proud. Would you believe it, sir, as I offered to go in just now, the rude porter pushed me back with his staff. I am at this present (thanks to Providence and my industry) worth twenty thousand pounds. I pay the fifth part of this to maintain the liberty of the nation ; and yet this slave, the impudent Swiss slave, offered to strike me !

Herm. Would. 'Twas hard, sir, very hard: and if they used a man of your substance so roughly, how will they manage me, that am not worth a groat?

Fair. I would not willingly defraud your hopes of what may happen. If you can drink and swear; perhaps—

Herm. Would. I shall not pay that price for his lordship's bounty would it extend to half he's worth. Sir, I give you thanks for your caution, and shall steer another course.

Fair. Sir, you look like an honest, modest gentleman. Come home with me; I am as able to give you a dinner as my lord; and you shall be very welcome to eat at my table every day, till you are better provided.

Herm. Would. [*Aside.*] Good man!—[*Aloud.*] Sir, I must beg you to excuse me to-day: but I shall find a time to accept of your favours, or at least to thank you for 'em.

Fair. Sir, you shall be very welcome whenever you please. [*Exit.*

Herm. Would. Gramercy, citizen! Surely, if Justice were an herald, she would give this tradesman a nobler coat of arms than my brother.—But I delay: I long to vindicate the honour of my station, and to displace this bold usurper.—But one concern methinks is nearer still, my Constance! Should she, upon the rumour of my death, have fixed her heart elsewhere, —then I were dead indeed; but if she still proves true,—brother, sit fast.

I'll shake your strength, all obstacles remove,
Sustain'd by justice, and inspired by love.
[*Exit.*

SCENE III.

Constance's *Apartment.*

Constance *and* Aurelia *discovered.*

Con. For Heaven's sake, cousin, cease your impertinent consolation! it but makes me angry, and raises two passions in me instead of one. You see I commit no extravagance, my grief is silent enough: my tears make no noise to disturb anybody. I desire no companion in my sorrows: leave me to myself and you comfort me.

Aur. But, cousin, have you no regard to your reputation?—This immoderate concern for a young fellow—what will the world say? You lament him like a husband.

Con. No, you mistake: I have no rule nor method for my grief; no pomp of black and darkened rooms; no formal month for visits on my bed. I am content with the slight mourning of a broken heart; and all my form is tears.   [*Weeps.*

Enter Mrs. Mandrake.

Mrs. Man. Madam Aurelia, madam, don't disturb her. Everything must have its vent. 'Tis a hard case to be crossed in one's first love. But you should consider, madam, [*To* Constance] that we are all born to die; some young, some old.

Con. Better we all died young, than be plagued with age as I am. I find other folks' years are as troublesome to us as our own.

Mrs. Man. You have reason, you have cause to mourn : he was the handsomest man, and the sweetest babe, that I know. Though I must confess too, that Ben had much the finer complexion when he was born. But then Hermes—O yes, Hermes had the shape, that he had! But of all the infants that I ever beheld with my eyes, I think Ben had the finest ear! —waxwork, perfect waxwork! And then he did so sputter at the breast! His nurse was a hale, well-complexioned, sprightly jade as ever I saw; but her milk was a little too stale, though, at the same time, 'twas as blue and clear as a cambric.

Aur. Do you intend all this, madam, for a consolation to my cousin?

Mrs. Man. No, no, madam, that's to come.—I tell you, fair lady, you have only lost the man ; the estate and title are still your own ; and this very moment I would salute you Lady Wouldbe, if you pleased.

Con. Dear madam, your proposal is very tempting ; let me but consider till to-morrow, and I'll give you an answer.

Mrs. Man. I knew it, I knew it! I said, when you were born, you would be a lady; I knew it! To-morrow, you say?—My lord shall know it immediately. [*Exit.*

Aur. What d'ye intend to do, cousin ?

Con. To go into the country this moment, to be free from the impertinence of condolence, the persecution of that monster of a man, and that devil of a woman. O Aurelia, I long to be alone! I am become so fond of grief, that I would fly where I might enjoy it all, and have no interruption in my darling sorrow.

Enter Hermes Wouldbe *unperceived.*

Herm. Would. In tears! perhaps for me; I'll try.
[*Drops a miniature, and retires behind, listening.*

Aur. If there be aught in grief delightful, don't grudge me a share.

Con. No, my dear Aurelia, I'll engross it all. I loved him so, methinks I should be jealous if any mourned his death besides myself. What's here!—[*Takes up the miniature.*] Ha! see, cousin—the very face and features of the man! Sure, some officious angel has brought me this for a companion in my solitude! Now I'm fitted out for sorrow! With this I'll sigh, with this converse, gaze on his image till I grow blind with weeping!

Aur. I'm amazed! how came it here?

Con. Whether by miracle or human chance, 'tis all alike; I have it here: nor shall it ever separate from my breast. It is the only thing could give me joy, because it will increase my grief.

Herm. Would. [*Coming forward.*] Most glorious woman! now I am fond of life.

Aur. Ha! what's this!—Your business, pray, sir?

Herm. Would. With this lady.—[*Goes to* Constance, *takes her hand, and kneels.*] Here let me worship that perfection whose virtue might attract the listening angels, and make 'em smile to see such purity, so like themselves in human shape!

Con. Hermes!

Herm. Would. Your living Hermes, who shall die yours too!

Con. [*Aside.*] Now passion, powerful passion, would

bear me like a whirlwind to his arms!—But my sex has bounds.—[*Aloud.*] 'Tis wondrous, sir!

Herm. Would. Most wondrous are the works of fate for man; and most closely laid is the serpentine line that guides him into happiness! That hidden power which did permit those arts to cheat me of my birthright, had this surprise of happiness in store, well knowing that grief is the best preparative for joy.

Con. I never found the true sweets of love till this romantic turn.—Dead, and alive!—my stars are poetical! For Heaven's sake, sir, unriddle your fortune!

Herm. Would. That my dear brother must do; for he made the enigma.

Aur. Methinks I stand here like a fool all this while! would I had somebody or other to say a fine thing or two to me!

Herm. Would. Madam, I beg ten thousand pardons! I have my excuse in my hand.

Aur. My lord, I wish you joy!

Herm. Would. Pray, madam, don't trouble me with a title till I am better equipped for it. My peerage would look a little shabby in these robes.

Con. You have a good excuse, my lord: you can wear better when you please.

Herm. Would. I have a better excuse, madam: these are the best I have.

Con. How, my lord?

Herm. Would. Very true, madam; I am at present, I believe, the poorest peer in England. Heark'ee, Aurelia, prithee lend me a piece or two.

Aur. Ha! ha! ha! poor peer indeed! he wants a guinea.

Con. I'm glad on't, with all my heart!

Herm. Would. Why so, madam?

Con. Because I can furnish you with five thousand.

Herm. Would. Generous woman!

Enter Captain TRUEMAN.

Ha, my friend too!

True. I'm glad to find you here, my lord. Here's a current report about town that you were killed. I was afraid it might reach this family; so I came to disprove the story by your letter to me by the last post.

Aur. I'm glad he's come; now it will be my turn, cousin.   [*Aside.*

True. Now, my lord, I wish you joy; and I expect the same from you.

Herm. Would. With all my heart; but upon what score?

True. The old score—marriage.

Herm. Would. To whom?

True. To a neighbour lady here.

[*Looking at* AURELIA.

Aur. [*Aside.*] Impudence!—[*Aloud.*] The lady mayn't be so near as you imagine, sir.

True. The lady mayn't be so near as you imagine, madam.

Aur. Don't mistake me, sir; I did not care if the lady were in Mexico.

True. Nor I neither, madam.

Aur. You're very short, sir!

True. The shortest pleasures are the sweetest, you know.

Aur. Sir, you appear very different to me from what you were lately.

True. Madam, you appear very indifferent to me to what you were lately.

Aur. Strange!

[*This while* CONSTANCE *and* WOULDBE *converse in dumb-show.*

True. Miraculous!

Aur. I could never have believed it.

True. Nor I, as I hope to be saved!

Aur. Ill manners!

True. Worse.

Aur. How have I deserved it, sir?

True. How have I deserved it, madam?

Aur. What?

True. You.

Aur. Riddles!

True. Women!—My lord, you'll hear of me at White's.—Farewell! [*Runs off.*

Herm. Would. What, Trueman gone?

Aur. Yes. [*Walks about in disorder.*

Con. Bless me! what's the matter, cousin?

Aur. Nothing.

Con. Why are you uneasy?

Aur. Nothing.

Con. What ails you then?

Aur. Nothing.—I don't love the fellow!—yet, to be affronted—I can't bear it!

[*Bursts out a-crying, and runs off.*

Con. Your friend, my lord, has affronted Aurelia.

Herm. Would. Impossible! his regard to me were sufficient security for his good behaviour here, though it were in his nature to be rude elsewhere. She has certainly used him ill.

Con. Too well rather.

Herm. Would. Too well! have a care, madam! That, with some men, is the greatest provocation to a slight.

Con. Don't mistake, my lord; her usage never went further than mine to you; and I should take it very ill to be abused for it.

Herm. Would. I'll follow him, and know the cause of it.

Con. No, my lord, we'll follow her, and know it. Besides, your own affairs with your brother require you at present.   [*Exeunt.*

ACT IV.

SCENE I.

A Room in Lord WOULDBE'S *House.*

BENJAMIN WOULDBE *and* SUBTLEMAN *discovered.*

Ben. Would. Returned! who saw him? who spoke with him?—He can't be returned.

Sub. My lord, he's below at the gate parleying with the porter, who has private orders from me to admit nobody till you send him word, that we may have the more time to settle our affairs.

Ben. Would. 'Tis a hard case, Mr. Subtleman, that a man can't enjoy his right without all this trouble.

Sub. Ay, my lord, you see the benefit of law now, what an advantage it is to the public for securing of property! Had you not the law o' your side, who knows what devices might be practised to defraud you of your right!—But I have secured all.—The will is in true form; and you have two witnesses already to swear to the last words of your father.

Ben. Would. Then you have got another?

Sub. Yes, yes, a right one; and I shall pick up another time enough before the term: and I have planted three or four constables in the next room to take care of your brother if he should be boisterous.

Ben. Would. Then you think we are secure?

Sub. Ay, ay; let him come now when he pleases. I'll go down, and give orders for his admittance.

[Exit.

Ben. Would. Unkind brother! to disturb me thus, just in the swing and stretch of my full fortune! Where is the tie of blood and nature when brothers will do this? Had he but staid till Constance had been mine, his presence or his absence had been then indifferent.

Enter Mrs. MANDRAKE.

Mrs. Man. Well, my lord,—[*Pants as out of breath*] you'll ne'er be satisfied till you have broken my poor heart. I have had such ado yonder about you with Madam Constance—but she's our own.

Ben. Would. How! my own! Ah, my dear helpmate, I'm afraid we are routed in that quarter: my brother's come home.

Mrs. Man. Your brother come home! then I'll go travel. *[Going.*

Ben. Would. Hold, hold, madam, we are all secure; we have provided for his reception; your nephew Subtleman has stopped up all passages to the estate.

Mrs. Man. Ay, Subtleman is a pretty, thriving, ingenious boy. Little do you think who is the father of him! I'll tell you;—Mr. Moabite, the rich Jew in Lombard Street.

Ben. Would. Moabite the Jew!

Mrs. Man. You shall hear, my lord. One evening as I was very grave in my own house, reading the— *Weekly Preparation*—ay, it was the *Weekly Preparation*, I do remember particularly well—what hears me

I—but pat, pat, pat, very softly at the door. Come in, cries I; and presently enters Mr. Moabite, followed by a snug-chair, the windows close drawn, and in it a fine young virgin just upon the point of being delivered. We were all in a great hurly-burly for a while, to be sure; but our production was a fine boy. I had fifty guineas for my trouble, the lady was wrapped up very warm, placed in her chair, and reconveyed to the place she came from. Who she was, or what she was, I could never learn, though my maid said that the chair went through the Park—but the child was left with me. The father would have made a Jew on't presently, but I swore, if he committed such a barbarity on the infant, that I would discover all. So I had him brought up a good Christian, and bound prentice to an attorney.

Ben. Would. Very well!

Mrs. Man. Ah, my lord! there's many a pretty fellow in London that knows as little of their true father and mother as he does: I have had several such jobs in my time;—there was one Scotch nobleman that brought me four in half a year.

Ben. Would. Four! and how were they all provided for?

Mrs. Man. Very handsomely indeed; they were two sons and two daughters; the eldest son rides in the first troop of guards, and the other is a very pretty fellow, and his father's valet-de-chambre.

Ben. Would. And what is become of the daughters, pray?

Mrs. Man. Why, one of 'em is a manteau-maker, and the youngest has got into the playhouse.—Ay, ay, my lord, let Subtleman alone, I'll warrant he'll manage your brother.—Ads my life, here's somebody coming ! I would not be seen.

Ben. Would. 'Tis my brother, and he'll meet you upon the stairs ; 'adso, get into this closet till he be gone.   [*Shuts her into the closet.*

Re-enter SUBTLEMAN *with* HERMES WOULDBE.

My brother ! dearest brother, welcome !
                     [*Runs and embraces him.*
Herm. Would. I can't dissemble, sir, else I would return your false embrace.

Ben. Would. False embrace ! still suspicious of me ! I thought that five years' absence might have cooled the unmanly heats of our childish days. That I am overjoyed at your return, let this testify ; this moment I resign all right and title to your honour, and salute you, lord.

Herm. Would. I want not your permission to enjoy my right ; here I am lord and master without your resignation : and the first use I make of my authority is, to discard that rude, bull-faced fellow at the door.—Where's my steward ?

Enter CLEARACCOUNT.

Mr. Clearaccount, let that pampered sentinel below this minute be discharged.—Brother, I wonder you could feed such a swarm of lazy, idle drones about you, and leave the poor industrious bees, that fed you from their hives, to starve for want.—Steward, look to't ; if I have not discharges for every farthing of my father's debts upon my toilet to-morrow morning, you shall follow the tipstaff, I can assure you.

Ben. Would. Hold, hold, my lord, you usurp too large a power, methinks, o'er my family.

Herm. Would. Your family!

Ben. Would. Yes, my family: you have no title to lord it here.—Mr. Clearaccount, you know your master.

Herm. Would. How! a combination against me! —brother, take heed how you deal with one that, cautious of your falsehood, comes prepared to meet your arts, and can retort your cunning to your infamy. Your black, unnatural designs against my life, before I went abroad, my charity can pardon: but my prudence must remember to guard me from your malice for the future.

Ben. Would. Our father's weak and fond surmise! which he upon his death-bed owned: and to recompense me for that injurious, unnatural suspicion, he left me sole heir to his estate. Now, my lord, my house and servants are—at your service.

Herm. Would. Villany beyond example! Have I not letters from my father, of scarce a fortnight's date, where he repeats his fears for my return, lest it should again expose me to your hatred?

Sub. Well, well, these are no proofs, no proofs, my lord; they won't pass in court against positive evidence. Here is your father's will, *signatum et sigillatum*, besides his last words to confirm it, to which I can take my positive oath in any court of Westminster.

Herm. Would. What are you, sir?

Sub. Of Clifford's Inn, my lord; I belong to the law.

Herm. Would. Thou art the worm and maggot

of the law, bred in the bruised and rotten parts, and now art nourished on the same corruption that produced thee. The English law, as planted first, was like the English oak, shooting its spreading arms around, to shelter all that dwelt beneath its shade : but now whole swarms of caterpillars, like you, hang in such clusters upon every branch, that the once thriving tree now sheds infectious vermin on our heads.

Ben. Would. My lord, I have some company above ; if your lordship will drink a glass of wine, we shall be proud of the honour ; if not, I shall attend you at any court of judicature, whenever you please to summon me. [*Going.*

Herm. Would. Hold, sir !—[*Aside.*] Perhaps my father's dying weakness was imposed on, and he has left him heir ; if so, his will shall freely be obeyed.— [*Aloud.*] Brother, you say you have a will?

Sub. Here it is. [*Showing a parchment.*

Herm. Would. Let me see it.

Sub. There's no precedent for that, my lord.

Herm. Would. Upon my honour, I'll restore it.

Ben. Would. Upon my honour, but you shan't.

[*Takes it from* SUBTLEMAN *and puts it in his pocket.*

Herm. Would. This over-caution, brother, is suspicious.

Ben. Would. Seven thousand pound a year is worth looking after.

Herm. Would. Therefore you can't take it ill, that I am a little inquisitive about it.—Have you witnesses to prove my father's dying words ?

Ben. Would. A couple in the house.

Herm. Would. Who are they?

Sub. Witnesses, my lord! 'tis unwarrantable to inquire into the merits of the cause out of court. My client shall answer no more questions.

Herm. Would. Perhaps, sir, upon a satisfactory account of his title, I intend to leave your client to the quiet enjoyment of his right, without troubling any court with the business; I therefore desire to know what kind of persons are these witnesses.

Sub. [*Aside.*] Oho, he's a coming about!—[*Aloud.*] I told your lordship already that I am one; another is in the house, one of my lord's footmen.

Herm. Would. Where is this footman?

Ben. Would. Forthcoming.

Herm. Would. Produce him.

Sub. That I shall presently.—[*Aside to* BENJAMIN WOULDBE.] The day's our own, sir—[*To* HERMES WOULDBE.] But you shall engage first to ask him no cross questions.

Herm. Would. I am not skilled in such.—[*Exit* SUBTLEMAN.] But pray, brother, did my father quite forget me? left me nothing!

Ben. Would. Truly, my lord, nothing. He spoke but little; left no legacies.

Herm. Would. 'Tis strange! he was extremely just, and loved me too;—but perhaps—

Re-enter SUBTLEMAN *with* TEAGUE.

Sub. My lord, here's another evidence.

Herm. Would. Teague!

Ben. Would. My brother's servant!

[*They all four stare upon one another.*

Sub. His servant!

Teague. Maishter! see here, maishter, I did get all dish—[*Chinks money*] for being an evidensh, dear joy! an be me shoule, I will give the half of it to you, if you will give me your permission to maake swear against you.

Herm. Would. My wonder is divided between the villany of the fact, and the amazement of the discovery! Teague! my very servant! sure I dream.

Teague. Fet, dere ish no dreaming in the cashe; I'm sure the croon pieceish are awake, for I have been taaking with dem dish half hour.

Ben. Would. Ignorant, unlucky man, thou hast ruined me! why had not I a sight of him before?

                        [*Aside to* SUBTLEMAN.

Sub. I thought the fellow had been too ignorant to be a knave.

Teague. Be me shoule, you lee, dear joy. I can be a knave as well as you, fen I think it conveniency.

Herm. Would. Now, brother!—Speechless!—Your oracle too silenced!—Is all your boasted fortune sunk to the guilty blushing for a crime?—But I scorn to insult: let disappointment be your punishment.— But for your lawyer there—Teague, lay hold of him.

Sub. Let none dare to attach me without a legal warrant.

Teague. Attach! no, dear joy, I cannot attach you —but I can catch you by the troat, after the fashion of Ireland.   [*Takes* SUBTLEMAN *by the throat.*

Sub. An assault! an assault!

Teague. No, no, 'tish nothing but choking, nothing but choking.

Herm. Would. Hold him fast, Teague.—[*To* BEN-

JAMIN WOULDBE.] Now, sir, because I was your brother, you would have betrayed me ; and because I am your brother I forgive it :—dispose yourself as you think fit. I'll order Mr. Clearaccount to give you a thousand pounds. Go take it, and pay me by your absence.

Ben. Would. I scorn your beggarly benevolence ! had my designs succeeded, I would not have allowed you the weight of a wafer, and therefore will accept none.—As for that lawyer, he deserves to be pilloried, not for his cunning in deceiving you, but for his ignorance in betraying me. The villain has defrauded me of seven thousand pounds a year. Farewell—

[Going.

Re-enter Mrs. MANDRAKE, and runs to
BENJAMIN WOULDBE.

Mrs. Man. [*Kneeling.*] My lord ! my dear lord Wouldbe, I beg you ten thousand pardons !

Ben. Would. What offence hast thou done to me ?

Mrs. Man. An offence the most injurious. I have hitherto concealed a secret in my breast to the offence of justice, and the defrauding your lord-ship of your true right and title. You, Benjamin Wouldbe, with the crooked back, are the eldest-born, and true heir to the estate and dignity.

All. How !

Teague. Arah, how ?

Mrs. Man. None, my lord, can tell better than I, who brought you both into the world. My deceased lord, upon the sight of your deformity, engaged me by a considerable reward, to say you were the last born, that the beautiful twin, likely to be the greater ornament to the family, might succeed him in his honour. This secret my conscience has long struggled with. Upon the news that you were left heir to the estate, I thought justice was satisfied, and I was resolved to keep it a secret still; but by strange chance, overhearing what passed just now, my poor conscience was racked, and I was forced to declare the truth.

Ben. Would. By all my forward hopes, I could have sworn it! I found the spirit of eldership in my blood; my pulses beat, and swelled for seniority. —Mr. Hermes Wouldbe,—I'm your most humble servant. 　　　　　　　　　　*[Foppishly.*

Herm. Would. Hermes is my name, my Christian name; of which I am prouder than of all titles that honour gives, or flattery bestows. But thou, vain bubble, puffed up with the empty breath of that more empty woman; to let thee see how I despise thy pride, I'll call thee lord, dress thee up in titles like a king at arms; you shall be blazoned round, like any church in Holland; thy pageantry shall exceed the lord mayor's; and yet this Hermes, plain Hermes, shall despise thee.

Sub. Well, well, this is nothing to the purpose.— Mistress, will you make an affidavit of what you have said, before a master in Chancery?

Mrs. Man. That I can, though I were to die the next minute after it.

Teague. Den, dear joy, you would be dam the next minute after dat.

Herm. Would. All this is trifling: I must purge my house of this nest of villainy at once.—Here, Teague!—[*Whispers* TEAGUE.] Go, make haste!

Teague. Dat I can.

[*As he runs out,* BENJAMIN WOULDBE *stops him.*

Ben. Would. Where are you going, sir?

Teague. Only for a pot of ale, dear joy, for you and my maishter, to drink friends.

Ben. Would. You lie, sirrah!   [*Pushes him back.*

Teague. Fet, I do so.

Herm. Would. What! violence to my servant! Nay, then, I'll force him a passage.   [*Draws.*

Sub. An assault! an assault upon the body of a peer!—Within there!

Enter Constables, *one of them with a black patch on his eye. They disarm* HERMES WOULDBE, *and secure* TEAGUE.

Herm. Would. This plot was laid for my reception. —Unhand me, constable!

Ben. Would. Have a care, Mr. Constable, the man is mad; he's possessed with an odd frenzy, that he's my brother, and my elder too: so, because I would not very willingly resign my house and estate, he attempted to murder me.

Sub. Gentlemen, take care of that fellow: he made an assault upon my body, *vi et armis.*

Teague. Arah, fat is dat *wy at armish?*

Sub. No matter, sirrah; I shall have you hanged.

Teague. Hanged! dat is nothing, dear joy:—we are used to't.

Herm. Would. Unhand me, villains! or by all—

Teague. Have a caar, dear maishter, don't swear; we shall be had in the croon-offish.—You know dere ish sharpers about us.

[*Looking about on them that hold him.*

Ben. Would. Mr. Constable, you know your directions; away with 'em!

Herm. Would. Hold!—

Constab. No, no; force him away.

> [*Exeunt all but* BENJAMIN WOULDBE *and*
> Mrs. MANDRAKE.

Ben. Would. Now, my dear prophetess, my sibyl, by all my dear desires and ambitions, I do believe you have spoken the truth!—I am the elder.

Mrs. Man. No, no, sir, the devil a word on't is true. I would not wrong my conscience neither; for, faith and troth, as I am an honest woman, you were born above three-quarters of an hour after him; —but I don't much care if I do swear that you are the eldest.—What a blessing it was that I was in the closet at that pinch! Had I not come out that moment, you would have sneaked off; your brother had been in possession, and then we had lost all; but now you are established: possession gets your money, that gets you law, and law, you know—Down on your knees, sirrah, and ask me blessing.

Ben. Would. No, my dear mother, I'll give thee a blessing, a rent-charge of five hundred pound a year, upon what part of the estate you will, during your life.

Mrs. Man. Thank you, my lord: that five hundred a year will afford me a leisurely life, and a handsome retirement in the country, where I mean to repent me of my sins, and die a good Christian: for, Heaven knows, I am old, and ought to bethink me of another life.—Have you none of the cordial left that we had in the morning?

Ben. Would. Yes, yes, we'll go to the fountain-head.　　　　　　　　　　　　　　　　　[*Exeunt.*

SCENE II.

A Street.

Enter TEAGUE.

Teague. Deel tauke me but dish ish a most shweet business indeed! Maishters play the fool, and shervants must shuffer for it. I am prishoner in the constable's house, be me shoule, and shent abrode to fetch some bail for my maishter; but foo shall bail poor Teague agra?

Enter CONSTANCE.

Oh, dere ish my maishter's old love. Indeed, I fear dish bishness will spoil his fortune.

Con. Who's here, Teague?   [*He turns from her.*

Teague. [*Aside.*] Deel tauke her, I did tought she could not know me again.—[CONSTANCE *goes about to look him in the face. He turns from her.*] Dish ish not shivil, be me shoule, to know a shentleman fither he will or no.

Con. Why this, Teague? what's the matter? are you ashamed of me, or yourself, Teague?

Teague. Of bote, be my shoule.

Con. How does your master, sir?

Teague. Very well, dear joy, and in prishon.

Con. In prison! how? where?

Teague. Why, in the little Bashtile yonder, at the end of the street.

Con. Show me the way immediately.

Teague. Fet, I can show you the house yonder: she yonder; be me shoule, I she his faace yonder, peeping troo the iron glash window!

Con. I'll see him, though a dungeon were his con-finement.   [*Runs out.*

Teague. Ah! auld kindnesh, be my shoule, cannot be forgotten. Now, if my maishter had but grash enough to get her with child, her word would go for two; and she would bail him and I bote.   [*Exit.*

SCENE III.

A meanly furnished Room in a Spunging-House.

HERMES WOULDBE *is discovered sitting at a table writing.*

Herm. Would. The Tower confines the great,
  The spunging-house the poor;
Thus there are degrees of state
  That even the wretched must endure.

Virgil, though cherish'd in courts,
  Relates but a splenetic tale :
Cervantes revels and sports,
  Although he writ in a jail.

Then hang reflections !—[*Starts up.*] I'll go write a comedy.—Ho, within there ! Tell the lieutenant of the Tower that I would speak with him.

Enter Constable.

Constab. Ay, ay, the man is mad : lieutenant o' th' Tower ! ha ! ha ! ha !—Would you could make your words good, master.

Herm. Would. Why, am not I a prisoner there ? I know it by the stately apartments. What is that, pray, that hangs streaming down upon the wall yonder ?

Constab. Yonder ! 'tis cobweb, sir.

Herm. Would. 'Tis false, sir! 'tis as fine tapestry as any in Europe.

Constab. The devil it is!

Herm. Would. Then your damask bed, here; the flowers are so bold, I took 'em for embroidery; and then the headwork! *Pointe de Venise,* I protest.

Constab. As good Kidderminster as any in England, I must confess; and though the sheets be a little soiled, yet I can assure you, sir, that many an honest gentleman has lain in them.

Herm. Would. Pray, sir, what did those two Indian pieces cost, that are fixed up in the corner of the room?

Constab. Indian pieces! What the devil, sir, they are my old jack boots, my militia boots!

Herm. Would. I took 'em for two china jars, upon my word! But heark'ee, friend, art thou content that these things should be as they are?

Constab. Content! ay, sir.

Herm. Would. Why then should I complain?

Servant. [*Without.*] Mr. Constable, here's a woman will force her way upon us: we can't stop her.

Constab. Knock her down then, knock her down; let no woman come up, the man's mad enough already.

Enter CONSTANCE.

Con. Who dares oppose me?

[*Throws him a handful of money.*

Constab. Not I truly, madam.

[*Gathers up the money.*

Herm. Would. My Constance! my guardian angel here! Then naught can hurt me.

Constab. Heark'ee, sir, you may suppose the bed to be a damask bed for half an hour if you please.

Con. No, no, sir, your prisoner must along with me.

Constab. Ay, faith, the woman's madder than the man.

Enter Captain Trueman *and* Teague.

Herm. Would. Ha! Trueman too! I'm proud to think that many a prince has not so many true friends in his palace, as I have here in prison.— Two such—

Teague. Tree, be my shoule.

True. My lord, just as I heard of your confinement, I was going to make myself a prisoner. Behold the fetters! I had just bought the wedding ring.

Con. I hope they are golden fetters, captain?

True. They weigh four thousand pound, madam, besides the purse, which is worth a million.—My lord, this very evening was I to be married; but the news of your misfortune has stopped me: I would not gather roses in a wet hour.

Herm. Would. Come, the weather shall be clear; the thoughts of your good fortune will make me easy, more than my own can do, if purchased by your disappointment.

True. Do you think, my lord, that I can go to the bed of pleasure whilst you lie in a hovel?— Here, where is this constable? How dare you do this, insolent rascal?

Constab. Insolent rascal! do you know who you speak to, sir?

True. Yes, sirrah, don't I call you by your proper name? How dare you confine a peer of the realm?

Constab. Peer of the realm! you may give good words though, I hope.

Herm. Would. Ay, ay, Mr. Constable is in the right, he did but his duty; I suppose he had twenty guineas for his pains.

Constab. No, I had but ten.

Herm. Would. Heark'ee, Trueman, this fellow must be soothed, he'll be of use to us; I must employ you too in this affair with my brother.

True. Say no more, my lord, I'll cut his throat, 'tis but flying the kingdom.

Herm. Would. No, no, 'twill be more revenge to worst him at his own weapons. Could I but force him out of his garrison, that I might get into possession, his claim would vanish immediately. Does my brother know you?

True. Very little, if at all.

Herm. Would. Heark'ee.   [*Whispers.*

True. It shall be done.—Look'ee, constable, you're drawn into a wrong cause, and it may prove your destruction if you don't change sides immediately. We desire no favour, but the use of your coat, wig, and staff, for half an hour.

Constab. Why truly, sir, I understand now, by this gentlewoman that I know to be our neighbour, that he is a lord, and I heartily beg his worship's pardon, and if I can do your honour any service, your grace may command me.

Herm. Would. I'll reward you.—But we must have the black patch for the eye too.

Teague. I can give your lordship wan; here fet, 'tis a plaishter for a shore finger, and I have worn it but twice.

Con. But pray, captain, what was your quarrel at Aurelia to-day?

True. With your permission, madam, we'll mind my lord's business at present; when that's done, we'll mind the lady's.—My lord, I shall make an excellent constable; I never had the honour of a civil employment before. We'll equip ourselves in another place.—Here, you Prince of Darkness, have you ne'er a better room in your house? these iron grates frighten the lady.

Constab. I have a handsome, neat parlour below, sir.

True. Come along then, you must conduct us.— [*Aside.*] We don't intend to be out of your sight, that you mayn't be out of ours.   [*Exeunt.*

SCENE IV.

AURELIA'S *Apartment.*

Enter AURELIA, RICHMORE *following.*

Aur. Follow me not! age and deformity, with quiet, were preferable to this vexatious persecution. For Heaven's sake, Mr. Richmore, what have I ever shown to vindicate this presumption of yours?

Rich. You show it now, madam; your face, your wit, your shape, are all temptations to undergo even the rigour of your disdain, for the bewitching pleasure of your company.

Aur. Then be assured, sir, you shall reap no other benefit by my company; and if you think it a pleasure to be constantly slighted, ridiculed, and affronted, you shall have admittance to such entertainment whenever you will.

Rich. I take you at your word, madam; I am armed with submission against all the attacks of your severity, and your ladyship shall find that my resignation can bear much longer than your rigour can inflict.

Aur. That is, in plain terms, your sufficiency will presume much longer than my honour can resist. Sir, you might have spared the unmannerly declaration to my face, having already taken care to let me know your opinion of my virtue, by your impudent settlement, proposed by Mrs. Mandrake.

Rich. By those fair eyes, I'll double the proposal! This soft, this white, this powerful hand—[*Takes her hand*] shall write its own conditions.

Aur. Then it shall write this—[*Strikes him*] and if you like the terms, you shall have more another time.
[*Exit.*

Rich. Death and madness! a blow!—Twenty thousand pound sterling for one night's revenge upon her dear, proud, disdainful person!—Am I rich as many a sovereign prince, wallow in wealth, yet can't command my pleasure?—Woman!—If there be power in gold, I yet shall triumph o'er thy pride.

Enter Mrs. MANDRAKE.

Mrs. Man. O' my troth, and so you shall, if I can help it.

Rich. Madam, madam, here, here, here's money, gold, silver! take, take, all, all, my rings too! All shall be yours, make me but happy in this presumptuous beauty; I'll make thee rich as avarice can crave; if not, I'll murder thee, and myself too.

Mrs. Man. Your bounty is too large, too large indeed, sir.

Rich. Too large! no, 'tis beggary without her. Lordships, manors, acres, rents, tithes and trees, all, all shall fly for my dear sweet revenge!

Mrs. Man. Say no more, this night I'll put you in a way.

Rich. This night!

Mrs. Man. The lady's aunt is very near her time— she goes abroad this evening a-visiting; in the meantime I send to your mistress, that her aunt is fallen in labour at my house: she comes in a hurry, and then—

Rich. Shall I be there to meet her?

Mrs. Man. Perhaps.

Rich. In a private room?

Mrs. Man. Mum.

Rich. No creature to disturb us?

Mrs. Man. Mum, I say; but you must give me your word not to ravish her; nay, I can tell you she won't be ravished.

Rich. Ravish!—Let me see, I'm worth five thousand pound a year, twenty thousand guineas in my pocket, and may not I force a toy that's scarce worth fifteen hundred pound?   I'll do't.

Her beauty sets my heart on fire; beside
The injurious blow has set on fire my pride;
The bare fruition were not worth my pain,
The joy will be to humble her disdain;
Beyond enjoyment will the transport last
In triumph when the ecstacy is past.   [*Exeunt.*

ACT V.

SCENE I.

A room in Lord Wouldbe's *House.*

Benjamin Wouldbe *discovered alone.*

Ben. Would. Show me that proud stoic that can bear success and champagne : philosophy can support us in hard fortune, but who can have patience in prosperity? The learned may talk what they will of human bodies, but I am sure there is not one atom in mine but what is truly epicurean. My brother is secured, I guarded with my friends, my lewd and honest midnight friends—Holla, who waits there?

Enter Footman.

Foot. My lord?

Ben. Would. A fresh battalion of bottles to reinforce the cistern. Are the ladies come?

Foot. Half an hour ago, my lord ; they're below in the bathing-chamber.

Ben. Would. Where did you light on 'em?

Foot. One in the passage at the old playhouse, my lord—I found another very melancholy paring her nails by Rosamond's Pond,*—and a couple I got at

---

* Rosamond's Pond was a small sheet of water at the end of Birdcage Walk, and was a famous place for assignations.

the Chequer ale-house in Holborn; the two last came to town yesterday in a west-country waggon.

Ben. Would. Very well, order Baconface to hasten supper; and, d'ye hear? and bid the Swiss admit no stranger without acquainting me.—[*Exit* Footman.] Now, Fortune, I defy thee; this night's my own at least.

Re-enter Footman.

Foot. My lord, here's the constable below with the black eye, and he wants to speak with your lordship in all haste.

Ben. Would. Ha! the constable!—Should Fortune jilt me now?—Bid him come up.—[*Exit* Footman.] I fear some cursed chance to thwart me.

Enter Captain TRUEMAN, *disguised as a* Constable.

True. Ah! my lord, here is sad news—your brother is—

Ben. Would. Got away, made his escape, I warrant you.

True. Worse, worse, my lord.

Ben. Would. Worse, worse! what can be worse?

True. I dare not speak it.

Ben. Would. Death and hell, fellow, don't distract me!

True. He's dead.

Ben. Would. Dead!

True. Positively.

Ben. Would. *Coup de grace, ciel grandmerci!*

True. Villain, I understand you.   [*Aside.*

Ben. Would. But, how, how, Mr. Constable? speak it aloud, kill me with the relation.

True. I don't know how; the poor gentleman was

very melancholy upon his confinement, and so he desired me to send for a gentlewoman that lives hard by here : mayhap your worship may know her.

Ben. Would. At the gilt balcony in the square?

True. The very same, a smart woman truly. I went for her myself, but she was otherwise engaged ; not she truly ! she would not come. Would you believe it, my lord, at hearing of this the poor man was like to drop down dead.

Ben. Would. Then he was but likely to drop dead?

True. Would it were no more ! Then I left him, and coming about two hours after, I found him hanged in his sword-belt.

Ben. Would. Hanged !

True. Dangling.

Ben. Would. Le coup d'éclat! done like the noblest Roman of 'em all !—But are you sure he's past all recovery? Did you send for no surgeon to bleed him ?

True. No, my lord, I forgot that—but I'll send immediately.

Ben. Would. No, no, Mr. Constable, 'tis too late now, too late.—And the lady would not come, you say?

True. Not a step would she stir.

Ben. Would. Inhuman ! barbarous !—dear, delicious woman, thou now art mine.—Where is the body, Mr. Constable? I must see it.

True. By all means, my lord ; it lies in my parlour: there's a power of company come in, and among the rest one, one, one Trueman, I think they call him ; a devilish hot fellow, he had like to have pulled the house down about our ears, and swears. I told him he should pay for his swearing; he gave me a slap in the face, said he was in the army, and had a commission for't.

Ben. Would. Captain Trueman? a blustering kind of rakehelly officer?

True. Ay, my lord, one of those scoundrels that we pay wages to for being knocked o' th' head for us.

Ben. Would. Ay, ay, one of those fools that have only brains to be knocked out.

True. [*Aside.*] Son of a whore.—[*Aloud.*] He's a plaguy impudent fellow, my lord; he swore that you were the greatest villain upon the earth.

Ben. Would. Ay, ay, but he durst not say that to my face, Mr. Constable.

True. No, no, hang him, he said it behind your back, to be sure. And he swore, moreover,—have a care, my lord,—he swore that he would cut your throat whenever he met you.

Ben. Would. Will you swear that you heard him say so?

True. Heard him! ay, as plainly as you hear me: he spoke the very words that I speak to your lordship.

Ben. Would. Well, well, I'll manage him.—But now I think on't, I won't go see the body; it will but increase my grief. Mr. Constable, do you send for the coroner: they must find him *non compos.* He was mad before, you know. Here—something for your trouble. [*Gives money.*

True. Thank your honour.—But pray, my lord, have a care of that Trueman; he swears that he'll cut your throat, and he will do't, my lord, he will do't.

Ben. Would. Never fear, never fear.

True. But he swore it, my lord, and he will certainly do't.   Pray have a care.   [*Exit.*

Ben. Would. Well, well,—so,—the devil's in't if I ben't the eldest now.   What a pack of civil relations have I had here!   My father takes a fit of the apoplexy, makes a face, and goes off one way; my brother takes a fit of the spleen, makes a face, and goes off t'other way.—Well, I must own he has found the way to mollify me, and I do love him now with all my heart; since he was so very civil to justle into the world before me, I think he did very civilly to justle out of it before me.—But now my joys!— Without there—hollo!—Take off the inquisition of the gate; the heir may now enter unsuspected.

> The wolf is dead, the shepherds may go play:
> Ease follows care; so rolls the world away.

'Tis a question whether adversity or prosperity makes the most poets.

Re-enter Footman.

Foot. My lord, a footman brought this letter, and waits for an answer.

Ben. Would. Nothing from the Elysian fields, I hope.—[*Opening the letter.*]   What do I see, *CONSTANCE!*   Spells and magic in every letter of the name!—Now for the sweet contents.

My Lord,

I'm pleased to hear of your happy change of fortune, and shall be glad to see your lordship this evening to wish you joy.

CONSTANCE.

Now the devil's in this Mandrake! she told me this

afternoon that the wind was chopping about; and has it got into the warm corner already?—Here, my coach-and-six to the door: I'll visit my sultana in state. As for the seraglio below stairs, you, my bashaws, may possess 'em.

[*Exit*, Footman *following.*

SCENE II.

The Street before Mrs. MANDRAKE'S *House.*

Enter TEAGUE *carrying a lantern*, Captain TRUEMAN *following, disguised as a* Constable.

True. Blockhead, thou hast led us out of the way; we have certainly passed the constable's house.

Teague. Be me shoule, dear joy, I am never out of my ways; for poor Teague has been a vanderer ever since he was borned.

True. Hold up the lantern.—What sign is that? the St. Albans tavern ! *—Why, you blundering fool, you have led me directly to St. James's Square, when you should have gone towards Soho.—[*Shrieking within.*] Hark! what noise is that over the way? a woman's cry !

Teague. Fet is it; shome daumsel in distress I believe, that has no mind to be relieved.

True. I'll use the privilege of my office to know what the matter is.

Teague. Hold, hold, maishter captain, be me fet, dat ish not the way home.

---

* The famous tavern in which the Roxburghe Club was originated a century later, after the great sale of the Duke of Roxburghe's library.

Aur. [*Within.*] Help! help! murder! help.

True. Ha! here must be mischief.—Within there, open the door in the king's name, or I'll force it open.—Here, Teague, break down the door.

[TEAGUE *takes the staff, thumps at the door.*

Teague. Deel tauke him, I have knock so long as I am able. Arah, maishter, get a great long ladder to get in the window of the firsht room, and sho open the door, and let in yourshelf.

Aur. [*Within.*] Help! help! help!

True. Knock harder; let's raise the mob.

Teague. O maishter, I have tink just now of a brave invention to maake dem come out; and be St. Patrick, dat very bushiness did maake my nown shelf and my fader run like de devil out of my nown hoose in my nown country:—be me shoule, set the hoose a-fire.

Enter Mob.

Mob. What's the matter, master constable?

True. Gentlemen, I command your assistance in the king's name to break into the house: there is murder cried within.

Mob. Ay, ay, break open the door.

Mrs. Man. [*From the balcony.*] What noise is that below?

Teague. Arah, vat noise ish dat above?

Mrs. Man. Only a poor gentlewoman in labour; 'twill be over presently.—Here, Mr. Constable; there's something for you to drink.

[*Throws down a purse,* TEAGUE *takes it up.*

Teague. Come, maishter, we have no more to shay, be me shoule.—[*Going.*] Arah, if you vill play the constable right now, fet you vill come away.

True. No, no; there must be villany by this bribe.—Who lives in this house?

Mob. A midwife, a midwife; 'tis none of our business: let us be gone.

Aur. [*Looking out at a window.*] Gentleman, dear gentleman, help!—A rape! a rape! villany!

True. Ha! that voice I know.—Give me the staff; I'll make a breach, I warrant you.

> [*Breaks open the door and enters*, TEAGUE *and* Mob *following*.

SCENE III.

A Room in Mrs. MANDRAKE'S *House.*

Enter Captain TRUEMAN *and* Mob.

True. Gentlemen, search all about the house; let not a soul escape.

> [*Enter* AURELIA, *running out of breath, and her hair dishevelled.*

Aur. Dear Mr. Constable—had you—staid but a moment longer—I had been ruined.

True. [*Aside.*] Aurelia! [*Aloud.*] Are you safe, madam?

Aur. Yes, yes; I am safe—I think—but with enough ado: he's a devilish strong fellow.

True. Where is the villain that attempted it?

Aur. Psha!—never mind the villain;—look out the woman of the house, the devil, the monster, that decoyed me hither.

Enter TEAGUE, *haling in* Mrs. MANDRAKE *by the hair.*

Teague. Be me shoule, I have taaken my shaare of the plunder. Let me she fat I have gotten.—[*Takes her to the light.*] Ububboo, a witch! a witch! the very saame witch dat would swear my maishter was the youngest.

True. [*Aside.*] How! Mandrake! this was the luckiest disguise—[*Aloud.*] Come, my dear Proserpine, I'll take care of you.

Mrs. Man. Pray, sir, let me speak with you.

True. No, no; I'll talk with you before a magistrate.—A cart, Bridewell,—you understand me?—Teague, let her be your prisoner: I'll wait on this lady.

Aur. Mr. Constable, I'll reward you.

Teague. It ish convenient noo by the law of armsh, that I search my prishoner, for fear she may have some pocket-pishtols.—Dere is a joak for you!

[*Searches her pockets.*

Mrs. Man. Ah! don't use an old woman so barbarously.

Teague. Dear joy, den fy vere you an old woman? dat is your falt, not mine, joy!—Uboo, here ish nothing but scribble-scrabble papers, I tink.

[*Pulls out a handful of letters.*

True. Let me see 'em; they may be of use.—[*Looks over the letters.*] *For Mr. Richmore*—Ay! does he traffic hereabouts?

Aur. That is the villain that would have abused me.

True. [*Aside.*] Ha! then he has abused you? Villain indeed!—[*Aloud.*] Was his name Richmore, mistress? a lusty, handsome man?

Aur. Ay, ay, the very same : a lusty, ugly fellow.

True. Let me see—[*Opening a letter*] whose scrawl is this?—[*Aside.*] Death and confusion to my sight ! Clelia, my bride, his whore !—I've passed a precipice unseen, which to look back upon, shivers me with terror.—This night, this very moment, had not my friend been in confinement, had not I worn this dress, had not Aurelia been in danger, had not Teague found this letter, had the least minutest circumstance been omitted, what a monster had I been !—[*Aloud.*] Mistress, is this same Richmore in the house still, think'ee ?

Aur. 'Tis very probable he may.

True. Very well.—Teague, take these ladies over to the tavern, and stay there till I come to you.— [*To* AURELIA.] Madam, fear no injury ; your friends are near you.

Aur. What does he mean ?   [*Aside.*

Teague. Come, dear joy, I vill give you a pot of wine out of your own briberies here.

> [*Hales out* Mrs. MANDRAKE, AURELIA *and* Mob
>   *following.*

Enter RICHMORE.

Rich. [*Aside.*] Since my money won't prevail on this cross fellow, I'll try what my authority can do.— [*Aloud.*] What's the meaning of this riot, constable? I have the commission of the peace, and can command you. Go about your business, and leave your prisoners with me.

True. No, sir ; the prisoners shall go about their business, and I'll be left with you.—Look'ee, master, we don't use to make up these matters before company: so you and I must be in private a little.—You say, sir, that you are a justice of peace?

Rich. Yes, sir; I have my commission in my pocket.

True. I believe it.—Now, sir, one good turn deserves another: and, if you will promise to do me a kindness, why, you shall have as good as you bring.

Rich. What is it?

True. You must know, sir, there is a neighbour's daughter that I had a woundy kindness for. She had a very good repute all over the parish, and might have married very handsomely, that I must say; but, I don't know how, we came together after a very kindly, natural manner, and I swore, that I must say, I did swear confoundedly, that I would marry her; but, I don't know how, I never cared for marrying of her since.

Rich. How so?

True. Why, because I did my business without it: that was the best way, I thought. The truth is, she has some foolish reasons to say she's with child, and threatens mainly to have me taken up with a warrant, and brought before a justice of peace. Now, sir, I intend to come before you, and I hope your worship will bring me off.

Rich. Look'ee, sir, if the woman prove with child, and you swore to marry her, you must do't.

True. Ay, master; but I am for liberty and property. I vote for parliament men: I pay taxes, and, truly, I don't think matrimony consistent with the liberty of the subject.

Rich. But, in this case, sir, both law and justice will oblige you.

True. Why, if it be the law of the land—I found a letter here—I think it is for your worship.

Rich. Ay, sir; how came you by it?

True. By a very strange accident truly.—Clelia— she says here you swore to marry her. Eh!—Now, sir, I suppose that what is law for a petty-constable may be law for a justice of peace.

Rich. This is the oddest fellow—

True. Here was the t'other lady that cried out so —I warrant now, if I were brought before you for ravishing a woman—the gallows would ravish me for't.

Rich. But I did not ravish her.

True. That I'm glad to hear: I wanted to be sure of that.   [*Aside.*

Rich. [*Aside.*] I don't like this fellow.—[*Aloud.*] Come, sir, give me my letter, and go about your business; I have no more to say to you.

True. But I have something to say to you.

[*Coming up to him.*

Rich. What?

True. Dog!   [*Strikes him.*

Rich. Ha! struck by a peasant!—[*Draws.*] Slave, thy death is certain.   [*Runs at* Captain TRUEMAN.

True. O brave Don John, rape and murder in one night!   [*Disarms him.*

Rich. Rascal, return my sword, and acquit your prisoners, else will I prosecute thee to beggary. I'll give some pettifogger a thousand pound to starve thee and thy family according to law.

True. I'll lay you a thousand pound you won't.

[*Discovering himself.*

Rich. Ghosts and apparitions! Trueman!

True. Words are needless to upbraid you : my very looks are sufficient ; and, if you have the least sense of shame, this sword would be less painful in your heart than my appearance is in your eye.

Rich. Truth, by Heavens !

True. Think on the contents of this,—[*Showing a letter*] think next on me ; reflect upon your villany to Aurelia, then view thyself.

Rich. Trueman, canst thou forgive me ?

True. Forgive thee !—[*A long pause.*]   Do one thing, and I will.

Rich. Anything :—I'll beg thy pardon.

True. The blow excuses that.

Rich. I'll give thee half my estate.

True. Mercenary !

Rich. I'll make thee my sole heir.

True. I despise it.

Rich. What shall I do?

True. You shall—marry Clelia.

Rich. How ! that's too hard.

True. Too hard ! why was it then imposed on me ? If you marry her yourself, I shall believe you intended me no injury ; so your behaviour will be justified, my resentment appeased, and the lady's honour repaired.

Rich. 'Tis infamous.

True. No, by Heavens, 'tis justice ! and what is just is honourable : if promises from man to man have force, why not from man to woman ? Their very weakness is the charter of their power, and they should not be injured because they can't return it.

Rich. Return my sword.

True. In my hand 'tis the sword of justice, and I should not part with it.

Rich. Then sheathe it here; I'll die before I consent so basely.

True. Consider, sir, the sword is worn for a distinguishing mark of honour: promise me one, and receive t'other.

Rich. I'll promise nothing, till I have that in my power.

True. Take it.   [*Throws him his sword.*

Rich. I scorn to be compelled even to justice; and now, that I may resist, I yield. Trueman, I have injured thee, and Clelia I have severely wronged.

True. Wronged indeed, sir;—and, to aggravate the crime, the fair afflicted loves you. Marked you with what confusion she received me? She wept, the injured Innocence wept, and, with a strange reluctance, gave consent; her moving softness pierced my heart, though I mistook the cause.

Rich. Your youthful virtue warms my breast, and melts it into tenderness.

True. Indulge it, sir; justice is noble in any form: think of the joys and raptures will possess her when she finds you instead of me: you, the dear dissembler, the man she loves, the man she gave for lost, to find him true, returned, and in her arms.

Rich. No new possession can give equal joy. It shall be done, the priest that waits for you shall tie the knot this moment; in the morning I'll expect you'll give me joy.   [*Exit.*

True. So, is not this better now than cutting of throats? I have got my revenge, and the lady will have hers without bloodshed.   [*Exit.*

SCENE IV.

CONSTANCE'S *Apartment.*

CONSTANCE *and* Footman *discovered,*

Foot. He's just a-coming up, madam.   [*Exit.*

Con. My civility to this man will be as great a con-
straint upon me as rudeness would be to his brother:
but I must bear it a little, because our designs require it.

Enter BENJAMIN WOULDBE.

—[*Aside.*] His appearance shocks me.—[*Aloud.*] My
lord, I wish you joy.

Ben. Would. Madam, 'tis only in your power to
give it; and would you honour me with a title to
be really proud of, it should be that of your humblest servant.

Con. I never admitted anybody to the title of an
humble servant, that I did not intend should command me; if your lordship will bear with the slavery,
you shall begin when you please, provided you take
upon you the authority when I have a mind.

Ben. Would. Our sex, madam, make much better
lovers than husbands; and I think it highly unreasonable, that you should put yourself in my power, when
you can so absolutely keep me in yours.

Con. No, my lord, we never truly command till we
have given our promise to obey; and we are never
in more danger of being made slaves, than when we
have 'em at our feet.

Ben. Would. True, madam, the greatest empires
are in most danger of falling; but it is better to be

absolute there, than to act by a prerogative that's confined.

Con. Well, well, my lord, I like the constitution we live under; I'm for a limited power, or none at all.

Ben. Would. You have so much the heart of the subject, madam, that you may rule as you please; but you have weak pretences to a limited sway, where your eyes have already played the tyrant. I think one privilege of the people is to kiss their sovereign's hand.   *[Taking her hand.*

Con. Not till they have taken the oaths, my lord; and he that refuses them in the form the law prescribes, is, I think, no better than a rebel.

Ben. Would. [*Kneeling.*] By shrines and altars! by all that you think just, and I hold good! by this, [*Taking her hand*] the fairest, and the dearest vow—
      [Kisses her hand.

Con. Fy, my lord!   *[Seemingly yielding.*

Ben. Would. Your eyes are mine, they bring me tidings from your heart that this night I shall be happy.

Con. Would not you despise a conquest so easily gained?

Ben. Would. Yours will be the conquest, and I shall despise all the world but you.

Con. But will you promise to make no attempts upon my honour?

Ben. Would. [*Aside.*] That's foolish. [*Aloud.*] Not angels sent on messages to earth shall visit with more innocence.

Con. [*Aside.*] Ay, ay, to be sure. [*Aloud.*] My lord, I'll send one to conduct you.   *[Exit.*

Ben. Would. Ha! ha! ha! no atttempts upon her honour! When I can find the place where it lies, I'll tell her more of my mind. Now do I feel ten thousand Cupids tickling me all over with the points of their arrows. Where's my deformity now? I have read somewhere these lines:—

> Though Nature cast me in a rugged mould,
> Since fate has changed the bullion into gold:
> Cupid returns, breaks all his shafts of lead,
> And tips each arrow with a golden head.
> Feather'd with title, the gay lordly dart
> Flies proudly on, whilst every virgin's heart
> Swells with ambition to receive the smart.

Enter HERMES WOULDBE *behind him.*

Herm. Would. Thus to adorn dramatic story,
> Stage-hero struts in borrowed glory,
> Proud and august as ever man saw,
> And ends his empire in a stanza.

> > *[Slaps him on the shoulder.*

Ben. Would. Ha! my brother!

Herm. Would. No, perfidious man; all kindred and relation I disown! The poor attempts upon my fortune I could pardon, but thy base designs upon my love I never can forgive. My honour, birthright, riches, all I could more freely spare, than the least thought of thy prevailing here.

Ben. Would. How! my hopes deceived! Cursed be the fair delusions of her sex! whilst only man opposed my cunning, I stood secure; but soon as woman interposed, luck changed hands, and the devil was immediately on her side. Well, sir, much good may do you with your mistress, and may you love, and live, and starve together. [*Going.*

Herm. Would. Hold, sir! I was lately your prisoner, now you are mine; when the ejectment is executed, you shall be at liberty.

Ben Would. Ejectment!

Herm. Would. Yes, sir; by this time, I hope, my friends have purged my father's house of that debauched and riotous swarm that you had hived together.

Ben. Would. Confusion! Sir, let me pass; I am the elder, and will be obeyed. [*Draws.*

Herm. Would. Darest thou dispute the eldership so nobly?

Ben. Would. I dare, and will, to the last drop of my inveterate blood. [*They fight.*

Enter Captain TRUEMAN *and* TEAGUE.

True. [*Striking down their swords.*] Hold, hold, my lord! I have brought those shall soon decide the controversy.

Ben. Would. If I mistake not, that is the villain that decoyed me abroad.

[*Runs at* Captain TRUEMAN, TEAGUE *catches his arm behind, and takes away his sword.*

Teague. Ay, be me shoule, thish ish the besht guard upon the rules of fighting, to catch a man behind his back.

True. My lord, a word.— [*Whispers* HERMES WOULDBE.] Now, gentlemen, please to hear this venerable lady.

[*Goes to the door, and brings in* Mrs. MANDRAKE.

Herm. Would. Mandrake in custody!

Teague. In my custody, fet.

True. Now, madam, you know what punishment is destined for the injury offered to Aurelia, if you don't immediately confess the truth.

Mrs. Man. Then I must own, (Heaven forgive me !)—[*Weeping*] I must own, that Hermes, as he was still esteemed, so he is the first-born.

Teague. A very honesht woman, be me shoule !

Ben. Would. That confession is extorted by fear, and therefore of no force.

True. Ay, sir ; but here is your letter to her, with the ink scarce dry, where you repeat your offer of five hundred pound a year to swear in your behalf.

Teague. Dat was Teague's finding out, and, I believe, St. Patrick put it in my toughts to pick her pockets.

Enter CONSTANCE *and* AURELIA.

Con. I hope, Mr. Wouldbe, you will make no attempts upon my person.

Ben. Would. Damn your person !

Herm. Would. But pray, madam, where have you been all this evening ?　　　　　[*To* AURELIA.

Aur. Very busy, I can assure you, sir. Here's an honest constable that I could find in my heart to marry, had the greasy rogue but one drop of genteel blood in his veins ; what's become of him?

[*Looking about.*

Con. Bless me, cousin, marry a constable !

Aur. Why truly, madam, if that constable had not come in a very critical minute, by this time I had been glad to marry anybody.

True. I take you at your word, madam, you shall

marry him this moment; and if you don't say that I have genteel blood in my veins by to-morrow morning—

Aur. And was it you, sir?

True. Look'ee, madam, don't be ashamed; I found you a little in the *déshabillé*, that's the truth on't, but you made a brave defence.

Aur. I am obliged to you; and though you were a little whimsical to-day, this late adventure has taught me how dangerous it is to provoke a gentleman by ill usage; therefore, if my lord and this lady will show us a good example, I think we must follow our leaders, captain.

True. As boldly as when honour calls.

Con. My lord, there was taken among your brother's jovial crew, his friend Subtleman, whom we have taken care to secure.

Herm. Would. For him the pillory. — For you, madam—   [*To* Mrs. MANDRAKE.

Teague. Be me shoule, she shall be married to maishter Fuller.*

Herm. Would. For you, brother—

Ben. Would. Poverty and contempt—

To which I yield as to a milder fate,

Than obligations from the man I hate.   [*Exit.*

Herm. Would. Then take thy wish.—And now, I hope, all parties have received their due rewards and punishments?

---

* I suppose this is an allusion to William Fuller, the notorious informer and spy, who was at this time in prison. I am the more inclined to this opinion, because one of Fuller's "cock-and-bull" stories bore some resemblance to Mrs. Mandrake's pretended confession of the substitution of one child for another.

Teague. But what will you do for poor Teague, maishter?

Herm. Would. What shall I do for thee?—

Teague. Arah, maak me a justice of peash, dear joy.

Herm. Would. Justice of peace! thou art not qualified, man.

Teague. Yest, fet am I—I can take the oats, and write my mark—I can be an honesht man myshelf, and keep a great rogue for my clark.

Herm. Would. Well, well, you shall be taken care of.—And now, captain, we set out for happiness :—

Let none despair whate'er their fortunes be,
Fortune must yield, would men but act like me.
Choose a brave friend as partner of your breast,
Be active when your right is in contest;
Be true to love, and fate will do the rest.

[*Exeunt omnes.*

EPILOGUE.

SPOKEN BY MRS. HOOK.

OUR poet open'd with a loud warlike blast,
But now weak woman is his safest cast,
To bring him off with quarter at the last:
Not that he's vain to think that I can say,
Or he can write, fine things to help the play.
The various scenes have drain'd his strength and
    art;
And I, you know, had a hard struggling part:
But then he brought me off with life and limb;
Ah, would that I could do as much for him!—
Stay, let me think—your favours to excite,
I still must act the part I play'd to-night.
For whatsoe'er may be your sly pretence,
You like those best that make the best defence:
But this is needless—'tis in vain to crave it.
If you have damn'd the play, no power can save it.
Not all the wits of Athens, and of Rome;
Not Shakspeare, Jonson, could revoke its doom:
Nay, what is more—if once your anger rouses,
Not all the courted beauties of both houses.
He would have ended here—but I thought meet,
To tell him there was left one safe retreat,
Protection sacred, at the ladies' feet.
To that he answer'd in submissive strain,
He paid all homage to this female reign,
And therefore turn'd his satire 'gainst the men.
From your great queen this sovereign right ye draw,
To keep the wits, as she the world, in awe:

To her bright sceptre your bright eyes they bow ;
Such awful splendour sits on every brow,
All scandal on the sex were treason now.
The play can tell with what poetic care
He labour'd to redress the injured fair,
And if you won't protect, the men will damn him
    there.
Then save the Muse, that flies to ye for aid ;
Perhaps my poor request may some persuade
Because it is the first I ever made.

THE RECRUITING OFFICER.

Captique dolis, *donisque* coacti.
       —VIRGIL: *Æneid*, ii. 196.

This comedy was first produced on April 8, 1706, at Drury Lane, and was very successful. It is one of the liveliest plays in our language: the plot carefully constructed and held together by amusing yet probable incidents, the scenes illustrative of certain phases of social life ignored by the historian, and the dialogue, if not supremely witty, always genial and vivacious. It is the truest picture we have of the recruiting service at the close of the seventeenth century, and shows the arts that were once used to fire the ambition and appeal to the ignorance of our country bumpkins. The swagger and sentiments of the rival captains serve as excellent foils to each other. According to tradition, the character of Plume was intended by the author for a picture of himself, but the tradition is probably untrustworthy.

The original cast was:—*Captain Plume*, WILKS; *Captain Brazen*, CIBBER; *Serjeant Kite*, ESTCOURT; *Bullock*, BULLOCK; *Justice Balance*, KEEN; *Worthy*, WILLIAMS; *Costar Pearmain*, NORRIS; *Thomas Appletree*, FAIRBANK; *Sylvia*, Mrs. OLDFIELD; *Melinda*, Mrs. ROGERS; *Rose*, Mrs. MOUNTFORT; *Lucy*, Mrs. SAPSFORD.

TO ALL FRIENDS ROUND THE WREKIN.

My Lords and Gentlemen,—Instead of the mercenary expectations that attend addresses of this nature, I humbly beg, that this may be received as an acknowledgment for the favours you have already conferred. I have transgressed the rules of dedication in offering you anything in that style, without first asking your leave: but the entertainment I found in Shropshire commands me to be grateful, and that's all I intend.

'Twas my good fortune to be ordered some time ago into the place which is made the scene of this comedy; I was a perfect stranger to everything in Salop, but its character of loyalty, the number of its inhabitants, the alacrity of the gentlemen in recruiting the army, with their generous and hospitable reception of strangers.

This character I found so amply verified in every particular, that you made recruiting, which is the greatest fatigue upon earth to others, to be the greatest pleasure in the world to me.

The kingdom cannot show better bodies of men, better inclinations for the service, more generosity, more good understanding, nor more politeness, than is to be found at the foot of the Wrekin.

Some little turns of humour that I met with almost within the shade of that famous hill, gave the rise to this comedy; and people were apprehensive that, by the example of some others, I would make the town merry at the expense of the country-gentlemen. But they forgot that I was to write a comedy, not a libel; and that whilst I held to nature, no person of any character in your country could suffer by being exposed. I have drawn the justice and the clown in their *puris naturalibus:* the one an apprehensive, sturdy, brave blockhead; and the other a worthy, honest, generous gentleman, hearty in his country's cause, and of as good an understanding as I could give him, which I must confess is far short of his own.

I humbly beg leave to interline a word or two of the adventures of the Recruiting Officer upon the stage. Mr. Rich, who commands the company for which those recruits were raised, has desired me to acquit him before the world of a charge which he thinks lies heavy upon him, for acting this play on Mr. Durfey's third night.

Be it known unto all men by these presents, that it was my act and deed, or rather Mr. Durfey's; for he *would* play his third night against the first of mine. He brought down a huge flight of frightful birds upon me ; when (Heaven knows !) I had not a feathered fowl in my play, except one single *Kite;* but I presently made *Plume* a bird, because of his name, and *Brazen* another, because of the feather in his hat ; and with these three I engaged his whole empire, which I think was as great a *Wonder* as any *in the Sun.*[*]

But to answer his complaints more gravely, the season was far advanced ; the officers that made the greatest figures in my play were all commanded to their posts abroad, and waited only for a wind, which might possibly turn in less time than a day : and I know none of Mr. Durfey's birds that had posts abroad but his *Woodcocks,* and their season is over ; so that he might put off a day with less prejudice than the Recruiting Officer could ; who has this farther to say for himself, that he was posted before the other spoke, and could not with credit recede from his station.

These and some other rubs this comedy met with before it appeared. But, on the other hand, it had powerful helps to set it forward. The Duke of Ormond encouraged the author, and the Earl of Orrery approved the play. My recruits were reviewed by my general and my colonel, and could not fail to pass muster ; and still to add to my success, they were raised among my friends round the Wrekin.

This health has the advantage over our other celebrated toasts, never to grow worse for the wearing : 'tis a lasting beauty, old without age, and common without scandal. That you may live long to set it cheerfully round, and to enjoy the abundant pleasures of your fair and plentiful country, is the hearty wish of, my Lords and Gentlemen, your most obliged, and most obedient servant,

G. FARQUHAR.

---

[*] Durfey's opera bore the title of *Wonders in the Sun,* or, *the Kingdom of the Birds.*

DRAMATIS PERSONÆ.

JUSTICE BALANCE,
JUSTICE SCRUPLE, } *three Justices of the Peace.*
JUSTICE SCALE,
MR. WORTHY, *a Gentleman of Shropshire.*
CAPTAIN PLUME,
CAPTAIN BRAZEN, } *two Recruiting Officers.*
SERJEANT KITE, *Serjeant to* CAPTAIN PLUME.
BULLOCK, *a Country Clown, Brother to* ROSE.
COSTAR PEARMAIN,
THOMAS APPLETREE, } *two Recruits.*
PLUCK, *a Butcher.*
THOMAS, *a Smith.*
MELINDA, *a Lady of Fortune, beloved by* MR. WORTHY.
SILVIA, *Daughter to* JUSTICE BALANCE, *in love with* CAPTAIN
 PLUME.
LUCY, *Maid to* MELINDA.
ROSE, *a Country Girl, Sister to* BULLOCK.
Steward, Drummer, Recruits, Constables, Watch, Mob, Ser-
 vants, &c. &c.

SCENE,—SHREWSBURY.

PROLOGUE.

In ancient times when Helen's fatal charms
Roused the contending universe to arms,
The Grecian council happily deputes
The sly Ulysses forth—to raise recruits.
The artful captain found, without delay,
Where great Achilles, a deserter, lay.
Him fate had warn'd to shun the Trojan blows :
Him Greece required—against their Trojan foes.
All the recruiting arts were needful here,
To raise this great, this timorous volunteer.
Ulysses well could talk : he stirs, he warms
The warlike youth.—He listens to the charms
Of plunder, fine laced coats, and glittering arms.
Ulysses caught the young aspiring boy,
And listed him who wrought the fate of Troy.
Thus by recruiting was bold Hector slain :
Recruiting thus fair Helen did regain.
If for one Helen such prodigious things
Were acted, that they even listed kings ;
If for one Helen's artful, vicious charms,
Half the transported world was found in arms ;
What for so many Helens may we dare,
Whose minds as well as faces are so fair ?
If by one Helen's eyes old Greece could find,
Its Homer fired to write—even Homer blind ;
The Britons sure beyond compare may write,
That view so many Helens every night.

THE RECRUITING OFFICER.

ACT I.

SCENE I.

The Market Place.

Enter Drummer, *beating the* "*Grenadier's March*," Serjeant KITE, COSTAR PEARMAIN, THOMAS APPLETREE, *and* Mob *following*.

Kite [*Making a speech*]. If any gentlemen, soldiers, or others, have a mind to serve her majesty, and pull down the French king: if any prentices have severe masters, any children have undutiful parents: if any servants have too little wages, or any husband too much wife: let them repair to the noble serjeant Kite, at the sign of the Raven in this good town of Shrewsbury, and they shall receive present relief and entertainment.—Gentlemen, I don't beat my drums here to ensnare or inveigle any man; for you must know, gentlemen, that I am a man of honour. Besides, I don't beat up for common soldiers; no, I list only grenadiers—grenadiers, gentlemen. Pray, gentlemen, observe this cap. This is the cap of honour, it dubs a man a gentle-

man in the drawing of a tricker; and he that has
the good fortune to be born six foot high, was born
to be a great man.—[*To* Costar Pearmain.] Sir,
will you give me leave to try this cap upon your
head?

Pear. Is there no harm in't? Won't the cap
list me?

Kite. No, no, no more than I can.—Come, let me
see how it becomes you?

Pear. Are you sure there be no conjuration in it?
no gunpowder plot upon me?

Kite. No, no, friend; don't fear, man.

Pear. My mind misgives me plaguily.—Let me
see it.—[*Going to put it on.*] It smells woundily of
sweat and brimstone. Pray, serjeant, what writing
is this upon the face of it?

Kite. The crown, or the bed of honour.

Pear. Pray now, what may be that same bed of
honour?

Kite. Oh! a mighty large bed! bigger by half than
the great bed of Ware *—ten thousand people may lie
in it together, and never feel one another.

Pear. My wife and I would do well to lie in't, for
we don't care for feeling one another.—But do folk
sleep sound in this same bed of honour?

Kite. Sound! ay, so sound that they never wake.

Pear. Wauns! I wish again that my wife lay there.

Kite. Say you so? then, I find, brother—

Pear. Brother! hold there, friend; I am no
kindred to you that I know of yet. Look'ee, serjeant,

* This famous bed was twelve feet square, and was capable of
holding twenty-four persons. Tradition assigned it to the Earl
of Warwick, the King-maker. Shakespeare alludes to it in *Twelfth
Night*, act iii. sc. 2.

no coaxing, no wheedling, d'ye see: if I have a mind
to list, why so; if not, why 'tis not so, therefore take
your cap and your brothership back again, for I an't
disposed at this present writing.—No coaxing, no
brothering me, faith !

Kite. I coax ! I wheedle ! I'm above it ! sir, I
have served twenty campaigns.   But, sir, you talk
well, and I must own that you are a man every inch
of you, a pretty young sprightly fellow.   I love a
fellow with a spirit; but I scorn to coax, 'tis base :
though I must say, that never in my life have I seen
a better built man ; how firm and strong he treads !
he steps like a castle ; but I scorn to wheedle any
man.—Come, honest lad, will you take share of a
pot ?

Pear. Nay, for that matter, I'll spend my penny
with the best he that wears a head, that is, begging
your pardon, sir, and in a fair way.

Kite. Give me your hand then ; and now, gentlemen, I have no more to say, but this—here's a purse
of gold, and there is a tub of humming ale at my
quarters ! 'tis the queen's money, and the queen's
drink.—She's a generous queen, and loves her subjects—I hope, gentlemen, you won't refuse the queen's
health ?

Mob. No, no, no !

Kite. Huzza then ! huzza for the queen, and the
honour of Shropshire !

Mob. Huzza !

Kite. Beat drum.

[*Exeunt,* Drummer *beating the* " *Grenadier's March.*"

Enter Captain PLUME.

Plume. By the Grenadier March, that should be my drum, and by that shout, it should beat with success.—Let me see—four o'clock.—[*Looking on his watch.*] At ten yesterday morning I left London.—A hundred and twenty miles in thirty hours is pretty smart riding, but nothing to the fatigue of recruiting.

Re-enter Serjeant KITE.

Kite. Welcome to Shrewsbury, noble captain! From the banks of the Danube to the Severn side, noble captain, you're welcome!

Plume. A very elegant reception indeed, Mr. Kite! I find you are fairly entered into your recruiting strain: pray, what success?

Kite. I have been here but a week, and I have recruited five.

Plume. Five! pray what are they?

Kite. I have listed the strong man of Kent, the king of the gipsies, a Scotch pedlar, a scoundrel attorney, and a Welsh parson.

Plume. An attorney! wert thou mad? List a lawyer! Discharge him, discharge him this minute.

Kite. Why, sir?

Plume. Because I will have nobody in my company that can write; a fellow that can write, can draw petitions.—I say this minute discharge him.

Kite. And what shall I do with the parson?

Plume. Can he write?

Kite. Hum! He plays rarely upon the fiddle.

Plume. Keep him by all means.—But how stands the country affected? were the people pleased with the news of my coming to town?

Kite. Sir, the mob are so pleased with your honour, and the justices and better sort of people are so delighted with me, that we shall soon do our business.—But, sir, you have got a recruit here that you little think of.

Plume. Who?

Kite. One that you beat up for last time you were in the country: you remember your old friend Molly at the Castle?

Plume. She's not with child, I hope?

Kite. No, no, sir—she was brought to bed yesterday.

Plume. Kite, you must father the child.

Kite. And so her friends will oblige me to marry the mother!

Plume. If they should, we'll take her with us; she can wash, you know, and make a bed upon occasion.

Kite. Ay, or unmake it upon occasion. But your honour knows that I am married already.

Plume. To how many.

Kite. I can't tell readily—I have set them down here upon the back of the muster-roll.—[*Draws it out.*] Let me see,—*Imprimis*, Mrs. Sheely Snikereyes; she sells potatoes upon Ormond Key in Dublin —Peggy Guzzle, the brandy-woman at the Horse-guard at Whitehall—Dolly Waggon, the carrier's daughter at Hull—Mademoiselle Van-Bottomflat at the Buss.—Then Jenny Oakham, the ship-carpenter's widow, at Portsmouth; but I don't reckon upon her, for she was married at the same time to two lieutenants of marines, and a man-of-war's boatswain.

Plume. A full company!—You have named five—

come, make 'em half-a-dozen, Kite. Is the child a
boy or a girl?

Kite. A chopping boy.

Plume. Then set the mother down in your list, and
the boy in mine: Enter him a grenadier by the name
of Francis Kite, absent upon furlough. I'll allow you
a man's pay for his subsistence; and now go comfort
the wench in the straw.

Kite. I shall, sir.

Plume. But hold; have you made any use of your
German doctor's habit since you arrived?

Kite. Yes, yes, sir, and my fame's all about the
country for the most famous fortune-teller that ever
told a lie.—I was obliged to let my landlord into the
secret, for the convenience of keeping it so; but he's
an honest fellow, and will be trusty to any roguery
that is confided to him. This device, sir, will get you
men, and me money, which, I think, is all we want at
present.—But yonder comes your friend Mr. Worthy.
—Has your honour any farther commands?

Plume. None at present.—[*Exit* Serjeant KITE.]
'Tis indeed the picture of Worthy, but the life's de-
parted.

Enter Mr. WORTHY.

What! arms a-cross, Worthy! Methinks, you should
hold 'em open when a friend's so near.—The man
has got the vapours in his ears, I believe: I must
expel this melancholy spirit.

Spleen, thou worst of fiends below,

Fly, I conjure thee by this magic blow.

[*Slaps* Mr. WORTHY *on the shoulder.*

Wor. Plume! my dear captain, welcome. Safe
and sound returned?

Plume. I 'scaped safe from Germany, and sound, I hope, from London; you see I have lost neither leg, arm, nor nose; then for my inside, 'tis neither troubled with sympathies nor antipathies; and I have an excellent stomach for roast-beef.

Wor. Thou art a happy fellow; once I was so.

Plume. What ails thee, man? No inundations nor earthquakes in Wales, I hope? Has your father rose from the dead, and reassumed his estate?

Wor. No.

Plume. Then you are married, surely?

Wor. No.

Plume. Then you are mad, or turning quaker?

Wor. Come, I must out with it.—Your once gay, roving friend is dwindled into an obsequious, thoughtful, romantic, constant coxcomb.

Plume. And, pray, what is all this for?

Wor. For a woman.

Plume. Shake hands, brother; if you go to that, behold me as obsequious, as thoughtful, and as constant a coxcomb as your worship.

Wor. For whom?

Plume. For a regiment.—But for a woman!— 'Sdeath! I have been constant to fifteen at a time, but never melancholy for one; and can the love of one bring you into this pickle? Pray, who is this miraculous Helen?

Wor. A Helen indeed, not to be won under a ten years' siege, as great a beauty, and as great a jilt.

Plume. A jilt! pho! is she as great a whore?

Wor. No, no.

Plume. 'Tis ten thousand pities. But who is she? do I know her?

Wor. Very well.

Plume. Impossible !—I know no woman that will hold out a ten years' siege.

Wor. What think you of Melinda?

Plume. Melinda! why, she began to capitulate this time twelvemonth, and offered to surrender upon honourable terms ; and I advised you to propose a settlement of five hundred pounds a-year to her, before I went last abroad.

Wor. I did, and she hearkened to't, desiring only one week to consider : when, beyond her hopes, the town was relieved, and I forced to turn my siege into a blockade.

Plume. Explain, explain !

Wor. My lady Richly, her aunt, in Flintshire dies, and leaves her, at this critical time, twenty thousand pounds.

Plume. Oh ! the devil ! what a delicate woman was there spoiled ! But, by the rules of war now, Worthy, your blockade was foolish. After such a convoy of provisions was entered the place, you could have no thought of reducing it by famine ; you should have redoubled your attacks, taken the town by storm, or have died upon the breach.

Wor. I did make one general assault, and pushed it with all my forces ; but I was so vigorously repulsed, that, despairing of ever gaining her for a mistress, I have altered my conduct, given my addresses the obsequious and distant turn, and court her now for a wife.

Plume. So as you grew obsequious, she grew haughty ; and because you approached her as a goddess, she used you like a dog ?

Wor. Exactly.

Plume. 'Tis the way of 'em all. Come, Worthy, your obsequious and distant 'airs will never bring you together ; you must not think to surmount her pride by your humility. Would you bring her to better thoughts of you, she must be reduced to a meaner opinion of herself. Let me see; the very first thing that I would do, should be to lie with her chamber-maid, and hire three or four wenches in the neighbour-hood to report that I had got them with child. Suppose we lampooned all the pretty women in town, and left her out? Or, what if we made a ball, and forgot to invite her with one or two of the ugliest?

Wor. These would be mortifications, I must con-fess ; but we live in such a precise, dull place, that we can have no balls, no lampoons, no——

Plume. What! no bastards! and so many recruit-ing officers in town! I thought 'twas a maxim among them to leave as many recruits in the country as they carried out.

Wor. Nobody doubts your good-will, noble captain, in serving your country with your best blood ; witness our friend Molly at the Castle. There have been tears in town about that business, captain.

Plume. I hope Silvia has not heard of 't?

Wor. O sir, have you thought of her? I began to fancy you had forgot poor Silvia.

Plume. Your affairs had put my own quite out of my head. 'Tis true, Silvia and I had once agreed to go to bed together, could we have adjusted pre-liminaries ; but she would have the wedding before consummation, and I was for consummation before the wedding ; we could not agree. She was a pert, obstinate fool, and would lose her maidenhead her own way, so she may keep it for Plume.

Wor. But do you intend to marry upon no other conditions?

Plume. Your pardon, sir, I'll marry upon no conditions at all. If I should, I am resolved never to bind myself to a woman for my whole life, till I know whether I shall like her company for half an hour. Suppose I married a woman that wanted a leg! such a thing might be, unless I examined the goods beforehand. If people would but try one another's constitutions before they engaged, it would prevent all these elopements, divorces, and the devil knows what.

Wor. Nay, for that matter, the town did not stick to say, that——

Plume. I hate country towns for that reason. If your town has a dishonourable thought of Silvia it deserves to be burned to the ground. I love Silvia, I admire her frank, generous disposition. There's something in that girl more than woman, her sex is but a foil to her. The ingratitude, dissimulation, envy, pride, avarice, and vanity of her sister females, do but set off their contraries in her. In short, were I once a general I would marry her.

Wor. Faith, you have reason; for were you but a corporal she would marry you. But my Melinda coquettes it with every fellow she sees. I'll lay fifty pound she makes love to you.

Plume. I'll lay fifty pound that I return it, if she does. Look'ee, Worthy, I'll win her, and give her to you afterwards.

Wor. If you win her you shall wear her, faith; I

would not give a fig for the conquest without the credit of the victory.

Re-enter Serjeant KITE.

Kite. Captain, captain, a word in your ear.

Plume. You may speak out, here are none but friends.

Kite. You know, sir, that you sent me to comfort the good woman in the straw, Mrs. Molly—my wife, Mr. Worthy.

Wor. O ho! very well! I wish you joy, Mr. Kite.

Kite. Your worship very well may, for I have got both a wife and a child in half-an-hour. But, as I was a-saying, you sent me to comfort Mrs. Molly, my wife, I mean ; but what d'ye think, sir? she was better comforted before I came.

Plume. As how?

Kite. Why, sir, a footman in a blue livery had brought her ten guineas to buy her baby-clothes.

Plume. Who, in the name of wonder, could send them?

Kite. Nay, sir, I must whisper that—Mrs. Silvia.

[*Whispers.*

Plume. Silvia! generous creature!

Wor. Silvia! impossible!

Kite. Here be the guineas, sir; I took the gold as part of my wife's portion. Nay, farther, sir, she sent word that the child should be taken all imaginable care of, and that she intended to stand godmother. The same footman, as I was coming to you with this news, called after me, and told me, that his lady would speak with me. I went, and, upon hearing that you were come to town, she gave me half-a-guinea for the news; and ordered me to tell you, that justice Balance, her father, who is just come out of the country, would be glad to see you.

Plume. There's a girl for you, Worthy! Is there anything of woman in this? No, 'tis noble and generous, manly friendship. Show me another woman that would lose an inch of her prerogative, that way, without tears, fits, and reproaches! The common jealousy of her sex, which is nothing but their avarice of pleasure, she despises; and can part with the lover, though she dies for the man. Come, Worthy: where's the best wine? for there I'll quarter.

Wor. Horton has a fresh pipe of choice Barcelona, which I would not let him pierce before, because I reserved the maidenhead of it for your welcome to town.

Plume. Let's away then.—Mr. Kite, wait on the lady with my humble service, and tell her I shall only refresh a little, and wait upon her.

Wor. Hold, Kite!—Have you seen the other recruiting-captain?

Kite. No, sir.

Plume. Another! who is he?

Wor. My rival in the first place, and the most unaccountable fellow—but I'll tell you more as we go.

[*Exeunt.*

SCENE II.

MELINDA'S *Apartment.*

Enter MELINDA *and* SILVIA *meeting.*

Mel. Welcome to town, cousin Silvia—[*Salute*]. I envied you your retreat in the country; for Shrewsbury, methinks, and all your heads of shires, are the most irregular places for living. Here we have smoke, noise, scandal, affectation, and pretension ; in short, everything to give the spleen—and nothing to divert it. Then the air is intolerable.

Silv. O madam! I have heard the town commended for its air.

Mel. But you don't consider, Silvia, how long I have lived in't! for I can assure you, that to a lady, the least nice in her constitution, no air can be good above half a year. Change of air I take to be the most agreeable of any variety in life.

Silv. As you say, cousin Melinda, there are several sorts of airs.

Mel. Psha! I talk only of the air we breathe, or more properly of that we taste. Have not you, Silvia, found a vast difference in the taste of airs?

Silv. Pray, cousin, are not vapours a sort of air? taste air! you might as well tell me, I may feed upon air. But prithee, my dear Melinda, don't put on such an air to me. Your education and mine were just the same ; and I remember the time when we never troubled our heads about air, but when the sharp air from the Welsh mountains made our fingers ache in a cold morning at the boarding-school.

Mel. Our education, cousin, was the same, but our temperaments had nothing alike ; you have the constitution of a horse.

Silv. So far as to be troubled with neither spleen, colic, nor vapours ; I need no salts for my stomach, no hartshorn for my head, nor wash for my complexion ; I can gallop all the morning after the hunting-horn, and all the evening after a fiddle. In short,

I can do everything with my father, but drink, and shoot flying; and I am sure, I can do everything my mother could, were I put to the trial.

Mel. You are in a fair way of being put to't; for I am told your captain is come to town.

Silv. Ay, Melinda, he is come, and I'll take care he shan't go without a companion.

Mel. You are certainly mad, cousin !

Silv. And there's a pleasure sure, in being mad,
      Which none but madmen know.

Mel. Thou poor romantic Quixote. Hast thou the vanity to imagine that a young sprightly officer, that rambles over half the globe in half a year, can confine his thoughts to the little daughter of a country-justice, in an obscure corner of the world?

Silv. Psha! what care I for his thoughts? I should not like a man with confined thoughts, it shows a narrowness of soul. Constancy is but a dull sleepy quality at best, they will hardly admit it among the manly virtues; nor do I think it deserves a place with bravery, knowledge, policy, justice, and some other qualities that are proper to that noble sex. In short, Melinda, I think a petticoat a mighty simple thing, and I am heartily tired of my sex.

Mel. That is, you are tired of an appendix to our sex, that you can't so handsomely get rid of in petticoats, as if you were in breeches. O' my conscience, Silvia, hadst thou been a man, thou hadst been the greatest rake in Christendom.

Silv. I should have endeavoured to know the world, which a man can never do thoroughly without half a hundred friendships, and as many amours. But now I think on't, how stands your affair with Mr. Worthy ?

Mel. He's my aversion !

Silv. Vapours !

Mel. What do you say, madam ?

Silv. I say, that you should not use that honest fellow so inhumanly. He's a gentleman of parts and fortune ; and besides that he's my Plume's friend, and by all that's sacred, if you don't use him better, I shall expect satisfaction.

Mel. Satisfaction ! you begin to fancy yourself in breeches in good earnest. But to be plain with you, I like Worthy the worse for being so intimate with your captain, for I take him to be a loose, idle, unmannerly coxcomb.

Silv. O madam ! you never saw him, perhaps, since you were mistress of twenty-thousand pound ; you only knew him when you were capitulating with Worthy for a settlement, which perhaps might encourage him to be a little loose, and unmannerly with you.

Mel. What do you mean, madam ?

Silv. My meaning needs no interpretation, madam.

Mel. Better it had, madam ; for methinks you are too plain.

Silv. If you mean the plainness of my person, I think your ladyship as plain as me to the full.

Mel. Were I sure of that, I would be glad to take up with a rakehelly officer as you do.

Silv. Again !—Look'ee, madam, you're in your own house.

Mel. And if you had kept in yours, I should have excused you.

Silv. Don't be troubled, madam, I shan't desire to have my visit returned.

Mel. The sooner, therefore, you make an end of this the better.

Silv. I am easily persuaded to follow my inclinations, so, madam, your humble servant.   [*Exit.*

Mel. Saucy thing !

Enter LUCY.

Lucy. What's the matter, madam ?

Mel. Did you not see the proud nothing, how she swells upon the arrival of her fellow ?

Lucy. Her fellow has not been long enough arrived to occasion any great swelling, madam ; I don't believe she has seen him yet.

Mel. Nor shan't if I can help it.—Let me see—I have it !—Bring me pen and ink.—Hold, I'll go write in my closet.

Lucy. An answer to this letter, I hope, madam.

[*Presents a letter.*

Mel. Who sent it ?

Lucy. Your captain, madam.

Mel. He's a fool, and I am tired of him. Send it back unopened.

Lucy. The messenger's gone, madam.

Mel. Then how shall I send an answer ? Call him back immediately, while I go write.   [*Exeunt.*

ACT II.

SCENE I.

A Room in Justice BALANCE'S *House.*

Enter Justice BALANCE *and* Captain PLUME.

Bal. Look'ee, captain, give us but blood for our money, and you shan't want men. I remember that for some years of the last war,* we had no blood nor wounds, but in the officers' mouths; nothing for our millions but newspapers not worth a reading. Our armies did nothing but play at prison bars, and hide-and-seek with the enemy; but now ye have brought us colours, and standards, and prisoners. Ads, my life, captain, get us but another mareschal of France,† and I'll go myself for a soldier.

Plume. Pray, Mr. Balance, how does your fair daughter?

Bal. Ah, Captain! what is my daughter to a mareschal of France? We're upon a nobler subject, I want to have a particular description of the battle of Hochstadt.

---

* An allusion to the French war of 1689–1697, which ended with the Peace of Ryswick, and was not marked by any very brilliant successes, except the Siege of Namur, which practically concluded it. The succeeding war, which was in progress when this comedy was written, was quite a different matter owing to Marlborough's brilliant successes.

† Marshal Tallard was taken prisoner at Blenheim, August 13, 1704.

Plume. The battle, sir, was a very pretty battle as one should desire to see, but we were all so intent upon victory, that we never minded the battle. All that I know of the matter is, our general commanded us to beat the French, and we did so; and if he pleases but to say the word, we'll do't again. But pray, sir, how does Mrs. Silvia?

Bal. Still upon Silvia! For shame, captain! you are engaged already, wedded to the war; victory is your mistress, and 'tis below a soldier to think of any other.

Plume. As a mistress, I confess, but as a friend, Mr. Balance.

Bal. Come, come, captain, never mince the matter, would not you debauch my daughter if you could?

Plume. How, sir! I hope she's not to be debauched.

Bal. Faith, but she is, sir; and any woman in England of her age and complexion, by a man of your youth and vigour. Look'ee, captain, once I was young, and once an officer as you are; and I can guess at your thoughts now, by what mine were then; and I remember very well, that I would have given one of my legs to have deluded the daughter of an old plain country gentleman, as like me as I was then like you.

Plume. But, sir, was that country gentleman your friend and benefactor?

Bal. Not much of that.

Plume. There the comparison breaks: the favours, sir, that——

Bal. Pho, I hate speeches! If I have done you any service, captain, 'twas to please myself, for I love thee; and if I could part with my girl you should have her as soon as any young fellow I know. But I hope you have more honour than to quit the service, and she more prudence than to follow the camp; but she's at her own disposal, she has fifteen hundred pound in her pocket, and so—Silvia, Silvia! [*Calls.*

Enter SILVIA.

Silv. There are some letters, sir, come by the post from London; I left them upon the table in your closet.

Bal. And here is a gentleman from Germany.— [*Presents* Captain PLUME *to her.*] Captain, you'll excuse me, I'll go read my letters, and wait on you.

[*Exit.*

Silv. Sir, you're welcome to England.

Plume. You are indebted to me a welcome, madam, since the hopes of receiving it from this fair hand was the principal cause of my seeing England.

Silv. I have often heard that soldiers were sincere, shall I venture to believe public report?

Plume. You may, when 'tis backed by private insurance: for I swear, madam, by the honour of my profession, that whatever dangers I went upon, it was with the hope of making myself more worthy of your esteem; and, if ever I had thoughts of preserving my life, 'twas for the pleasure of dying at your feet.

Silv. Well, well, you shall die at my feet, or where you will; but you know, sir, there is a certain will and testament to be made beforehand.

Plume. My will, madam, is made already, and there it is [*Gives her a parchment*]; and if you please to open that parchment, which was drawn the evening

before the battle of Blenheim, you will find whom I
left my heir.

Silv. [*Opens the will and reads.*]   *Mrs. Silvia
Balance.*—Well, Captain, this is a handsome and a
substantial compliment; but I can assure you, I am
much better pleased with the bare knowledge of your
intention, than I should have been in the possession
of your legacy.   But methinks, sir, you should have
left something to your little boy at the Castle.

Plume. [*Aside.*] That's home!—[*Aloud.*] My little
boy!   Lack-a-day, madam, that alone may convince
you 'twas none of mine.   Why the girl, madam, is
my serjeant's wife, and so the poor creature gave out
that I was father, in hopes that my friends might
support her in case of necessity—that was all,
madam.—My boy! no, no, no.

Enter Servant.

Ser. Madam, my master has received some ill news
from London, and desires to speak with you immediately, and he begs the captain's pardon, that he
can't wait on him as he promised.   [*Exit.*

Plume. Ill news!   Heavens avert it, nothing could
touch me nearer than to see that generous worthy
gentleman afflicted.   I'll leave you to comfort him,
and be assured, that if my life and fortune can be
any way serviceable to the father of my Silvia, she
shall freely command both.

Silv. The necessity must be very pressing that
would engage me to endanger either.

                              [*Exeunt severally.*

SCENE II.

Another room in the same.

Justice BALANCE *and* SILVIA *discovered.*

Silv. Whilst there is life there is hope, sir ; perhaps my brother may recover.

Bal. We have but little reason to expect it ; doctor Kilman acquaints me here, that before this comes to my hands, he fears I shall have no son.   Poor Owen ! —But the decree is just, I was pleased with the death of my father, because he left me an estate, and now I'm punished with the loss of an heir to inherit mine. I must now look upon you as the only hopes of my family, and I expect that the augmentation of your fortune will give you fresh thoughts, and new prospects.

Silv. My desire of being punctual in my obedience, requires that you would be plain in your commands, sir.

Bal. The death of your brother makes you sole heiress to my estate, which you know is about twelve hundred pounds a year.   This fortune gives you a fair claim to quality and a title ; you must set a just value upon yourself, and, in plain terms, think no more of Captain Plume.

Silv. You have often commended the gentleman, sir.

Bal. And I do so still ; he's a very pretty fellow ; but though I liked him well enough for a bare son-in-law, I don't approve of him for an heir to my estate and family.   Fifteen hundred pounds indeed I might trust in his hands, and it might do the young fellow a kindness ; but, ods my life ! twelve hundred pounds a-year would ruin him—quite turn his brain! A captain of foot worth twelve hundred pounds a year! 'tis a prodigy in nature. Besides this, I have five or six thousand pounds in woods upon my estate; oh, that would make him stark mad! For you must know, that all captains have a mighty aversion to timber; they can't endure to see trees standing. Then I should have some rogue of a builder, by the help of his damned magic art, transform my noble oaks and elms into cornices, portals, sashes, birds, beasts, and devils, to adorn some maggotty, new-fashioned bauble upon the Thames; and then you should have a dog of a gardener bring a *habeas corpus* for my *terra firma*, remove it to Chelsea or Twittenham, and clap it into grass-plats and gravel-walks.

Enter Servant.

Ser. Sir, here's one below with a letter for your worship, but he will deliver it into no hands but your own.

Bal. Come, show me the messenger.

          [*Exit with* Servant.

Silv. Make the dispute between love and duty, and I am prince Prettyman * exactly. If my brother dies, ah poor brother! if he lives, ah poor sister! 'Tis bad both ways; I'll try again. Follow my own inclinations, and break my father's heart; or obey his commands, and break my own? worse and worse. Suppose I take it thus? a moderate fortune, a pretty fellow, and a pad; or a fine estate, a coach-and-six, and an ass. That will never do neither.

* Prince Prettyman in *The Rehearsal;* but Farquhar surely meant to write "Prince Volscius" in the same play, who has a famous soliloquy on Love and Duty. (*Rehearsal*, act iii., sc. 5.)

Re-enter Justice BALANCE *and* Servant.

Bal. [*To* Servant.] Put four horses into the coach. —[*Exit* Servant.] Silvia!

Silv. Sir.

Bal. How old were you when your mother died?

Silv. So young that I don't remember I ever had one; and you have been so careful, so indulgent to me since, that indeed I never wanted one.

Bal. Have I ever denied you anything you asked of me?

Silv. Never that I remember.

Bal. Then, Silvia, I must beg that, once in your life, you would grant me a favour.

Silv. Why should you question it, sir?

Bal. I don't; but I would rather counsel than command. I don't propose this with the authority of a parent, but as the advice of your friend; that you would take the coach this moment, and go into the country.

Silv. Does this advice proceed from the contents of the letter you received just now?

Bal. No matter; I shall be with you in three or four days, and then give you my reasons. But before you go, I expect you will make me one solemn promise.

Silv. Propose the thing, sir.

Bal. That you will never dispose of yourself to any man without my consent.

Silv. I promise.

Bal. Very well; and to be even with you, I promise that I will never dispose of you without your own consent; and so, Silvia, the coach is ready;

farewell!—[*Leads her to the door, and returns.*]   Now she's gone, I'll examine the contents of this letter a little nearer.   [*Reads.*

Sir,

My intimacy with Mr. Worthy has drawn a secret from him that he had from his friend Captain Plume; and my friendship and relation to your family oblige me to give you timely notice of it: the Captain has dishonourable designs upon my cousin Silvia. Evils of this nature are more easily prevented than amended; and that you would immediately send my cousin into the country, is the advice of, sir, your humble servant,

MELINDA.

Why, the devil's in the young fellows of this age! they are ten times worse than they were in my time. Had he made my daughter a whore, and forswore it like a gentleman, I could have almost pardoned it; but to tell tales beforehand is monstrous.   Hang it, I can fetch down a woodcock or a snipe, and why not a hat and feather?   I have a case of good pistols, and have a good mind to try.

Enter Mr. WORTHY.

Worthy, your servant.

Wor. I'm sorry, sir, to be the messenger of ill news.

Bal. I apprehend it, sir; you have heard that my son Owen is past recovery.

Wor. My advices say he's dead, sir.

Bal. He's happy, and I'm satisfied.   The strokes of Heaven I can bear, but injuries from men, Mr. Worthy, are not so easily supported.

Wor. I hope, sir, you're under no apprehension of wrong from anybody?

Bal. You know I ought to be.

Wor. You wrong my honour, sir, in believing I could know anything to your prejudice without resenting it as much as you should.

Bal. This letter, sir, which I tear in pieces to conceal the person that sent it, informs me that Plume has a design upon Silvia, and that you are privy to't.

[*Tears the letter.*

Wor. Nay then, sir, I must do myself justice, and endeavour to find out the author.—[*Takes up a fragment of the letter.*] Sir, I know the hand, and if you refuse to discover the contents, Melinda shall tell me. [*Going.*

Bal. Hold, sir! the contents I have told you already, only with this circumstance, that her intimacy with Mr. Worthy had drawn the secret from him.

Wor. Her intimacy with me!—Dear sir, let me pick up the pieces of this letter; 'twill give me such a hank upon her pride, to have her own an intimacy under hand.—[*Gathering up the letter.*] 'Twas the luckiest accident! The aspersion, sir, was nothing but malice, the effect of a little quarrel between her and Mrs. Silvia.

Bal. Are you sure of that, sir?

Wor. Her maid gave me the history of part of the battle just now, as she overheard it. But I hope, sir, your daughter has suffered nothing upon the account?

Bal. No, no, poor girl; she's so afflicted with the news of her brother's death, that to avoid company she begged leave to be gone into the country.

Wor. And is she gone?

Bal. I could not refuse her, she was so pressing; the coach went from the door the minute before you came.

Wor. So pressing to be gone, sir! I find her fortune will give her the same airs with Melinda, and then Plume and I may laugh at one another.

Bal. Like enough; women are as subject to pride as we are, and why mayn't great women, as well as great men, forget their old acquaintance? But come, where's this young fellow? I love him so well, it would break the heart of me to think him a rascal.— [*Aside.*] I'm glad my daughter's gone fairly off, though —[*Aloud.*] Where does the captain quarter?

Wor. At Horton's; I'm to meet him there two hours hence, and we should be glad of your company.

Bal. Your pardon, dear Worthy; I must allow a day or two to the death of my son; the decorum of mourning is what we owe the world, because they pay it to us afterwards. I'm yours over a bottle, or how you will.

Wor. Sir, I'm your humble servant.

[Exeunt severally.

SCENE III.

A Street.

Enter Serjeant KITE, *leading* COSTAR PEARMAIN *in one hand, and* THOMAS APPLETREE *in the other, both drunk.*

Serjeant KITE *sings.*

Our prentice Tom may now refuse
To wipe his scoundrel master's shoes;

For now he's free to sing and play—
Over the hills and far away.

Chorus.

Over the hills, and over the main,
To Flanders, Portugal, or Spain:
The queen commands, and we'll obey—
Over the hills and far away.

We all shall lead more happy lives,
By getting rid of brats and wives,
That scold and brawl both night and day—
Over the hills and far away.

Chorus.

Over the hills, &c.

Hey, boys! thus we soldiers live; drink, sing, dance, play! We live, as one should say—we live—'tis impossible to tell how we live. We are all princes. Why—why, you are a king, you are an emperor, and I'm a prince. Now, an't we—

Apple. No, serjeant, I'll be no emperor.

Kite. No!

Apple. No, I'll be a justice of peace.

Kite. A justice of peace, man!

Apple. Ay, wauns will I; for since this pressing act, they are greater than any emperor under the sun.

Kite. Done! you are a justice of peace, and you are a king, and I am a duke; and a rum duke, an't I?

Pear. Ay, but I'll be no king.

Kite. What then?

Pear. I'll be a queen.

Kite. A queen!

Pear. Ay, Queen of England ; that's greater than any king of 'em all.

Kite. Bravely said, faith ! Huzza for the queen !— [*Huzza.*] But heark'ee, you Mr. Justice, and you Mr. Queen, did you ever see the queen's picture?

Both. No ! no ! no !

Kite. I wonder at that ; I have two of 'em set in gold, and as like her majesty, God bless the mark !— See here, they are set in gold.

[*Takes two broad-pieces out of his pocket, and gives one to each.*

Apple. The wonderful works of Nature !

[*Looking at it.*

Pear. What's this written about? Here's a posy, I believe,—*Ca-ro-lus.*—What's that, serjeant?

Kite. Oh, Carolus !—Why, **Carolus** is Latin for Queen Anne,—that's all.

Pear. 'Tis a fine thing to be a scollard !—Serjeant, will you part with this? I'll buy it on you, if it come within the compass of a crown.

Kite. A crown ! never talk of buying ; 'tis the same thing among friends, you know ; I present them to ye both : you shall give me as good a thing. Put 'em up, and remember your old friend, when I am— *Over the hills and far away !*

[*They sing and put up the money.*

Enter Captain **PLUME,** *singing.*

Plume. *Over the hills, and over the main,*
    To Flanders, Portugal, or Spain :
    The queen commands, and we'll obey—
    Over the hills and far away.

Come on, my men of mirth, away with it, I'll make one among ye.—Who are these hearty lads?

Kite. Off with your hats; 'ounds, off with your hats! This is the captain, the captain.

Apple. We have seen captains afore now, mun.

Pear. Ay, and lieutenant-captains too; flesh, I'se keep on my nab!

Apple. And I'se scarcely doff mine for any captain in England. My vether's a freeholder.

Plume. Who are these jolly lads, serjeant?

Kite. A couple of honest brave fellows, that are willing to serve the queen: I have entertained 'em just now as volunteers under your honour's command.

Plume. And good entertainment they shall have. Volunteers are the men I want, those are the men fit to make soldiers, captains, generals!

Pear. Wauns, Tummas, what's this! are you listed?

Apple. Flesh, not I: are you, Costar?

Pear. Wauns, not I!

Kite. What, not listed! Ha! ha! ha! a very good jest, i'faith!

Pear. Come, Tummas, we'll go home.

Apple. Ay, ay, come.

Kite. Home! for shame, gentlemen, behave your-selves better before your captain! Dear Tummas, honest Costar—

Apple. No, no, we'll be gone.

Kite. Nay then, I command you to stay: I place you both sentinels in this place for two hours to watch the motion of St. Mary's clock, you; and you the motion of St. Chad's: and he that dares stir from his post till he be relieved, shall have my sword in his guts the next minute.

Plume. What's the matter, serjeant? I'm afraid you are too rough with these gentlemen.

Kite. I'm too mild, sir: they disobey command, sir, and one of 'em should be shot for an example to the other.

Pear. Shot, Tummas!

Plume. Come, gentlemen, what's the matter?

Pear. We don't know; the noble serjeant is pleased to be in a passion, sir, but—

Kite. They disobey command; they deny their being listed.

Apple. Nay, serjeant, we don't downright deny it neither; that we dare not do, for fear of being shot: but we humbly conceive in a civil way, and begging your worship's pardon, that we may go home.

Plume. That's easily known. Have either of you received any of the queen's money?

Pear. Not a brass farthing, sir.

Kite. Sir, they have each of them received three-and-twenty shillings and sixpence, and 'tis now in their pockets.

Pear. Wauns, if I have a penny in my pocket but a bent sixpence, I'll be content to be listed, and shot into the bargain!

Apple. And I. Look ye here, sir.

Pear. Ay, here's my stock too: nothing but the queen's picture, that the serjeant gave me just now.

Kite. See there, a broad-piece! three-and-twenty shillings and sixpence; t'other has the fellow on't.

Plume. The case is plain, gentlemen; the goods are found upon you. Those pieces of gold are worth three-and-twenty and sixpence each.

[Whispers Serjeant KITE.

Pear. So it seems that *Carolus* is three-and-twenty shillings and sixpence in Latin.

Apple. 'Tis the same thing in Greek, for we are listed.

Pear. Flesh, but we an't, Tummas!—I desire to be carried before the mayor, captain.

Plume. [*Aside to* KITE.] 'Twill never do, Kite— your damned tricks will ruin me at last.—I won't lose the fellows though, if I can help it.—[*Aloud.*] Well, gentlemen, there must be some trick in this: my serjeant offers here to take his oath that you are fairly listed.

Apple. Why, captain, we know that you soldiers have more liberty of conscience than other folks; but for me or neighbour Costar here to take such an oath, 'twould be a downright perjuration.

Plume. [*To* KITE.] Look'ee, you rascal! you villain! if I find that you have imposed upon these two honest fellows, I'll trample you to death, you dog! Come, how was't?

Apple. Nay, then, we will speak. Your serjeant, as you say, is a rogue, begging your worship's pardon, and—

Pear. Nay, Tummas, let me speak; you know I can read.—And so, sir, he gave us those two pieces of money for pictures of the queen, by way of a present.

Plume. How! by way of a present! The son of a whore! I'll teach him to abuse honest fellows like you!—Scoundrel, rogue, villain!

[*Beats off* Serjeant KITE, *and follows.*

Both. O brave noble captain! Huzza! a brave captain, faith!

Pear. Now, Tummas, *Carolus* is Latin for a beating. This is the bravest captain I ever saw.—Wauns, I have a month's mind to go with him!

Re-enter Captain PLUME.

Plume. A dog, to abuse two such pretty fellows as you!—Look'ee, gentlemen, I love a pretty fellow: I come among you as an officer to list soldiers, not as a kidnapper, to steal slaves.

Pear. Mind that, Tummas.

Plume. I desire no man to go with me but as I went myself: I went a volunteer, as you, or you, may do; for a little time carried a musket, and now I command a company.

Apple. Mind that, Costar.—A sweet gentleman!

Plume. 'Tis true, gentlemen, I might take an advantage of you; the queen's money was in your pockets, my serjeant was ready to take his oath you were listed; but I scorn to do a base thing, you are both of you at your liberty.

Pear. Thank you, noble captain.—Ecod, I can't find in my heart to leave him, he talks so finely.

Apple. Ay, Costar, would he always hold in this mind.

Plume. Come, my lads, one thing more I'll tell you: you're both young tight fellows, and the army is the place to make you men for ever: every man has his lot, and you have yours. What think you now of a purse full of French gold out of a monsieur's pocket, after you have dashed out his brains with the butt of your firelock, eh?

Pear. Wauns! I'll have it, captain—give me a shilling, I'll follow you to the end of the world.

Apple. Nay, dear Costar, do'na; be advised.

Plume. Here, my hero, here are two guineas for thee, as earnest of what I'll do farther for thee.

Apple. Do'na take it; do'na, dear Costar!

[*Cries, and pulls back his arm.*

Pear. I wull! I wull!—Wauns, my mind gives me, that I shall be a captain myself.—I take your money, sir, and now I am a gentleman.

Plume. Give me thy hand, and now you and I will travel the world o'er, and command wherever we tread. —[*Aside to* COSTAR PEARMAIN.] Bring your friend with you, if you can.

Pear. Well, Tummas, must we part?

Apple. No, Costar, I canno leave thee.—Come, captain, I'll e'en go along too; and if you have two honester simpler lads in your company than we twa been, I'll say no more.

Plume. Here, my lad.—[*Gives him money.*] Now, your name?

Apple. Tummas Appletree.

Plume. And yours?

Pear. Costar Pearmain.

Plume. Born where?

Apple. Both in Herefordshire.

Plume. Very well; courage, my lads!—Now we'll sing, *Over the hills and far away.* [Sings.

> *Courage, boys, 'tis one to ten,*
> *But we return all gentlemen;*
> *While conquering colours we display,*
> *Over the hills and far away.*
> *Over the hills, &c.* [Exeunt singing.

ACT III.

SCENE I.

The Market-place.

Enter Captain PLUME *and* Mr. WORTHY.

Wor. I cannot forbear admiring the equality of our two fortunes. We loved two ladies, they met us half way, and just as we were upon the point of leaping into their arms, fortune drops into their laps, pride possesses their hearts, a maggot fills their heads, madness takes 'em by the tails; they snort, kick up their heels, and away they run.

Plume. And leave us here to mourn upon the shore—a couple of poor melancholy monsters.—What shall we do?

Wor. I have a trick for mine; the letter, you know, and the fortune-teller.

Plume. And I have a trick for mine.

Wor. What is't?

Plume. I'll never think of her again.

Wor. No!

Plume. No; I think myself above administering to the pride of any woman, were she worth twelve thousand a year, and I han't the vanity to believe I shall ever gain a lady worth twelve hundred. The generous good-natured Silvia in her smock I admire,

but the haughty scornful Silva, with her fortune, I
despise. [*Sings.*

Come, fair one, be kind ;
You never shall find
A fellow so fit for a lover ;
The world shall view
My passion for you,
But never your passion discover.

I still will complain
Of your frowns and disdain,
Though I revel through all your charms :
The world shall declare,
That I die with despair,
When I only die in your arms.

I still will adore,
And love more and more,
But, by Jove, if you chance to prove cruel,
I'll get me a miss
That freely will kiss,
Though I afterwards drink water-gruel.

What, sneak out o' town, and not so much as a word,
a line, a compliment ! 'Sdeath, how far off does she
live ? I'll go and break her windows.

Wor. Ha ! ha ! ha ! ay, and the window-bars too
to come at her. Come, come, friend, no more of
your rough military airs.

Enter Serjeant KITE.

Kite. Captain ! sir ! look yonder, she's a-coming
this way : 'tis the prettiest, cleanest little tit !

Plume. Now, Worthy, to show you how much I am

in love.—Here she comes; and what is that great
country fellow with her?

Kite. I can't tell, sir.

Enter Rose, *a basket on her arm, and* Bullock.

Rose. Buy chickens! young and tender! young
and tender chickens!

Plume. Here, you chickens!

Rose. Who calls?

Plume. Come hither, pretty maid.

Rose. Will you please to buy, sir?

Wor. Yes, child, we'll both buy.

Plume. Nay, Worthy, that's not fair, market for
yourself.—Come, child, I'll buy all you have.

Rose. Then all I have is at your sarvice. [*Curtsies.*

Wor. Then I must shift for myself, I find. [*Exit.*

Plume. Let me see; young and tender you say!
[*Chucks her under the chin.*

Rose. As ever you tasted in your life, sir.

Plume. Come, I must examine your basket to the
bottom, my dear.

Rose. Nay, for that matter, put in your hand;
feel, sir; I warrant my ware as good as any in the
market.

Plume. And I'll buy it all, child, were it ten times
more.

Rose. Sir, I can furnish you.

Plume. Come, then, we won't quarrel about the
price, they're fine birds.—Pray what's your name,
pretty creature?

Rose. Rose, sir. My father is a farmer within
three short mile o' the town; we keep this market;

I sell chickens, 'eggs, and butter, and my brother Bullock there sells corn.

Bull. Come, sister, haste ye, we shall be leat a hoame. [*Whistles about the stage.*

Plume. Kite!—[*Tips him the wink, he returns it.*] Pretty Mrs. Rose—you have, let me see—how many?

Rose. A dozen, sir, and they are richly worth a crawn.

Bull. Come, Ruose, Ruose! I sold fifty strake o' barley to-day in half this time; but you will higgle and higgle for a penny more than the commodity is worth.

Rose. What's that to you, oaf? I can make as much out of a groat as you can out of fourpence, I'm sure. The gentleman bids fair, and when I meet with a chapman I know how to make the best on him; and so, sir, I say, for a crawn-piece, the bargain's yours.

Plume. Here's a guinea, my dear.

Rose. I can't change your money, sir.

Plume. Indeed, indeed, but you can: my lodging is hard by, you shall bring home the chickens, and we'll make change there.

[*Goes off,* ROSE *follows him.*

Kite. So, sir, as I was telling you, I have seen one of these hussars eat up a ravelin for his breakfast, and afterwards pick his teeth with a palisado.

Bull. Ay, you soldiers see very strange things. But pray, sir, what is a ravelin?

Kite. Why, 'tis like a modern minced pie, but the crust is confounded hard, and the plums are somewhat hard of digestion.

Bull. Then your palisado, pray what may he be?—Come, Ruose, pray ha' done.

Kite. Your palisado is a pretty sort of bodkin, about the thickness of my leg.

Bull. [*Aside.*] That's a fib, I believe.—[*Aloud.*] Eh! where's Ruose? Ruose! Ruose! 'sflesh, where's Ruose gone?

Kite. She's gone with the captain.

Bull. The captain! wauns, there's no pressing of women, sure?

Kite. But there is, sir.

Bull. If the captain should press Ruose I should be ruined! Which way went she? Oh, the devil take your rablins and palisadoes! [*Exit.*

Kite. You shall be better acquainted with them, honest Bullock, or I shall miss of my aim.

Re-enter Mr. WORTHY.

Wor. Why, thou art the most useful fellow in nature to your captain; admirable in your way, I find.

Kite. Yes, sir, I understand my business, I will say it.—You must know, sir, I was born a gipsy, and bred among that crew till I was ten year old. There I learnt canting and lying. I was bought from my mother, Cleopatra, by a certain nobleman for three pistoles; who, liking my beauty, made me his page; there I learned impudence and pimping. I was turned off for wearing my lord's linen, and drinking my lady's ratafia; and then turned bailiff's follower: there I learned bullying and swearing. I at last got into the army, and there I learned whoring and drinking: so that if your worship pleases to cast up the whole sum, viz., canting, lying, impudence, pimping, bullying, swearing, whoring, drinking, and a halberd, you will find the sum total amount to a recruiting serjeant.

Wor. And pray what induced you to turn soldier?

Kite. Hunger and ambition, the fears of starving, and hopes of a truncheon, led me along to a gentleman, with a fair tongue and a fair periwig, who loaded me with promises; but egad, it was the lightest load that ever I felt in my life. He promised to advance me, and indeed he did so—to a garret in the Savoy. I asked him why he put me in prison; he called me lying dog, and said I was in garrison; and, indeed, 'tis a garrison that may hold out till doomsday before I should desire to take it again. But here comes Justice Balance.

Enter Justice BALANCE *and* BULLOCK.

Bal. Here, you serjeant, where's your captain? Here's a poor foolish fellow comes clamouring to me with a complaint that your captain has pressed his sister.—Do you know anything of this matter, Worthy?

Wor. Ha! ha! ha! I know his sister is gone with Plume to his lodging, to sell him some chickens.

Bal. Is that all? the fellow's a fool.

Bull. I know that, an't please you; but if your worship pleases to grant me a warrant to bring her before you, for fear of the worst.

Bal. Thou'rt mad, fellow; thy sister's safe enough.

Kite. I hope so too. [*Aside.*

Wor. Hast thou no more sense, fellow, than to believe that the captain can list women?

Bull. I know not whether they list them, or what they do with them, but, I am sure, they carry as many women as men with them out of the country.

Bal. But how came you not to go along with your sister?

Bull. Luord, sir, I thought no more of her going than I do of the day I shall die; but this gentleman here, not suspecting any hurt neither, I believe—[*To* KITE.] You thought no harm, friend, did ye?

Kite. Lackaday, sir, not I !—[*Aside.*] Only that I believe I shall marry her to-morrow.

Bal. I begin to smell powder.—Well, friend, but what did that gentleman with you?

Bull. Why, sir, he entertained me with a fine story of a great fight between the Hungarians, I think it was, and the Irish; and so, sir, while we were in the heat of the battle—the captain carried off the baggage.

Bal. Serjeant, go along with this fellow to your captain, give him my humble service, and I desire him to discharge the wench, though he has listed her.

Bull. Ay, and if he ben't free for that, he shall have another man in her place.

Kite. Come, honest friend.—[*Aside*]. You shall go to my quarters instead of the captain's.

[Exit with BULLOCK.

Bal. We must get this mad captain his complement of men, and send him a-packing, else he'll overrun the country.

Wor. You see, sir, how little he values your daughter's disdain.

Bal. I like him the better; I was just such another

fellow at his age. I never set my heart upon any woman so much as to make myself uneasy at the disappointment; but what was very surprising both to myself and friends, I changed o' th' sudden from the most fickle lover to the most constant husband in the world. But how goes your affair with Melinda?

Wor. Very slowly. Cupid had formerly wings, but I think, in this age, he goes upon crutches; or, I fancy Venus has been dallying with her cripple Vulcan when my amour commenced, which has made it go on so lamely; my mistress has got a captain too, but such a captain! As I live, yonder he comes?

Bal. Who? that bluff fellow in the sash! I don't know him.

Wor. But I engage he knows you, and everybody at first sight: his impudence were a prodigy were not his ignorance proportionable. He has the most universal acquaintance of any man living; for he won't be alone, and nobody will keep him company twice. Then he's a Cæsar among the women, *Vini, vidi, vici,* that's all: if he has but talked with the maid, he swears he has lain with the mistress. But the most surprising 'part of his character is his memory, which is the most prodigious and the most trifling in the world.

Bal. I have met with such men; and I take this good-for-nothing memory to proceed from a certain contexture of the brain, which is purely adapted to impertinences, and there they lodge secure, the owner having no thoughts of his own to disturb them. I have known a man as perfect as a chronologer as to the day and year of most important transactions, but be altogether ignorant of the causes, springs, or consequences of any one thing of moment. I have known another acquire so much by travel as to tell you the names of most places in Europe, with their distances of miles, leagues, or hours, as punctually as a postboy; but for anything else, as ignorant as the horse that carries the mail.

Wor. This is your man, sir, add but the traveller's privilege of lying; and even that he abuses. This is the picture, behold the life.

Enter Captain BRAZEN.

Braz. Mr. Worthy, I am your servant, and so forth.—Hark'ee, my dear.

Wor. Whispering, sir, before company is not manners, and when nobody's by 'tis foolish.

Braz. Company! *Mort de ma vie!* I beg the gentleman's pardon; who is he?

Wor. Ask him.

Braz. So I will.—My dear, I am your servant, and so forth—your name, my dear?

Bal. Very laconic, sir!

Braz. Laconic! a very good name, truly; I have known several of the Laconics abroad.—Poor Jack Laconic! he was killed at the battle of Landen. I remember that he had a blue ribbon in his hat that very day, and after he fell we found a piece of neat's tongue in his pocket.

Bal. Pray, sir, did the French attack us, or we them, at Landen?

Braz. The French attack us! Oons, sir, are you a Jacobite?

Bal. Why that question ?

Braz. Because none but a Jacobite could think that the French durst attack us. No, sir, we attacked them on the—I have reason to remember the time, for I had two-and-twenty horses killed under me that day.

Wor. Then, sir, you must have rid mighty hard.

Bal. Or perhaps, sir, like my countrymen, you rid upon half-a-dozen horses at once.

Braz. What do you mean, gentlemen ? I tell you they were killed, all torn to pieces by cannon-shot, except six I staked to death upon the enemies *chevaux-de-frise.*

Bal. Noble captain, may I crave your name !

Braz. Brazen, at your service.

Bal. Oh, Brazen, a very good name ; I have known several of the Brazens abroad.

Wor. Do you know Captain Plume, sir ?

Braz. Is he anything related to Frank Plume in Northamptonshire ?—Honest Frank ! many, many a dry bottle have we cracked hand to fist. You must have known his brother Charles that was concerned in the India Company ; he married the daughter of old Tonguepad, the Master in Chancery, a very pretty woman, only squinted a little. She died in childbed of her first child, but the child survived ; 'twas a daughter, but whether 'twas called Margaret or Margery, upon my soul, I can't remember.—[*Looking on his watch.*] But, gentlemen, I must meet a lady, a twenty thousand pounder, presently, upon the walk by the water.—Worthy, your servant.—Laconic, yours. [*Exit.*

Bal. If you can have so mean an opinion of

Melinda as to be jealous of this fellow, I think she ought to give you cause to be so.

Wor. I don't think she encourages him so much for gaining herself a lover, as to set me up a rival. Were there any credit to be given to his words, I should believe Melinda had made him this assignation. I must go see; sir, you'll pardon me.

Bal. Ay, ay, sir, you're a man of business.—[*Exit* Mr. WORTHY.] But what have we got here?

Re-enter ROSE, *singing.*

Rose. And I shall be a lady, a captain's lady, and ride single upon a white horse with a star, upon a velvet side-saddle; and I shall go to London, and see the tombs, and the lions, and the queen.—Sir, an please your worship, I have often seen your worship ride through our grounds a-hunting, begging your worship's pardon—pray what may this lace be worth a yard?   [*Showing some lace.*

Bal. Right Mechlin, by this light! Where did you get this lace, child?

Rose. No matter for that, sir; I came honestly by it.

Bal. I question it much.

Rose. And see here, sir, a fine Turkey-shell snuff-box, and fine mangery, see here.—[*Takes snuff affectedly.*] The captain learned me how to take it with an air.

Bal. Oho! the captain! now the murder's out. And so the captain taught you to take it with an air?

Rose. Yes, and give it with an air too.—Will your worship please to taste my snuff.

[*Offers the box affectedly.*

Bal. You are a very apt scholar, pretty maid. And pray, what did you give the captain for these fine things?

Rose. He's to have my brother for a soldier, and two or three sweethearts that I have in the country, they shall all go with the captain. Oh, he's the finest man, and the humblest withal! Would you believe it, sir, he carried me up with him to his own chamber, with as much fam-mam-mill-yara-rality as if I had been the best lady in the land!

Bal. Oh! he's a mighty familiar gentleman, as can be.

Rose. But I must beg your worship's pardon, I must go seek out my brother Bullock.

[Runs off singing.

Bal. If all officers took the same method of recruiting with this gentleman, they might come in time to be fathers as well as captains of their companies.

Re-enter Captain PLUME, singing, with his arm round ROSE.

Plume. *But it is not so*
With those that go,
Through frost and snow.
Most apropos,
My maid with the milking-pail.

—[*Aside*]. How, the Justice! then I'm arraigned, condemned, and executed.

Bal. Oh, my noble captain!

Rose. And my noble captain too, sir.

Plume. [*Aside to* ROSE.] 'Sdeath, child! are you

mad?—[*Aloud.*] Mr. Balance, I am so full of business about my recruits, that I han't a moment's time to—I have just now three or four people to—

Bal. Nay, captain, I must speak to you.

Rose. And so must I too, captain.

Plume. Any other time, sir—I cannot for my life, sir—

Bal. Pray, sir—

Plume. Twenty thousand things—I would—but now, sir, pray—devil take me—I cannot—I must—

[Breaks away.

Bal. Nay, I'll follow you.　　　　　[*Exit.*

Rose. And I too.　　　　　　　　　[*Exit.*

SCENE II.

A Walk by the Severn.

Enter MELINDA *and* LUCY.

Mel. And pray was it a ring, or buckle, or pendants, or knots? or in what shape was the almighty gold transformed that has bribed you so much in his favour?

Lucy. Indeed, madam, the last bribe I had was from the captain, and that was only a small piece of Flanders edging for pinners.

Mel. Ay, Flanders lace is as constant a present from officers to their women as something else is from their women to them. They every year bring over a cargo of lace, to cheat the queen of her duty, and her subjects of their honesty.

Lucy. They only barter one sort of prohibited goods for another, madam.

Mel. Has any of 'em been bartering with you, Mrs. Pert, that you talk so like a trader?

Lucy. Madam, you talk as peevishly to me as if it were my fault; the crime is none of mine, though I pretend to excuse it: though he should not see you this week, can I help it? But as I was saying, madam—his friend, Captain Plume, has so taken him up these two days.

Mel. Psha! would his friend, the captain, were tied upon his back! I warrant he has never been sober since that confounded captain came to town. The devil take all officers, I say! they do the nation more harm by debauching us at home than they do good by defending us abroad. No sooner a captain comes to town but all the young fellows flock about him, and we can't keep a man to ourselves.

Lucy. One would imagine, madam, by your concern for Worthy's absence, that you should use him better when he's with you.

Mel. Who told you, pray, that I was concerned for his absence? I'm only vexed that I've had nothing said to me these two days. One may like the love and despise the lover, I hope; as one may love the treason and hate the traitor. Oh, here comes another captain, and a rogue that has the confidence to make love to me; but, indeed, I don't wonder at that, when he has the assurance to fancy himself a fine gentleman.

Lucy. If he should speak o' th' assignation I should be ruined.   [*Aside.*

Enter Captain BRAZEN.

Braz. [*Aside.*] True to the touch, faith !—[*Aloud.*] Madam, I am your humble servant, and all that, madam.—A fine river this same Severn.—Do you love fishing, madam ?

Mel. 'Tis a pretty melancholy amusement for lovers.

Braz. I'll go buy hooks and lines presently; for you must know, madam, that I have served in Flanders against the French, in Hungary against the Turks, and in Tangier against the Moors, and I was never so much in love before; and split me, madam, in all the campaigns I ever made, I have not seen so fine a woman as your ladyship.

Mel. And from all the men I ever saw I never had so fine a compliment; but you soldiers are the best bred men, that we must allow.

Braz. Some of us, madam.—But there are brutes among us too, very sad brutes; for my own part, I have always had the good luck to prove agreeable.— I have had very considerable offers, madam—I might have married a German princess, worth fifty thousand crowns a year, but her stove disgusted me.—The daughter of a Turkish bashaw fell in love with me too, when I was prisoner among the Infidels; she offered to rob her father of his treasure, and make her escape with me; but I don't know how, my time was not come; hanging and marriage, you know, go by destiny; fate has reserved me for a Shropshire lady with twenty thousand pounds.—Do you know any such person, madam ?

Mel. [*Aside.*] Extravagant coxcomb !—[*Aloud.*] To

be sure, a great many ladies of that fortune would be proud of the name of Mrs. Brazen.

Braz. Nay, for that matter, madam, there are women of very good quality of the name of Brazen.

Enter Mr. WORTHY.

Mel. [*Aside.*] Oh, are you there, gentlemen?— [*Aloud.*] Come, captain, we'll walk this way, give me your hand.

Braz. My hand, heart's blood, and guts are at your service.—Mr. Worthy, your servant, my dear.

> [*Exit, leading* MELINDA, LUCY *following.*

Wor. Death and fire, this is not to be borne!

Enter Captain PLUME.

Plume. No more it is, faith.

Wor. What?

Plume. The March beer at the Raven. I have been doubly serving the queen—raising men, and raising the excise. Recruiting and elections are rare friends to the excise.

Wor. You an't drunk?

Plume. No, no, whimsical only; I could be mighty foolish, and fancy myself mighty witty. Reason still keeps its throne, but it nods a little, that's all.

Wor. Then you're just fit for a frolic.

Plume. As fit as close pinners [1] for a punk in the pit.

Wor. There's your play, then, recover me that vessel from that Tangerine.

Plume. She's well rigged, but how is she manned?

----

[1] The lappets of a head-dress, apparently affected by prostitutes at this time.

Wor. By Captain Brazen, that I told you of to-day. She is called the Melinda, a first-rate, I can assure you; she sheered off with him just now, on purpose to affront me; but according to your advice I would take no notice, because I would seem to be above a concern for her behaviour.—But have a care of a quarrel.

Plume. No, no, I never quarrel with anything in my cups but an oyster wench, or a cookmaid; and if they ben't civil, I knock 'em down. But heark'ee, my friend, I'll make love, and I must make love. I tell you what, I'll make love like a platoon.

Wor. Platoon, how's that?

Plume. I'll kneel, stoop, and stand, faith; most ladies are gained by platooning.

Wor. Here they come; I must leave you.   [*Exit.*

Plume. So! now must I look as sober and as demure as a whore at a christening.

Re-enter Captain Brazen *and* Melinda.

Braz. Who's that, madam?

Mel. A brother officer of yours, I suppose, sir.

Braz. Ay!—[*To* Plume.] My dear!

Plume. My dear!   [*Run and embrace.*

Braz. My dear boy, how is't? Your name, my dear? If I be not mistaken, I have seen your face.

Plume. I never saw yours in my life, my dear.— But there's a face well known, as the sun's that shines on all, and is by all adored.

Braz. Have you any pretensions, sir?

Plume. Pretensions!

Braz. That is, sir, have you ever served abroad?

Plume. I have served at home, sir, for ages served this cruel fair—and that will serve the turn, sir.

Mel. So, between the fool and the rake I shall bring a fine spot of work upon my hands!—I see Worthy yonder—I could be content to be friends with him, would he come this way.   [*Aside.*

Braz. Will you fight for the lady, sir?

Plume. No, sir, but I'll have her notwithstanding.

Thou peerless princess of Salopian plains,
Envied by nymphs, and worshipp'd by the swains!

Braz. Oons, sir, not fight for her!

Plume. Prithee be quiet—I shall be out—

Behold, how humbly does the Severn glide,
To greet thee princess of the Severn side!

Braz. Don't mind him, madam.—If he were not so well dressed, I should take him for a poet.—But I'll show the difference presently.—Come, madam, we'll place you between us; and now the longest sword carries her.   [*Draws :* MELINDA *shrieks.*

Re-enter Mr. WORTHY.

Mel. Oh! Mr. Worthy! save me from these mad-men.   [*Exit with* WORTHY.

Plume. Ha! ha! ha! why don't you follow, sir, and fight the bold ravisher?

Braz. No, sir, you are my man.

Plume. I don't like the wages, and I won't be your man.

Braz. Then you're not worth my sword.

Plume. No! pray what did it cost?

Braz. It cost me twenty pistoles in. France, and my enemies thousands of lives in Flanders.

Plume. Then they had a dear bargain.

Enter SILVIA *in male apparel.*

Silv. Save ye, save ye, gentlemen !

Braz. My dear, I'm yours.

Plume. Do you know the gentleman?

Braz. No, but I will presently.—[*To* SILVIA.] Your name, my dear?

Silv. Wilful; Jack Wilful, at your service.

Braz. What, the Kentish Wilfuls, or those of Staffordshire?

Silv. Both, sir, both; I'm related to all the Wilfuls in Europe, and I'm head of the family at present.

Plume. Do you live in this country, sir?

Silv. Yes, sir, I live where I stand; I have neither home, house, nor habitation, beyond this spot of ground.

Braz. What are you, sir?

Silv. A rake.

Plume. In the army, I presume.

Silv. No, but I intend to list immediately.—Look'ee, gentlemen, he that bids me fairest shall have me.

Braz. Sir, I'll prefer you, I'll make you a corporal this minute.

Plume. Corporal ! I'll make you my companion; you shall eat with me.

Braz. You shall drink with me.

Plume. You shall lie with me, you young rogue.

[Kisses her.

Braz. You shall receive your pay, and do no duty.

Silv. Then you must make me a field officer.

Plume. Pho! pho! I'll do more than all this; I'll make you a corporal, and give you a brevet for sergeant.

Braz. Can you read and write, sir?

Silv. Yes.

Braz. Then your business is done—I'll make you chaplain to the regiment.

Silv. Your promises are so equal, that I'm at a loss to choose. There is one Plume, that I hear much commended, in town; pray, which of you is Captain Plume?

Plume. I am Captain Plume.

Braz. No, no, I am Captain Plume.

Silv. Heyday!

Plume. Captain Plume! I'm your servant, my dear.

Braz. Captain Brazen! I am yours.—[*Aside.*] The fellow dare not fight.

Enter Serjeant KITE.

Kite. [*To* Captain PLUME.] Sir, if you please—

Plume. No, no, there's your captain.—Captain Plume, your serjeant here has got so drunk, he mistakes me for you.

Braz. He's an incorrigible sot!—[*To* SILVIA.] Here, my Hector of Holborn, forty shillings for you.

Plume. I forbid the banns.—Look'ee, friend, you shall list with Captain Brazen.

Silv. I will see Captain Brazen hanged first! I will list with Captain Plume. I am a freeborn Englishman, and will be a slave my own way.—[*To* Captain BRAZEN.] Look'ee, sir, will you stand by me?

Braz. I warrant you, my lad.

Silv. [*To* Captain PLUME.] Then I will tell you, Captain Brazen, that you are an ignorant, pretending, impudent coxcomb.

Braz. Ay, ay, a sad dog.

Silv. A very sad dog.—Give me the money, noble Captain Plume.

Plume. Then you won't list with Captain Brazen?

Silv. I won't.

Braz. Never mind him, child, I'll end the dispute presently.—Heark'ee, my dear.

[*Takes* Captain PLUME *to one side of the stage, and entertains him in dumb show.*

Kite. Sir, he in the plain coat is Captain Plume, I am his serjeant, and will take my oath on't.

Silv. What! are you Serjeant Kite?

Kite. At your service.

Silv. Then I would not take your oath for a farthing.

Kite. A very understanding youth of his age!—Pray, sir, let me look you full in the face?

Silv. Well, sir, what have you to say to my face.

Kite. The very image and superscription of my brother; two bullets of the same caliver were never so like: sure it must be Charles, Charles!

Silv. What d'ye mean by Charles?

Kite. The voice too, only a little variation in Effa ut * flat.—My dear brother, for I must call you so, if you should have the fortune to enter into the most noble society of the sword, I bespeak you for a comrade.

* *Ut* was the first note in Guido's musical scale, which we now call *Do*.

Silv. No, sir, I'll be your captain's comrade, if anybody's.

Kite. Ambition there again! 'Tis a noble passion for a soldier; by that I gained this glorious halberd. Ambition! I see a commission in his face already. Pray, noble captain, give me leave to salute you.

[*Offers to kiss her.*

Silv. What, men kiss one another!

Kite. We officers do : 'tis our way; we live together like man and wife, always either kissing or fighting.— But I see a storm coming.

Silv. Now, serjeant, I shall see who is your captain by your knocking down the t'other.

Kite. My captain scorns assistance, sir.

Braz. How dare you contend for anything, and not dare to draw your sword? But you're a young fellow, and have not been much abroad; I excuse that, but prithee resign the man, prithee do; you're a very honest fellow.

Plume. You lie; and you are a son of a whore.

[*Draws and makes up to* Captain BRAZEN.

Braz. Hold! hold! did not you refuse to fight the lady? [*Retiring.*

Plume. I always do—but for a man I'll fight knee deep: so you lie again.

[PLUME *and* BRAZEN *fight a traverse or two about the stage;* SILVIA *draws, and is held by* KITE, *who sounds to arms with his mouth; takes* SILVIA *in his arms, and carries her off.*

Braz. Hold! where's the man?

Plume. Gone.

Braz. Then what do we fight for?—[*Puts up.*] Now let's embrace, my dear.

Plume. [*Putting up.*] With all my heart, my dear. —[*Aside.*] I suppose Kite has listed him by this time.

[*They embrace.*

Braz. You are a brave fellow. I always fight with a man before I make him my friend; and if once I find he will fight, I never quarrel with him afterwards. And now I'll tell you a secret, my dear friend; that lady that we frighted out of the walk just now I found in bed this morning—so beautiful, so inviting!—I presently locked the door—but I am a man of honour. —But I believe I shall marry her nevertheless; her twenty thousand pound, you know, will be a pretty convenience.—I had an assignation with her here, but your coming spoiled my sport. Curse you, my dear, but don't do so again.

Plume. No, no, my dear, men are my business at present. [*Exeunt severally.*

ACT IV.

SCENE I.

The Walk by the Severn.

Enter ROSE *and* BULLOCK, *meeting.*

Rose. Where have you been, you great booby? you're always out o' the way in the time of preferment.

Bull. Preferment! who should prefer me?

Rose. I would prefer you! who should prefer a man but a woman? Come, throw away that great club, hold up your head, cock your hat, and look big.

Bull. Ah, Ruose, Ruose, I fear somebody will look big sooner than folk think of! this genteel breeding never comes into the country without a train of followers.—Here has been Cartwheel, your sweetheart, what will become of him?

Rose. Look'ee, I'm a great woman, and will provide for my relations. I told the captain how finely he could play upon the tabor and pipe, so he has set him down for drum-major.

Bull. Nay, sister, why did not you keep that place for me? you know I always loved to be a-drumming, if it were but on a table or on a quart pot. ,

Enter SILVIA.

Silv. Had I but a commission in my pocket, I fancy my breeches would become me as well as any ranting fellow of 'em all; for I take a bold step, a rakish toss, a smart cock, and an impudent air, to be the principal ingredients in the composition of a captain.—What's here: Rose! my nurse's daughter! —I'll go and practice.—Come, child, kiss me at once. —[*Kisses* ROSE.] And her brother too!—[*To* BULLOCK.] Well, honest dungfork, do you know the difference between a horse-cart, and a cart-horse, eh?

Bull. I presume that your worship is a captain by your clothes and your courage.

Silv. Suppose I were, would you be contented to list, friend?

Rose. No, no, though your worship be a handsome man, there be others as fine as you; my brother is engaged to Captain Plume.

Silv. Plume! do you know Captain Plume?

Rose. Yes, I do, and he knows me. He took the very ribbons out of his shirt-sleeves, and put 'em into my shoes. See there—I can assure you, that I can do anything with the captain.

Bull. That is, in a modest way, sir.—Have a care what you say, Ruose, don't shame your parentage.

Rose. Nay, for that matter, I am not so simple as to say that I can do anything with the captain but what I may do with anybody else.

Silv. So! and pray what do you expect from this captain, child?

Rose. I expect, sir—I expect—but he ordered me to tell nobody.—But suppose that he should promise to marry me.

Silv. You should have a care, my dear, men will promise anything beforehand.

Rose. I know that, but he promised to marry me afterwards.

Bull. Wauns, Ruose, what have you said?

Silv. Afterwards! after what?

Rose. After I had sold him my chickens.—I hope there's no harm in that.

Enter Captain PLUME.

Plume. What, Mr. Wilful, so close with my market-woman!

Silv. [*Aside.*] I'll try if he loves her.—[*Aloud.*] Close, sir! ay, and closer yet, sir.—Come, my pretty maid, you and I will withdraw a little.

Plume. No, no, friend, I han't done with her yet.

Silv. Nor have I begun with her, so I have as good right as you have.

Plume. Thou art a bloody impudent fellow.

Silv. Sir, I would qualify myself for the service.

Plume. Hast thou really a mind to the service?

Silv. Yes, sir: so let her go.

Rose. Pray, gentlemen, don't be so violent.

Plume. Come, leave it to the girl's own choice.—Will you belong to me or to that gentleman?

Rose. Let me consider, you are both very handsome.

Plume. Now the natural unconstancy of her sex begins to work. [*Aside.*

Rose. Pray, sir, what will you give me?

Bull. Don't be angry, sir, that my sister should be mercenary, for she's but young.

Silv. Give thee, child! I'll set thee above scandal; you shall have a coach with six before and six behind, an equipage to make vice fashionable, and put virtue out of countenance.

Plume. Pho ! that's easily done.—I'll do more for thee, child ; I'll buy you a furbelow scarf, and give you a ticket to see a play.

Bull. A play !   Wauns, Ruose, take the ticket, and let's see the show.

Silv. Look'ee, captain, if you won't resign, I'll go list with Captain Brazen this minute.

Plume. Will you list with me if I give up my title ?

Silv. I will.

Plume. Take her : I'll change a woman for a man at any time.

Rose. I have heard before, indeed, that you captains used to sell your men.

Bull. Pray, captain, do not send Ruose to the West Indies.   [*Cries.*

Plume. Ha ! ha ! ha ! West Indies !—No, no, my honest lad, give me thy hand ; nor you nor she shall move a step further than I do.   This gentleman is one of us, and will be kind to you, Mrs. Rose.

Rose. But will you be so kind to me, sir, as the captain would ?

Silv. I can't be altogether so kind to you, my circumstances are not so good as the captain's ; but I'll take care of you, upon my word.

Plume. Ay, ay, we'll all take care of her ; she shall live like a princess, and her brother here shall be — What would you be ?

Bull. Oh, sir ! if you had not promised the place of drum-major—

Plume. Ay, that is promised.   But what think you of barrack-master ? You are a person of understanding,

and barrack-master you shall be.—But what's become
of this same Cartwheel you told me of, my dear?

Rose. We'll go fetch him.—Come, brother barrack-
master.—We shall find you at home, noble captain?

Plume. Yes, yes.—[*Exeunt* ROSE *and* BULLOCK.]
And now, sir, here are your forty shillings.

Silv. Captain Plume, I despise your listing money;
if I do serve, 'tis purely for love—of that wench, I
mean. For you must know, that, among my other
sallies, I have spent the best part of my fortune in
search of a maid, and could never find one hitherto:
so you may be assured I'd not sell my freedom under
a less purchase than I did my estate. So, before I
list, I must be certified that this girl is a virgin.

Plume. Mr. Wilful, I can't tell you how you can be
certified in that point till you try; but, upon my
honour, she may be a vestal for aught that I know
to the contrary. I gained her heart, indeed, by some
trifling presents and promises, and, knowing that the
best security for a woman's soul is her body, I would
have made myself master of that too, had not the
jealousy of my impertinent landlady interposed.

Silv. So you only want an opportunity for accom-
plishing your designs upon her?

Plume. Not at all; I have already gained my ends,
which were only the drawing in one or two of her
followers. The women, you know, are the loadstones
everywhere; gain the wives, and you are caressed by
the husbands; please the mistresses, and you are
valued by the gallants; secure an interest with the
finest women at court, and you procure the favour
of the greatest men: so, kiss the prettiest country
wenches, and you are sure of listing the lustiest

fellows. Some people may call this artifice, but I term it stratagem, since it is so main a part of the service. Besides, the fatigue of recruiting is so intolerable, that, unless we could make ourselves some pleasure amidst the pain, no mortal man would be able to bear it.

Silv. Well, sir, I am satisfied as to the point in debate; but now let me beg you to lay aside your recruiting airs, put on the man of honour, and tell me plainly what usage I must expect when I am under your command.

Plume. You must know, in the first place, then, that I hate to have gentlemen in my company; for they are always troublesome and expensive, sometimes dangerous; and 'tis a constant maxim amongst us, that those who know the least obey the best. Notwithstanding all this, I find something so agreeable about you, that engages me to court your company; and I can't tell how it is, but I should be uneasy to see you under the command of anybody else. Your usage will chiefly depend upon your behaviour; only this you must expect, that if you commit a small fault I will excuse it, if a great one I'll discharge you; for something tells me I shall not be able to punish you.

Silv. And something tells me, that if you do discharge me, 'twill be the greatest punishment you can inflict; for were we this moment to go upon the greatest dangers in your profession, they would be less terrible to me than to stay behind you.—And now your hand, this lists me—and now you are my captain.

Plume. [*Kissing her.*] Your friend.—[*Aside.*] 'Sdeath! there's something in this fellow that charms me.

Silv. One favour I must beg.   This affair will make some noise, and I have some friends that would censure my conduct if I threw myself into the circumstance of a private sentinel of my own head : I must therefore take care to be impressed by the act of parliament ; you shall leave that to me.

Plume. What you please as to that.—Will you lodge at my quarters in the meantime? you shall have part of my bed.

Silv. O fy! lie with a common soldier! Would not you rather lie with a common woman ?

Plume. No, faith, I'm not that rake that the world imagines ; I have got an air of freedom, which people mistake for lewdness in me, as they mistake formality in others for religion.   The world is all a cheat ; only I take mine, which is undesigned, to be more excusable than theirs, which is hypocritical.   I hurt nobody but myself, and they abuse all mankind.—Will you lie with me ?

Silv. No, no, captain, you forget Rose ; she's to be my bedfellow, you know.

Plume. I had forgot ; pray be kind to her.

[*Exeunt severally.*

SCENE II.

The same.

Enter MELINDA *and* LUCY.

Mel. [*Aside.*] 'Tis the greatest misfortune in nature for a woman to want a confidant! We are so weak that we can do nothing without assistance, and then a secret racks us worse than the colic.   I am at this minute so sick of a secret, that I'm ready to faint away.—[*Aloud.*] Help me, Lucy!

Lucy. Bless me, madam! what's the matter?

Mel. Vapours only, I begin to recover.—[*Aside.*] If Silvia were in town I could heartily forgive her faults for the ease of discovering my own.

Lucy. You're thoughtful, madam; am not I worthy to know the cause?

Mel. You are a servant, and a secret would make you saucy.

Lucy. Not unless you should find fault without a cause, madam.

Mel. Cause or not cause, I must not lose the pleasure of chiding when I please; women must discharge their vapours somewhere, and before we get husbands our servants must expect to bear with 'em.

Lucy. Then, madam, you had better raise me to a degree above a servant. You know my family, and that five hundred pounds would set me upon the foot of a gentlewoman, and make me worthy the confidence of any lady in the land; besides, madam, 'twill extremely encourage me in the great design I now have in hand.

Mel. I don't find that your design can be of any great advantage to you. 'Twill please me, indeed, in the humour I have of being revenged on the fool for his vanity of making love to me, so I don't much care if I do promise you five hundred pound the day of my marriage.

Lucy. That is the way, madam, to make me diligent in the vocation of a confidant, which I think is generally to bring people together.

Mel. O Lucy! I can hold my secret no longer. You must know, that hearing of the famous fortune-teller in town, I went disguised to satisfy a curiosity, which has cost me dear. That fellow is certainly the devil, or one of his bosom favourites; he has told me the most surprising things of my past life—

Lucy. Things past, madam, can hardly be reckoned surprising, because we know them already. Did he tell you anything surprising that was to come?

Mel. One thing very surprising; he said I should die a maid!

Lucy. Die a maid! come into the world for nothing! Dear madam, if you should believe him, it might come to pass, for the bare thought on't might kill one in four-and-twenty hours.—And did you ask him any questions about me?

Mel. You! why, I passed for you.

Lucy. So 'tis I that am to die a maid!—But the devil was a liar from the beginning; he can't make me die a maid.—[*Aside.*] I have put it out of his power already.

Mel. I do but jest. I would have passed for you, and called myself Lucy; but he presently told me my name, my quality, my fortune, and gave me the whole history of my life. He told me of a lover I had in this country, and described Worthy exactly, but in nothing so well as in his present indifference. I fled to him for refuge here to-day; he never so much as encouraged me in my fright, but coldly told me that he was sorry for the accident, because it might give the town cause to censure my conduct; excused his not waiting on me home, made me a careless bow, and walked off. 'Sdeath! I could have stabbed him, or myself, 'twas the same thing.—Yonder he comes—I will so use him!

Lucy. Don't exasperate him; consider what the fortune-teller told you. Men are scarce, and as times go, it is not impossible for a woman to die a maid.

Mel. No matter.

Enter MR. WORTHY.

Wor. [*Aside.*] I find she's warmed; I must strike while the iron is hot.—[*Aloud.*] You have a great deal of courage, madam, to venture into the walks where you were so lately frightened.

Mel. And you have a quantity of impudence to appear before me, that you have so lately affronted.

Wor. I had no design to affront you, nor appear before you either, madam: I left you here, because I had business in another place, and came hither, thinking to meet another person.

Mel. Since you find yourself disappointed, I hope you'll withdraw to another part of the walk.

Wor. The walk is as free for me as you, madam, and broad enough for us both.—[*They walk by one another, he with his hat cocked, she fretting and tearing her fan.*] Will you please to take snuff, madam?

[*Offers her his box, she strikes it out of his hand; while he is gathering it up,*

Enter Captain BRAZEN.

Braz. What, here before me, my dear!

[*Clasps* MELINDA *round the waist.*

Mel. What means this insolence?

[*Gives him a box on the ear.*

Lucy. Are you mad? don't you see Mr. Worthy?

[*To* Captain BRAZEN.

Braz. No, no, I'm struck blind.—Worthy! odso! well turned!—My mistress has wit at her fingers' ends.—Madam, I ask your pardon, 'tis our way abroad.—Mr. Worthy, you are the happy man.

Wor. I don't envy your happiness very much, if the lady can afford no other sort of favours but what she has bestowed upon you.

Mel. I am sorry the favour miscarried, for it was designed for you, Mr. Worthy; and be assured, 'tis the last and only favour you must expect at my hands. —Captain, I ask your pardon.

Braz. I grant it.—[*Exeunt* MELINDA *and* LUCY.] You see, Mr. Worthy, 'twas only a random-shot; it might have taken off your head as well as mine. Courage, my dear! 'tis the fortune of war.—But the enemy has thought fit to withdraw, I think.

Wor. Withdraw! oons, sir! what d'ye mean by withdraw?

Braz. I'll show you. [*Exit.*

Wor. She's lost, irrecoverably lost, and Plume's advice has ruined me! 'Sdeath! why should I, that knew her haughty spirit, be ruled by a man that's a stranger to her pride?

Enter Captain PLUME.

Plume. Ha! ha! ha! a battle-royal. Don't frown so, man; she's your own, I tell you; I saw the fury of her love in the extremity of her passion: the wildness of her anger is a certain sign that she loves you to madness. That rogue Kite began the battle with abundance of conduct, and will bring you off victorious, my life on't; he plays his part admirably; she's to be with him again presently.

Wor. But what could be the meaning of Brazen's familiarity with her?

Plume. You are no logician, if you pretend to draw consequences from the actions of fools: there's no arguing by the rule of reason upon a science without principles, and such is their conduct. Whim, unaccountable whim, hurries 'em on like a man drunk with brandy before ten o'clock in the morning.—But we lose our sport: Kite has opened above an hour ago, let's away.   [*Exeunt.*

SCENE III.

Serjeant KITE's *Quarters.*

Serjeant KITE, *in a conjurer's habit, discovered sitting at a table, whereon are a globe and books.*

Kite. [*Rising.*] By the position of the heavens, gained from my observation upon these celestial globes, I find that Luna was a tidewaiter, Sol a surveyor, Mercury a thief, Venus a whore, Saturn an alderman, Jupiter a rake, and Mars a serjeant of grenadiers; and this is the system of Kite the conjurer.

Enter Captain PLUME *and* Mr. WORTHY.

Plume. Well, what success?

Kite. I have sent away a shoemaker and a tailor already; one's to be a captain of marines, and the other a major of dragoons: I am to manage them at night.—Have you seen the lady, Mr. Worthy?

Wor. Ay, but it won't do. Have you showed her her name, that I tore off from the bottom of the letter?

Kite. No, sir, I reserve that for the last stroke.

Plume. What letter?

Wor. One that I would not let you see, for fear that you should break Melinda's windows in good earnest. [*Knocking at the door.*

Kite. Officers, to your posts. [PLUME *and* WORTHY *conceal themselves behind a screen.*]—Tycho, mind the door. [Servant *opens the door.*

Enter THOMAS.

Thos. Well, master, are you the cunning man?

Kite. I am the learned Copernicus.

Thos. Well, master Coppernose, I'm but a poor man, and I can't afford above a shilling for my fortune.

Kite. Perhaps that is more than 'tis worth.

Thos. Look'ee, doctor, let me have something that's good for my shilling, or I'll have my money again.

Kite. If there be faith in the stars, you shall have your shilling forty-fold.—Your hand, countryman, you're by trade a smith.

Thos. How the devil should you know that?

Kite. Because the devil and you are brother-tradesmen—you were born under Forceps.

Thos. Forceps, what's that?

Kite. One of the signs. There's Leo, Sagitarius, Forceps, Furnes, Dixmude, Namur, Brussels, Charleroy, and so forth—twelve of 'em.—Let me see—did you ever make any bombs or cannon-bullets?

Thos. Not I.

Kite. You either have or will. The stars have decreed that you shall be—I must have more money, sir, your fortune's great.

Thos. Faith, doctor, I have no more.

Kite. O sir, I'll trust you, and take it out of your arrears.

Thos. Arrears ! what arrears?

Kite. The five hundred pound that's owing to you from the government.

Thos. Owing me?

Kite. Owing you, sir.—Let me see your t'other hand.—I beg your pardon, it will be owing to you : and the rogue of an agent will demand fifty per cent. for a fortnight's advance.

Thos. I'm in the clouds, doctor, all this while.

Kite. Sir, I am above 'em, among the stars. In two years, three months, and two hours, you will be made captain of the forges to the grand train of artillery, and will have ten shillings a day, and two servants. 'Tis the decree of the stars, and of the fixed stars, that are as immovable as your anvil ; strike, sir, while the iron is hot. Fly, sir ! begone !

Thos. What, what would you have me do, doctor? I wish the stars would put me in a way for this fine place.

Kite. The stars do.—Let me see—ay, about an hour hence walk carelessly into the market-place, and you'll see a tall, slender gentleman, cheapening a pennyworth of apples, with a cane hanging upon his button. This gentleman will ask you what's o'clock. He's your man, and the maker of your fortune ! follow him, follow him.—And now go

home, and take leave of your wife and children ;
an hour hence exactly is your time.

Thos. A tall slender gentleman, you say, with a
cane ? pray, what sort of head has the cane ?

Kite. An amber head with a black ribbon.

Thos. And pray of what employment is the
gentleman ?

Kite. Let me see ; he's either a collector of the
excise, a plenipotentiary, or a captain of grenadiers,
I can't tell exactly which. But he'll call you honest
—your name is—

Thos. Thomas.

Kite. Right ! He'll call you honest Tom.

Thos. But how the devil should he know my
name ?

Kite. Oh, there are several sorts of Toms ! Tom
o' Lincoln, Tom-tit, Tom Tell-troth, Tom o'Bedlam,
and Tom Fool.—[*Knocking at the door.*] Begone !—
an hour hence precisely.

Thos. You say he'll ask me what's o'clock ?

Kite. Most certainly.—And you'll answer you don't
know :—and be sure you look at St. Mary's dial ; for
the sun won't shine, and if it should, you won't be
able to tell the figures.

Thos. I will, I will.   [*Exit.*

Plume. [*Behind.*] Well done, conjurer ! go on and
prosper.

Kite. As you were.

Enter PLUCK.

[*Aside.*] What, my old friend Pluck the butcher ! I
offered the surly bull-dog five guineas this morning,
and he refused it.

Pluck. So, Master Conjurer, here's half-a-crown.—
And now you must understand—

Kite. Hold, friend, I know your business beforehand.

Pluck. You're devilish cunning then, for I don't
well know it myself.

Kite. I know more than you, friend.—You have a
foolish saying, that such a one knows no more than
the man in the moon : I tell you, the man in the
moon knows more than all the men under the sun.
Don't the moon see all the world ?

Pluck. All the world see the moon, I must confess.

Kite. Then she must see all the world, that's certain.—Give me your hand.—You're by trade, either
a butcher or a surgeon.

Pluck. True, I am a butcher.

Kite. And a surgeon you will be, the employments
differ only in the name : he that can cut up an ox,
may dissect a man ; and the same dexterity that
cracks a marrow-bone, will cut off a leg or an arm.

Pluck. What d'ye mean, doctor, what d'ye mean ?

Kite. Patience, patience, Mr. Surgeon-General ;
the stars are great bodies, and move slowly.

Pluck. But what d'ye mean by surgeon-general,
doctor ?

Kite. Nay, sir, if your worship won't have patience,
I must beg the favour of your worship's absence.

Pluck. My worship ! my worship ! but why my
worship ?

Kite. Nay then, I have done.　　　　[*Sits down.*

Pluck. Pray, doctor—

Kite. Fire and fury, sir !—[*Rises in a passion.*]　Do
you think the stars will be hurried ?　Do the stars

owe you any money, sir, that you dare to dun their lordships at this rate? Sir, I am porter to the stars, and I am ordered to let no dun come near their doors.

Pluck. Dear doctor, I never had any dealings with the stars, they don't owe me a penny. But since you are their porter, please to accept of this half-crown to drink their healths, and don't be angry.

Kite. Let me see your hand then once more.— Here has been gold—five guineas, my friend, in this very hand this morning.

Pluck. Nay, then he is the devil!—Pray, doctor, were you born of a woman? or, did you come into the world of your own head?

Kite. That's a secret.—This gold was offered you by a proper handsome man, called Hawk, or Buzzard, or—

Pluck. Kite, you mean.

Kite. Ay, ay, Kite.

Pluck. As arrant a rogue as ever carried a halberd! The impudent rascal would have decoyed me for a soldier!

Kite. A soldier! a man of your substance for a soldier! Your mother has a hundred pound in hard money, lying at this minute in the hands of a mercer, not forty yards from this place.

Pluck. Oons! and so she has, but very few know so much.

Kite. I know it, and that rogue, what's his name, Kite, knew it, and offered you five guineas to list, because he knew your poor mother would give the hundred for your discharge.

Pluck. There's a dog now!—Flesh, doctor, I'll

give you t'other half-crown, and tell me that this same Kite will be hanged.

Kite. He's in as much danger as any man in the county of Salop.

Pluck. There's your fee.——But you have forgot the surgeon-general all this while.

Kite. You put the stars in a passion.—[*Looks on his books.*] But now they are pacified again:—Let me see, did you never cut off a man's leg?

Pluck. No.

Kite. Recollect, pray.

Pluck. I say, no.

Kite. That's strange! wonderful strange! but nothing is strange to me, such wonderful changes have I seen.—The second, or third, ay, the third campaign that you make in Flanders, the leg of a great officer will be shattered by a great shot, you will be there accidentally, and with your cleaver chop off the limb at a blow: in short, the operation will be performed with so much dexterity, that with the general applause you will be made surgeon-general of the whole army.

Pluck. Nay, for the matter of cutting off a limb, I'll do't, I'll do't with any surgeon in Europe, but I have no thoughts of making a campaign.

Kite. You have no thoughts! what's matter for your thoughts? The stars have decreed it, and you must go.

Pluck. The stars decree it! oons, sir, the justices can't press me!

Kite. Nay, friend, 'tis none of my business—I ha' done; only mind this, you'll know more an hour and a half hence—that's all, farewell!   [*Going.*

Pluck. Hold, hold, doctor!—Surgeon-general! what is the place worth, pray?

Kite. Five hundred pounds a year, besides guineas for claps.

Pluck. Five hundred pounds a year!—An hour and a half hence, you say?

Kite. Prithee, friend, be quiet, don't be so troublesome. Here's such a work to make a booby butcher accept of five hundred pound a year!—But if you must hear it—I'll tell you in short, you'll be standing in your stall an hour and half hence, and a gentleman will come by with a snuff-box in his hand, and the tip of his handkerchief hanging out of his right pocket; he'll ask you the price of a loin of veal, and at the same time stroke your great dog upon the head, and call him Chopper.

Pluck. Mercy on us! Chopper is the dog's name.

Kite. Look'ee there—what I say is true—things that are to come must come to pass. Get you home, sell off your stock, don't mind the whining and the snivelling of your mother and your sister—women always hinder preferment—make what money you can, and follow that gentleman, his name begins with a P, mind that.—There will be the barber's daughter, too, that you promised marriage to—she will be pulling and haling you to pieces.

Pluck. What! know Sally too? He's the devil, and he needs must go that the devil drives.— [*Going.*] The tip of his handkerchief out of his left pocket?

Kite. No, no, his right pocket; if it be the left, 'tis none of the man.

Pluck. Well, well, I'll mind him. [*Exit.*

Plume. [*Behind.*] The right pocket, you say?

[*Knocking at the door.*

Kite. I hear the rustling of silks. Fly, sir! 'tis Madam Melinda.

Enter MELINDA *and* LUCY.

Tycho, chairs for the ladies. [*Calls to* Servant.

Mel. Don't trouble yourself, we shan't stay, doctor.

Kite. Your ladyship is to stay much longer than you imagine.

Mel. For what?

Kite. For a husband.—[*To* LUCY.] For your part, madam, you won't stay for a husband.

Lucy. Pray, doctor, do you converse with the stars, or with the devil?

Kite. With both. When I have the destinies of men in search, I consult the stars; when the affairs of women come under my hands, I advise with my t'other friend.

Mel. And have you raised the devil upon my account?

Kite. Yes, madam, and he's now under the table.

Lucy. Oh, Heavens protect us! Dear madam, let's be gone.

Kite. If you be afraid of him, why do you come to consult him?

Mel. [*To* LUCY.] Don't fear, fool.—[*To* KITE.] Do you think, sir, that because I am a woman, I'm to be fooled out of my reason, or frighted out of my senses? Come, show me this devil.

Kite. He's a little busy at present; but when he has done, he shall wait on you.

Mel. What is he doing?

Kite. Writing your name in his pocket-book.

Mel. Ha! ha! my name! Pray, what have you or he to do with my name?

Kite. Look'ee, fair lady, the devil is a very modest person, he seeks nobody unless they seek him first; he's chained up like a mastiff, and can't stir unless he be let loose. You come to me to have your fortune told—do you think, madam, that I can answer you of my own head? No, madam, the affairs of women are so irregular, that nothing less than the devil can give any account of 'em. Now to convince you of your incredulity, I'll show you a trial of my skill.—Here, you *Cacodemon del fuego*—exert your power, draw me this lady's name, the word Melinda, in the proper letters and character of her own handwriting.—Do it at three motions—one—two—three—'tis done.—Now, madam, will you please to send your maid to fetch it?

Lucy. I fetch it! the devil fetch me if I do!

Mel. My name in my own handwriting! that would be convincing indeed.

Kite. Seeing's believing.—[*Goes to the table, lifts up the carpet.*] Here, Tre, Tre, poor Tre, give me the bone, sirrah.—[*He puts his hand under the table,* PLUME *steals to the other side of the table, and catches him by the hand.*] Oh! oh! the devil! the devil in good earnest! My hand! my hand! the devil! my hand!—[MELINDA *and* LUCY *shriek, and run to a corner of the stage.* KITE *discovers* PLUME, *and gets away his hand.*] A plague o' your pincers! he has fixed his nails in my very flesh.—O madam! you put the demon in such a passion with your scruples, that it has almost cost me my hand.

Mel. It has cost us our lives almost—but have you got the name?

Kite. Got it! ay, madam, I have got it here—I'm sure the blood comes.—But there's your name upon that square piece of paper—behold!

Mel. 'Tis wonderful! my very letters to a tittle!

Lucy. 'Tis like your hand, madam, but not so like your hand neither, and now I look nearer, 'tis not like your hand at all.

Kite. Here a chambermaid now that will outlie the devil!

Lucy. Look'ee, madam, they shan't impose upon us; people can't remember their hands, no more than they can their faces.—Come, madam, let us be certain, write your name upon this paper, then we'll compare the two names.

[*Takes out a paper, and folds it.*

Kite. Anything for your satisfaction, madam— here's pen and ink.

[MELINDA *writes,* LUCY *holds the paper.*

Lucy. Let me see it, madam; 'tis the same—the very same.—[*Aside.*] But I'll secure one copy for my own affairs.

Mel. This is demonstration.

Kite. 'Tis so, madam.—The word demonstration comes from Demon, the father of lies.

Mel. Well, doctor, I am convinced; and now, pray, what account can you give me of my future fortune?

Kite. Before the sun has made one course round this earthly globe, your fortune will be fixed for happiness or misery.

Mel. What! so near the crisis of my fate!

Kite. Let me see—about the hour of ten to-morrow

morning you will be saluted by a gentleman, who will come to take his leave of you, being designed for travel; his intention of going abroad is sudden, and the occasion a woman. Your fortune and his are like the bullet and the barrel, one runs plump into the other. In short, if the gentleman travels, he will die abroad; and if he does you will die before he comes home.

Mel. What sort of man is he?

Kite. Madam, he's a fine gentleman and a lover, that is, a man of very good sense, and a very great fool.

Mel. How is that possible, doctor?

Kite. Because, madam—because it is so.—A woman's reason is the best for a man's being a fool.

Mel. Ten o'clock, you say?

Kite. Ten—about the hour of tea-drinking throughout the kingdom.

Mel. Here, doctor.—[*Gives money.*] Lucy, have you any questions to ask?

Lucy. O madam! a thousand.

Kite. I must beg your patience till another time; for I expect more company this minute; besides, I must discharge the gentleman under the table.

Lucy. Oh, pray, sir, discharge us first!

Kite. Tycho, wait on the ladies down stairs.

> [*Exeunt* MELINDA *and* LUCY. PLUME *and*
> WORTHY *come forward laughing.*

Kite. Ay, you may well laugh, gentlemen, not all the cannon of the French army could have frighted me so much as that gripe you gave me under the table.

Plume. I think, Mr. Doctor, I out-conjured you that bout.

Kite. I was surprised, for I should not have taken a captain for a conjurer.

Plume. No more than I should a serjeant for a wit.

Kite. Mr. Worthy, you were pleased to wish me joy to-day, I hope to be able to return the compliment to-morrow.

Wor. I'll make it the best compliment to you that you ever made in your life, if you do. But I must be a traveller, you say?

Kite. No farther than the chops of the Channel, I presume, sir.

Plume. That we have concerted already.—[*Loud knocking at the door.*] Heyday! you don't profess midwifery, doctor.

Kite. Away to your ambuscade!

[PLUME *and* WORTHY *retire as before.*

Enter Captain BRAZEN.

Braz. Your servant, servant, my dear.

Kite. Stand off, I have my familiar already.

Braz. Are you bewitched, my dear?

Kite. Yes, my dear; but mine is a peaceable spirit, and hates gunpowder. Thus I fortify myself—[*Draws a circle round him.*] And now, captain, have a care how you force my lines.

Braz. Lines! what dost talk of lines! You have something like a fishing-rod there, indeed; but I come to be acquainted with you, man.—What's your name, my dear?

Kite. Conundrum.

Braz. Conundrum! rat me, I knew a famous doctor in London of your name!—Where were you born?

Kite. I was born in Algebra.

Braz. Algebra! 'tis no country in Christendom, I'm sure, unless it be some pitiful place in the Highlands of Scotland.

Kite. Right, I told you I was bewitched.

Braz. So am I, my dear: I am going to be married. I have had two letters from a lady of fortune that loves me to madness, fits, colic, spleen, and vapours: shall I marry her in four-and-twenty hours, ay, or no?

Kite. I must have the year and day of the month when these letters were dated.

Braz. Why, you old bitch, did you ever hear of love-letters dated with the year and day o' the month? Do you think billets-doux are like bank bills?

Kite. They are not so good.—But if they bear no date, I must examine the contents.

Braz. Contents! that you shall, old boy: here they be both.   [*Pulls out two letters.*

Kite. Only the last you received, if you please.— [*Takes one of the letters.*] Now, sir, if you please to let me consult my books for a minute, I'll send this letter inclosed to you with the determination of the stars upon it to your lodgings.

Braz. With all my heart—I must give him—[*Puts his hands in his pocket.*] Algebra! I fancy, doctor, 'tis hard to calculate the place of your nativity?— Here.—[*Gives him money.*] And if I succeed, I'll build a watch-tower upon the top of the highest mountain in Wales for the study of astrology, and the benefit of Conundrums.

                    [*Exit.* PLUME *and* WORTHY *come forward.*

Wor. O doctor! that letter's worth a million.   Let me see it.—[*Takes the letter.*] And now I have it, I'm afraid to open it.

Plume. Pho! let me see it.—[*Snatches the letter from* WORTHY *and opens it.*] If she be a jilt—damn her, she is one! there's her name at the bottom on't.

Wor. How! then I'll travel in good earnest.— [*Looking at the letter.*] By all my hopes, 'tis Lucy's hand!

Plume. Lucy's!

Wor. Certainly; 'tis no more like Melinda's character than black is to white.

Plume. Then 'tis certainly Lucy's contrivance to draw in Brazen for a husband.—But are you sure 'tis not Melinda's hand?

Wor. You shall see.—[*To* KITE.] Where's the bit of paper I gave you just now that the devil writ Melinda upon?

Kite. Here, sir.

Plume. 'Tis plain they're not the same. And is this the malicious name that was subscribed to the letter, which made Mr. Balance send his daughter into the country?

Wor. The very same, the other fragments I showed you just now. I once intended it for another use, but I think I have turned it now to better advantage.

Plume. But 'twas barbarous to conceal this so long, and to continue me so many hours in the pernicious heresy of believing that angelic creature could change! —Poor Silvia!

Wor. Rich Silvia you mean, and poor captain, ha! ha! ha! Come, come, friend, Melinda is true and shall be mine; Silvia is constant, and may be yours.

Plume. No, she's above my hopes: but for her sake I'll recant my opinion of her sex.

By some the sex is blamed without design,
Light harmless censure, such as yours and mine,
Sallies of wit, and vapours of our wine.
Others the justice of the sex condemn,
And wanting merit to create esteem,
Would hide their own defects by censuring them.
But they, secure in their all-conquering charms,
Laugh at the vain efforts of false alarms ;
He magnifies their conquests who complains,
For none would struggle were they not in chains.

[*Exeunt.*

ACT V.

SCENE I.

An Anteroom adjoining SILVIA'S *Bedchamber ; A periwig, hat, and sword, upon the table.*

Enter SILVIA *in her nightcap.*

Silv. I have rested but indifferently, and I believe
my bedfellow was as little pleased ; poor Rose ! here
she comes—

Enter ROSE.

Good morrow, my dear, how d'ye this morning ?

Rose. Just as I was last night, neither better nor
worse for you.

Silv. What's the matter ? did you not like your
bedfellow ?

Rose. I don't know whether I had a bedfellow or
not.

Silv. Did not I lie with you ?

Rose. No : I wonder you could have the conscience
to ruin a poor girl for nothing.

Silv. I have saved thee from ruin, child ; don't be
melancholy, I can give you as many fine things as
the captain can.

Rose. But you can't, I'm sure.

[Knocking at the door.

Silv. Odso ! my accoutrements.—[*Puts on her periwig, hat, and sword.*]   Who's at the door ?

Constable. [*Without.*] Open the door, or we'll break it down.

Silv. Patience a little.   [*Opens the door.*

Enter Constable *and* Watch.

Con. We have 'em, we have 'em! the duck and the mallard both in the decoy.

Silv. What means this riot? Stand off!—[*Draws.*] The man dies that comes within reach of my point.

Con. That is not the point, master; put up your sword or I shall knock you down; and so I command the queen's peace.

Silv. You are some blockhead of a constable.

Con. I am so, and have a warrant to apprehend the bodies of you and your whore there.

Rose. Whore! never was poor woman so abused.

Enter BULLOCK *unbuttoned.*

Bull. What's the matter now?—O Mr. Bridewell! what brings you abroad so early?

Con. This, sir.—[*Lays hold of* BULLOCK.] You're the queen's prisoner.

Bull. Wauns, you lie, sir! I'm the queen's soldier.

Con. No matter for that, you shall go before Justice Balance.

Silv. [*Aside.*] Balance! 'tis what I wanted.— [*Aloud.*] Here, Mr. Constable, I resign my sword.

Rose. Can't you carry us before the captain, Mr. Bridewell?

Con. Captain! han't you got your bellyfull of captains yet?—Come, come, make way there.

                                        [*Exeunt.*

SCENE II.

A Room in Justice BALANCE'S *House.*

Enter Justice BALANCE *and* Justice SCALE.

Scale. I say 'tis not to be borne, Mr. Balance!

Bal. Look'ee, Mr. Scale, for my own part I shall be very tender in what regards the officers of the army; they expose their lives to so many dangers for us abroad, that we may give them some grains of allowance at home.

Scale. Allowance! this poor girl's father is my tenant; and, if I mistake not, her mother nursed a child for you. Shall they debauch our daughters to our faces?

Bal. Consider, Mr. Scale, that were it not for the bravery of these officers, we should have French dragoons among us, that would leave us neither liberty, property, wife, nor daughter. Come, Mr. Scale, the gentlemen are vigorous and warm, and may they continue so; the same heat that stirs them up to love, spurs them on to battle; you never knew a great general in your life, that did not love a whore. This I only speak in reference to Captain Plume—for the other spark I know nothing of.

Scale. Nor can I hear of anybody that does.—Oh, here they come.

Enter Constable *and* Watch, *with* SILVIA, BULLOCK, *and* ROSE.

Con. May it please your worships we took them in the very act, *re infecta*, sir. The gentleman, indeed, behaved himself like a gentleman; for he drew his sword and swore, and afterwards laid it down, and said nothing.

Bal. Give the gentleman his sword again—wait you without.—[*Exeunt* Constable *and* Watch.] I'm sorry, sir,—[*To* SILVIA] to know a gentleman upon such terms, that the occasion of our meeting should prevent the satisfaction of an acquaintance.

Silv. Sir, you need make no apology for your warrant, no more than I shall do for my behaviour: my innocence is upon an equal foot with your authority.

Scale. Innocence! have not you seduced that young maid?

Silv. No, Mr. Goosecap, she seduced me.

Bull. So she did, I'll swear—for she proposed marriage first.

Bal. What, then you are married, child?

[*To* ROSE.

Rose. Yes, sir, to my sorrow.

Bal. Who was witness?

Bull. That was I—I danced, threw the stocking, and spoke jokes by their bedside, I'm sure.

Bal. Who was the minister?

Bull. Minister! we are soldiers, and want no ministers. They were married by the Articles of War.

Bal. Hold thy prating, fool!—[*To* SILVIA.] Your appearance, sir, promises some understanding; pray what does this fellow mean?

Silv. He means marriage, I think—but that you know is so odd a thing, that hardly any two people under the sun agree in the ceremony; some make it a sacrament, others a convenience, and others make it a jest; but among soldiers 'tis most sacred. Our sword, you know, is our honour; that we lay down; the hero jumps over it first, and the amazon after—leap rogue, follow whore—the drum beats a ruff, and so to bed; that's all—the ceremony is concise.

Bull. And the prettiest ceremony, so full of pastime and prodigality!

Bal. What! are you a soldier?

Bull. Ay, that I am. Will your worship lend me your cane, and I'll show you how I can exercise.

Bal. [*Striking him over the head.*] Take it.—[*To* Silvia.] Pray, sir, what commission may you bear?

Silv. I'm called captain, sir, by all the coffeemen, drawers, whores, and groom-porters in London; for I wear a red coat, a sword, a hat *bien troussé*, a martial twist in my cravat, a fierce knot in my periwig, a cane upon my button, piquet in my head, and dice in my pocket.

Scale. Your name, pray, sir?

Silv. Captain Pinch: I cock my hat with a pinch, I take snuff with a pinch, pay my whores with a pinch. In short, I can do anything at a pinch, but fight and fill my belly.

Bal. And pray, sir, what brought you into Shropshire?

Silv. A pinch, sir: I knew you country gentlemen want wit, and you know that we town gentlemen want money, and so—

Bal. I understand you, sir.—Here, constable!

Re-enter Constable.

Take this gentleman into custody till farther orders.

Rose. Pray, your worship, don't be uncivil to him,

for he did me no hurt; he's the most harmless man in the world, for all he talks so.

Scale. Come, come, child, I'll take care of you.

Silv. What, gentlemen, rob me of my freedom, and my wife at once! 'Tis the first time they ever went together.

Bal. Heark'ee, constable!   [*Whispers him.*

Con. It shall be done, sir.—Come along, sir.

[*Exit with* BULLOCK *and* SILVIA.

Bal. Come, Mr. Scale, we'll manage the spark presently.   [*Exeunt.*

SCENE III.

MELINDA'S *Apartment.*

Enter MELINDA *and* WORTHY.

Mel. [*Aside.*] So far the prediction is right, 'tis ten exactly.—[*Aloud.*] And pray, sir, how long have you been in this travelling humour?

Wor. 'Tis natural, madam, for us to avoid what disturbs our quiet.

Mel. Rather the love of change, which is more natural, may be the occasion of it.

Wor. To be sure, madam, there must be charms in variety, else neither you nor I should be so fond of it.

Mel. You mistake, Mr. Worthy, I am not so fond of variety as to travel for't, nor do I think it prudence in you to run yourself into a certain expense and danger, in hopes of precarious pleasures, which at best never answer expectation; as 'tis evident from the example of most travellers, that long more to return to their own country than they did to go abroad.

Wor. What pleasures I may receive abroad are indeed uncertain ; but this I am sure of, I shall meet with less cruelty among the most barbarous nations than I have found at home.

Mel. Come, sir, you and I have been jangling a great while ; I fancy if we made up our accounts, we should the sooner come to an agreement.

Wor. Sure, madam, you won't dispute your being in my debt ? My fears, sighs, vows, promises, assiduities, anxieties, jealousies, have run on for a whole year without any payment.

Mel. A year! oh, Mr. Worthy! what you owe to me is not to be paid under a seven years' servitude. How did you use me the year before? when, taking the advantage of my innocence and necessity, you would have made me your mistress, that is, your slave. Remember the wicked insinuations, artful baits, deceitful arguments, cunning pretences ; then your impudent behaviour, loose expressions, familiar letters, rude visits,—remember those! those, Mr. Worthy!

Wor. [*Aside.*] I do remember, and am sorry I made no better use of 'em.—[*Aloud.*] But you may remember, madam, that—

Mel. Sir, I'll remember nothing—'tis your interest that I should forget : you have been barbarous to me, I have been cruel to you ; put that and that together, and let one balance the other. Now if you will begin upon a new score, lay aside your adventuring airs, and behave yourself handsomely till Lent be over ; here's my hand, I'll use you as a gentleman should be.

Wor. And if I don't use you as a gentlewoman should be, may this be my poison.

[*Kissing her hand.*

Enter Servant.

Ser. Madam, the coach is at the door. [*Exit.*

Mel. I am going to Mr. Balance's country-house to see my cousin Silvia; I have done her an injury, and can't be easy till I have asked her pardon.

Wor. I dare not hope for the honour of waiting on you.

Mel. My coach is full; but if you will be so gallant as to mount your own horses and follow us, we shall be glad to be overtaken; and if you bring Captain Plume with you, we shan't have the worse reception.

Wor. I'll endeavour it. [*Exit leading* MELINDA.

SCENE IV.

The Market-Place.

Enter Captain PLUME *and* Serjeant KITE.

Plume. A baker, a tailor, a smith, and a butcher— I believe the first colony planted in Virginia had not more trades in their company than I have in mine.

Kite. The butcher, sir, will have his hands full; for we have two sheep-stealers among us. I hear of a fellow too committed just now for stealing of horses.

Plume. We'll dispose of him among the dragoons. Have we ne'er a poulterer among us?

Kite. Yes, sir, the king of the gipsies is a very good one, he has an excellent hand at a goose or a turkey.

Here's Captain Brazen, sir, I must go look after the men.				[*Exit.*

Enter Captain' BRAZEN, *reading a letter.*

Braz. Um, um, um, the canonical hour—Um, um, very well.—My dear Plume! give me a buss.

Plume. Half a score, if you will, my dear. What hast got in thy hand, child?

Braz. 'Tis a project for laying out a thousand pound.

Plume. Were it not requisite to project first how to get it in?

Braz. You can't imagine, my dear, that I want twenty thousand pound; I have spent twenty times as much in the service. Now, my dear, pray advise me, my head runs much upon architecture; shall I build a privateer or a playhouse?

Plume. An odd question—a privateer or a playhouse! 'Twill require some consideration.—Faith, I'm for a privateer.

Braz. I'm not of your opinion, my dear.—For in the first place a privateer may be ill built.

Plume. And so may a playhouse.

Braz. But a privateer may be ill manned.

Plume. And so may a playhouse.

Braz. But a privateer may run upon the shallows.

Plume. Not so often as a playhouse.

Braz. But you know a privateer may spring a leak.

Plume. And I know that a playhouse may spring a great many.

Braz. But suppose the privateer come home with a rich booty, we should never agree about our shares.

Plume. 'Tis just so in a playhouse:—so, by my advice, you shall fix upon the privateer.

Braz. Agreed!—But if this twenty thousand should not be in specie—

Plume. What twenty thousand?

Braz. Heark'ee.   [*Whispers.*

Plume. Married!

Braz. Presently, we're to meet about half a mile out of town at the water-side—and so forth.—[*Reads.*] *For fear I should be known by any of Worthy's friends, you must give me leave to wear my mask till after the ceremony, which will make me for ever yours.*—Look'ee there, my dear dog.

    [*Shows the bottom of the letter to* PLUME.

Plume. Melinda!—and by this light, her own hand! —Once more, if you please, my dear.—Her hand exactly!—Just now, you say?

Braz. This minute I must be gone.

Plume. Have a little patience, and I'll go with you.

Braz. No, no, I see a gentleman coming this way, that may be inquisitive; 'tis Worthy, do you know him?

Plume. By sight only.

Braz. Have a care, the very eyes discover secrets.

         [*Exit.*

Enter Mr. WORTHY.

Wor. To boot and saddle, captain, you must mount.

Plume. Whip and spur, Worthy, or you won't mount.

Wor. But I shall: Melinda and I are agreed, she's gone to visit Silvia, we are to mount and follow; and could we carry a parson with us, who knows what might be done for us both?

Plume. Don't trouble your head; Melinda has secured a parson already.

Wor. Already! do you know more than I?

Plume. Yes, I saw it under her hand.—Brazen and she are to meet half a mile hence at the water-side, there to take boat, I suppose to be ferried over to the Elysian fields, if there be any such thing in matrimony.

Wor. I parted with Melinda just now; she assured me she hated Brazen, and that she resolved to discard Lucy for daring to write letters to him in her name.

Plume. Nay, nay, there's nothing of Lucy in this— I tell ye, I saw Melinda's hand, as surely as this is mine.

Wor. But I tell you she's gone this minute to Justice Balance's country-house.

Plume. But I tell you she's gone this minute to the water-side.

Enter SERVANT.

Ser. [*To* WORTHY.] Madam Melinda has sent word that you need not trouble yourself to follow her, because her journey to Justice Balance's is put off, and she's gone to take the air another way.

Wor. How! her journey put off!

Plume. That is, her journey was a put-off to you.

Wor. 'Tis plain, plain!—But how, where, when is she to meet Brazen?

Plume. Just now, I tell you, half a mile hence, at the water-side.

Wor. Up or down the water?

Plume. That I don't know.

Wor. I'm glad my horses are ready.—Jack, get 'em out.   [*Exit* Servant.

Plume. Shall I go with you?

Wor. Not an inch; I shall return presently.

Plume. You'll find me at the hall; the justices are sitting by this time, and I must attend them.

[*Exeunt severally.*

SCENE V.

A Court of Justice.

Justices BALANCE, SCALE, *and* SCRUPLE *discovered upon the bench;* Serjeant KITE, Constable, *and* Mob *in attendance.*

Kite. [*Aside to* Constable.] Pray, who are those honourable gentlemen upon the bench?

Con. He in the middle is Justice Balance, he on the right is Justice Scale, and he on the left is Justice Scruple; and I am Mr. Constable:—four very honest gentlemen.

Kite. O dear sir! I am your most obedient servant.—[*Saluting him.*] I fancy, sir, that your employment and mine are much the same; for my business is to keep people in order, and if they disobey, to knock 'em down; and then we are both staff-officers.

Con. Nay, I'm a serjeant myself—of the militia. Come, brother, you shall see me exercise. Suppose this a musket now: now I am shouldered.

[*Puts his staff on his right shoulder.*

Kite. Ay, you are shouldered pretty well for a

constable's staff; but for a musket, you must put it on t'other shoulder, my dear.

Con. Adso! that's true.—Come, now give the word of command.

Kite. Silence!

Con. Ay, ay, so we will—we will be silent.

Kite. Silence, you dog, silence!

[*Strikes him over the head with his halberd.*

Con. That's the way to silence a man with a witness! What d'ye mean, friend?

Kite. Only to exercise you, sir.

Con. Your exercise differs so from ours, that we shall ne'er agree about it. If my own captain had given me such a rap, I had taken the law of him.

Enter Captain PLUME.

Bal. Captain, you're welcome.

Plume. Gentlemen, I thank you.

Scrup. Come, honest captain, sit by me.—[PLUME *takes his seat upon the bench.*] Now produce your prisoners.—Here, that fellow there—set him up.—Mr. Constable, what have you to say against this man?

Con. I have nothing to say against him, an please you.

Bal. No! what made you bring him hither?

Con. I don't know, an please your worship.

Scale. Did not the contents of your warrant direct you what sort of men to take up?

Con. I can't tell, an please ye; I can't read.

Scrup. A very pretty constable truly!—I find we have no business here.

Kite. May it please the worshipful bench, I desire to be heard in this case, as being counsel for the queen.

Bal. Come, serjeant, you shall be heard, since nobody else will speak; we won't come here for nothing.

Kite. This man is but one man; the country may spare him, and the army wants him; besides, he's cut out by nature for a grenadier; he's five foot ten inches high; he shall box, wrestle, or dance the Cheshire round with any man in the country; he gets drunk every sabbath day, and he beats his wife.

Wife. You lie, sirrah! you lie!—An please your worship, he's the best-natur'dst, pains-taking'st man in the parish, witness my five poor children.

Scrup. A wife and five children!—You, constable, you rogue, how durst you impress a man that has a wife and five children?

Scale. Discharge him! discharge him!

Bal. Hold, gentlemen!—Hark'ee, friend, how do you maintain your wife and children?

Plume. They live upon wildfowl and venison, sir; the husband keeps a gun, and kills all the hares and partridges within five miles round.

Bal. A gun! nay, if he be so good at gunning, he shall have enough on't. He may be of use against the French, for he shoots flying, to be sure.

Scrup. But his wife and children, Mr. Balance!

Wife. Ay, ay, that's the reason you would send him away; you know I have a child every year, and you are afraid they should come upon the parish at last.

Plume. Look'ee there, gentlemen, the honest woman

has spoke it at once; the parish had better maintain five children this year, than six or seven the next. That fellow, upon his high feeding, may get you two or three beggars at a birth.

Wife. Look'ee, Mr. Captain, the parish shall get nothing by sending him away, for I won't lose my teeming-time, if there be a man left in the parish.

Bal. Send that woman to the house of correction —and the man—

Kite. I'll take care o' him, if you please.

[*Takes him down.*

Scale. Here, you constable, the next:—set up that black-faced fellow, he has a gunpowder look. What can you say against this man, constable?

Con. Nothing, but that he is a very honest man.

Plume. Pray, gentlemen, let me have one honest man in my company, for the novelty's sake.

Bal. What are you, friend?

Mob. A collier; I work in the coal-pits.

Scrup. Look'ee, gentlemen, this fellow has a trade, and the act of parliament here expresses, that we are to impress no man that has any visible means of a livelihood.

Kite. May it please your worships, this man has no visible means of livelihood, for he works under-ground.

Plume. Well said, Kite! Besides, the army wants miners.

Bal. Right, and had we an order of government for't, we could raise you in this, and the neighbouring county of Stafford, five hundred colliers, that would run you underground like moles, and do more service in a siege than all the miners in the army.

Scrup. Well, friend, what have you to say for yourself?

Mob. I'm married.

Kite. Lack-a-day, so am I!

Mob. Here's my wife, poor woman.

Bal. Are you married, good woman?

Wom. I'm married in conscience.

Kite. May it please your worship, she's with child in conscience.

Scale. Who married you, mistress?

Wom. My husband—we agreed that I should call him husband to avoid passing for a whore, and that he should call me wife, to shun going for a soldier.

Scrup. A very pretty couple! Pray, captain, will you take 'em both?

Plume. What say you, Mr. Kite? will you take care of the woman?

Kite. Yes, sir; she shall go with us to the seaside, and there, if she has a mind to drown herself, we'll take care that nobody shall hinder her.

Bal. Here, constable, bring in my man.—[*Exit* Constable.] Now, captain, I'll fit you with a man, such as you ne'er listed in your life.

Re-enter Constable *with* SILVIA.

Oh! my friend Pinch, I'm very glad to see you.

Silv. Well, sir, and what then?

Scale. What then! is that your respect to the bench?

Silv. Sir, I don't care a farthing for you nor your bench neither.

Scrup. Look'ee, gentlemen, that's enough: he's a very impudent fellow, and fit for a soldier.

Scale. A notorious rogue, I say, and very fit for a soldier.

Con. A whoremaster, I say, and therefore fit to go.

Bal. What think you, captain?

Plume. I think he's a very pretty fellow, and therefore fit to serve.

Silv. Me for a soldier! send your own lazy, lubberly sons at home, fellows that hazard their necks every day in pursuit of a fox, yet dare not peep abroad to look an enemy in the face.

Con. May it please your worships, I have a woman at the door to swear a rape against this rogue.

Silv. Is it your wife or daughter, booby? I ravished 'em both yesterday.

Bal. Pray, captain, read the Articles of War, we'll see him listed immediately.

Plume. [Reads.] *Articles of War against mutiny and desertion—*

Silv. Hold, sir!—Once more, gentlemen, have a care what you do, for you shall severely smart for any violence you offer to me; and you, Mr. Balance, I speak to you particularly, you shall heartily repent it.

Plume. Look'ee, young spark, say but one word more, and I'll build a horse for you as high as the ceiling, and make you ride the most tiresome journey that ever you made in your life.

Silv. You have made a fine speech, good Captain Huffcap, but you had better be quiet; I shall find a way to cool your courage.

Plume. Pray, gentlemen, don't mind him, he's distracted.

Silv. 'Tis false! I am descended of as good a

family as any in your county; my father is as good
a man as any upon your bench, and I am heir to
twelve hundred pound a year.

Bal. He's certainly mad!—Pray, captain, read the
Articles of War.

Silv. Hold once more!—Pray, Mr. Balance, to you
I speak; suppose I were your child, would you use
me at this rate?

Bal. No, faith, were you mine, I would send you
to Bedlam first, and into the army afterwards.

Silv. But consider my father, sir, he's as good, as
generous, as brave, as just a man as ever served his
country; I'm his only child, perhaps the loss of me
may break his heart.

Bal. He's a very great fool if it does.—Captain, if
you don't list him this minute, I'll leave the court.

Plume. Kite, do you distribute the levy-money to
the men while I read.

Kite. Ay, sir.—Silence, gentlemen!

      [Captain PLUME *reads the Articles of War.*

Bal. Very well; now, captain, let me beg the
favour of you, not to discharge this fellow upon any
account whatsoever.—Bring in the rest.

Con. There are no more, an't please your worship.

Bal. No more! there were five two hours ago.

Silv. 'Tis true, sir, but this rogue of a constable
let the rest escape for a bribe of eleven shillings a
man; because he said the act allowed him but ten,
so the odd shilling was clear gains.

Justices. How!

Silv. Gentlemen, he offered to let me get away for
two guineas, but I had not so much about me; this
is truth, and I'm ready to swear it.

Kite. And I'll swear it; give me the book, 'tis for the good of the service.

Mob. May it please your worship, I gave him half-a-crown to say that I was an honest man; but now, since that your worships have made me a rogue, I hope I shall have my money again.

Bal. 'Tis my opinion that this constable be put into the captain's hands, and if his friends don't bring four good men for his ransom by to-morrow night—captain, you shall carry him to Flanders.

Scale. Scrup. Agreed! agreed!

Plume. Mr. Kite, take the constable into custody.

Kite. Ay, ay, sir.—[*To* Constable.] Will you please to have your office taken from you? or will you handsomely lay down your staff, as your betters have done before you?   [Constable *drops his staff.*

Bal. Come, gentlemen, there needs no great ceremony in adjourning this court.—Captain, you shall dine with me.

Kite. [*To* Constable.] Come, Mr. Militia Serjeant, I shall silence you now, I believe, without your taking the law of me.   [*Exeunt.*

SCENE VI.

The Fields.

Enter Captain Brazen *leading* Lucy *masked.*

Braz. The boat is just below here.

Enter Mr. Worthy *with a case of pistols under his arm.*

Wor. Here, sir, take your choice.
            [*Going between them, and offering the pistols.*

Braz. What! pistols! are they charged, my dear?

Wor. With a brace of bullets each.

Braz. But I'm a foot-officer, my dear, and never use pistols, the sword is my way—and I won't be put out of my road to please any man.

Wor. Nor I neither; so have at you.

> [*Cocks one pistol.*

Braz. Look'ee, my dear, I don't care for pistols. —Pray, oblige me, and let us have a bout at sharps; damn it, there's no parrying these bullets!

Wor. Sir, if you han't your bellyfull of these, the swords shall come in for second course.

Braz. Why, then, fire and fury! I have eaten smoke from the mouth of a cannon, sir; don't think I fear powder, for I live upon't. Let me see—[*Takes one.*] And now, sir, how many paces distant shall we fire?

Wor. Fire you when you please, I'll reserve my shot till I'm sure of you.

Braz. Come, where's your cloak?

Wor. Cloak! what d'ye mean?

Braz. To fight upon; I always fight upon a cloak, 'tis our way abroad.

Lucy. Come, gentlemen, I'll end the strife.

> [*Unmasks.*

Wor. Lucy!—take her.

Braz. The devil take me if I do! Huzza!—[*Fires his pistol.*] D'ye hear, d'ye hear, you plaguy harridan, how those bullets whistle! suppose they had been lodged in my gizzard now!

Lucy. Pray, sir, pardon me.

Braz. I can't tell, child, till I know whether my money be safe.—[*Searching his pockets.*] Yes, yes, I do pardon you, but if I had you in the Rose Tavern,* Covent-Garden, with three or four hearty rakes, and three or four smart napkins, I would tell you another story, my dear. [*Exit.*

Wor. And was Melinda privy to this?

Lucy. No, sir, she wrote her name upon a piece of paper at the fortune-teller's last night, which I put in my pocket, and so writ above it to the captain.

Wor. And how came Melinda's journey put off?

Lucy. At the town's end she met Mr. Balance's steward, who told her that Mrs. Silvia was gone from her father's, and nobody could tell whither.

Wor. Silvia gone from her father's! This will be news to Plume.—Go home, and tell your lady how near I was being shot for her. [*Exeunt severally.*

SCENE VII.

A Room in Justice BALANCE'S *House.*

Enter Justice BALANCE *and* Steward.

Stew. We did not miss her till the evening, sir; and then, searching for her in the chamber that was my young master's, we found her clothes there; but the suit that your son left in the press, when he went to London, was gone.

Bal. The white trimmed with silver?

Stew. The same.

Bal. You han't told that circumstance to anybody?

Stew. To none but your worship.

* The Rose Tavern was a noted haunt of bad characters, especially those of the female sex. It was situated near Drury Lane Theatre, and was a favourite place of resort after the play.

Bal. And be sure you don't. Go into the dining-room, and tell Captain Plume that I beg to speak with him.

Stew. I shall. [*Exit.*

Bal. Was ever man so imposed upon! I had her promise, indeed, that she should never dispose of herself without my consent. I have consented with a witness, given her away as my act and deed. And this, I warrant, the captain thinks will pass; no, I shall never pardon him the villainy, first of robbing me of my daughter, and then the mean opinion he must have of me, to think that I could be so wretchedly imposed upon; her extravagant passion might encourage her in the attempt, but the contrivance must be his. I'll know the truth presently.

Enter Captain PLUME.

Pray, captain, what have you done with your young gentleman soldier?

Plume. He's at my quarters, I suppose, with the rest of my men.

Bal. Does he keep company with the common soldiers?

Plume. No, he's generally with me.

Bal. He lies with you, I presume?

Plume. No, faith, I offered him part of my bed; but the young rogue fell in love with Rose, and has lain with her, I think, since he came to town.

Bal. So that, between you both, Rose has been finely managed.

Plume. Upon my honour, sir, she had no harm from me.

Bal. [*Aside.*] All's safe, I find!—[*Aloud.*] Now,

captain, you must know that the young fellow's impudence in court was well grounded; he said I should heartily repent his being listed, and so I do from my soul.

Plume. Ay! for what reason?

Bal. Because he is no less than what he said he was, born of as good a family as any in this county, and is heir to twelve hundred pound a year.

Plume. I'm very glad to hear it—for I wanted but a man of that quality to make my company a perfect representative of the whole commons of England.

Bal. Won't you discharge him?

Plume. Not under a hundred pound sterling.

Bal. You shall have it, for his father is my intimate friend.

Plume. Then you shall have him for nothing.

Bal. Nay, sir, you shall have your price.

Plume. Not a penny, sir; I value an obligation to you much above a hundred pound.

Bal. Perhaps, sir, you shan't repent your generosity. —Will you please to write his discharge in my pocket-book?—[*Gives his book.*] In the meantime, we'll send for the gentleman.—Who waits there?

Enter Servant.

Go to the captain's lodging and inquire for Mr. Wilful; tell him his captain wants him here immediately.

Ser. Sir, the gentleman's below at the door, inquiring for the captain.

Plume. Bid him come up.—[*Exit* Servant.] Here's the discharge, sir.

Bal. Sir, I thank you.—[*Aside.*] 'Tis plain he had no hand in't.

Enter SILVIA.

Silv. I think, captain, you might have used me better than to leave me yonder among your swearing drunken crew. And you, Mr. Justice, might have been so civil as to have invited me to dinner, for I have eaten with as good a man as your worship.

Plume. Sir, you must charge our want of respect upon our ignorance of your quality.—But now you are at liberty—I have discharged you.

Silv. Discharged me!

Bal. Yes, sir, and you must once more go home to your father.

Silv. My father! then I am discovered.—O sir! [*Kneeling.*] I expect no pardon.

Bal. Pardon! no, no, child, your crime shall be your punishment.—Here, captain, I deliver her over to the conjugal power for her chastisement; since she will be a wife, be you a husband, a very husband. When she tells you of her love, upbraid her with her folly; be modishly ungrateful, because she has been unfashionably kind, and use her worse than you would anybody else, because you can't use her so well as she deserves.

Plume. And are you Silvia, in good earnest?

Silv. Earnest! I have gone too far to make it a jest, sir.

Plume. And do you give her to me in good earnest?

Bal. If you please to take her, sir.

Plume. Why then I have saved my legs and arms, and lost my liberty; secure from wounds, I am prepared for the gout; farewell subsistence, and welcome taxes!—Sir, my liberty, and hopes of being a general, are much dearer to me than your twelve hundred pound a year.—But to your love, madam, I resign my freedom, and to your beauty my ambition: greater in obeying at your feet, than commanding at the head of an army.

Enter Mr. WORTHY.

Wor. I am sorry to hear, Mr. Balance, that your daughter is lost.

Bal. So am not I, sir, since an honest gentleman has found her.

Enter MELINDA.

Mel. Pray, Mr. Balance, what's become of my cousin Silvia?

Bal. Your cousin Silvia is talking yonder with your cousin Plume.

Mel. Wor. How!

Silv. Do you think it strange, cousin, that a woman should change? but, I hope you'll excuse a change that has proceeded from constancy. I altered my outside, because I was the same within; and only laid by the woman to make sure of my man; that's my history.

Mel. Your history is a little romantic, cousin; but since success has crowned your adventures, you will have the world o' your side, and I shall be willing to go with the tide, provided you'll pardon an injury I offered you in the letter to your father.

Plume. That injury, madam, was done to me, and the reparation I expect shall be made to my friend; make Mr. Worthy happy, and I shall be satisfied.

Mel. A good example, sir, will go a great way: when my cousin is pleased to surrender, 'tis probable I shan't hold out much longer.

Enter Captain BRAZEN.

Braz. Gentlemen, I am yours.—Madam, I am not yours.

Mel. I'm glad on't, sir.

Braz. So am I.—You have got a pretty house here, Mr. Laconic.

Bal. 'Tis time to right all mistakes.—My name, sir, is Balance.

Braz. Balance! Sir, I am your most obedient!— I know your whole generation. Had not you an uncle that was governor of the Leeward Islands some years ago?

Bal. Did you know him?

Braz. Intimately, sir. He played at billiards to a miracle. You had a brother, too, that was captain of a fireship—poor Dick—he had the most engaging way with him—of making punch—and then his cabin was so neat—but his boy Jack was the most comical bastard—ha! ha! ha! ha! ha! a pickled dog, I shall never forget him.

Plume. Well, captain, are you fixed in your project yet? are you still for the privateer?

Braz. No, no, I had enough of a privateer just now; I had like to have been picked up by a cruiser under false colours, and a French pickaroon for aught I know.

Plume. But have you got your recruits, my dear?

Braz. Not a stick, my dear.

Plume. Probably I shall furnish you.

Enter ROSE *and* BULLOCK.

Rose. Captain, captain, I have got loose once more, and have persuaded my sweetheart Cartwheel to go with us; but you must promise not to part with me again.

Silv. I find Mrs. Rose has not been pleased with her bedfellow.

Rose. Bedfellow! I don't know whether I had a bedfellow or not.

Silv. Don't be in a passion, child; I was as little pleased with your company as you could be with mine.

Bull. Pray, sir, dunna be offended at my sister, she's something underbred; but if you please, I'll lie with you in her stead.

Plume. I have promised, madam, to provide for this girl; now will you be pleased to let her wait upon you? or shall I take care of her?

Silv. She shall be my charge, sir; you may find it business enough to take care of me.

Bull. Ay, and of me, captain; for wauns! if ever you lift your hand against me, I'll desert.

Plume. Captain Brazen shall take care o' that.— [*To* Captain BRAZEN.] My dear, instead of the twenty thousand pound you talked of, you shall have the twenty brave recruits that I have raised, at the rate they cost me.—My commission I lay down, to be taken up by some braver fellow, that has more merit and less good fortune, whilst I endeavour, by the example of this worthy gentleman, to serve my queen and country at home.

With some regret I quit the active field,
Where glory full reward for life does yield;

But the recruiting trade, with all its train
Of lasting plague, fatigue, and endless pain,
I gladly quit, with my fair spouse to stay,
And raise recruits the matrimonial way.

[*Exeunt omnes.*

EPILOGUE.

ALL ladies and gentlemen that are willing to see the
comedy, called the *Recruiting Officer*, let them repair
to-morrow night, by six o'clock, to the sign of the
Theatre Royal in Drury Lane, and they shall be
kindly entertained.

> We scorn the vulgar ways to bid you come,
> Whole Europe now obeys the call of drum.
> The soldier, not the poet, here appears,
> And beats up for a corps of volunteers :
> He finds that music chiefly does delight ye,
> And therefore chooses music to invite ye.

Beat the Grenadier March.—Row, row, tow !—
Gentlemen, this piece of music, called *An overture to
a Battle*, was composed by a famous Italian master,
and was performed with wonderful success at the
great operas of Vigo, Schellenberg, and Blenheim *—
it came off with the applause of all Europe, excepting
France; the French found it a little too rough for
their *delicatesse*.

---

* Sir George Rooke, with the combined English and Dutch fleets,
attacked the French fleet and the Spanish galleons in the port of
Vigo, October 12, 1702, when several men-of-war and galleons were
taken and destroyed, and a large quantity of plate fell into the
hands of the conquerors.

At Schellenberg, in Upper Bavaria, Marlborough defeated the
Duke of Bavaria.

Blenheim—here the French and Bavarians were defeated by the
English and Imperialists, August 2, 1704, under the Duke of Marlborough and Prince Eugene.

> Some that have acted on those glorious stages,
> Are here to witness to succeeding ages,
> That no music like the grenadier's engages.

Ladies, we must own, that this music of ours is not altogether so soft as Bononcini's;* yet, we dare affirm, that it has laid more people asleep than all the *Camillas* † in the world; and, you'll condescend to own, that it keeps one awake better than any opera that ever was acted.

The Grenadier March seems to be a composure excellently adapted to the genius of the English, for no music was ever followed so far by us, nor with so much alacrity; and, with all deference to the present subscription, we must say, that the Grenadier March has been subscribed for by the whole Grand Alliance; and, we presume to inform the ladies, that it always has a pre-eminence abroad, and is constantly heard by the tallest, handsomest men in the whole army. In short, to gratify the present taste, our author is now adapting some words to the Grenadier March, which he intends to have performed to-morrow, if the lady who is to sing it should not happen to be sick.

> This he concludes to be the surest way
> To draw you hither; for you'll all obey
> Soft music's call, though you should damn his play.

---

* Giovanni Bononcini, an Italian musician who flourished at the close of the seventeenth century.

† *Camilla* was an opera the libretto of which was written by Owen Swiney.

THE BEAUX-STRATAGEM.

A Comedy.

This comedy, the best constructed of all Farquhar's plays, was produced on 8th March 1707, at the Theatre Royal or Queen's Theatre (as it was variously styled) in the Haymarket, on the site of which Her Majesty's now stands. The plot is well conceived, and gives rise to numerous lively and amusing adventures. The idea of two embarrassed gentlemen coming down into the country disguised as master and servant is most humorously worked out, and furnishes scenes which are full of incident and lit up with trenchant and sparkling dialogue. The characters introduced are natural, yet each with an individuality of its own. Boniface the landlord, Cherry, Squire Sullen, the amusing Scrub, and the Irish-French Jesuit, are excellently drawn, and throughout the eighteenth century were always great favourites with the stage. The tone of the play is not high, but, as is the case with all the comedies of this writer, though human nature is represented as loose and unscrupulous, care is taken not to render it cruel or malignant.

The original cast was :—*Archer*, WILKS ; *Scrub*, NORRIS ; *Aimwell*, MILLS ; *Foigard*, BOWEN ; *Boniface*, BULLOCK ; *Sullen*, VERBRUGGEN ; *Gibbet*, CIBBER ; *Count Bellair*, BOMAN ; *Sir Charles Freeman*, KEEN ; *Mrs. Sullen*, MRS. OLDFIELD ; *Cherry*, MRS. BICKNELL ; *Dorinda*, MRS. BRADSHAW.

THE reader may find some faults in this play, which my illness
prevented the amending of; but there is great amends made in the
representation, which cannot be matched, no more than the friendly
and indefatigable care of Mr. Wilks, to whom I chiefly owe the
success of the play.

G. FARQUHAR.

AIMWELL, } *two Gentlemen of broken Fortunes, the first as*
ARCHER, }   *Master, and the second as Servant.*
COUNT BELLAIR, *a French Officer, Prisoner at Lichfield.*
SQUIRE SULLEN, *a Country Blockhead, brutal to his Wife.*
SIR CHARLES FREEMAN, *Brother to* MRS. SULLEN.
FOIGARD, *a Priest, Chaplain to the French Officers.*
BONIFACE, *an Innkeeper.*
GIBBET, }
HOUNSLOW, } *three Highwaymen.*
BAGSHOT, }
SCRUB, *Servant to* SQUIRE SULLEN.
LADY BOUNTIFUL, *an old, civil, Country Gentlewoman, that
cures all her Neighbours of all distempers, and foolishly fond
of her Son,* SQUIRE SULLEN.
DORINDA, *Daughter to* LADY BOUNTIFUL.
MRS. SULLEN, *Wife to* SQUIRE SULLEN.
GIPSY, *Maid to the Ladies.*
CHERRY, *Daughter to* BONIFACE.

*Tapster, Coach-passengers, Countryman, Countrywoman, and
Servants.*

SCENE.—LICHFIELD.'

PROLOGUE.

WHEN strife disturbs, or sloth corrupts an age,
Keen satire is the business of the stage,
When the Plain-Dealer * writ, he lash'd those
    crimes,
Which then infested most the modish times :
But now, when faction sleeps, and sloth is fled,
And all our youth in active fields are bred ;
When through Great Britain's fair extensive round,
The trumps of fame, the notes of union sound ; †
When Anna's sceptre points the laws their course,
And her example gives her precepts force :
There scarce is room for satire ; all our lays
Must be, or songs of triumph, or of praise.
But as in grounds best cultivated, tares
And poppies rise among the golden ears ;
Our product so, fit for the field or school,
Must mix with nature's favourite plant—a fool :
A weed that has to twenty summers ran,
Shoots up in stalk, and vegetates to man.
Simpling our author goes from field to field,
And culls such fools as may diversion yield ;

* Wycherley.
† England and Scotland had just been united.

And, thanks to nature, there's no want of those,
For rain or shine, the thriving coxcomb grows.
Follies to-night we show ne'er lash'd before,
Yet such as nature shows you every hour;
Nor can the pictures give a just offence,
For fools are made for jests to men of sense.

THE BEAUX-STRATAGEM.

ACT I.

SCENE I.

A Room in BONIFACE'S *Inn.*

Enter BONIFACE *running.*

Bon. Chamberlain! maid! Cherry! daughter Cherry! all asleep? all dead?

Enter CHERRY *running.*

Cher. Here, here! why d'ye bawl so, father? d'ye think we have no ears?

Bon. You deserve to have none, you young minx! The company of the Warrington coach has stood in the hall this hour, and nobody to show them to their chambers.

Cher. And let 'em wait, father; there's neither red-coat in the coach, nor footman behind it.

Bon. But they threaten to go to another inn to-night.

Cher. That they dare not, for fear the coachman should overturn them to-morrow.—Coming! coming! —Here's the London coach arrived.

Enter Coach-passengers *with trunks, bandboxes, and other luggage, and cross the stage.*

Bon. Welcome, ladies !

Cher. Very welcome, gentlemen !—Chamberlain, show the Lion and the Rose. [*Exit with the company.*

Enter AIMWELL *and* ARCHER, *the latter carrying a portmantle.*

Bon. This way, this way, gentlemen !

Aim. [*To* ARCHER.] Set down the things ; go to the stable, and see my horses well rubbed.

Arch. I shall, sir.   [*Exit.*

Aim. You're my landlord, I suppose ?

Bon. Yes, sir ; I'm old Will Boniface, pretty well known upon this road, as the saying is.

Aim. O Mr. Boniface, your servant !

Bon. O sir !—What will your honour please to drink, as the saying is ?

Aim. I have heard your town of Lichfield much famed for ale ; I think I'll taste that.

Bon. Sir, I have now in my cellar ten tun of the best ale in Staffordshire ; 'tis smooth as oil, sweet as milk, clear as amber, and strong as brandy ; and will be just fourteen year old the fifth day of next March, old style.

Aim. You're very exact, I find, in the age of your ale.

Bon. As punctual, sir, as I am in the age of my children.   I'll show you such ale !—Here, tapster, broach number 1706, as the saying is.—Sir, you shall taste my *Anno Domini.*—I have lived in Lichfield, man and boy, above eight-and-fifty years, and, I believe, have not consumed eight-and-fifty ounces of meat.

Aim. At a meal, you mean, if one may guess your sense by your bulk.

Bon. Not in my life, sir, I have fed purely upon ale; I have eat my ale, drank my ale, and I always sleep upon ale.

Enter Tapster *with a bottle and glass, and exit.*

Now, sir, you shall see!—[*Pours out a glass.*] Your worship's health.—Ha! delicious, delicious! fancy it burgundy, only fancy it, and 'tis worth ten shillings a quart.

Aim. [*Drinks.*] 'Tis confounded strong!

Bon. Strong! it must be so, or how should we be strong that drink it?

Aim. And have you lived so long upon this ale, landlord?

Bon. Eight-and-fifty years, upon my credit, sir— but it killed my wife, poor woman, as the saying is.

Aim. How came that to pass?

Bon. I don't know how, sir; she would not let the ale take its natural course, sir; she was for qualifying it every now and then with a dram, as the saying is; and an honest gentleman that came this way from Ireland, made her a present of a dozen bottles of usquebaugh—but the poor woman was never well after: but, howe'er, I was obliged to the gentleman, you know.

Aim. Why, was it the usquebaugh that killed her?

Bon. My Lady Bountiful said so. She, good lady, did what could be done; she cured her of three tympanies, but the fourth carried her off. But she's happy, and I'm contented, as the saying is.

Aim. Who's that Lady Bountiful you mentioned?

Bon. Ods my life, sir, we'll drink her health.— [*Drinks.*] My Lady Bountiful is one of the best of women. Her last husband, Sir Charles Bountiful, left her worth a thousand pound a year; and, I believe, she lays out one-half on't in charitable uses for the good of her neighbours. She cures rheumatisms, ruptures, and broken shins in men; green-sickness, obstructions, and fits of the mother, in women; the king's evil, chincough, and chilblains, in children; in short, she has cured more people in and about Lichfield within ten years than the doctors have killed in twenty; and that's a bold word.

Aim. Has the lady been any other way useful in her generation?

Bon. Yes, sir; she has a daughter by Sir Charles, the finest woman in all our country, and the greatest fortune. She has a son too, by her first husband, Squire Sullen, who married a fine lady from London t'other day; if you please, sir, we'll drink his health.

Aim. What sort of a man is he?

Bon. Why, sir, the man's well enough; says little, thinks less, and does—nothing at all, faith. But he's a man of great estate, and values nobody.

Aim. A sportsman, I suppose?

Bon. Yes, sir, he's a man of pleasure; he plays at whisk and smokes his pipe eighty-and-forty hours together sometimes.

Aim. And married, you say?

Bon. Ay, and to a curious woman, sir. But he's a —he wants it; here, sir. [*Pointing to his forehead.*

Aim. He has it there, you mean?

Bon. That's none of my business; he's my land-lord, and so a man, you know, would not—But—ecod, he's no better than—Sir, my humble service to you.—[*Drinks.*] Though I value not a farthing what he can do to me; I pay him his rent at quarter-day; I have a good running trade; I have but one daughter, and I can give her—but no matter for that.

Aim. You're very happy, Mr. Boniface. Pray, what other company have you in town?

Bon. A power of fine ladies; and then we have the French officers.

Aim. Oh, that's right, you have a good many of those gentlemen: pray, how do you like their company?

Bon. So well, as the saying is, that I could wish we had as many more of 'em; they're full of money, and pay double for everything they have. They know, sir, that we paid good round taxes for the taking of 'em, and so they are willing to reimburse us a little. One of 'em lodges in my house.

Re-enter ARCHER.

Arch. Landlord, there are some French gentlemen below that ask for you.

Bon. I'll wait on 'em.—[*Aside to* ARCHER.] Does your master stay long in town, as the saying is?

Arch. I can't tell, as the saying is.

Bon. Come from London?

Arch. No.

Bon. Going to London, mayhap?

Arch. No.

Bon. [*Aside.*] An odd fellow this.—[*To* AIMWELL.]

I beg your worship's pardon, I'll wait on you in half a minute.   [*Exit.*

Aim. The coast's clear, I see.—Now, my dear Archer, welcome to Lichfield.

Arch. I thank thee, my dear brother in iniquity.

Aim. Iniquity! prithee, leave canting; you need not change your style with your dress.

Arch. Don't mistake me, Aimwell, for 'tis still my maxim, that there is no scandal like rags, nor any crime so shameful as poverty.

Aim. The world confesses it every day in its practice, though men won't own it for their opinion. Who did that worthy lord, my brother, single out of the side-box to sup with him t'other night?

Arch. Jack Handicraft, a handsome, well-dressed, mannerly, sharping rogue, who keeps the best company in town.

Aim. Right! And, pray, who married my lady Manslaughter t'other day, the great fortune?

Arch. Why, Nick Marrabone, a professed pickpocket, and a good bowler; but he makes a handsome figure, and rides in his coach, that he formerly used to ride behind.

Aim. But did you observe poor Jack Generous in the Park last week?

Arch. Yes, with his autumnal periwig, shading his melancholy face, his coat older than anything but its fashion, with one hand idle in his pocket, and with the other picking his useless teeth; and, though the Mall was crowded with company, yet was poor Jack as single and solitary as a lion in a desert.

Aim. And as much avoided, for no crime upon earth but the want of money.

Arch. And that's enough. Men must not be poor; idleness is the root of all evil; the world's wide enough, let 'em bustle. Fortune has taken the weak under her protection, but men of sense are left to their industry.

Aim. Upon which topic we proceed, and, I think, luckily hitherto. Would not any man swear now, that I am a man of quality, and you my servant, when if our intrinsic value were known—

Arch. Come, come, we are the men of intrinsic value who can strike our fortunes out of ourselves, whose worth is independent of accidents in life, or revolutions in government; we have heads to get money and hearts to spend it.

Aim. As to our hearts, I grant ye, they are as willing tits as any within twenty degrees; but I can have no great opinion of our heads from the service they have done us hitherto, unless it be that they have brought us from London hither to Lichfield, made me a lord and you my servant.

Arch. That's more than you could expect already. But what money have we left?

Aim. But two hundred pound.

Arch. And our horses, clothes, rings, &c.—Why, we have very good fortunes now for moderate people; and, let me tell you, that this two hundred pound, with the experience that we are now masters of, is a better estate than the ten we have spent. Our friends, indeed, began to suspect that our pockets were low, but we came off with flying colours, showed no signs of want either in word or deed.

Aim. Ay, and our going to Brussels was a good pretence enough for our sudden disappearing; and,

I warrant you, our friends imagine that we are gone a-volunteering.

Arch. Why, faith, if this prospect fails, it must e'en come to that. I am for venturing one of the hundreds, if you will, upon this knight-errantry; but, in case it should fail, we'll reserve the t'other to carry us to some counterscarp, where we may die, as we lived, in a blaze.

Aim. With all my heart; and we have lived justly, Archer; we can't say that we have spent our fortunes, but that we have enjoyed 'em.

Arch. Right! so much pleasure for so much money. We have had our pennyworths; and, had I millions, I would go to the same market again.—Oh London! London!—Well, we have had our share, and let us be thankful: past pleasures, for aught I know, are best, such as we are sure of; those to come may disappoint us.

Aim. It has often grieved the heart of me to see how some inhuman wretches murder their kind fortunes; those that, by sacrificing all to the one appetite, shall starve all the rest. You shall have some that live only in their palates, and in their sense of tasting shall drown the other four: others are only epicures in appearances, such who shall starve their nights to make a figure a days, and famish their own to feed the eyes of others: a contrary sort confine their pleasures to the dark, and contract their spacious acres to the circuit of a muff-string.

Arch. Right! But they find the Indies in that spot where they consume 'em, and, I think, your kind keepers have much the best on't; for they indulge the most senses by one expense, there's the seeing, hearing, and feeling, amply gratified ; and, some philosophers will tell you, that from such a commerce there arises a sixth sense, that gives infinitely more pleasure than the other five put together.

Aim. And to pass to the other extremity, of all keepers I think those the worst that keep their money.

Arch. Those are the most miserable wights in being, they destroy the rights of nature, and disappoint the blessings of Providence. Give me a man that keeps his five senses keen and bright as his sword, that has 'em always drawn out in their just order and strength, with his reason as commander at the head of 'em, that detaches 'em by turns upon whatever party of pleasure agreeably offers, and commands 'em to retreat upon the least appearance of disadvantage or danger ! For my part, I can stick to my bottle while my wine, my company, and my reason, holds good ; I can be charmed with Sappho's singing without falling in love with her face : I love hunting, but would not, like Actæon, be eaten up by my own dogs ; I love a fine house, but let another keep it ; and just so I love a fine woman.

Aim. In that last particular you have the better of me.

Arch. Ay, you're such an amorous puppy, that I'm afraid you'll spoil our sport ; you can't counterfeit the passion without feeling it.

Aim. Though the whining part be out of doors in town, 'tis still in force with the country ladies : and let me tell you, Frank, the fool in that passion shall outdo the knave at any time.

Arch. Well, I won't dispute it now ; you command

for the day, and so I submit: at Nottingham, your know, I am to be master.

Aim. And at Lincoln, I again.

Arch. Then, at Norwich I mount, which, I think shall be our last stage; for, if we fail there, we'll embark for Holland, bid adieu to Venus, and welcome Mars.

Aim. A match!—Mum!

Re-enter BONIFACE.

Bon. What will your worship please to have for supper?

Aim. What have you got?

Bon. Sir, we have a delicate piece of beef in the pot, and a pig at the fire.

Aim. Good supper-meat, I must confess. I can't eat beef, landlord.

Arch. And I hate pig.

Aim. Hold your prating, sirrah! do you know who you are?

Bon. Please to bespeak something else; I have everything in the house.

Aim. Have you any veal?

Bon. Veal! sir, we had a delicate loin of veal on Wednesday last.

Aim. Have you got any fish or wildfowl?

Bon. As for fish, truly, sir, we are an inland town, and indifferently provided with fish, that's the truth on't; and then for wildfowl—we have a delicate couple of rabbits.

Aim. Get me the rabbits fricasseed.

Bon. Fricasseed! Lard, sir, they'll eat much better smothered with onions.

Arch. Psha! damn your onions!

Aim. Again, sirrah!—Well, landlord, what you please. But hold, I have a small charge of money, and your house is so full of strangers, that I believe it may be safer in your custody than mine; for when this fellow of mine gets drunk he minds nothing.— Here, sirrah, reach me the strong-box.

Arch. Yes, sir.—[*Aside.*] This will give us a reputation.   [*Gives* AIMWELL *a box.*

Aim. Here, landlord; the locks are sealed down both for your security and mine; it holds somewhat above two hundred pound; if you doubt it, I'll count it to you after supper; but be sure you lay it where I may have it at a minute's warning; for my affairs are a little dubious at present; perhaps I may be gone in half an hour, perhaps I may be your guest till the best part of that be spent; and pray order your ostler to keep my horses always saddled. But one thing above the rest I must beg, that you would let this fellow have none of your *Anno Domini*, as you call it; for he's the most insufferable sot.—Here, sirrah, light me to my chamber.

        [*Exit lighted by* ARCHER.

Bon. Cherry! daughter Cherry!

Re-enter CHERRY.

Cher. D'ye call, father?

Bon. Ay, child, you must lay by this box for the gentleman; 'tis full of money.

Cher. Money! all that money! why, sure, father, the gentleman comes to be chosen parliament-man. Who is he?

Bon. I don't know what to make of him ; he talks of keeping his horses ready saddled, and of going perhaps at a minute's warning, or of staying perhaps till the best part of this be spent.

Cher. Ay, ten to one, father, he's a highwayman.

Bon. A highwayman ! upon my life, girl, you have hit it, and this box is some new-purchased booty. Now, could we find him out, the money were ours.

Cher. He don't belong to our gang.

Bon. What horses have they ?

Cher. The master rides upon a black.

Bon. A black ! ten to one the man upon the black mare ; and since he don't belong to our fraternity, we may betray him with a safe conscience ; I don't think it lawful to harbour any rogues but my own. Look'ee, child, as the saying is, we must go cunningly to work, proofs we must have ; the gentleman's servant loves drink, I'll ply him that way, and ten to one loves a wench ; you must work him t'other way.

Cher. Father, would you have me give my secret for his ?

Bon. Consider, child, there's two hundred pound to boot.—[*Ringing without.*] Coming !—coming !— Child, mind your business.　　　　　　　[*Exit.*

Cher. What a rogue is my father ! My father ! I deny it. My mother was a good, generous, free-hearted woman, and I can't tell how far her good-nature might have extended for the good of her children. This landlord of mine, for I think I can call him no more, would betray his guest, and debauch his daughter into the bargain—by a footman too !

Re-enter ARCHER.

Arch. What footman, pray, mistress, is so happy as to be the subject of your contemplation?

Cher. Whoever he is, friend, he'll be but little the better for't.

Arch. I hope so, for, I'm sure, you did not think of me.

Cher. Suppose I had?

Arch. Why then you're but even with me; for the minute I came in, I was a considering in what manner I should make love to you.

Cher. Love to me, friend!

Arch. Yes, child.

Cher. Child! manners!—If you kept a little more distance, friend, it would become you much better.

Arch. Distance! good-night, sauce-box.   [*Going.*

Cher. [*Aside.*] A pretty fellow! I like his pride. —[*Aloud.*] Sir, pray, sir, you see, sir, [ARCHER *returns*] I have the credit to be entrusted with your master's fortune here, which sets me a degree above his footman; I hope, sir, you an't affronted?

Arch. Let me look you full in the face, and I'll tell you whether you can affront me or no. 'Sdeath, child, you have a pair of delicate eyes, and you don't know what to do with 'em!

Cher. Why, sir, don't I see everybody?

Arch. Ay, but if some women had 'em, they would kill everybody. Prithee, instruct me, I would fain make love to you, but I don't know what to say.

Cher. Why, did you never make love to anybody before?

Arch. Never to a person of your figure, I can

assure you, madam ; my addresses have been always confined to people within my own sphere. I never aspired as high before. [*Sings.*

> But you look so bright,
> And are dress'd so tight,
> That a man would swear you're right,
> As arm was e'er laid over.
> Such an air
> You freely wear
> To ensnare,
> As makes each guest a lover !
>
> Since then, my dear, I'm your guest,
> Prithee give me of the best
> Of what is ready drest :
> Since then, my dear, &c.

Cher. [*Aside.*] What can I think of this man ?—[*Aloud.*] Will you give me that song, sir ?

Arch. Ay, my dear, take it while 'tis warm.—[*Kisses her.*] Death and fire ! her lips are honeycombs.

Cher. And I wish there had been bees too, to have stung you for your impudence.

Arch. There's a swarm of Cupids, my little Venus, that has done the business much better.

Cher. [*Aside.*] This fellow is misbegotten as well as I.—[*Aloud.*] What's your name, sir ?

Arch. [*Aside.*] Name ! egad, I have forgot it.—[*Aloud.*] Oh ! Martin.

Cher. Where were you born ?

Arch. In St. Martin's parish.

Cher. What was your father ?

Arch. St. Martin's parish.

Cher. Then, friend, good night.

Arch. I hope not.

Cher. You may depend upon't.

Arch. Upon what?

Cher. That you're very impudent.

Arch. That you're very handsome.

Cher. That you're a footman.

Arch. That you're an angel.

Cher. I shall be rude.

Arch. So shall I.   [*Seizes her hand.*

Cher. Let go my hand.

Arch. Give me a kiss.   [*Kisses her.*

Bon. [*Without.*] Cherry! Cherry!

Cher. I'm—my father calls; you plaguy devil, how durst you stop my breath so? Offer to follow me one step, if you dare.   [*Exit.*

Arch. A fair challenge, by this light! this is a pretty fair opening of an adventure; but we are knight-errants, and so Fortune be our guide.   [*Exit.*

ACT II.

SCENE I.

A Gallery in Lady Bountiful's *House.*

Enter Mrs. Sullen *and* Dorinda, *meeting.*

Dor. Morrow, my dear sister; are you for church this morning?

Mrs. Sul. Anywhere to pray; for Heaven alone can help me. But I think, Dorinda, there's no form of prayer in the liturgy against bad husbands.

Dor. But there's a form of law in Doctors-Commons; and I swear, sister Sullen, rather than see you thus continually discontented, I would advise you to apply to that: for besides the part that I bear in your vexatious broils, as being sister to the husband, and friend to the wife, your example gives me such an impression of matrimony, that I shall be apt to condemn my person to a long vacation all its life. But supposing, madam, that you brought it to a case of separation, what can you urge against your husband? My brother is, first, the most constant man alive.

Mrs. Sul. The most constant husband, I grant ye.

Dor. He never sleeps from you.

Mrs. Sul. No, he always sleeps with me.

Dor. He allows you a maintenance suitable to your quality.

Mrs. Sul. A maintenance! do you take me, madam, for an hospital child, that I must sit down, and bless my benefactors for meat, drink, and clothes? As I take it, madam, I brought your brother ten thousand pounds, out of which I might expect some pretty things, called pleasures.

Dor. You share in all the pleasures that the country affords.

Mrs. Sul. Country pleasures! racks and torments! Dost think, child, that my limbs were made for leaping of ditches, and clambering over stiles? or that my parents, wisely foreseeing my future happiness in country-pleasures, had early instructed me in rural accomplishments of drinking fat ale, playing at whisk, and smoking tobacco with my husband? or of spreading of plasters, brewing of diet-drinks, and stilling rosemary-water, with the good old gentlewoman my mother-in-law?

Dor. I'm sorry, madam, that it is not more in our power to divert you; I could wish, indeed, that our entertainments were a little more polite, or your taste a little less refined. But, pray, madam, how came the poets and philosophers, that laboured so much in hunting after pleasure, to place it at last in a country life?

Mrs. Sul. Because they wanted money, child, to find out the pleasures of the town. Did you ever see a poet or philosopher worth ten thousand pound? If you can show me such a man, I'll lay you fifty pound you'll find him somewhere within the weekly bills.* Not that I disapprove rural pleasures, as the poets

* The Weekly Bills of Mortality, I presume, which were instituted as early as 1592.

have painted them; in their landscape, every Phillis
has her Corydon, every murmuring stream, and every
flowery mead, gives fresh alarms to love. Besides,
you'll find, that their couples were never married :—
but yonder I see my Corydon, and a sweet swain it
is, Heaven knows! Come, Dorinda, don't be angry,
he's my husband, and your brother; and between
both, is he not a sad brute?

Dor. I have nothing to say to your part of him,
you're the best judge.

Mrs. Sul. O sister, sister! if ever you marry, beware of a sullen, silent sot, one that's always musing,
but never thinks. There's some diversion in a talking
blockhead; and since a woman must wear chains, I
would have the pleasure of hearing 'em rattle a little.
Now you shall see, but take this by the way. He
came home this morning at his usual hour of four,
wakened me out of a sweet dream of something else,
by tumbling over the tea-table, which he broke all to
pieces; after his man and he had rolled about the
room, like sick passengers in a storm, he comes
flounce into bed, dead as a salmon into a fishmonger's
basket; his feet cold as ice, his breath hot as a
furnace, and his hands and his face as greasy as his
flannel nightcap. O matrimony! He tosses up the
clothes with a barbarous swing over his shoulders,
disorders the whole economy of my bed, leaves me
half naked, and my whole night's comfort is the tune-
able serenade of that wakeful nightingale, his nose!
Oh, the pleasure of counting the melancholy clock by
a snoring husband! But now, sister, you shall see
how handsomely, being a well-bred man, he will beg
my pardon.

Enter Squire SULLEN.

Squire Sul. My head aches consumedly.

Mrs. Sul. Will you be pleased, my dear, to drink tea with us this morning? it may do your head good.

Squire Sul. No.

Dor. Coffee, brother?

Squire Sul. Psha!

Mrs. Sul. Will you please to dress, and go to church with me? the air may help you.

Squire Sul. Scrub! [*Calls.*

Enter SCRUB.

Scrub. Sir!

Squire Sul. What day o' th' week is this?

Scrub. Sunday, an't please your worship.

Squire Sul. Sunday! bring me a dram; and d'ye hear, set out the venison-pasty, and a tankard of strong beer upon the hall-table, I'll go to break-fast. [*Going.*

Dor. Stay, stay, brother, you shan't get off so; you were very naught last night, and must make your wife reparation; come, come, brother, won't you ask pardon?

Squire Sul. For what?

Dor. For being drunk last night.

Squire Sul. I can afford it, can't I?

Mrs. Sul. But I can't, sir.

Squire Sul. Then you may let it alone.

Mrs. Sul. But I must tell you, sir, that this is not to be borne.

Squire Sul. I'm glad on't.

Mrs. Sul. What is the reason, sir, that you use me thus inhumanly?

Squire Sul. Scrub!

Scrub. Sir!

Squire Sul. Get things ready to shave my head.

[*Exit.*

Mrs. Sul. Have a care of coming near his temples, Scrub, for fear you meet something there that may turn the edge of your razor.—[*Exit* SCRUB.] Inveterate stupidity! did you ever know so hard, so obstinate, a spleen as his? O sister, sister! I shall never ha' good of the beast till I get him to town; London, dear London, is the place for managing and breaking a husband.

Dor. And has not a husband the same opportunities there for humbling a wife?

Mrs. Sul. No, no, child, 'tis a standing maxim in conjugal discipline, that when a man would enslave his wife, he hurries her into the country; and when a lady would be arbitrary with her husband she wheedles her booby up to town. A man dare not play the tyrant in London, because there are so many examples to encourage the subject to rebel. O Dorinda! Dorinda! a fine woman may do anything in London: o' my conscience, she may raise an army of forty thousand men.

Dor. I fancy, sister, you have a mind to be trying your power that way here in Lichfield; you have drawn the French count to your colours already.

Mrs. Sul. The French are a people that can't live without their gallantries.

Dor. And some English that I know, sister, are not adverse to such amusements.

Mrs. Sul. Well, sister, since the truth must out, it may do as well now as hereafter; I think, one way to rouse my lethargic, sottish husband is to give him a rival: security begets negligence in all people, and men must be alarmed to make 'em alert in their duty. Women are like pictures, of no value in the hands of a fool, till he hears men of sense bid high for the purchase.

Dor. This might do, sister, if my brother's understanding were to be convinced into a passion for you; but I fancy, there's a natural aversion of his side; and I fancy, sister, that you don't come much behind him, if you dealt fairly.

Mrs. Sul. I own it, we are united contradictions, fire and water: but I could be contented, with a great many other wives, to humour the censorious mob, and give the world an appearance of living well with my husband, could I bring him but to dissemble a little kindness to keep me in countenance.

Dor. But how do you know, sister, but that, instead of rousing your husband by this artifice to a counterfeit kindness, he should awake in a real fury?

Mrs. Sul. Let him: if I can't entice him to the one, I would provoke him to the other.

Dor. But how must I behave myself between ye?

Mrs. Sul. You must assist me.

Dor. What, against my own brother?

Mrs. Sul. He's but half a brother, and I'm your entire friend. If I go a step beyond the bounds of honour, leave me; till then, I expect you should go along with me in everything; while I trust my honour in your hands, you may trust your brother's in mine.   The count is to dine here to-day.

Dor. 'Tis a strange thing, sister, that I can't like that man.

Mrs. Sul. You like nothing; your time is not come ; love and death have their fatalities, and strike home one time or other : you'll pay for all one day, I warrant ye.   But come, my lady's tea is ready, and 'tis almost church time.   [*Exeunt.*

SCENE II.

A Room in Boniface's *Inn.*

Aimwell *and* Archer *discovered.*

Aim. And was she the daughter of the house ?

Arch. The landlord is so blind as to think so ; but I dare swear she has better blood in her veins.

Aim. Why dost think so ?

Arch. Because the baggage has a pert *je ne sais quoi ;* she reads plays, keeps a monkey, and is troubled with vapours.

Aim. By which discoveries I guess that you know more of her.

Arch. Not yet, faith ; the lady gives herself airs ; forsooth, nothing under a gentleman !

Aim. Let me take her in hand.

Arch. Say one word more o' that, and I'll declare myself, spoil your sport there, and everywhere else ; look ye, Aimwell, every man in his own sphere.

Aim. Right ; and therefore you must pimp for your master.

Arch. In the usual forms, good sir, after I have

served myself.—But to our business. You are so well dressed, Tom, and make so handsome a figure, that I fancy you may do execution in a country church; the exterior part strikes first, and you're in the right to make that impression favourable.

Aim. There's something in that which may turn to advantage. The appearance of a stranger in a country church draws as many gazers as a blazing-star; no sooner he comes into the cathedral, but a train of whispers runs buzzing round the congregation in a moment. *Who is he? Whence comes he? Do you know him?* Then I, sir, tips me the verger with half-a-crown; he pockets the simony, and inducts me into the best pew in the church; I pull out my snuff-box, turn myself round, bow to the bishop or the dean, if he be the commanding officer; single out a beauty, rivet both my eyes to hers, set my nose a-bleeding by the strength of imagination, and show the whole church my concern, by my endeavouring to hide it; after the sermon, the whole town gives me to her for a lover, and by persuading the lady that I am a-dying for her, the tables are turned, and she in good earnest falls in love with me.

Arch. There's nothing in this, Tom, without a precedent; but instead of riveting your eyes to a beauty, try and fix 'em upon a fortune; that's our business at present.

Aim. Psha! no woman can be a beauty without a fortune. Let me alone, for I am a marksman.

Arch. Tom!

Aim. Ay.

Arch. When were you at church before, pray?

Aim. Um—I was there at the coronation.

Arch. And how can you expect a blessing by going to church now?

Aim. Blessing! nay, Frank, I ask but for a wife.

[*Exit.*

Arch. Truly, the man is not very unreasonable in his demands.   [*Exit at the opposite door.*

SCENE III.

Another Room in the same.

BONIFACE *and* CHERRY *discovered.*

Bon. Well, daughter, as the saying is, have you brought Martin to confess?

Cher. Pray, father, don't put me upon getting anything out of a man; I'm but young, you know, father, and I don't understand wheedling.

Bon. Young! why, you jade, as the saying is, can any woman wheedle that is not young? your mother was useless at five-and-twenty. Not wheedle! would you make your mother a whore, and me a cuckold, as the saying is? I tell you, his silence confesses it, and his master spends his money so freely, and is so much a gentleman every manner of way, that he must be a highwayman.

Enter GIBBET.

Gib. Landlord, landlord, is the coast clear?

Bon. O Mr. Gibbet, what's the news?

Gib. No matter, ask no questions, all fair and honourable.—Here, my dear Cherry.—[*Gives her a bag.*] Two hundred sterling pounds, as good as any that ever hanged or saved a rogue; lay 'em by with

the rest ; and here—three wedding or mourning rings,
'tis much the same, you know—here, two silver-hilted
swords ; I took those from fellows that never show
any part of their swords but the hilts—here is a
diamond necklace which the lady hid in the privatest
place in the coach, but I found it out—this gold watch
I took from a pawnbroker's wife ; it was left in her
hands by a person of quality, there's the arms upon
the case.

Cher. But who had you the money from ?

Gib. Ah ! poor woman ! I pitied her ;—from a
poor lady just eloped from her husband. She had
made up her cargo, and was bound for Ireland, as
hard as she could drive ; she told me of her husband's
barbarous usage, and so I left her half-a-crown. But
I had almost forgot, my dear Cherry, I have a present
for you.

Cher. What is't ?

Gib. A pot of ceruse, my child, that I took out of
a lady's under-pocket.

Cher. What, Mr. Gibbet, do you think that I
paint ?

Gib. Why, you jade, your betters do ; I'm sure the
lady that I took it from had a coronet upon her
handkerchief. Here, take my cloak, and go, secure
the premises.

Cher. I will secure 'em.   *[Exit.*

Bon. But, heark'ee, where's Hounslow and Bagshot ?

Gib. They'll be here to-night.

Bon. D'ye know of any other gentlemen o' the pad
on this road ?

Gib. No.

Bon. I fancy that I have two that lodge in the house just now.

Gib, The devil! how d'ye smoke 'em?

Bon. Why, the one is gone to church.

Gib. That's suspicious, I must confess.

Bon. And the other is now in his master's chamber; he pretends to be servant to the other.   We'll call him out and pump him a little.

Gib. With all my heart.

Bon. Mr. Martin, Mr. Martin!   [*Calls.*

Enter ARCHER, *combing a periwig and singing.*

Gib. The roads are consumed deep, I'm as dirty as old Brentford at Christmas.—A good pretty fellow that; whose servant are you, friend?

Arch. My master's.

Gib. Really!

Arch. Really.

Gib. That's much.—The fellow has been at the bar by his evasions.—But, pray, sir, what is your master's name?

Arch. Tall, all, dall!—[*Sings and combs the periwig.*] This is the most obstinate curl—

Gib. I ask you his name?

Arch. Name, sir—tall all, dall!—I never asked him his name in my life.—Tall, all, dall!

Bon. What think you now?   [*Aside to* GIBBET.

Gib. [*Aside to* BONIFACE.] Plain, plain, he talks now as if he were before a judge.—[*To* ARCHER.] But pray, friend, which way does your master travel?

Arch. A-horseback.

Gib. [*Aside.*] Very well again, an old offender,

right.—[*To* ARCHER.] But, I mean, does he go upwards or downwards?

Arch. Downwards, I fear, sir.—Tall, all!

Gib. I'm afraid my fate will be a contrary way.

Bon. Ha! ha! ha! Mr. Martin, you're very arch. This gentleman is only travelling towards Chester, and would be glad of your company, that's all.—Come, captain, you'll stay to-night, I suppose? I'll show you a chamber—come, captain.

Gib. Farewell, friend!

Arch. Captain, your servant.—[*Exeunt* BONIFACE *and* GIBBET.] Captain! a pretty fellow! 'Sdeath, I wonder that the officers of the army don't conspire to beat all scoundrels in red but their own.

Re-enter CHERRY.

Cher. [*Aside.*] Gone, and Martin here! I hope he did not listen; I would have the merit of the discovery all my own, because I would oblige him to love me.— [*Aloud.*] Mr. Martin, who was that man with my father?

Arch. Some recruiting serjeant, or whipped-out trooper, I suppose.

Cher. All's safe, I find. [*Aside.*

Arch. Come, my dear, have you conned over the catechise I taught you last night?

Cher. Come, question me.

Arch. What is love?

Cher. Love is I know not what, it comes I know not how, and goes I know not when.

Arch. Very well, an apt scholar.—[*Chucks her under the chin.*] Where does love enter?

Cher. Into the eyes.

Arch. And where go out?

Cher. I won't tell ye.

Arch. What are the objects of that passion?

Cher. Youth, beauty, and clean linen.

Arch. The reason?

Cher. The two first are fashionable in nature, and the third at court.

Arch. That's my dear.—[*Pats her cheek.*] What are the signs and tokens of that passion?

Cher. A stealing look, a stammering tongue, words improbable, designs impossible, and actions impracticable.

Arch. That's my good child, kiss me.—What must a lover do to obtain his mistress?

Cher. He must adore the person that disdains him, he must bribe the chambermaid that betrays him, and court the footman that laughs at him. He must— he must—

Arch. Nay, child, I must whip you if you don't mind your lesson; he must treat his—

Cher. O ay!—he must treat his enemies with respect, his friends with indifference, and all the world with contempt; he must suffer much, and fear more; he must desire much, and hope little; in short, he must embrace his ruin, and throw himself away.

Arch. Had ever man so hopeful a pupil as mine!— Come, my dear, why is love called a riddle?

Cher. Because, being blind, he leads those that see, and, though a child, he governs a man.

Arch. Mighty well!—And why is Love pictured blind?

Cher. Because the painters out of the weakness or

privilege of their art chose to hide those eyes that they could not draw.

Arch. That's my dear little scholar, kiss me again. —And why should Love, that's a child, govern a man?

Cher. Because that a child is the end of love.

Arch. And so ends Love's catechism.—And now, my dear, we'll go in and make my master's bed.

Cher. Hold, hold, Mr. Martin! You have taken a great deal of pains to instruct me, and, what d'ye think I have learned by it?

Arch. What?

Cher. That your discourse and your habit are contradictions, and it would be nonsense in me to believe you a footman any longer.

Arch. 'Oons, what a witch it is!

Cher. Depend upon this, sir, nothing in this garb shall ever tempt me; for, though I was born to servitude, I hate it. Own your condition, swear you love me, and then—

Arch. And then we shall go make the bed?

Cher. Yes.

Arch. You must know then, that I am born a gentleman, my education was liberal; but I went to London, a younger brother, fell into the hands of sharpers, who stripped me of my money, my friends disowned me, and now my necessity brings me to what you see.

Cher. Then take my hand—promise to marry me before you sleep, and I'll make you master of two thousand pounds.

Arch. How!

Cher. Two thousand pounds that I have this

minute in my own custody ; so, throw off your livery this instant, and I'll go find a parson.

Arch. What said you ? a parson !

Cher. What ! do you scruple ?

Arch. Scruple ! no, no, but—Two thousand pound, you say ?

Cher. And better.

Arch. [*Aside.*] 'Sdeath, what shall I do ?—[*Aloud.*] But heark'ee, child, what need you make me master of yourself and money, when you may have the same pleasure out of me, and still keep your fortune in your hands.

Cher. Then you won't marry me ?

Arch. I would marry you, but—

Cher. O, sweet sir, I'm your humble servant, you're fairly caught ! Would you persuade me that any gentleman who could bear the scandal of wearing a livery would refuse two thousand pound, let the condition be what it would ? no, no, sir. But I hope you'll pardon the freedom I have taken, since it was only to inform myself of the respect that I ought to pay you.

Arch. [*Aside.*] Fairly bit, by Jupiter !—[*Aloud.*] Hold ! hold !—And have you actually two thousand pounds ?

Cher. Sir, I have my secrets as well as you ; when you please to be more open I shall be more free, and be assured that I have discoveries that will match yours, be what they will. In the meanwhile, be satisfied that no discovery I make shall ever hurt you ; but beware of my father ! [*Exit.*

Arch. So ! we're like to have as many adventures in our inn as Don Quixote had in his. Let me see

—two thousand pounds—if the wench would promise to die when the money were spent, egad, one would marry her; but the fortune may go off in a year or two, and the wife may live—Lord knows how long. Then an innkeeper's daughter; ay, that's the devil— there my pride brings me off.

> For whatsoe'er the sages charge on pride,
> The angels' fall, and twenty faults beside,
> On earth, I'm sure, 'mong us of mortal calling,
> Pride saves man oft, and woman too from falling.

[*Exit.*

ACT III.

SCENE I.

The Gallery in Lady BOUNTIFUL'S *House.*

Enter Mrs. SULLEN *and* DORINDA.

Mrs. Sul. Ha! ha! ha! my dear sister, let me embrace thee! now we are friends indeed; for I shall have a secret of yours as a pledge for mine—now you'll be good for something, I shall have you conversable in the subjects of the sex.

Dor. But do you think that I am so weak as to fall in love with a fellow at first sight?

Mrs. Sul. Psha! now you spoil all; why should not we be as free in our friendships as the men? I warrant you the gentleman has got to his confidant already, has avowed his passion, toasted your health, called you ten thousand angels, has run over your lips, eyes, neck, shape, air, and everything in a description that warms their mirth to a second enjoyment.

Dor. Your hand, sister, I an't well.

Mrs. Sul. So—she's breeding already—come, child, up with it—hem a little—so—now tell me, don't you like the gentleman that we saw at church just now?

Dor. The man's well enough.

Mrs. Sul. Well enough! is he not a demigod, a Narcissus, a star, the man i' the moon?

Dor. O sister, I'm extremely ill !

Mrs. Sul. Shall I send to your mother, child, for a little of her cephalic plaster to put to the soles of your feet, or shall I send to the gentleman for something for you ? Come, unlace your stays, unbosom yourself. The man is perfectly a pretty fellow, I saw him when he first came into church.

Dor. I saw him too, sister, and with an air that shone, methought, like rays about his person.

Mrs. Sul. Well said, up with it !

Dor. No forward coquette behaviour, no airs to set him off, no studied looks nor artful posture,—but nature did it all—

Mrs. Sul. Better and better !—one touch more— come !

Dor. But then his looks—did you observe his eyes ?

Mrs. Sul. Yes, yes, I did.—His eyes, well, what of his eyes ?

Dor. Sprightly, but not wandering ; they seemed to view, but never gazed on anything but me.—And then his looks so humble were, and yet so noble, that they aimed to tell me that he could with pride die at my feet, though he scorned slavery anywhere else.

Mrs. Sul. The physic works purely !—How d'ye find yourself now, my dear ?

Dor. Hem ! much better, my dear.—Oh, here comes our Mercury !

Enter SCRUB.

Well, Scrub, what news of the gentleman ?

Scrub. Madam, I have brought you a packet of news.

Dor. Open it quickly, come.

Scrub. In the first place I inquired who the gentleman was; they told me he was a stranger. Secondly, I asked what the gentleman was; they answered and said, that they never saw him before. Thirdly, I inquired what countryman he was; they replied, 'twas more than they knew. Fourthly, I demanded whence he came; their answer was, they could not tell. And fifthly, I asked whither he went; and they replied, they knew nothing of the matter,—and this is all I could learn.

Mrs. Sul. But what do the people say? can't they guess?

Scrub. Why, some think he's a spy, some guess he's a mountebank, some say one thing, some another; but for my own part, I believe he's a Jesuit.

Dor. A Jesuit! why a Jesuit?

Scrub. Because he keeps his horses always ready saddled, and his footman talks French.

Mrs. Sul. His footman!

Scrub. Ay, he and the count's footman were gabbering French like two intriguing ducks in a mill-pond; and I believe they talked of me, for they laughed consumedly.

Dor. What sort of livery has the footman?

Scrub. Livery! Lord, madam, I took him for a captain, he's so bedizened with lace! And then he has tops on his shoes up to his mid leg, a silver-headed cane dangling at his knuckles; he carries his hands in his pockets just so—[*Walks about foppishly*] and has a fine long periwig tied up in a bag.—Lord, madam, he's clear another sort of man than I!

Mrs. Sul. That may easily be.—But what shall we do now, sister?

Dor. I have it—this fellow has a world of simplicity, and some cunning, the first hides the latter by abundance.—Scrub!

Scrub. Madam!

Dor. We have a great mind to know who this gentleman is, only for our satisfaction.

Scrub. Yes, madam, it would be a satisfaction, no doubt.

Dor. You must go and get acquainted with his footman, and invite him hither to drink a bottle of your ale because you're butler to-day.

Scrub. Yes, madam, I am butler every Sunday.

Mrs. Sul. O brave! sister, o' my conscience, you understand the mathematics already. 'Tis the best plot in the world; your mother, you know, will be gone to church, my spouse will be got to the ale-house with his scoundrels, and the house will be our own—so we drop in by accident, and ask the fellow some questions ourselves. In the country, you know, any stranger is company, and we're glad to take up with the butler in a country-dance and happy if he'll do us the favour.

Scrub. O madam, you wrong me! I never refused your ladyship the favour in my life.

Enter GIPSY.

Gip. Ladies, dinner's upon table.

Dor. Scrub, we'll excuse your waiting—go where we ordered you.

Scrub. I shall. [*Exeunt.*

SCENE II.

A Room in BONIFACE'S *Inn.*

AIMWELL *and* ARCHER *discovered.*

Arch. Well, Tom, I find you're a marksman.

Aim. A marksman! who so blind could be, as not discern a swan among the ravens?

Arch. Well, but hark'ee, Aimwell!

Aim. Aimwell! call me Oroondates, Cesario, Amadis, all that romance can in a lover paint, and then I'll answer. O Archer! I read her thousands in her looks, she looked like Ceres in her harvest: corn, wine and oil, milk and honey, gardens, groves, and purling streams played on her plenteous face.

Arch. Her face! her pocket, you mean; the corn, wine and oil, lies there. In short, she has ten thousand pound, that's the English on't.

Aim. Her eyes —

Arch. Are demi-canons, to be sure; so I won't stand their battery. [*Going.*

Aim. Pray excuse me, my passion must have vent.

Arch. Passion! what a plague, d'ye think these romantic airs will do our business? Were my temper as extravagant as yours, my adventures have something more romantic by half.

Aim. Your adventures!

Arch. Yes,

The nymph that with her twice ten hundred pounds,
With brazen engine hot, and quoif clear starched,
Can fire the guest in warming of the bed—
There's a touch of sublime Milton for you, and the

subject but an inn-keeper's daughter ! I can play with a girl as an angler does with his fish ; he keeps it at the end of his line, runs it up the stream, and down the stream, till at last he brings it to hand, tickles the trout, and so whips it into his basket.

Enter BONIFACE.

Bon. Mr. Martin, as the saying is—yonder's an honest fellow below, my Lady Bountiful's butler, who begs the honour that you would go home with him and see his cellar.

Arch. Do my *baise-mains* to the gentleman, and tell him I will do myself the honour to wait on him immediately.   [*Exit* BONIFACE.

Aim. What do I hear?
Soft Orpheus play, and fair Toftida* sing !

Arch. Psha ! damn your raptures ; I tell you, here's a pump going to be put into the vessel, and the ship will get into harbour, my life on't. You say, there's another lady very handsome there ?

Aim. Yes, faith.

Arch. I'm in love with her already.

Aim. Can't you give me a bill upon Cherry in the meantime ?

Arch. No, no, friend, all her corn, wine and oil, is ingrossed to my market. And once more I warn you, to keep your anchorage clear of mine ; for if you fall foul of me, by this light you shall go to the bottom ! What ! make prize of my little frigate, while I am upon the cruise for you !—

Aim. Well, well, I won't.—   [*Exit* ARCHER.

---

* Mrs. Tofts, the most famous English songstress of the day.

Re-enter BONIFACE.

Landlord, have you any tolerable company in the house, I don't care for dining alone?

Bon. Yes, sir, there's a captain below, as the saying is, that arrived about an hour ago.

Aim. Gentlemen of his coat are welcome everywhere; will you make him a compliment from me, and tell him I should be glad of his company?

Bon. Who shall I tell him, sir, would—

Aim. [*Aside.*] Ha! that stroke was well thrown in! —[*Aloud.*] I'm only a traveller like himself, and would be glad of his company, that's all.

Bon. I obey your commands, as the saying is.

[*Exit.*

Re-enter ARCHER.

Arch. 'Sdeath! I had forgot; what title will you give yourself?

Aim. My brother's, to be sure; he would never give me anything else, so I'll make bold with his honour this bout!—you know the rest of your cue.

Arch. Ay, ay.   [*Exit.*

Enter GIBBET.

Gib. Sir, I'm yours.

Aim. 'Tis more than I deserve, sir, for I don't know you.

Gib. I don't wonder at that, sir, for you never saw me before—[*Aside*] I hope.

Aim. And pray, sir, how came I by the honour of seeing you now?

Gib. Sir, I scorn to intrude upon any gentleman— but my landlord—

Aim. O sir, I ask your pardon, you're the captain he told me of?

Gib. At your service, sir.

Aim. What regiment, may I be so bold?

Gib. A marching regiment, sir, an old corps.

Aim. [*Aside.*] Very old, if your coat be regimental. —[*Aloud.*] You have served abroad, sir?

Gib. Yes, sir, in the plantations; 'twas my lot to be sent into the worst service. I would have quitted it indeed, but a man of honour, you know.—Besides, 'twas for the good of my country that I should be abroad:—anything for the good of one's country— I'm a Roman for that.

Aim. [*Aside.*] One of the first; I'll lay my life. [*Aloud.*] You found the West Indies very hot, sir?

Gib. Ay, sir, too hot for me.

Aim. Pray, sir, han't I seen your face at Wills' coffee-house?

Gib. Yes, sir, and at White's too.

Aim. And where is your company now, captain?

Gib. They han't come yet.

Aim. Why, d'ye expect 'em here?

Gib. They'll be here to-night, sir.

Aim. Which way do they march?

Gib. Across the country.—[*Aside.*] The devil's in't, if I han't said enough to 'encourage him to declare! But I'm afraid he's not right, I must tack about.

Aim. Is your company to quarter in Lichfield?

Gib. In this house, sir.

Aim. What! all?

Gib. My company's but thin, ha! ha! ha! we are but three, ha! ha! ha!

Aim. You're merry, sir.

Gib. Ay, sir, you must excuse me, sir, I understand the world, especially the art of travelling: I don't care, sir, for answering questions directly upon the road—for I generally ride with a charge about me.

Aim. Three or four, I believe.　　　　*[Aside.*

Gib. I am credibly informed that there are highwaymen upon this quarter, not, sir, that I could suspect a gentleman of your figure—but truly, sir, I have got such a way of evasion upon the road, that I don't care for speaking truth to any man.

Aim. [*Aside.*] Your caution may be necessary.—[*Aloud.*] Then I presume you're no captain?

Gib. Not I, sir, captain is a good travelling name, and so I take it; it stops a great many foolish inquiries that are generally made about gentlemen that travel, it gives a man an air of something, and makes the drawers obedient:—and thus far I am a captain, and no farther.

Aim. And pray, sir, what is your true profession?

Gib. O sir, you must excuse me!—upon my word, sir, I don't think it safe to tell ye.

Aim. Ha! ha! ha! upon my word, I commend you.

Re-enter BONIFACE.

Well, Mr. Boniface, what's the news?

Bon. There's another gentleman below, as the saying is, that hearing you were but two, would be glad to make the third man, if you would give him leave.

Aim. What is he?

Bon. A clergyman, as the saying is.

Aim. A clergyman! is he really a clergyman? or is it only his travelling name, as my friend the captain has it?

Bon. O sir, he's a priest, and chaplain to the French officers in town.

Aim. Is he a Frenchman?

Bon. Yes, sir, born at Brussels.

Gib. A Frenchman, and a priest! I won't be seen in his company, sir; I have a value for my reputation, sir.

Aim. Nay, but, captain, since we are by ourselves—can he speak English, landlord?

Bon. Very well, sir; you may know him, as the saying is, to be a foreigner by his accent, and that's all.

Aim. Then he has been in England before?

Bon. Never, sir; but he's a master of languages, as the saying is; he talks Latin—it does me good to hear him talk Latin.

Aim. Then you understand Latin, Mr. Boniface?

Bon. Not I, sir, as the saying is; but he talks it so very fast, that I'm sure it must be good.

Aim. Pray, desire him to walk up.

Bon. Here he is, as the saying is.

Enter FOIGARD.

Foi. Saave you, gentlemens, bote.

Aim. [*Aside.*] A Frenchman!—[*To* FOIGARD.] Sir, your most humble servant.

Foi. Och, dear joy, I am your most faithful shervant, and yours alsho.

Gib. Doctor, you talk very good English, but you have a mighty twang of the foreigner.

Foi. My English is very vell for the vords, but we foreigners, you know, cannot bring our tongues about the pronunciation so soon.

Aim. [*Aside.*] A foreigner! a downright Teague, by this light!—[*Aloud.*] Were you born in France, doctor?

Foi. I was educated in France, but I was borned at Brussels; I am a subject of the King of Spain, joy.

Gib. What King of Spain, sir? speak!

Foi. Upon my shoul, joy, I cannot tell you as yet.

Aim. Nay, captain, that was too hard upon the doctor, he's a stranger.

Foi. Oh, let him alone, dear joy, I am of a nation that is not easily put out of countenance.

Aim. Come, gentlemen, I'll end the dispute.— Here, landlord, is dinner ready?

Bon. Upon the table, as the saying is.

Aim. Gentlemen—pray—that door—

Foi. No, no, fait, the captain must lead.

Aim. No, doctor, the church is our guide.

Gib. Ay, ay, so it is.   [*Exit, the others following.*

SCENE III.

The Gallery in Lady BOUNTIFUL'S *House.*

Enter ARCHER *and* SCRUB *singing, and hugging one another, the latter with a tankard in his hand.* GIPSY *listening behind.*

Scrub. Tall, all, dall!—Come, my dear boy, let's have that song once more.

Arch. No, no, we shall disturb the family.—But will you be sure to keep the secret?

Scrub. Pho! upon my honour, as I'm a gentleman.

Arch. 'Tis enough. You must know then, that my master is the Lord Viscount Aimwell; he fought a duel t'other day in London, wounded his man so dangerously, that he thinks fit to withdraw till he hears whether the gentleman's wounds be mortal or not. He never was in this part of England before, so he chose to retire to this place, that's all.

Gip. And that's enough for me.   [*Exit.*

Scrub. And where were you when your master fought?

Arch. We never know of our masters' quarrels.

Scrub. No! if our masters in the country here receive a challenge, the first thing they do is to tell their wives; the wife tells the servants, the servants alarm the tenants, and in half an hour you shall have the whole county in arms.

Arch. To hinder two men from doing what they have no mind for.—But if you should chance to talk now of my business?

Scrub. Talk! ay, sir, had I not learned the knack of holding my tongue, I had never lived so long in a great family.

Arch. Ay, ay, to be sure there are secrets in all families.

Scrub. Secrets! ay;—but I'll say no more. Come, sit down, we'll make an end of our tankard: here—
                    [*Gives* ARCHER *the tankard.*

Arch. With all my heart; who knows but you and I may come to be better acquainted, eh? Here's

your ladies' healths ; you have three, I think, and
to be sure there must be secrets among 'em.

[Drinks.

Scrub. Secrets! ay, friend.—I wish I had a
friend!—

Arch. Am not I your friend? come, you and I
will be sworn brothers.

Scrub. Shall we?

Arch. From this minute. Give me a kiss :—and
now, brother Scrub—

Scrub. And now, brother Martin, I will tell you
a secret that will make your hair stand on end. You
must know that I am consumedly in love.

Arch. That's a terrible secret, that's the truth on't.

Scrub. That jade, Gipsy, that was with us just now
in the cellar, is the arrantest whore that ever wore a
petticoat; and I'm dying for love of her.

Arch. Ha! ha! ha!—Are you in love with her
person or her virtue, brother Scrub?

Scrub. I should like virtue best, because it is
more durable than beauty; for virtue holds good
with some women long, and many a day after they
have lost it.

Arch. In the country, I grant ye, where no women's
virtue is lost till a bastard be found.

Scrub. Ay, could I bring her to a bastard, I
should have her all to myself; but I dare not put
it upon that lay, for fear of being sent for a soldier.
Pray, brother, how do you gentlemen in London like
that same Pressing Act?[1]

---

[1] The Impressment Acts passed in Queen Anne's reign had some
rather curious provisions. Criminals were allowed to join the army
before their sentences were run out, receiving thus a sort of ticket-

Arch. Very ill, brother Scrub; 'tis the worst that ever was made for us. Formerly I remember the good days, when we could dun our masters for our wages, and if they refused to pay us, we could have a warrant to carry 'em before a justice : but now if we talk of eating, they have a warrant for us, and carry us before three justices.

Scrub. And to be sure we go, if we talk of eating ; for the justices won't give their own servants a bad example. Now this is my misfortune—I dare not speak in the house, while that jade Gipsy dings about like a fury.—Once I had the better end of the staff.

Arch. And how comes the change now ?

Scrub. Why, the mother of all this mischief is a priest !

Arch. A priest !

Scrub. Ay, a damned son of a whore of Babylon, that came over hither to say grace to the French officers, and eat up our provisions. There's not a day goes over his head without a dinner or supper in this house.

Arch. How came he so familiar in the family ?

Scrub. Because he speaks English as if he had lived here all his life, and tells lies as if he had been a traveller from his cradle.

Arch. And this priest, I'm afraid, has converted the affections of your Gipsy.

Scrub. Converted ! ay, and perverted, my dear friend : for, I'm afraid, he has made her a whore

of-leave. Persons having no apparent means of livelihood were liable to be impressed, and we see from the instances given in the text that the law was sometimes applied in very lax fashion.

and a papist! But this is not all; there's the French count and Mrs. Sullen, they're in the confederacy, and for some private ends of their own, to be sure.

Arch. A very hopeful family yours, brother Scrub! I suppose the maiden lady has her lover too?

Scrub. Not that I know! She's the best on 'em, that's the truth on't: but they take care to prevent my curiosity, by giving me so much business, that I'm a perfect slave. What d'ye think is my place in this family?

Arch. Butler, I suppose.

Scrub. Ah, Lord help you! I'll tell you. Of a Monday I drive the coach, of a Tuesday I drive the plough, on Wednesday I follow the hounds, a Thursday I dun the tenants, on Friday I go to market, on Saturday I draw warrants, and a Sunday I draw beer.

Arch. Ha! ha! ha! if variety be a pleasure in life, you have enough on't, my dear brother.

Enter MRS. SULLEN *and* DORINDA.

But what ladies are those?

Scrub. Ours, ours; that upon the right hand is Mrs. Sullen, and the other is Mrs. Dorinda. Don't mind 'em, sit still, man.

Mrs. Sul. I have heard my brother talk of my Lord Aimwell; but they say that his brother is the finer gentleman.

Dor. That's impossible, sister.

Mrs. Sul. He's vastly rich, but very close, they say.

Dor. No matter for that; if I can creep into his

heart, I'll open his breast, I warrant him: I have heard say, that people may be guessed at by the behaviour of their servants; I could wish we might talk to that fellow.

Mrs. Sul. So do I; for I think he's a very pretty fellow. Come this way, I'll throw out a lure for him presently.

> [DORINDA *and* Mrs. SULLEN *walk towards the opposite side of the stage.*

Arch. [*Aside.*] Corn, wine, and oil indeed!—But I think the wife has the greatest plenty of flesh and blood; she should be my choice.—Ay, ay, say you so!—[Mrs. SULLEN *drops her glove, which he picks up and presents to her.*] Madam—your ladyship's glove.

Mrs. Sul. O sir, I thank you!—[*To* DORINDA.] What a handsome bow the fellow has!

Dor. Bow! why I have known several footmen come down from London set up here for dancing-master, and carry off the best fortunes in the country.

Arch. [*Aside.*] That project, for aught I know, had been better than ours.—[*To* SCRUB.] Brother Scrub, why don't you introduce me?

Scrub. Ladies, this is the strange gentleman's servant that you see at church to-day; I understood he came from London, and so I invited him to the cellar, that he might show me the newest flourish in whetting my knives.

Dor. And I hope you have made much of him?

Arch. O yes, madam, but the strength of your ladyship's liquor is a little too potent for the constitution of your humble servant.

Mrs. Sul. What then, you don't usually drink ale?

Arch. No, madam; my constant drink is tea, or a

little wine and water. 'Tis prescribed me by the physician for a remedy against the spleen.

Scrub. O la! O la! a footman have the spleen!

Mrs. Sul. I thought that distemper had been only proper to people of quality?

Arch. Madam, like all other fashions it wears out, and so descends to their servants; though in a great many of us, I believe, it proceeds from some melancholy particles in the blood, occasioned by the stagnation of wages.

Dor. [*Aside to* Mrs. SULLEN.] How affectedly the fellow talks!—[*To* ARCHER.] How long, pray, have you served your present master?

Arch. Not long; my life has been mostly spent in the service of the ladies.

Mrs. Sul. And pray, which service do you like best?

Arch. Madam, the ladies pay best; the honour of serving them is sufficient wages; there is a charm in their looks that delivers a pleasure with their commands, and gives our duty the wings of inclination.

Mrs. Sul. [*Aside.*] That flight was above the pitch of a livery.—[*Aloud.*] And, sir, would not you be satisfied to serve a lady again?

Arch. As a groom of the chamber, madam, but not as a footman.

Mrs. Sul. I suppose you served as footman before?

Arch. For that reason I would not serve in that post again; for my memory is too weak for the load of messages that the ladies lay upon their servants in London. My Lady Howd'ye, the last mistress I served, called me up one morning, and told me, Martin, go to my Lady Allnight with my humble

service ; tell her I was to wait on her ladyship yesterday, and left word with Mrs. Rebecca, that the pre-
liminaries of the affair she knows of are stopped till
we know the concurrence of the person that I know
of, for which there are circumstances wanting which
we shall accommodate at the old place ; but that in
the meantime there is a person about her ladyship,
that from several hints and surmises, was accessory at
a certain time to the disappointments that naturally
attend things, that to her knowledge are of more
importance—

Mrs. Sul. Dor. Ha ! ha ! ha ! where are you
going, sir ?

Arch. Why, I han't half done !—The whole howd'ye
was about half an hour long ; so I happened to mis-
place two syllables, and was turned off, and rendered
incapable.

Dor. [*Aside to* Mrs. SULLEN.] The pleasantest
fellow, sister, I ever saw !—[*To* ARCHER.] But, friend,
if your master be married, I presume you still serve
a lady ?

Arch. No, madam, I take care never to come into
a married family ; the commands of the master and
mistress are always so contrary, that 'tis impossible to
please both.

Dor. There's a main point gained : my lord is not
married, I find. [*Aside.*

Mrs. Sul. But I wonder, friend, that in so many
good services, you had not a better provision made
for you.

Arch. I don't know how, madam. I had a
lieutenancy offered me three or four times ; but that
is not bread, madam—I live much better as I do.

Scrub. Madam, he sings rarely! I was thought to
do pretty well here in the country till he came; but
alack a day, I'm nothing to my brother Martin!

Dor. Does he?—Pray, sir, will you oblige us with
a song?

Arch. Are you for passion or humour?

Scrub. O le! he has the purest ballad about a
trifle—

Mrs Sul. A trifle! pray, sir, let's have it.

Arch. I'm ashamed to offer you a trifle, madam;
but since you command me—   [*Sings.*

> A trifling song you shall hear,
> Begun with a trifle and ended :
> All trifling people draw near,
> And I shall be nobly attended.
>
> Were it not for trifles, a few,
> That lately have come into play ;
> The men would want something to do,
> And the women want something to say.
>
> What makes men trifle in dressing ?
> Because the ladies (they know)
> Admire, by often possessing,
> That eminent trifle a beau.
>
> When the lover his moments has trifled,
> The trifle of trifles to gain :
> No sooner the virgin is rifled,
> But a trifle shall part 'em again.
>
> What mortal man would be able
> At White's half-an-hour to sit ?
> Or who could bear a tea-table,
> Without talking of trifles for wit ?

The court is from trifles secure,
Gold keys are no trifles, we see !
White rods are no trifles, I'm sure,
Whatever their bearers may be.

But if you will go to the place,
Where trifles abundantly breed,
The levee will show you his grace
Makes promises trifles indeed.

A coach with six footmen behind,
I count neither trifle nor sin :
But, ye gods ! how oft do we find
A scandalous trifle within.

A flask of champagne, people think it
A trifle, or something as bad :
But if you'll contrive how to drink it,
You'll find it no trifle, egad !

A parson's a trifle at sea,
A widow's a trifle in sorrow :
A peace is a trifle to-day,
Who knows what may happen to-morrow !

A black coat a trifle may cloke,
Or to hide it, the red may endeavour :
But if once the army is broke,
We shall have more trifles than ever.

The stage is a trifle, they say,
The reason, pray carry along,
Because at every new play,
The house they with trifles so throng.

But with people's malice to trifle,
And to set us all on a foot:
The author of this is a trifle,
And his song is a trifle to boot.

Mrs. Sul. Very well, sir, we're obliged to you.— Something for a pair of gloves. [*Offering him money.*

Arch. I humbly beg leave to be excused: my master, madam, pays me; nor dare I take money from any other hand, without injuring his honour, and disobeying his commands.   [*Exit with* SCRUB.

Dor. This is surprising! Did you ever see so pretty a well-bred fellow?

Mrs. Sul. The devil take him for wearing that livery!

Dor. I fancy, sister, he may be some gentleman, a friend of my lord's, that his lordship has pitched upon for his courage, fidelity, and discretion, to bear him company in this dress, and who ten to one was his second too.

Mrs. Sul. It is so, it must be so, and it shall be so!—for I like him.

Dor. What! better than the count?

Mrs. Sul. The count happened to be the most agreeable man upon the place; and so I chose him to serve me in my design upon my husband. But I should like this fellow better in a design upon myself.

Dor. But now, sister, for an interview with this lord and this gentleman; how shall we bring that about?

Mrs. Sul. Patience! you country ladies give no quarter if once you be entered. Would you prevent

their desires, and give the fellows no wishing-time?
Look'ee, Dorinda, if my Lord Aimwell loves you or
deserves you, he'll find a way to see you, and there
we must leave it.   My business comes now upon the
tapis.   Have you prepared your brother?

Dor. Yes, yes.

Mrs. Sul. And how did he relish it?

Dor. He said little, mumbled something to himself, promised to be guided by me—but here he
comes.

Enter Squire SULLEN.

Squire Sul. What singing was that I heard just now?

Mrs. Sul. The singing in your head, my dear, you
complained of it all day.

Squire Sul. You're impertinent.

Mrs. Sul. I was ever so, since I became one flesh
with you.

Squire Sul. One flesh! rather two carcasses joined
unnaturally together.

Mrs. Sul. Or rather a living soul coupled to a
dead body.

Dor. So, this is fine encouragement for me!

Squire Sul. Yes, my wife shows you what you
must do.

Mrs. Sul. And my husband shows you what you
must suffer.

Squire Sul. 'Sdeath, why can't you be silent?

Mrs. Sul. 'Sdeath, why can't you talk?

Squire Sul. Do you talk to any purpose?

Mrs. Sul. Do you think to any purpose?

Squire Sul. Sister, heark'ee!—[*Whispers.*] I shan't
be home till it be late.   [*Exit.*

Mrs. Sul. What did he whisper to ye?

Dor. That he would go round the back way, come into the closet, and listen as I directed him. But let me beg you once more, dear sister, to drop this project; for as I told you before, instead of awaking him to kindness, you may provoke him to a rage; and then who knows how far his brutality may carry him?

Mrs. Sul. I'm provided to receive him, I warrant you. But here comes the count, vanish!

[*Exit* DORINDA.

Enter Count BELLAIR.

Don't you wonder, monsieur le comte, that I was not at church this afternoon?

Count Bel. I more wonder, madam, that you go dere at all, or how you dare to lift those eyes to heaven that are guilty of so much killing.

Mrs. Sul. If Heaven, sir, has given to my eyes with the power of killing the virtue of making a cure, I hope the one may atone for the other.

Count Bel. Oh, largely, madam, would your ladyship be as ready to apply the remedy as to give the wound. Consider, madam, I am doubly a prisoner; first to the arms of your general, then to your more conquering eyes. My first chains are easy, there a ransom may redeem me, but from your fetters I never shall get free.

Mrs. Sul. Alas, sir! why should you complain to me of your captivity, who am in chains myself? You know, sir, that I am bound, nay, must be tied up in that particular that might give you ease: I am like you, a prisoner of war,—of war, indeed—I have given my parole of honour; would you break yours to gain your liberty?

Count Bel. Most certainly I would, were I a prisoner among the Turks; dis is your case, you're a slave, madam, slave to the worst of Turks, a husband.

Mrs. Sul. There lies my foible, I confess; no fortifications, no courage, conduct, nor vigilancy, can pretend to defend a place, where the cruelty of the governor forces the garrison to mutiny.

Count Bel. And where de besieger is resolved to die before de place.—Here will I fix;—[*Kneels*] with tears, vows, and prayers assault your heart and never rise till you surrender; or if I must storm—Love and St. Michael!—And so I begin the attack.

Mrs. Sul. Stand off!—[*Aside.*] Sure he hears me not!—And I could almost wish—he did not!—The fellow makes love very prettily.—[*Aloud.*] But, sir, why should you put such a value upon my person, when you see it despised by one that knows it so much better?

Count Bel. He knows it not, though he possesses it; if he but knew the value of the jewel he is master of, he would always wear it next his heart, and sleep with it in his arms.

Mrs. Sul. But since he throws me unregarded from him—

Count Bel. And one that knows your value well comes by and takes you up, is not justice?

[*Goes to lay hold of her.*

Enter Squire SULLEN *with his sword drawn.*

Squire Sul. Hold, villain, hold!

Mrs. Sul. [*Presenting a pistol.*] Do you hold!

Squire Sul. What ! murder your husband, to defend your bully !

Mrs. Sul. Bully ! for shame, Mr. Sullen, bullies wear long swords, the gentleman has none, he's a prisoner, you know. I was aware of your outrage, and prepared this to receive your violence ; and, if occasion were, to preserve myself against the force of this other gentleman.

Count Bel. O madam, your eyes be bettre firearms than your pistol ; they nevre miss.

Squire Sul. What ! court my wife to my face !

Mrs. Sul. Pray, Mr. Sullen, put up ; suspend your fury for a minute.

Squire Sul. To give you time to invent an excuse !

Mrs. Sul. I need none.

Squire Sul. No, for I heard every syllable of your discourse.

Count Bel. Ah ! and begar, I tink the dialogue was vera pretty.

Mrs. Sul. Then I suppose, sir, you heard something of your own barbarity ?

Squire Sul. Barbarity ! oons, what does the woman call barbarity ? do I ever meddle with you ?

Mrs. Sul. No.

Squire Sul. As for you, sir, I shall take another time.

Count Bel. Ah, begar, and so must I.

Squire Sul. Look'ee, madam, don't think that my anger proceeds from any concern I have for your honour, but for my own, and if you can contrive any way of being a whore without making me a cuckold, do it and welcome.

Mrs. Sul. Sir, I thank you kindly, you would

allow me the sin but rob me of the pleasure. No, no, I'm resolved never to venture upon the crime without the satisfaction of seeing you punished for't.

Squire Sul. Then will you grant me this, my dear? Let anybody else do you the favour but that Frenchman, for I mortally hate his whole generation. [*Exit.*

Count Bel. Ah, sir, that be ungrateful, for begar, I love some of yours, madam— [*Approaching her.*

Mrs. Sul. No, sir.

Count Bel. No, sir: garzoon, madam, I am not your husband.

Mrs. Sul. 'Tis time to undeceive you, sir. I believed your addresses to me were no more than an amusement, and I hope you will think the same of my complaisance; and to convince you that you ought, you must know, that I brought you hither only to make you instrumental in setting me right with my husband, for he was planted to listen by my appointment.

Count Bel. By your appointment?

Mrs. Sul. Certainly.

Count Bel. And so, madam, while I was telling twenty stories to part you from your husband, begar, I was bringing you together all the while?

Mrs. Sul. I ask your pardon, sir, but I hope this will give you a taste of the virtue of the English ladies.

Count Bel. Begar, madam, your virtue be vera great, but garzoon, your honeste be vera little.

Re-enter DORINDA.

Mrs. Sul. Nay, now, you're angry, sir.

Count Bel. Angry!—*Fair Dorinda* [*Sings and ad-*

dresses DORINDA.] Madam, when your ladyship want a fool, send for me. *Fair Dorinda, Revenge, &c.*

[*Exit singing.*

Mrs. Sul. There goes the true humour of his nation —resentment with good manners, and the height of anger in a song! Well, sister, you must be judge, for you have heard the trial.

Dor. And I bring in my brother guilty.

Mrs. Sul. But I must bear the punishment. 'Tis hard, sister.

Dor. I own it ; but you must have patience.

Mrs. Sul. Patience! the cant of custom—Providence sends no evil without a remedy. Should I lie groaning under a yoke I can shake off, I were accessary to my ruin, and my patience were no better than self-murder.

Dor. But how can you shake off the yoke? your divisions don't come within the reach of the law for a divorce.

Mrs. Sul. Law! what law can search into the remote abyss of nature? what evidence can prove the unaccountable disaffections of wedlock? Can a jury sum up the endless aversions that are rooted in our souls, or can a bench 'give judgment upon antipathies?

Dor. They never pretended, sister; they never meddle, but in case of uncleanness.

Mrs. Sul. Uncleanness! O sister ! casual violation is a transient injury, and may possibly be repaired, but can radical hatreds be ever reconciled? No, no, sister, nature is the first lawgiver, and when she has set tempers opposite, not all the golden links of wedlock nor iron manacles of law can keep 'em fast.

Wedlock we own ordained by Heaven's decree,
But such as Heaven ordained it first to be ;—
Concurring tempers in the man and wife
As mutual helps to draw the load of life.
View all the works of Providence above,
The stars with harmony and concord move ;
View all the works of Providence below,
The fire, the water, earth and air, we know,
All in one plant agree to make it grow.
Must man, the chiefest work of art divine,
Be doomed in endless discord to repine ?
No, we should injure Heaven by that surmise,
Omnipotence is just, were man but wise. [*Exeunt.*

ACT IV.

SCENE I.

The Gallery in Lady BOUNTIFUL'S *House.*

Mrs. SULLEN *discovered alone.*

Mrs. Sul. Were I born an humble Turk, where women have no soul nor property, there I must sit contented. But in England, a country whose women are its glory, must women be abused ? where women rule, must women be enslaved? Nay, cheated into slavery, mocked by a promise of comfortable society into a wilderness of solitude ! I dare not keep the thought about me. Oh, here comes something to divert me.

Enter a Countrywoman.

Wom. I come, an't please your ladyship—you're my Lady Bountiful, an't ye ?

Mrs. Sul. Well, good woman, go on.

Wom. I come seventeen long mail to have a cure for my husband's sore leg.

Mrs. Sul. Your husband ! what, woman, cure your husband !

Wom. Ay, poor man, for his sore leg won't let him stir from home.

Mrs. Sul. There, I confess, you have given me a reason. Well, good woman, I'll tell you what you must do. You must lay your husband's leg upon a table, and with a chopping-knife you must lay it open as broad as you can, then you must take out the bone, and beat the flesh soundly with a rolling-pin, then take salt, pepper, cloves, mace and ginger, some sweet-herbs, and season it very well, then roll it up like brawn, and put it into the oven for two hours.

Wom. Heavens reward your ladyship!—I have two little babies too that are piteous bad with the graips, an't please ye.

Mrs. Sul. Put a little pepper and salt in their bellies, good woman.

Enter Lady BOUNTIFUL.

I beg your ladyship's pardon for taking your business out of your hands; I have been a-tampering here a little with one of your patients.

Lady Boun. Come, good woman, don't mind this mad creature; I am the person that you want, I suppose. What would you have, woman?

Mrs. Sul. She wants something for her husband's sore leg.

Lady Boun. What's the matter with his leg, goody?

Wom. It come first, as one might say, with a sort of dizziness in his foot, then he had a kind of laziness in his joints, and then his leg broke out, and then it swelled, and then it closed again, and then it broke out again, and then it festered, and then it grew better, and then it grew worse again.

Mrs. Sul. Ha! ha! ha!

Lady Boun. How can you be merry with the misfortunes of other people?

Mrs. Sul. Because my own make me sad, madam.

Lady Boun. The worst reason in the world,

daughter; your own misfortunes should teach you to pity others.

Mrs. Sul. But the woman's misfortunes and mine are nothing alike; her husband is sick, and mine, alas! is in health.

Lady Boun. What! would you wish your husband sick?

Mrs. Sul. Not of a sore leg, of all things.

Lady Boun. Well, good woman, go to the pantry, get your bellyful of victuals, then I'll give you a receipt of diet-drink for your husband. But d'ye hear, goody, you must not let your husband move too much.

Wom. No, no, madam, the poor man's inclinable enough to lie still.   [*Exit.*

Lady Boun. Well, daughter Sullen, though you laugh, I have done miracles about the country here with my receipts.

Mrs. Sul. Miracles indeed, if they have cured any-body; but I believe, madam, the patient's faith goes farther toward the miracle than your prescription.

Lady Boun. Fancy helps in some cases; but there's your husband, who has as little fancy as anybody, I brought him from death's door.

Mrs. Sul. I suppose, madam, you made him drink plentifully of ass's milk.

Enter DORINDA, *who runs to* Mrs. SULLEN.

Dor. News, dear sister! news! news!

Enter ARCHER, *running.*

Arch. Where, where is my Lady Bountiful?— Pray, which is the old lady of you three?

Lady Boun. I am.

Arch. O madam, the fame of your ladyship's charity,

goodness, benevolence, skill and ability, have drawn me hither to implore your ladyship's help in behalf of my unfortunate master, who is this moment breathing his last.

Lady Boun. Your master! where is he?

Arch. At your gate, madam. Drawn by the appearance of your handsome house to view it nearer, and walking up the avenue within five paces of the courtyard, he was taken ill of a sudden with a sort of I know not what, but down he fell, and there he lies.

Lady Boun. Here, Scrub, Gipsy, all run, get my easy-chair downstairs, put the gentleman in it, and bring him in quickly! quickly!

Arch. Heaven will reward your ladyship for this charitable act.

Lady Boun. Is your master used to these fits?

Arch. O yes, madam, frequently: I have known him have five or six of a night.

Lady Boun. What's his name?

Arch. Lord, madam, he's a-dying! a minute's care or neglect may save or destroy his life.

Lady Boun. Ah, poor gentleman!—Come, friend, show me the way; I'll see him brought in myself.

[Exit with ARCHER.

Dor. O sister, my heart flutters about strangely! I can hardly forbear running to his assistance.

Mrs. Sul. And I'll lay my life he deserves your assistance more than he wants it. Did not I tell you that my lord would find a way to come at you? Love's his distemper, and you must be the physician; put on all your charms, summon all your fire into your eyes, plant the whole artillery of your looks against his breast, and down with him.

Dor. O sister! I'm but a young gunner; I shall be afraid to shoot, for fear the piece should recoil, and hurt myself.

Mrs. Sul. Never fear, you shall see me shoot before you, if you will.

Dor. No, no, dear sister; you have missed your mark so unfortunately, that I shan't care for being instructed by you.

Enter AIMWELL, *carried in a chair by* ARCHER *and* SCRUB, *and counterfeiting a swoon :* Lady BOUNTI-FUL *and* GIPSY *following.*

Lady Boun. Here, here, let's see the hartshorn drops.—Gipsy, a glass of fair water! His fit's very strong.—Bless me, how his hands are clinched!

Arch. For shame, ladies, what d'ye do? why don't you help us?—[*To* DORINDA.] Pray, madam, take his hand, and open it, if you can, whilst I hold his head.   [DORINDA *takes his hand.*

Dor. Poor gentleman!—Oh!—he has got my hand within his. and he squeezes it unmercifully—

Lady Boun. 'Tis the violence of his convulsion, child.

Arch. Oh, madam, he's perfectly possessed in these cases—he'll bite if you don't have a care.

Dor. Oh, my hand! my hand!

Lady Boun. What's the matter with the foolish girl? I have got this hand open you see with a great deal of ease.

Arch. Ay, but, madam, your daughter's hand is somewhat warmer than your ladyship's, and the heat of it draws the force of the spirits that way.

Mrs. Sul. I find, friend, you're very learned in these sorts of fits.

Arch. 'Tis no wonder, madam, for I'm often troubled with them myself; I find myself extremely ill at this minute. [*Looking hard at* Mrs. SULLEN.

Mrs. Sul. I fancy I could find a way to cure you.

[*Aside.*

Lady Boun. His fit holds him very long.

Arch. Longer than usual, madam.—Pray, young lady, open his breast, and give him air.

Lady Boun. Where did his illness take him first, pray?

Arch. To-day, at church, madam.

Lady Boun. In what manner was he taken?

Arch. Very strangely, my lady. He was of a sudden touched with something in his eyes, which, at the first, he only felt, but could not tell whether 'twas pain or pleasure.

Lady Boun. Wind, nothing but wind!

Arch. By soft degrees it grew and mounted to his brain, there his fancy caught it; there formed it so beautiful, and dressed it up in such gay, pleasing colours, that his transported appetite seized the fair idea, and straight conveyed it to his heart. That hospitable seat of life sent all its sanguine spirits forth to meet, and opened all its sluicy gates to take the stranger in.

Lady Boun. Your master should never go without a bottle to smell to.—Oh,—he recovers!—The lavender water—some feathers to burn under his nose —Hungary water to rub his temples.—Oh, he comes to himself!—Hem a little, sir, hem.—Gipsy! bring the cordial-water. [AIMWELL *seems to awake in amaze.*

Dor. How d'ye, sir?

Aim. Where am I?　　　　　　　　　　[*Rising.*

Sure I have pass'd the gulf of silent death,
And now I land on the Elysian shore!—
Behold the goddess of those happy plains,
Fair Proserpine—
Let me adore thy bright divinity.

　　　　　　[*Kneels to* DORINDA, *and kisses her hand.*

Mrs. Sul. So, so, so! I knew where the fit would end!

Aim. Eurydice perhaps—

How could thy Orpheus keep his word,
And not look back upon thee?
No treasure but thyself could sure have bribed him
To look one minute off thee.

Lady Boun. Delirious, poor gentleman!

Arch. Very delirious, madam, very delirious.

Aim. Martin's voice, I think.

Arch. Yes, my lord.—How does your lordship?

Lady Boun. Lord! did you mind that, girls?

　　　　　　[*Aside to* Mrs. SULLEN *and* DORINDA.

Aim. Where am I?

Arch. In very good hands, sir. You were taken just now with one of your old fits, under the trees, just by this good lady's house; her ladyship had you taken in, and has miraculously brought you to yourself, as you see.

Aim. I am so confounded with shame, madam, that I can now only beg pardon; and refer my acknowledgments for your ladyship's care till an opportunity offers of making some amends. I dare be no longer troublesome.—Martin! give two guineas to the servants.　　　　　　　　　　[*Going.*

Dor. Sir, you may catch cold by going so soon into the air; you don't look, sir, as if you were perfectly recovered.

[*Here* ARCHER *talks to* Lady BOUNTIFUL *in dumb show.*

Aim. That I shall never be, madam; my present illness is so rooted that I must expect to carry it to my grave.

Mrs. Sul. Don't despair, sir; I have known several in your distemper shake it off with a fortnight's physic.

Lady Boun. Come, sir, your servant has been telling me that you're apt to relapse if you go into the air: your good manners shan't get the better of ours —you shall sit down again, sir. Come, sir, we don't mind ceremonies in the country—here, sir, my service t'ye.—You shall taste my water; 'tis a cordial I can assure you, and of my own making—drink it off, sir. —[AIMWELL *drinks.*] And how d'ye find yourself now, sir?

Aim. Somewhat better—though very faint still.

Lady Boun. Ay, ay, people are always faint after these fits.—Come, girls, you shall show the gentleman the house.—'Tis but an old family building, sir; but you had better walk about, and cool by degrees, than venture immediately into the air. You'll find some tolerable pictures.—Dorinda, show the gentleman the way. I must go to the poor woman below. [*Exit.*

Dor. This way, sir.

Aim. Ladies, shall I beg leave for my servant to wait on you, for he understands pictures very well?

Mrs. Sul. Sir, we understand originals as well as he does pictures, so he may come along.

[*Exeunt all but* SCRUB, AIMWELL *leading* DORINDA.

Enter FOIGARD.

Foi. Save you, Master Scrub!

Scrub. Sir, I won't be saved your way—I hate a priest, I abhor the French, and I defy the devil. Sir, I'm a bold Briton, and will spill the last drop of my blood to keep out popery and slavery.

Foi. Master Scrub, you would put me down in politics, and so I would be speaking with Mrs. Shipsy.

Scrub. Good Mr. Priest, you can't speak with her, she's sick, sir, she's gone abroad, sir, she's—dead two months ago, sir.

Re-enter GIPSY.

Gip. How now, impudence! how dare you talk so saucily to the doctor?—Pray, sir, don't take it ill; for the common people of England are not so civil to strangers, as—

Scrub. You lie! you lie! 'tis the common people that are civillest to strangers.

Gip. Sirrah, I have a good mind to—get you out, I say!

Scrub. I won't.

Gip. You won't, sauce-box!—Pray, doctor, what is the captain's name that came to your inn last night?

Scrub. [*Aside.*] The captain! ah, the devil, there she hampers me again; the captain has me on one side, and the priest on t'other: so between the gown and the sword, I have a fine time on't—But, *Cedunt arma togæ.*

Gip. What, sirrah, won't you march?

Scrub. No, my dear, I won't march—but I'll walk.
—[*Aside.*] And I'll make bold to listen a little too.

[*Retires behind, listening.*

Gip. Indeed, doctor, the count has been barbarously treated, that's the truth on't.

Foi. Ah, Mrs. Gipsy, upon my shoule, now, gra, his complainings would mollify the marrow in your bones, and move the bowels of your commiseration ! He veeps, and he dances, and he fistles, and he swears, and he laughs, and he stamps, and he sings : in conclusion, joy, he's afflicted *à-la-Française*, and a stranger would not know whider to cry or to laugh with him.

Gip. What would you have me do, doctor ?

Foi. Noting, joy, but only hide the count in Mrs. Sullen's closet when it is dark.

Gip. Nothing ! is that nothing ? it would be both a sin and a shame, doctor.

Foi. Here is twenty louis-d'ors, joy, for your shame ; and I will give you an absolution for the shin.

Gip. But won't that money look like a bribe ?

Foi. Dat is according as you shall tauk it. If you receive the money beforehand, 'twill be *logice*, a bribe ; but if you stay till afterwards, 'twill be only a gratification.

Gip. Well, doctor, I'll take it *logice*. But what must I do with my conscience, sir ?

Foi. Leave dat wid me, joy ; I am your priest, gra ; and your conscience is under my hands.

Gip. But should I put the count into the closet—

Foi. Vel, is dere any shin for a man's being in a closhet ? one may go to prayers in a closhet.

Gip. But if the lady should come into her chamber, and go to bed?

Foi. Vel, and is dere any shin in going to bed, joy?

Gip. Ay, but if the parties should meet, doctor?

Foi. Vel den—the parties must be responsible. Do you be after putting the count in the closhet, and leave the shins wid themselves. I will come with the count to instruct you in your chamber.

Gip. Well, doctor, your religion is so pure! Methinks I'm so easy after an absolution, and can sin afresh with so much security, that I am resolved to die a martyr to't. Here's the key of the garden door, come in the back-way when 'tis late, I'll be ready to receive you; but don't so much as whisper, only take hold of my hand; I'll lead you, and do you lead the count, and follow me.   [*Exeunt.*

Scrub. [*Coming forward.*] What witchcraft now have these two imps of the devil been a-hatching here? There's twenty louis-d'ors; I heard that, and saw the purse.—But I must give room to my betters.   [*Exit.*

Re-enter AIMWELL, *leading* DORINDA, *and making love in dumb show;* Mrs. SULLEN *and* ARCHER *following.*

Mrs. Sul. [*To* ARCHER.] Pray, sir, how d'ye like that piece?

Arch. Oh, 'tis Leda! You find, madam, how Jupiter comes disguised to make love—

Mrs. Sul. But what think you there of Alexander's battles?[1]

---

[1] Le Brun's famous pictures of the battles of Alexander the Great.

Arch. We want only a Le Brun, madam, to draw greater battles, and a greater general of our own. The Danube, madam, would make a greater figure in a picture than the Granicus; and we have our Ramilies to match their Arbela.

Mrs. Sul. Pray, sir, what head is that in the corner there?

Arch. O madam, 'tis poor Ovid in his exile.

Mrs. Sul. What was he banished for?

Arch. His ambitious love, madam.—[*Bowing.*] His misfortune touches me.

Mrs. Sul. Was he successful in his amours?

Arch. There he has left us in the dark.—He was too much a gentleman to tell.

Mrs. Sul. If he were secret, I pity him.

Arch. And if he were successful, I envy him.

Mrs. Sul. How d'ye like that Venus over the chimney?

Arch. Venus! I protest, madam, I took it for your picture; but now I look again, 'tis not handsome enough.

Mrs. Sul. Oh, what a charm is flattery! If you would see my picture there it is over that cabinet. How d'ye like it?

Arch. I must admire anything, madam, that has the least resemblance of you. But, methinks, madam —[*He looks at the picture and* Mrs. SULLEN *three or four times, by turns*] Pray, madam, who drew it?

Mrs. Sul. A famous hand, sir.

[*Here* AIMWELL *aad* DORINDA *go off.*

Arch. A famous hand, madam!—Your eyes, indeed, are featured there; but where's the sparkling moisture, shining fluid, in which they swim? The picture, in deed, has your dimples; but where's the swarm of killing Cupids that should ambush there? The lips too are figured out; but where's the carnation dew, the pouting ripeness, that tempts the taste in the original?

Mrs. Sul. Had it been my lot to have matched with such a man! [*Aside.*

Arch. Your breasts too—presumptuous man! what, paint Heaven!—Apropos, madam, in the very next picture is Salmoneus, that was struck dead with lightning, for offering to imitate Jove's thunder; I hope you served the painter so, madam?

Mrs. Sul. Had my eyes the power of thunder, they should employ their lightning better.

Arch. There's the finest bed in that room, madam! I suppose 'tis your ladyship's bedchamber.

Mrs. Sul. And what then, sir?

Arch. I think the quilt is the richest that ever I saw. I can't at this distance, madam, distinguish the figures of the embroidery; will you give me leave, madam? [*Goes into the chamber.*

Mrs. Sul. The devil take his impudence!—Sure, if I give him an opportunity, he durst not offer it?— I have a great mind to try.—[*Goes in after* ARCHER, *but returns hastily.*] 'Sdeath, what am I doing?— And alone, too!—Sister! sister! [*Runs out.*

Arch. [*Coming out.*] I'll follow her close—
For where a Frenchman durst attempt to <u>storm,</u>
A Briton sure may well the work perform.

[*Going.*

Re-enter SCRUB.

Scrub. Martin! brother Martin!

Arch. O brother Scrub, I beg your pardon, I was not a-going: here's a guinea my master ordered you.

Scrub. A guinea! hi! hi! hi! a guinea! eh—by this light it is a guinea! But I suppose you expect one and twenty shillings in change?

Arch. Not at all; I have another for Gipsy.

Scrub. A guinea for her! faggot and fire for the witch! Sir, give me that guinea, and I'll discover a plot.

Arch. A plot!

Scrub. Ay, sir, a plot, a horrid plot! First, it must be a plot, because there's a woman in't: secondly, it must be a plot, because there's a priest in't : thirdly, it must be a plot, because there's French gold in't : and fourthly, it must be a plot, because I don't know what to make on't.

Arch. Nor anybody else, I'm afraid, brother Scrub.

Scrub. Truly, I'm afraid so too; for where there's a priest and a woman, there's always a mystery and a riddle. This, I know, that here has been the doctor with a temptation in one hand and an absolution in the other, and Gipsy has sold herself to the devil; I saw the price paid down, my eyes shall take their oath on't.

Arch. And is all this bustle about Gipsy?

Scrub. That's not all; I could hear but a word here and there; but I remember they mentioned a count, a closet, a back-door, and a key.

Arch. The count!—Did you hear nothing of Mrs. Sullen?

Scrub. I did hear some word that sounded that way; but whether it was Sullen or Dorinda, I could not distinguish.

Arch. You have told this matter to nobody, brother?

Scrub. Told! no, sir, I thank you for that; I'm resolved never to speak one word *pro* nor *con*, till we have a peace.

Arch. You're i' the right, brother Scrub. Here's a treaty a foot between the count and the lady: the priest and the chambermaid are the plenipotentiaries. It shall go hard but I find a way to be included in the treaty.—Where's the doctor now?

Scrub. He and Gipsy are this moment devouring my lady's marmalade in the closet.

Aim. [*Without.*] Martin! Martin!

Arch. I come, sir, I come.

Scrub. But you forgot the other guinea, brother Martin.

Arch. Here, I give it with all my heart.

Scrub. And I take it with all my soul.—[*Exit* ARCHER.] Ecod, I'll spoil your plotting, Mrs. Gipsy! and if you should set the captain upon me, these two guineas will buy me off. [*Exit.*

Re-enter Mrs. SULLEN *and* DORINDA, *meeting.*

Mrs. Sul. Well, sister!

Dor. And well, sister!

Mrs. Sul. What's become of my lord?

Dor. What's become of his servant?

Mrs. Sul. Servant! he's a prettier fellow, and a finer gentleman by fifty degrees, than his master.

Dor. O' my conscience, I fancy you could beg that fellow at the gallows-foot!

Mrs. Sul. O' my conscience I could, provided I could put a friend of yours in his room.

Dor. You desired me, sister, to leave you when you transgressed the bounds of honour.

Mrs. Sul. Thou dear censorious country girl! what dost mean? You can't think of the man without the bedfellow, I find.

Dor. I don't find anything unnatural in that thought: while the mind is conversant with flesh and blood, it must conform to the humours of the company.

Mrs. Sul. How a little love and good company improves a woman! Why, child, you begin to live —you never spoke before.

Dor. Because I was never spoke to.—My lord has told me that I have more wit and beauty than any of my sex; and truly I begin to think the man is sincere.

Mrs. Sul. You're in the right, Dorinda; pride is the life of a woman, and flattery is our daily bread; and she's a fool that won't believe a man there, as much as she that believes him in anything else. But I'll lay you a guinea that I had finer things said to me than you had.

Dor. Done! What did your fellow say to ye?

Mrs. Sul. My fellow took the picture of Venus for mine.

Dor. But my lover took me for Venus herself.

Mrs. Sul. Common cant! Had my spark called me a Venus directly, I should have believed him a footman in good earnest.

Dor. But my lover was upon his knees to me.

Mrs. Sul. And mine was upon his tiptoes to me.

Dor. Mine vowed to die for me.

Mrs. Sul. Mine swore to die with me.

Dor. Mine spoke the softest moving things.

Mrs. Sul. Mine had his moving things too.

Dor. Mine kissed my hand ten thousand times.

Mrs Sul. Mine has all that pleasure to come.

Dor. Mine offered marriage.

Mrs. Sul. O Lard! d'ye call that a moving thing?

Dor. The sharpest arrow in his quiver, my dear sister! Why, my ten thousand pounds may lie brooding here this seven years, and hatch nothing at last but some ill-natured clown like yours? Whereas, if I marry my Lord Aimwell, there will be title, place, and precedence, the Park, the play, and the drawing-room, splendour, equipage, noise, and flambeaux.— *Hey, my Lady Aimwell's servants there!—Lights, lights to the stairs!—My Lady Aimwell's coach put forward! —Stand by, make room for her ladyship!*—Are not these things moving?—What! melancholy of a sudden?

Mrs. Sul. Happy, happy sister! your angel has been watchful for your happiness, whilst mine has slept regardless of his charge. Long smiling years of circling joys for you, but not one hour for me!

[*Weeps.*

Dor. Come, my dear, we'll talk of something else.

Mrs. Sul. O Dorinda! I own myself a woman, full of my sex, a gentle, generous soul, easy and yielding to soft desires; a spacious heart, where love and all his train might lodge. And must the fair apartment of my breast be made a stable for a brute to lie in?

Dor. Meaning your husband, I suppose?

Mrs. Sul. Husband! no; even husband is too soft a name for him.—But, come, I expect my brother here to-night or to-morrow; he was abroad when my father married me; perhaps he'll find a way to make me easy.

Dor. Will you promise not to make yourself easy in the meantime with my lord's friend?

Mrs. Sul. You mistake me, sister. It happens with us as among the men, the greatest talkers are the greatest cowards; and there's a reason for it; those spirits evaporate in prattle, which might do more mischief if they took another course.—Though, to confess the truth, I do love that fellow;—and if I meet him dressed as he should be, and I undressed as I should be—look'ee, sister, I have no super-natural gifts—I can't swear I could resist the tempta-tion; though I can safely promise to avoid it; and that's as much as the best of us can do. [*Exeunt.*

SCENE II.

A Room in BONIFACE'S *Inn.*

Enter AIMWELL *and* ARCHER, *laughing.*

Arch. And the awkward kindness of the good motherly old gentlewoman—

Aim. And the coming easiness of the young one— 'Sdeath, 'tis pity to deceive her!

Arch. Nay, if you adhere to those principles, stop where you are.

Aim. I can't stop; for I love her to distraction.

Arch. 'Sdeath, if you love her a hair's breadth be-yond discretion, you must go no farther.

Aim. Well, well, anything to deliver us from sauntering away our idle evenings at White's, Tom's or Will's, and be stinted to bear looking at our old acquaintance, the cards; because our impotent pockets can't afford us a guinea for the mercenary drabs.

Arch. Or be obliged to some purse-proud coxcomb for a scandalous bottle, where we must not pretend to our share of the discourse, because we can't pay our club o'th' reckoning.—Damn it, I had rather spunge upon Morris, and sup upon a dish of bohea scored behind the door!

Aim. And there expose our want of sense by talking criticisms, as we should our want of money by railing at the government.

Arch. Or be obliged to sneak into the side-box, and between both houses steal two acts of a play, and because we han't money to see the other three, we come away discontented, and damn the whole five.*

Aim. And ten thousand such rascally tricks—had we outlived our fortunes among our acquaintance.— But now—

Arch. Ay, now is the time to prevent all this:— strike while the iron is hot.—This priest is the luckiest part of our adventure; he shall marry you, and pimp for me.

Aim. But I should not like a woman that can be so fond of a Frenchman.

Arch. Alas, sir! Necessity has no law. The lady may be in distress; perhaps she has a confounded husband, and her revenge may carry her farther than her love. Egad, I have so good an opinion of her,

* An allusion to the strange practice which obtained in the theatres, by which any one who did not remain beyond the completion of the act of the play which was in progress when he entered, paid no admission-money; or, if he had paid, had his money returned.

and of myself, that I begin to fancy strange things; and we must say this for the honour of our women, and indeed of ourselves, that they do stick to their men as they do to their *Magna Charta.* If the plot lies as I suspect, I must put on the gentleman.—But here comes the doctor—I shall be ready. [*Exit.*

Enter FOIGARD.

Foi. Sauve you, noble friend.

Aim. O sir, your servant! Pray, doctor, may I crave your name?

Foi. Fat naam is upon me? My naam is Foigard, joy.

Aim. Foigard! a very good name for a clergyman. Pray, Doctor Foigard, were you ever in Ireland?

Foi. Ireland! no, joy. Fat sort of plaace is dat saam Ireland? Dey say de people are catched dere when dey are young.

Aim. And some of 'em when they're old:—as for example.—[*Takes* FOIGARD *by the shoulder.*] Sir, I arrest you as a traitor against the government; you're a subject of England, and this morning showed me a commission, by which you served as chaplain in the French army. This is death by our law, and your reverence must hang for't.

Foi. Upon my shoule, noble friend, dis is strange news you tell me! Fader Foigard a subject of England! de son of a burgomaster of Brussels a subject of England! ubooboo—

Aim. The son of a bog-trotter in Ireland! Sir, your tongue will condemn you before any bench in the kingdom.

Foi. And is my tongue all your evidensh, joy?

Aim. That's enough.

Foi. No, no, joy, for I vil never spake English no more.

Aim. Sir, I have other evidence.—Here, Martin.

Re-enter ARCHER.

You know this fellow?

Arch. [*In a brogue.*] Saave you, my dear cussen, how does your health?

Foi. [*Aside.*] Ah! upon my shoule dere is my countryman, and his brogue will hang mine.—[*To* ARCHER.] *Mynheer, Ick wet neat watt hey zacht, Ick universton ewe neat, sacramant!*

Aim. Altering your language won't do, sir; this fellow knows your person, and will swear to your face.

Foi. Faash! fey, is dere a brogue upon my faash too?

Arch. Upon my soulvation, dere ish, joy!—But cussen Mackshane, vil you not put a remembrance upon me?

Foi. Mackshane! by St. Paatrick, dat ish naame sure enough!   [*Aside.*

Aim. I fancy, Archer, you have it.

[*Aside to* ARCHER.

Foi. The devil hang you, joy! by fat acquaintance are you my cussen?

Arch. Oh, the devil hang yourshelf, joy! you know we were little boys togeder upon de school, and your foster-moder's son was married upon my nurse's chister, joy, and so we are Irish cussens.

Foi. De devil taake de relation! vel, joy, and fat school was it?

Arch. I tinks it vas—aay,—'twas Tipperary.

Foi. No, no, joy; it vas Kilkenny.

Aim. That's enough for us—self-confession,—come, sir, we must deliver you into the hands of the next magistrate.

Arch. He sends you to jail, you're tried next assizes, and away you go swing into purgatory.

Foi. And is it so wid you, cussen?

Arch. It vil be sho wid you, cussen, if you don't immediately confess the secret between you and Mrs. Gipsy. Look'ee, sir, the gallows or the secret, take your choice.

Foi. The gallows! upon my shoule I hate that saam gallow, for it is a diseash dat is fatal to our family. Vel, den, dere is nothing, shentlemens, but Mrs. Shullen would spaak wid the count in her chamber at midnight, and dere is no haarm, joy, for I am to conduct the count to the plash myshelf.

Arch. As I guessed.—Have you communicated the matter to the count?

Foi. I have not sheen him since.

Arch. Right again! Why then, doctor—you shall conduct me to the lady instead of the count.

Foi. Fat, my cussen to the lady! upon my shoule, gra, dat is too much upon the brogue.

Arch. Come, come, doctor; consider we have got a rope about your neck, and if you offer to squeak, we'll stop your windpipe, most certainly; we shall have another job for you in a day or two, I hope.

Aim. Here's company coming this way, let's into my chamber, and there concert our affair farther.

Arch. Come, my dear cussen, come along.

[Exeunt.

Enter Boniface, Hounslow, *and* Bagshot *at one
door,* Gibbet *at the opposite.*

Gib. Well, gentlemen, 'tis a fine night for our
enterprise.

Houn. Dark as hell.

Bag. And blows like the devil; our landlord here
has showed us the window where we must break in,
and tells us the plate stands in the wainscot cupboard
in the parlour.

Bon. Ay, ay, Mr. Bagshot, as the saying is, knives
and forks, and cups and cans, and tumblers and
tankards.   There's one tankard, as the saying is,
that's near upon as big as me; it was a present to the
squire from his godmother, and smells of nutmeg and
toast like an East-India ship.

Houn. Then you say we must divide at the stair-
head?

Bon. Yes, Mr. Hounslow, as the saying is.   At one
end of that gallery lies my Lady Bountiful and her
daughter, and at the other Mrs. Sullen.   As for the
squire—

Gib. He's safe enough, I have fairly entered him,
and he's more than half seas over already.   But such
a parcel of scoundrels are got about him now, that,
egad, I was ashamed to be seen in their company.

Bon. 'Tis now twelve, as the saying is—gentlemen,
you must set out at one.

Gib. Hounslow, do you and Bagshot see our arms
fixed, and I'll come to you presently.

Houn. Bag. We will.   [*Exeunt.*

Gib. Well, my dear Bonny, you assure me that
Scrub is a coward?

Bon. A chicken, as the saying is. You'll have no creature to deal with but the ladies.

Gib. And I can assure you, friend, there's a great deal of address and good manners in robbing a lady; I am the most a gentleman that way that ever travelled the road.—But, my dear Bonny, this prize will be a galleon, a Vigo business.—I warrant you we shall bring off three or four thousand pound.

Bon. In plate, jewels, and money, as the saying is, you may.

Gib. Why then, Tyburn, I defy thee! I'll get up to town, sell off my horse and arms, buy myself some pretty employment in the household, and be as snug and as honest as any courtier of 'em all.

Bon. And what think you then of my daughter Cherry for a wife?

Gib. Look'ee, my dear Bonny—Cherry *is the Goddess I adore*, as the song goes; but it is a maxim, that man and wife should never have it in their power to hang one another; for if they should, the Lord have mercy on 'em both!   [*Exeunt.*

ACT V.

SCENE I.

A Room in BONIFACE'S *Inn.*

Knocking without, enter BONIFACE.

Bon. Coming! coming!—A coach and six foaming horses at this time o'night! some great man, as the saying is, for he scorns to travel with other people.

Enter Sir CHARLES FREEMAN.

Sir Chas. What, fellow! a public house, and abed when other people sleep?

Bon. Sir, I an't abed, as the saying is.

Sir Chas. Is Mr. Sullen's family abed, think'ee?

Bon. All but the squire himself, sir, as the saying is, he's in the house.

Sir Chas. What company has he?

Bon. Why, sir, there's the constable, Mr. Gage the exciseman, the hunch-backed barber, and two or three other gentlemen.

Sir Chas. I find my sister's letters gave me the true picture of her spouse. [*Aside.*

Enter Squire SULLEN, *drunk.*

Bon. Sir, here's the squire.

Squire Sul. The puppies left me asleep—Sir!

Sir Chas. Well, sir.

Squire Sul. Sir, I am an unfortunate man—I have three thousand pound a year, and I can't get a man to drink a cup of ale with me.

Sir Chas. That's very hard.

Squire Sul. Ay, sir; and unless you have pity upon me, and smoke one pipe with me, I must e'en go home to my wife, and I had rather go to the devil by half.

Sir Chas. But I presume, sir, you won't see your wife to-night; she'll be gone to bed. You don't use to lie with your wife in that pickle?

Squire Sul. What! not lie with my wife! why, sir, do you take me for an atheist or a rake?

Sir Chas. If you hate her, sir, I think you had better lie from her.

Squire Sul. I think so too, friend. But I'm a justice of peace, and must do nothing against the law.

Sir Chas. Law! as I take it, Mr. Justice, nobody observes law for law's sake, only for the good of those for whom it was made.

Squire Sul. But, if the law orders me to send you to jail, you must lie there, my friend.

Sir Chas. Not unless I commit a crime to deserve it.

Squire Sul. A crime! oons, an't I married?

Sir Chas. Nay, sir, if you call marriage a crime, you must disown it for a law.

Squire Sul. Eh! I must be acquainted with you, sir.—But, sir, I should be very glad to know the truth of this matter.

Sir Chas. Truth, sir, is a profound sea, and few there be that dare wade deep enough to find out the bottom on't. Besides, sir, I'm afraid the line of your understanding mayn't be long enough.

Squire Sul. Look'ee, sir, I have nothing to say to your sea of truth, but, if a good parcel of land can entitle a man to a little truth, I have as much as any he in the country.

Bon. I never heard your worship, as the saying is, talk so much before.

Squire Sul. Because I never met with a man that I liked before.

Bon. Pray, sir, as the saying is, let me ask you one question : are not man and wife one flesh ?

Sir Chas. You and your wife, Mr. Guts, may be one flesh, because ye are nothing else ; but rational creatures have minds that must be united.

Squire Sul. Minds !

Sir Chas. Ay, minds, sir ; don't you think that the mind takes place of the body ?

Squire Sul. In some people.

Sir Chas. Then the interest of the master must be consulted before that of his servant.

Squire Sul. Sir, you shall dine with me to-morrow ! —Oons, I always thought that we were naturally one.

Sir Chas. Sir, I know that my two hands are naturally one, because they love one another, kiss one another, help one another in all the actions of life ; but I could not say so much if they were always at cuffs.

Squire Sul. Then 'tis plain that we are two.

Sir Chas. Why don't you part with her, sir ?

Squire Sul. Will you take her, sir ?

Sir Chas. With all my heart.

Squire Sul. You shall have her to-morrow morning, and a venison-pasty into the bargain.

Sir Chas. You'll let me have her fortune too ?

Squire Sul. Fortune! why, sir, I have no quarrel at her fortune : I only hate the woman, sir, and none but the woman shall go.

Sir Chas. But her fortune, sir—

Squire Sul. Can you play at whisk, sir?

Sir Chas. No, truly, sir.

Squire Sul. Nor at all-fours?

Sir Chas. Neither.

Squire Sul. [*Aside.*] Oons! where was this man bred?—[*Aloud.*] Burn me, sir! I can't go home, 'tis but two a clock.

Sir Chas. For half an hour, sir, if you please ; but you must consider 'tis late.

Squire Sul. Late! that's the reason I can't go to bed.—Come, sir!   [*Exeunt.*

SCENE II.

The Lobby before AIMWELL'S *Chamber in the same.*

Enter CHERRY, *runs across the stage, and knocks at the chamber-door. Enter* AIMWELL *in his nightcap and gown.*

Aim. What's the matter? you tremble, child, you're frighted.

Cher. No wonder, sir.—But, in short, sir, this very minute a gang of rogues are gone to rob my Lady Bountiful's house.

Aim. How!

Cher. I dogged 'em to the very door, and left 'em breaking in.

Aim. Have you alarmed anybody else with the news?

Cher. No, no, sir, I wanted to have discovered the whole plot, and twenty other things, to your man Martin; but I have searched the whole house, and can't find him! where is he?

Aim. No matter, child; will you guide me immediately to the house?

Cher. With all my heart, sir; my Lady Bountiful is my godmother, and I love Mrs. Dorinda so well—

Aim. Dorinda! the name inspires me, the glory and the danger shall be all my own.—Come, my life, let me but get my sword. [*Exeunt.*

SCENE III.

A Bedchamber in Lady BOUNTIFUL's *House.*

Mrs. SULLEN *and* DORINDA *discovered.*

Dor. 'Tis very late, sister, no news of your spouse yet?

Mrs. Sul. No, I'm condemned to be alone till towards four, and then perhaps I may be executed with his company.

Dor. Well, my dear, I'll leave you to your rest; you'll go directly to bed, I suppose?

Mrs. Sul. I don't know what to do.—Heigh-ho!

Dor. That's a desiring sigh, sister.

Mrs. Sul. This is a languishing hour, sister.

Dor. And might prove a critical minute if the pretty fellow were here.

Mrs. Sul. Here! what, in my bedchamber at two o'clock o' th' morning, I undressed, the family asleep, my hated husband abroad, and my lovely fellow at my feet!—O 'gad, sister!

Dor. Thoughts are free, sister, and them I allow you.—So, my dear, good night.

Mrs. Sul. A good rest to my dear Dorinda !—[*Exit* Dorinda.] Thoughts free ! are they so ? Why, then, suppose him here, dressed like a youthful, gay, and burning bridegroom,

Enter Archer *unperceived from a closet behind.*

with tongue enchanting, eyes bewitching, knees imploring.—[*Turns, and discovers* Archer *kneeling.*]—Ah !—[*Shrieks and runs to the other side of the stage.*] Have my thoughts raised a spirit ?—What are you, sir, a man or a devil ?

Arch. A man, a man, madam.   [*Rising.*

Mrs. Sul. How shall I be sure of it ?

Arch. Madam, I'll give you demonstration this minute.   [*Takes her hand.*

Mrs. Sul. What, sir ! do you intend to be rude ?

Arch. Yes, madam, if you please.

Mrs. Sul. In the name of wonder, whence came ye ?

Arch. From the skies, madam—I'm a Jupiter in love, and you shall be my Alcmena.

Mrs. Sul. How came you in ?

Arch. I flew in at the window, madam ; your cousin Cupid lent me his wings, and your sister Venus opened the casement.

Mrs. Sul. I'm struck dumb with admiration !

Arch. And I—with wonder !

      [*Looks passionately at her.*

Mrs. Sul. What will become of me ?

Arch. How beautiful she looks !—The teeming jolly Spring smiles in her blooming face, and, when

she was conceived, her mother smelt to roses, looked
on lilies—

Lilies unfold their white, their fragrant charms,
When the **warm sun** thus darts into their arms.

> [*Runs to her.*

Mrs. Sul. Ah!   [*Shrieks.*

Arch. Oons, madam, what d'ye mean? you'll raise
the house.

Mrs. Sul. Sir, I'll wake the **dead** before I bear
this!—What! approach me with the freedoms of
a keeper! I'm glad on't, your impudence has
cured me.

Arch. If this be impudence,—[*Kneels*] I leave to
your partial self; no panting pilgrim, after a tedious,
painful **voyage**, e'er bowed before his saint with more
devotion.

Mrs. Sul. [*Aside.*] Now, now, I'm ruined if he
kneels!—[*Aloud.*] Rise, thou prostrate engineer, not
all thy undermining skill shall reach my heart.—Rise,
and know I am a woman without my sex; I can love
to all the tenderness of wishes, sighs, and tears—but
go no farther.—Still, to convince you that I'm more
than woman, I can speak **my frailty, confess my weakness** even for you—but—

Arch. For me!   [*Going to lay hold on her.*

Mrs. Sul. Hold, sir! build not upon that; for my
most mortal hatred follows if you disobey what I
command you now.—Leave me this minute.—[*Aside.*]
If he denies I'm lost.

Arch. Then you'll promise—

Mrs. Sul. Anything another time.

Arch. When shall I come?

Mrs. Sul. To-morrow, when you will.

Arch. Your lips must seal the promise.

Mrs. Sul. Psha!

Arch. They must! they must!—[*Kisses her.*] Raptures and paradise!—And why not now, my angel? the time, the place, silence, and secrecy, all conspire—And the now conscious stars have pre-ordained this moment for my happiness.

[*Takes her in his arms.*

Mrs. Sul. You will not! cannot sure!

Arch. If the sun rides fast, and disappoints not mortals of to-morrow's dawn, this night shall crown my joys.

Mrs. Sul. My sex's pride assist me!

Arch. My sex's strength help me!

Mrs. Sul. You shall kill me first!

Arch. I'll die with you. [*Carrying her off.*

Mrs. Sul. Thieves! thieves! murder!—

Enter SCRUB *in his breeches and one shoe.*

Scrub. Thieves! thieves! murder! popery!

Arch. Ha! the very timorous stag will kill in rutting time. [*Draws, and offers to stab* SCRUB.

Scrub. [*Kneeling.*] O pray, sir, spare all I have, and take my life!

Mrs. Sul. [*Holding* ARCHER'S *hand.*] What does the fellow mean?

Scrub. O madam, down upon your knees, your marrowbones!—he's one of 'em.

Arch. Of whom?

Scrub. One of the rogues—I beg your pardon, one of the honest gentlemen that just now are broke into the house.

Arch. How!

Mrs. Sul. I hope you did not come to rob me?

Arch. Indeed I did, madam, but I would have taken nothing but what you might ha' spared; but your crying thieves has waked this dreaming fool, and so he takes 'em for granted.

Scrub. Granted! 'tis granted, sir, take all we have.

Mrs. Sul. The fellow looks as if he were broke out of Bedlam.

Scrub. Oons, madam, they're broke into the house with fire and sword! I saw them, heard them, they'll be here this minute.

Arch. What, thieves!

Scrub. Under favour, sir, I think so.

Mrs. Sul. What shall we do, sir?

Arch. Madam, I wish your ladyship a good night.

Mrs. Sul. Will you leave me?

Arch. Leave you! Lord, madam, did not you command me to be gone just now, upon pain of your immortal hatred?

Mrs. Sul. Nay, but pray, sir— [*Takes hold of him.*

Arch. Ha! ha! ha! now comes my turn to be ravished.—You see now, madam, you must use men one way or other; but take this by the way, good madam, that none but a fool will give you the benefit of his courage, unless you'll take his love along with it.—How are they armed, friend?

Scrub. With sword and pistol, sir.

Arch. Hush!—I see a dark lantern coming through the gallery.—Madam, be assured I will protect you, or lose my life.

Mrs. Sul. Your life! no, sir, they can rob me of nothing that I value half so much; therefore, now, sir, let me entreat you to be gone.

Arch. No, madam, I'll consult my own safety for the sake of yours; I'll work by stratagem. Have you courage enough to stand the appearance of 'em!

Mrs. Sul. Yes, yes, since I have 'scaped your hands, I can face anything.

Arch. Come hither, brother Scrub! don't you know me?

Scrub. Eh, my dear brother, let me kiss thee.

[*Kisses* ARCHER.

Arch. This way—here—

[ARCHER *and* SCRUB *hide behind the bed.*

Enter GIBBET, *with a dark lantern in one hand, and a pistol in the other.*

Gib. Ay, ay, this is the chamber, and the lady alone.

Mrs. Sul. Who are you, sir? what would you have? d'ye come to rob me?

Gib. Rob you! alack a day, madam, I'm only a younger brother, madam; and so, madam, if you make a noise, I'll shoot you through the head; but don't be afraid, madam.—[*Laying his lantern and pistol upon the table.*] These rings, madam, don't be concerned, madam, I have a profound respect for you, madam; your keys, madam; don't be frighted, madam, I'm the most of a gentleman. —[*Searching her pockets.*] This necklace, madam; I never was rude to a lady;—I have a veneration— for this necklace—

[*Here* ARCHER *having come round and seized the pistol, takes* GIBBET *by the collar, trips up his heels, and claps the pistol to his breast.*

Arch. Hold, profane villain, and take the reward of thy sacrilege!

Gib. Oh! pray, sir, don't kill me; I an't prepared.

Arch. How many is there of 'em, Scrub?

Scrub. Five-and-forty, sir.

Arch. Then I must kill the villain, to have him out of the way.

Gib. Hold, hold, sir, we are but three, upon my honour.

Arch. Scrub, will you undertake to secure him?

Scrub. Not I, sir; kill him, kill him!

Arch. Run to Gipsy's chamber, there you'll find the doctor; bring him hither presently.—[*Exit* SCRUB, *running.*] Come, rogue, if you have a short prayer, say it.

Gib. Sir, I have no prayer at all; the government has provided a chaplain to say prayers for us on these occasions.

Mrs. Sul. Pray, sir, don't kill him; you fright me as much as him.

Arch. The dog shall die, madam, for being the occasion of my disappointment.—Sirrah, this moment is your last.

Gib. I'll give you two hundred pounds to spare my life.

Arch. Have you no more, rascal?

Gib. Yes, sir, I can command four hundred, but I must reserve two of 'em to save my life at the sessions.

Re-enter SCRUB *with* FOIGARD.

Arch. Here, doctor, I suppose Scrub and you between you may manage him. Lay hold of him, doctor.   [FOIGARD *lays hold of* GIBBET.

Gib. What! turned over to the priest already!—Look'ee, doctor, you come before your time; I an't condemned yet, I thank ye.

Foi. Come, my dear joy, I vill secure your body and your shoule too; I vill make you a good catholic, and give you an absolution.

Gib. Absolution! can you procure me a pardon, doctor.

Foi. No, joy.

Gib. Then you and your absolution may go to the devil!

Arch. Convey him into the cellar, there bind him:—take the pistol, and if he offers to resist, shoot him through the head—and come back to us with all the speed you can.

Scrub Ay, ay, come, doctor, do you hold him fast, and I'll guard him.

[*Exit* FOIGARD *with* GIBBET, SCRUB *following.*

Mrs. Sul. But how came the doctor.

Arch. In short, madam —[*Shrieking without.*] 'Sdeath! the rogues are at work with the other ladies —I'm vexed I parted with the pistol; but I must fly to their assistance.—Will you stay here, madam, or venture yourself with me?

Mrs. Sul. [*Taking him by the arm.*] Oh, with you, dear sir, with you.　　　　　　　　　　[*Exeunt.*

SCENE IV.

Another Bedchamber in the same.

Enter HOUNSLOW *and* BAGSHOT, *with drawn swords, haling in* Lady BOUNTIFUL *and* DORINDA.

Houn. Come, come, your jewels, mistress!

Bag. Your keys, your keys, old gentlewoman!

Enter AIMWELL *and* CHERRY.

Aim. Turn this way, villains! I durst engage an army in such a cause.   [*He engages them both.*

Dor. O madam, had I but a sword to help the brave man!

Lady Boun. There's three or four hanging up in the hall; but they won't draw. I'll go fetch one, however.   [*Exit.*

Enter ARCHER *and* Mrs. SULLEN.

Arch. Hold, hold, my lord! every man his bird, pray.   [*They engage man to man,* HOUNSLOW *and* BAGSHOT *are thrown and disarmed.*

Cher. [*Aside.*] What! the rogues taken! then they'll impeach my father; I must give him timely notice.   [*Runs out.*

Arch. Shall we kill the rogues?

Aim. No, no, we'll bind them.

Arch. Ay, ay.—[*To* Mrs. SULLEN.] Here, madam, lend me your garter.

Mrs. Sul. [*Aside.*] The devil's in this fellow! he fights, loves, and banters, all in a breath.—[*Aloud.*] Here's a cord that the rogues brought with 'em, I suppose.

Arch. Right, right, the rogue's destiny, a rope to hang himself.—Come, my lord—this is but a scandalous sort of an office; [*Binding the* Highwaymen *together*] if our adventures should end in this sort of hangman-work; but I hope there is something in prospect, that—

Enter SCRUB.

Well, Scrub, have you secured your Tartar?

Scrub. Yes, sir, I left the priest and him disputing about religion.

Aim. And pray carry these gentlemen to reap the benefit of the controversy.

   [*Exit* Scrub *with the* Highwaymen *bound.*

Mrs. Sul. Pray, sister, how came my lord here?

Dor. And pray how came the gentleman here?

Mrs. Sul. I'll tell you the greatest piece of villainy—

     [*They talk in dumb show.*

Aim. I fancy, Archer, you have been more successful in your adventures than the housebreakers.

Arch. No matter for my adventure, yours is the principal.—Press her this minute to marry you—now while she's hurried between the palpitation of her fear and the joy of her deliverance, now while the tide of her spirits are at high-flood—throw yourself at her feet, speak some romantic nonsense or other—address her, like Alexander, in the height of his victory, confound her senses, bear down her reason, and away with her.—The priest is now in the cellar, and dare not refuse to do the work.

Re-enter Lady BOUNTIFUL.

Aim. But how shall I get off without being observed?

Arch. You a lover, and not find a way to get off! —Let me see—

Aim. You bleed, Archer.

Arch. 'Sdeath, I'm glad on't; this wound will do the business. I'll amuse the old lady and Mrs. Sullen about dressing my wound, while you carry off Dorinda.

Lady Boun. Gentlemen, could we understand how you would be gratified for the services—

Arch. Come, come, my lady, this is no time for compliments; I'm wounded, madam.

Lady Boun. Mrs. Sul. How! wounded!

Dor. I hope, sir, you have received no hurt.

Aim. None but what you may cure—

[*Makes love in dumb show.*

Lady Boun. Let me see your arm, sir—I must have some powder-sugar to stop the blood.—O me! an ugly gash; upon my word, sir, you must go into bed.

Arch. Ay, my lady, a bed would do very well.— [*To* Mrs. SULLEN.] Madam, will you do me the favour to conduct me to a chamber?

Lady Boun. Do, do, daughter—while I get the lint and the probe and the plaster ready.

[*Runs out one way,* AIMWELL *carries off* DORINDA *another.*

Arch. Come, madam, why don't you obey your mother's commands?

Mrs. Sul. How can you, after what is passed, have the confidence to ask me?

Arch. And if you go to that, how can you, after what is passed, have the confidence to deny me? Was not this blood shed in your defence, and my life exposed for your protection? Look'ee, madam, I'm none of your romantic fools, that fights giants and monsters for nothing; my valour is downright Swiss; I'm a soldier of fortune, and must be paid.

Mrs. Sul. 'Tis ungenerous in you, sir, to upbraid me with your services!

Arch. 'Tis ungenerous in you, madam, not to reward 'em.

Mrs. Sul. How! at the expense of my honour?

Arch. Honour! can honour consist with ingratitude? If you would deal like a woman of honour, do like a man of honour. D'ye think I would deny you in such a case?

Enter Servant.

Ser. Madam, my lady ordered me to tell you, that your brother is below at the gate.   [*Exit.*

Mrs. Sul. My brother! Heavens be praised!—Sir, he shall thank you for your services, he has it in his power.

Arch. Who is your brother, madam?

Mrs. Sul. Sir Charles Freeman.—You'll excuse me, sir; I must go and receive him.   [*Exit.*

Arch. Sir Charles Freeman! 'sdeath and hell! my old acquaintance. Now unless Aimwell has made good use of his time, all our fair machine goes souse into the sea like the Eddystone.*   [*Exit.*

SCENE V.

The Gallery in the same.

Enter AIMWELL *and* DORINDA.

Dor. Well, well, my lord, you have conquered; your late generous action will, I hope, plead for my easy yielding; though I must own, your lordship had a friend in the fort before.

Aim. The sweets of Hybla dwell upon her tongue!
—Here, doctor—

---

* During a terrible storm in 1703, the first Eddystone lighthouse, a wooden structure, was dashed into the sea.

Enter FOIGARD, *with a book in his hand.*

Foi. Are you prepared boat?

Dor. I'm ready. But first, my lord, one word—I have a frightful example of a hasty marriage in my own family; when I reflect upon't it shocks me. Pray, my lord, consider a little—

Aim. Consider! do you doubt my honour or my love?

Dor. Neither: I do believe you equally just as brave: and were your whole sex drawn out for me to choose, I should not cast a look upon the multitude if you were absent. But, my lord, I'm a woman; colours, concealments may hide a thousand faults in me, therefore know me better first; I hardly dare affirm I know myself in anything except my love.

Aim. [*Aside.*] Such goodness who could injure! I find myself unequal to the task of villain; she has gained my soul, and made it honest like her own—I cannot, cannot hurt her.—[*Aloud.*] Doctor, retire.—[*Exit* FOIGARD.] Madam, behold your lover and your proselyte, and judge of my passion by my conversion!—I'm all a lie, nor dare I give a fiction to your arms; I'm all counterfeit, except my passion.

Dor. Forbid it, Heaven! a counterfeit!

Aim. I am no lord, but a poor needy man, come with a mean, a scandalous design to prey upon your fortune; but the beauties of your mind and person have so won me from myself, that like a trusty servant, I prefer the interest of my mistress to my own.

Dor. Sure I have had the dream of some poor mariner, a sleepy image of a welcome port, and wake involved in storms!—Pray, sir, who are you?

Aim. Brother to the man whose title I usurped, but stranger to his honour or his fortune.

Dor. Matchless honesty!—Once I was proud, sir, of your wealth and title, but now am prouder that you want it: now I can show my love was justly levelled, and had no aim but love.—Doctor, come in.

Enter FOIGARD *at one door*, GIPSY *at another, who whispers* DORINDA.

[*To* FOIGARD.] Your pardon, sir, we shan't want you now.—[*To* AIMWELL.] Sir, you must excuse me—I'll wait on you presently. [*Exit with* GIPSY.

Foi. Upon my shoule, now, dis is foolish. [*Exit.*

Aim. Gone! and bid the priest depart!—It has an ominous look.

Enter ARCHER.

Arch. Courage, Tom!—Shall I wish you joy?

Aim. No.

Arch. Oons, man, what ha' you been doing?

Aim. O Archer! my honesty, I fear, has ruined me.

Arch. How!

Aim. I have discovered myself.

Arch. Discovered! and without my consent? What! have I embarked my small remains in the same bottom with yours, and you dispose of all without my partnership?

Aim. O Archer! I own my fault.

Arch. After conviction—'tis then too late for pardon.—You may remember, Mr. Aimwell, that you proposed this folly: as you begun, so end it. Henceforth I'll hunt my fortune single—so farewell!

Aim. Stay, my dear Archer, but a minute.

Arch. Stay! what, to be despised, exposed, and

laughed at! No, I would sooner change conditions with the worst of the rogues we just now bound, than bear one scornful smile from the proud knight that once I treated as my equal.

Aim. What knight?

Arch. Sir Charles Freeman, brother to the lady that I had almost—but no matter for that, 'tis a cursed night's work, and so I leave you to make the best on't.

Aim. Freeman!—One word, Archer. Still I have hopes; methought she received my confession with pleasure.

Arch. 'Sdeath, who doubts it?

Aim. She consented after to the match; and still I dare believe she will be just.

Arch. To herself, I warrant her, as you should have been.

Aim. By all my hopes she comes, and smiling comes!

Re-enter DORINDA.

Dor. Come, my dear lord—I fly with impatience to your arms—the minutes of my absence was a tedious year. Where's this priest?

Re-enter FOIGARD.

Arch. Oons, a brave girl!

Dor. I suppose, my lord, this gentleman is privy to our affairs?

Arch. Yes, yes, madam, I'm to be your father.

Dor. Come, priest, do your office.

Arch. Make haste, make haste, couple 'em any way.—[*Takes* AIMWELL'S *hand.*] Come, madam, I'm to give you—

Dor. My mind's altered; I won't.

Arch. Eh!—

Aim. I'm confounded!

Foi. Upon my shoule, and sho is myshelf.

Arch. What's the matter now, madam?

Dor. Look'ee, sir, one generous action deserves another.—This gentleman's honour obliged him to hide nothing from me; my justice engages me to conceal nothing from him. In short, sir, you are the person that you thought you counterfeited; you are the true Lord Viscount Aimwell, and I wish your lordship joy.—Now, priest, you may be gone; if my lord is pleased now with the match, let his lordship marry me in the face of the world.

Aim. Arch. What does she mean?

Dor. Here's a witness for my truth.

Enter Sir CHARLES FREEMAN *and* Mrs. SULLEN.

Sir. Chas. My dear Lord Aimwell, I wish you joy.

Aim. Of what?

Sir Chas. Of your honour and estate. Your brother died the day before I left London; and all your friends have writ after you to Brussels;—among the rest I did myself the honour.

Arch. Heark'ee, sir knight, don't you banter now?

Sir Chas. 'Tis truth, upon my honour.

Aim. Thanks to the pregnant stars that formed this accident!

Arch. Thanks to the womb of time that brought it forth!—away with it!

Aim. Thanks to my guardian angel that led me to the prize!   [*Taking* DORINDA'S *hand.*

Arch. And double thanks to the noble Sir Charles

Freeman.—My lord, I wish you joy.—My lady, I wish you joy.—Egad, Sir Freeman, you're the honestest fellow living !—'Sdeath, I'm grown strange airy upon this matter.—My lord, how d'ye ?—A word, my lord ; don't you remember something of a previous agreement, that entitles me to the moiety of this lady's fortune, which I think will amount to five thousand pounds ?

Aim. Not a penny, Archer ; you would ha' cut my throat just now, because I would not deceive this lady.

Arch. Ay, and I'll cut your throat again, if you should deceive her now.

Aim. That's what I expected ; and to end the dispute, the lady's fortune is ten thousand pounds, we'll divide stakes : take the ten thousand pounds or the lady.

Dor. How ! is your lordship so indifferent ?

Arch. No, no, no, madam ! his lordship knows very well that I'll take the money ; I leave you to his lordship, and so we're both provided for.

Enter Count BELLAIR.

Count Bel. Mesdames et Messieurs, I am your servant trice humble !   I hear you be robbed here.

Aim. The ladies have been in some danger, sir.

Count Bel. And, begar, our inn be rob too !

Aim. Our inn ! by whom ?

Count Bel. By the landlord, begar !—Garzoon, he has rob himself, and run away !

Arch. Robbed himself !

Count Bel. Ay, begar, and me too of a hundred pound.

Arch. A hundred pounds?

Count Bel. Yes, that I owed him.

Aim. Our money's gone, Frank.

Arch. Rot the money! my wench is gone.—[*To* Count BELLAIR.] *Savez-vous quelquechose de Mademoiselle* Cherry?

Enter a Countryman *with a box and a letter.*

Coun. Is there one Martin here?

Arch. Ay, ay—who wants him?

Coun. I have a box here, and letter for him.

[*Gives the box and letter to* ARCHER *and exit.*

Arch. Ha! ha! ha! what's here? Legerdemain! —By this light, my lord, our money again!—But this unfolds the riddle.—[*Opening the letter.*] Hum, hum, hum!—Oh, 'tis for the public good, and must be communicated to the company. [*Reads.*

Mr. Martin,

My father being afraid of an impeachment by the rogues that are taken to-night, is gone off; but if you can procure him a pardon, he'll make great discoveries that may be useful to the country. Could I have met you instead of your master to-night, I would have delivered myself into your hands, with a sum that much exceeds that in your strong-box, which I have sent you, with an assurance to my dear Martin that I shall ever be his most faithful friend till death.

CHERRY BONIFACE.

There's a billet-doux for you! As for the father, I think he ought to be encouraged; and for the daughter—pray, my lord, persuade your bride to take her into her service instead of Gipsy.

Aim. I can assure you, madam, your deliverance was owing to her discovery.

Dor. Your command, my lord, will do without the obligation. I'll take care of her.

Sir Chas. This good company meets opportunely in favour of a design I have in behalf of my unfortunate sister. I intend to part her from her husband—gentlemen, will you assist me?

Arch. Assist you! 'sdeath, who would not?

Count Bel. Assist! garzoon, we all assist!

Enter Squire SULLEN *and* SCRUB.

Squire Sul. What's all this? They tell me spouse, that you had like to have been robbed.

Mrs. Sul. Truly, spouse, I was pretty near it, had not these two gentlemen interposed.

Squire Sul. How came these gentlemen here?

Mrs. Sul. That's his way of returning thanks, you must know.

Count Bel. Garzoon, the question be apropos for all that.

Sir Chas. You promised last night, sir, that you would deliver your lady to me this morning.

Squire Sul. Humph!

Arch. Humph! what do you mean by humph? Sir, you shall deliver her—in short, sir, we have saved you and your family; and if you are not civil, we'll unbind the rogues, join with 'em, and set fire to your house. What does the man mean? not part with his wife!

Count Bel. Ay, garzoon, de man no understan common justice.

Mrs. Sul. Hold, gentlemen, all things here must move by consent, compulsion would spoil us; let my dear and I talk the matter over, and you shall judge it between us.

Squire Sul. Let me know first who are to be our judges. Pray, sir, who are you?

Sir Chas. I am Sir Charles Freeman, come to take away your wife.

Squire Sul. And you, good sir?

Aim. Charles Viscount Aimwell, come to take away your sister.

Squire Sul. And you, pray, sir?

Arch. Francis Archer, esquire, come—

Squire Sul. To take away my mother, I hope. Gentlemen, you're heartily welcome; I never met with three more obliging people since I was born! —And now, my dear, if you please, you shall have the first word.

Arch. And the last, for five pound!

Mrs. Sul. Spouse!

Squire Sul. Rib!

Mrs. Sul. How long have we been married?

Squire Sul. By the almanac, fourteen months; but by my account, fourteen years.

Mrs. Sul. 'Tis thereabout by my reckoning.

Count Bel. Garzoon, their account will agree.

Mrs. Sul. Pray, spouse, what did you marry for?

Squire Sul. To get an heir to my estate.

Sir Chas. And have you succeeded?

Squire Sul. No.

Arch. The condition fails of his side.—Pray, madam, what did you marry for?

Mrs. Sul. To support the weakness of my sex by

the strength of his, and to enjoy the pleasures of an agreeable society.

Sir Chas. Are your expectations answered?

Mrs. Sul. No.

Count Bel. A clear case! a clear case!

Sir Chas. What are the bars to your mutual contentment?

Mrs. Sul. In the first place, I can't drink ale with him.

Squire Sul. Nor can I drink tea with her.

Mrs. Sul. I can't hunt with you.

Squire Sul. Nor can I dance with you.

Mrs. Sul. I hate cocking and racing.

Squire Sul. And I abhor ombre and piquet.

Mrs. Sul. Your silence is intolerable.

Squire Sul. Your prating is worse.

Mrs. Sul. Have we not been a perpetual offence to each other! a gnawing vulture at the heart?

Squire Sul. A frightful goblin to the sight?

Mrs. Sul. A porcupine to the feeling?

Squire Sul. Perpetual wormwood to the taste?

Mrs. Sul. Is there on earth a thing we could agree in?

Squire Sul. Yes—to part.

Mrs. Sul. With all my heart.

Squire Sul. Your hand.

Mrs. Sul. Here.

Squire Sul. These hands joined us, these shall part us.—Away!

Mrs. Sul. North.

Squire Sul. South.

Mrs. Sul. East.

Squire Sul. West—far as the poles asunder.

Count Bel. Begar, the ceremony be vera pretty.

Sir Chas. Now, Mr. Sullen, there wants only my sister's fortune to make us easy.

Squire Sul. Sir Charles, you love your sister, and I love her fortune ; every one to his fancy.

Arch. Then you won't refund ?

Squire Sul. Not a stiver.

Arch. Then I find, madam, you must e'en go to your prison again.

Count Bel. What is the portion ?

Sir Chas. Ten thousand pound, sir.

Count Bel. Garzoon, I'll pay it, and she shall go home wid me.

Arch. Ha ! ha ! ha ! French all over.—Do you know, sir, what ten thousand pound English is ?

Count Bel. No, begar, not justement.

Arch. Why, sir, 'tis a hundred thousand livres.

Count Bel. A hundre tousand livres ! A garzoon, me canno' do't, your beauties and their fortunes are both too much for me.

Arch. Then I will.—This night's adventure has proved strangely lucky to us all—for Captain Gibbet in his walk had made bold, Mr. Sullen, with your study and escritoir, and had taken out all the writings of your estate, all the articles of marriage with your lady, bills, bonds, leases, receipts to an infinite value ; I took 'em from him, and I deliver 'em to Sir Charles.

> [*Gives* SIR CHARLES FREEMAN *a parcel of papers and parchments.*

Squire Sul. How, my writings !—my head aches consumedly.—Well, gentlemen, you shall have her fortune, but I can't talk. If you have a mind, Sir Charles, to be merry, and celebrate my sister's wed-

ding and my divorce, you may command my house—
but my head aches consumedly.—Scrub, bring me a
dram.

Arch. [*To* Mrs. SULLEN.] Madam, there's a country
dance to the trifle that I sung to-day; your hand, and
we'll lead it up.

A Dance.

'Twould be hard to guess which of these parties is
the better pleased, the couple joined, or the couple
parted; the one rejoicing in hopes of an untasted
happiness, and the other in their deliverance from an
experienced misery.

> Both happy in their several states we find,
> Those parted by consent, and those conjoined.
> Consent, if mutual, saves the lawyer's fee,
> Consent is law enough to set you free.

[*Exeunt omnes.*

EPILOGUE.

DESIGNED TO BE SPOKEN IN THE "BEAUX-STRATAGEM."

If to our play your judgment can't be kind,
Let its expiring author pity find :
Survey his mournful case with melting eyes,
Nor let the bard be damned before he dies.
Forbear, you fair, on his last scene to frown,
But his true exit with a plaudit crown ;
Then shall the dying poet cease to fear
The dreadful knell, while your applause he hears.
At Leuctra so the conquering Theban died,
Claimed his friends' praises, but their tears denied :
Pleased in the pangs of death he greatly thought
Conquest with loss of life but cheaply bought.
The difference this,—the Greek was one would fight,
As brave, though not so gay as Serjeant Kite ;
Ye sons of Will's, what's that to those who write ?
To Thebes alone the Grecian owed his bays,
You may the bard above the hero raise,
Since yours is greater than Athenian praise.

INDEX TO NOTES.

Admission to theatres without paying, ii. 320
Albemarle, Earl of, i. 235
Author's nights, ii. 10

Bandoleers, i. 184
Bank of England, i. 282
Basset, i. 211
Bergamot, i. 35
Blackmore, Sir Richard, i. 127
Blenheim, Battle of, ii. 234
Blue Posts Tavern, i. 170
Bona Roba, i. 172
Bononcini, Giovanni, ii. 235
Brett, Colonel Henry, ii. 3
Burgundy (a head-dress), i. 246

Camilla, opera, ii. 235
Cards, games of, i. 271
Carmarthen, Marquis of, i. 3
Chamberlain, Dr. Hugh, ii. 13
Charles II., King of Spain, i. 269
Charles XII., of Sweden, i. 278
Chocolate Houses, i. 141, 310
"Cocket," i. 161

Collier, Jeremy, i. 117
"Coupee," i. 193
Cremona, taking of, i. 422
Critics at the theatre, i. 79
Cully, i. 202
Cunning-man, i. 205

Danby, Earl of, i. 3

Eddystone Lighthouse, ii. 341
English Rogue, The, i. 64

Fleet Ditch, i. 253
Flying-Post, newspaper, ii. 12
Footmen's Gallery, i. 239
French goods smuggled into England, i. 131
Fuller, William, the spy, ii. 110

Gaming, love of, among ladies, i. 242
Gray's Inn pieces (base coins), i. 250

Groaning-cheese, i. 46
Groom-porter, i. 135

Haines, Joe, i. 7
High-head, i. 17.
" Hot-cockles," i. 255
Hungarian army, i. 132
Hungary water, i. 73

Impressment Acts, ii. 286

Joan, Pope, i. 113
Jones, Inigo, i. 177

Kidd, Captain, the pirate, i. 245

Landen, Battle of, i. 136
Le Brun's Battles of Alexander,
　ii. 312
Liége, ii. 10
Loach, i. 208
Locket's Ordinary, i. 230, 310
Long Lane, ii. 6

Masks, i. 12, 318
Monteth, i. 230
Moorfields, i. 89
Mourning Bride, i. 315

Namur, i. 163, 245
Nantes, Revocation of Edict of,
　i. 252
Neale, Thomas, Groom-porter,
　i. 135

Officers, disbanded, i. 258

Orangerie, i. 35
Oroonoko, i. 315

Piazza (Covent Garden), i. 177
" Pigsny," i. 22
Pinners, ii. 171
Pit of the theatre, i. 79
Powell, i. 7
Pressing, i. 289
Prinking, i. 217
Pulvil, i. 141
Punk, i. 71

Ratafia, i. 243
Rehearsal, The, ii. 144
Rival Queens, The, i. 210, 214
Rosamond's Pond, ii. 91
Rose Tavern, i. 230, ii. 226
Ruelle, i. 136
Rummer Tavern, i. 132
Ryswick, Peace of, i. 37, 227

St. Alban's Tavern, ii. 96
St. James's, houses opening on
　the Park, i. 297
" Sa ! Sa !" i. 193
Schellenberg, Battle of, ii. 234
Smyrna Chocolate House, i. 258
Snuff, i. 34, 35
Spanish snuff, i. 35
Standing Army, i. 131
Succubus, i. 206
Sun Tavern, i. 47

Tables, the game of, i. 65.
Tallard, Marshal, ii. 139

Thatched House Coffee House, i. 269

Tofts, Mrs., the singer, ii. 279

Tompion, Thomas, i. 409

Union of England and Scotland, ii. 241

Urwin, William, proprietor of Will's Coffee House, i. 45

"Ut," the first note in Guido's musical scale, ii. 176

Venloo, ii. 10

Vigo, Battle of, ii. 31

Vigo, ii. 234

Ware, the bed of, ii. 124

Wars, the French, of 1689 and following years, ii. 139

Weekly Bills of Mortality, ii. 259

White's, i. 243, 310

Wild Goose Chase, i. 422

Will's Coffee House, i. 45

Wonders in the Sun, an opera by Durfey, i. 118

Wycherley, ii. 241

"Zauns," i. 34

PRINTED BY BALLANTYNE, HANSON AND CO.
EDINBURGH AND LONDON.